# NAÏDA

# NAÏDA

SCOTT OVERTON

No Walls Publishing
SUDBURY, ONTARIO, CANADA

**Scott Overton/No Walls Publishing**
**Sudbury, Ontario, Canada**
**www.scottoverton.ca**

Publisher's Note: This is a work of fiction. Names, characters, places, and incidents are a product of the author's imagination. Locales and public names are sometimes used for atmospheric purposes. Any resemblance to actual people, living or dead, or to businesses, companies, events, institutions, or locales is completely coincidental.

Book Layout © 2017 BookDesignTemplates.com
Photo of Author: Shaun K. Overton

**Naïda/ Scott Overton**. -- 1st ed.
ISBN 978-1-7774308-2-5

We acknowledge the financial support of the Ontario Arts Council in the creation of this book.

To my Dad,

A lifelong fan of science fiction who made me one too. I hope you're somewhere watching me writing the kind of stories you loved and getting a kick out of it.

"The meeting of two personalities is like the contact of two chemical substances: if there is any reaction, both are transformed."

— CARL GUSTAV JUNG

# *PART ONE*

# 1

The green depths of the lake beckoned: a coyly inscrutable crystal ball, poised to reveal life-changing secrets.

Michael Hart sank into its liquid embrace, freed for a time from the world above the waves where past choices congealed around him. He became a different person when water closed over his head, as if he were rinsed of his life's mistakes and, through the element of danger, reborn as a hero.

A few meters away his scuba-diving buddy, Phil Rodriguez, was already clearing his mask. Rodriguez' mask always leaked a little when they dropped below the thermocline and the colder water made his face muscles contract. Michael questioned him with the circled thumb and forefinger of the OK sign, and Rodriguez returned it, ready to go deeper. They closed in to check each other's tank pressures: both had just over 2900 psi—plenty of air. Blissfully alien in the underwater realm, Michael exhaled and felt himself drop further, his finger poised on the inflator hose button of the vest-like Buoyancy Control Device he wore like a personal elevator in the water column. As the surrounding liquid darkened, he felt the shiver of his inner eight-year-old discovering a new cave. The bottom of Evergreen Lake was virgin territory, undisturbed by creatures of the land since long before the end of the last ice age.

He and Rodriguez had come in pursuit of a shadow: a tantalizing shape on the bottom of the lake seen by a water-bomber pilot as he'd lined up for a refill while fighting a nearby brush fire. Was it a deep hole? A wreck? No one knew. There'd never been any large-boat traffic on Evergreen. The ribbons of water linking it to adjoining lakes were no bigger than creeks. Maybe a derelict bus had been abandoned to sink through the spring ice, though Evergreen was a bitch to drive to. Michael hoped it was a downed plane. Now *that* would be interesting.

*The juvenile awakens.*

Gradual awareness of its surroundings follows. It is immersed in fluid.

Nearby, it senses the presence it knows as the Controller, also newly awakened, and consults it for more information. The environment is liquid water at an ambient temperature almost exactly midway between the values related to solid and gaseous states. This temperature is ninety-seven per cent warmer than conditions at the time stasis was initiated. Life forms are also present in much greater numbers: billions of micro-organisms suspended in the water, an indication of more abundant solar radiation.

Time has passed. Extensive time. *More than planned?*

The sun of the planet is visible through the water. Allowing for refractive interference, it appears the same size as before stasis. The wavelengths of radiated light are also in the same proportions.

Manageable time, then: thousands of sidereal years, but not millions. The Controller will make more exact calculations after nightfall using a comparison of star positions.

It is puzzling that none of the others has awakened from stasis. They are emitting no metabolic energy at all. No indication of biological viability.

Is it possible that too much time has passed? That the life processes of the companions have been terminated?

This is unexpected. Awakening alone.

There is something nearby, though. Two large life forms native to this world. They match a pre-stasis record of the planet's only sentient species. It can be assumed that their presence has triggered the awakening.

This is encouraging. There is a protocol for this.

The Controller begins to fill the water with welcoming light.

Michael pressed the inflator button to add more air to his vest and slow his descent. He pinched his nose and pushed air into his sinuses and ears to equalize the pressure. Their rate of cautious progress was trying his patience. Whatever they found might change the lake from a nearly forgotten pothole in the water-pocked northern Ontario landscape into a popular dive destination. He wanted the credit for that.

He swept his head back and forth as much as the stiff neoprene hood of his wetsuit would allow. They should have brought flashlights. It might be pretty dark at the bottom.

Michael glanced at Rodriguez, who always swam a couple of metres from his left shoulder and a little behind. The man was farther back than usual. Michael waved him forward. The gap didn't change.

What was he worried about?

Facing forward again, Michael saw a gleam beckoning from the darkness below. Steady. Yellow green. He gave his dive computer a quick check: twenty-two metres deep—a long way for sunlight to penetrate a northern Ontario lake. But there couldn't be a light source down there.

Unless somebody had beaten them to it.

No, it wasn't electric light. Chemical maybe, like the glow-sticks divers attached to their gear to keep each other in sight when night diving.

Drawn to the glow like a moth, he found that his mind wouldn't immediately accept what he saw: not an object illuminated by light, but an object that seemed to be made of light! His brain tried to tell him it was a nebulous afterimage, like the lingering trail of a child's sparkler waved through a night sky. But it didn't fade. It was stable, maybe solid: perhaps a structure of some kind, but a structure such as he'd never seen. An array of jelly-like geometric shapes jutted from the lake bottom: hexagons, or maybe octahedrons that were nearly transparent and produced their own eerie radiance.

Jellyfish did that, but they were creatures of the deep ocean. Did they have bioluminescent cousins that lived in fresh water? Not that he'd ever heard. These gelatinous sheets were the height of a man. A shot of air into his buoyancy vest brought Michael to a gentle hover, and he watched patterns of light and shadow ripple over the uneven array below, like an office of cubicles arranged by a drunken builder.

His wetsuit was no protection against a sudden chill.

Something clutched his arm and he nearly screamed into his mouthpiece.

It was Rodriguez, expressively pointing to his gauge pack. Could the man really have burned through that much air in—how long had it been—fifteen minutes? Aching cold could do that. Or fear.

Rodriguez' eyes were saucer wide behind his face mask, and clouds of bubbles burst from the first-stage regulator at the back of his neck every few seconds. Michael nodded again and gave the thumbs up sign. Together, they tipped up into a vertical position and gave a few kicks to start a carefully controlled ascent.

At five metres below the surface Rodriguez had calmed down enough to do their three-minute safety stop, and they hung motionless in the water, allowing time for absorbed nitrogen to leave their bloodstream before they surfaced. But their eyes were fixed on the direction of their fins, and the dark depths beyond. Michael felt his legs twitch.

The shore was only a ten-minute swim away along the surface. Once on land, they stripped off their gear in awkward silence. Michael cleared his throat. "That was something, huh? What do you think?" He struggled to keep his balance while tugging his left foot out of his wet suit.

Rodriguez only shrugged and hurriedly shoved his fins into his gear bag.

"You're not going to pretend we didn't see anything."

"I got no idea what we saw. Maybe we were narc'd."

"Shit, Phil, we've both been way deeper than that without any nitrogen symptoms. Only, what the hell was it? Toxic waste?"

"A joke. Somebody trying to pull our leg." Rodriguez went to dry the protective cap of his regulator with air from his tank, and the cap flew from his hands. The tank gave a scream of escaping air while he fumbled with the shut off valve.

Michael looked away and looped his hoses to fit in their carrying case. As they lugged the heavy gear up the hill toward his car, he stole a glance at his friend, at Rodriguez' stiff stance and staring eyes.

"That wasn't a gag. Or anything natural, either. I don't think it was…from here."

"*Jesus!* Let it go!" Rodriguez dropped his bags and stood bent over, breathing hard. Then he straightened but avoided looking at Michael. "Let's just get the hell out of here." The words were thick with pleading.

They drove home in silence, not even saying goodbye when Michael dropped Rodriguez off in his driveway. As he turned the wheel toward his own home, he thought about the green glow in the watery darkness, like something from a Stephen King novel, and swallowed hard.

# 2

Michael's apartment was in an older house transformed into a duplex: stucco below faded pale green wood siding, with white trim around a three-paned bow window that faced the street. His landlords, Gerry and Emma Smith, had rented out the upstairs once their kids left home. Michael had been there for eight months, pleased that the quiet street was a dead end. There was even a small balcony at the back where he liked to sit and grade papers. At least he had, until the neighbours had inherited a terrier of some fashionable crossbreed. He couldn't decide what was more incredible: that any living creature could make that much noise sixteen hours a day, or that its owners could possibly be so ignorant as to allow it.

Gerry had trimmed the lilac bushes again. With his constant attentions, it was a miracle that they ever had a chance to bloom.

Michael took the stairs two at a time and flung open the door of his apartment, wishing Nicole was there so he could tell her about his discovery. He pulled out his iPhone. A voicemail message said that she'd dropped by on her way home from City Hall, then gone to her own apartment for the night to catch up on paperwork. That meant she wouldn't want to be disturbed.

*Shit!* He itched to tell somebody.

Diving made him hungry. He opened a can of stew, made toast, and ate while he watched the last two thirds of *Jaws* on TV. He felt a new empathy for the embattled Chief Brody, trying to convince his willfully blind community of a deadly shark threat in their waters. Did Michael have some responsibility to report what he'd seen in Evergreen Lake? What if it really did have a harmless explanation? A practical joke, like Phil had claimed? Michael knew that he wouldn't do his prospects at the university any good by crying wolf.

Which was why he had to go back to Evergreen Lake.

He called Phil in the morning to carpool. Marcia Rodriguez told him that Phil had left early for some reason. Michael thanked her, and the last swallow of his coffee tasted bitter.

In the hallway to his office, one of the interns told him that his department head, Laura Wood, wanted to see him. Wood was big on "face time" with the faculty under her supervision, but she rarely had anything important to talk about, and her efforts to be chummy were painful. Maybe he'd go close to lunchtime so he'd have an excuse to keep it short.

Grace McDonald looked up from the more comfortable of the two chairs in the small office they shared.

"Hear about Harcourt's paper at the conference in Brussels?"

"Good morning to you, too. What's Harcourt on about this time? RNA degradation?"

"No, I think he let that bone drop for now. The results of his latest study, though—the one with victims of Catholic priests..."

"Alleged victims."

"Sure, alleged. He claims his results prove that such memories can be implanted unintentionally and are completely unreliable. Of course, he is Catholic. Maybe that's the field you should go into."

"The Catholic Church?"

She laughed. "Repressed memory. You could do a better job than Harcourt."

It was a reminder that Michael's research choice this year, the addictive implications of brain-computer interfaces, had exploded in popularity and the better-funded universities were leaving him behind. He might have to return to his previous field, the psychological implications of living in the high-stress artificial environments of submarines, spacecraft, and space habitats. He didn't resent Grace for bringing it up. She was only trying to help.

Repressed memory. Were his memories about Evergreen Lake reliable? He opened his mouth just as Grace slid her iPad across to him with Harcourt's executive summary displayed. The opening of the second paragraph and the graph below it caught his attention, and he forgot what he'd been about to say. Soon after that, another intern showed up with the department's preliminary scheduling sheets, and that work lasted until lunch time. He and Grace grabbed some club sandwiches at the Tim Horton's restaurant a few buildings over.

He had no classes that day, but he was pleased that his Psych courses were among the most popular. Students liked debating whether the comic strip kid in *Calvin and Hobbes* or the *X-Files*' FBI agent Fox Mulder was the most typical of the Dreamer personality profile. They liked seeing clips of *The Rocky Horror Picture Show* to illustrate the difference between extraverts and introverts, and exploring Jungian concepts via episodes of *Star Trek*. Not to mention that Michael did a mean Sigmund Freud imitation.

It had taken a couple of years to develop his style (and forget his fears of his late father watching over his shoulder), but the offbeat stuff was his way of finding pleasure in a career that had never been his first choice.

The afternoon filled itself with busywork; and when he pulled up at his apartment at 5:30, he realized that he hadn't got around to seeing Laura Wood. She'd be pissed.

Nicole arrived soon after him. She pulled her car in behind the Smiths' Subaru, a sign that she didn't expect to spend the night. It was a new BMW she'd bought a month after the election that made his ten-year-old gray Honda Civic look like a brick on wheels. He did his best not to be jealous—she worked hard for her toys.

A lot had changed since he'd first met Nicole, the night his brother Jay dragged him out to audition for a community-theatre group. Jay had done a few shows with them and got a big kick out of it. To Michael's surprise, his nerdy brother was actually a pretty good dancer and could hold a tune, though he only did chorus parts—no leads yet. Jay introduced him to a woman who'd done one show with the company—*The Sound of Music*—and nailed the part of the Baroness, though there was nothing aristocratically reserved about her. This time Nicole was auditioning for the bold and brassy lead in *Mame*, a much better fit. Michael wasn't surprised that she got it, but was astonished to find out he'd been cast as her husband Beauregard.

The part wasn't huge, but all of those nights singing "Loving You" turned fiction into fact. She was beautiful, smart, and sassy, thoroughly feminine but refreshingly earthy. He fell for her hard, and she returned his feelings with surprising passion. Three years later, he was still amazed that a woman like her had picked him.

At the time, she was working in the auditing department of the local taxation center and when she decided she could do a better job of running the city than the clowns in charge, her insightful criticism of the municipality's financial practices convinced the voters she was right, and she was elected mayor of the city. Michael had been thrilled.

He hadn't foreseen how the new job would change things.

"Hey, you. How come you didn't call me last night? Where were you anyway—cruising Elgin Street?"

The dig took some of the heat out of his kiss. A year earlier, eager to impress a class of grad students, he'd taken them out to interview some hookers and been caught in a police sweep. His explanation had satisfied the cops, but Nicole wouldn't let it go.

"Phil and I went for a dive south of town. Want to hear about it?"

"Got anything to eat?" She pulled the fridge door open for a few seconds then gave a slightly more thorough inspection of the freezer. "OK, pizza, then. Your pizza place or mine?"

The question was moot. Michael preferred Pizza Hut, but she always ordered from one of the hometown operations instead because it wouldn't do for the mayor's boyfriend to have any other kind of pizza boxes stacked in his recycling bin. She picked up the phone.

He tried to bring up the dive again while they ate, but she was obsessed with a public input session scheduled for the next night.

"We just finished the last goddamned budget and we're already asking people what we should do better next time. It'll be the same old shit: roads and health care and lower taxes. As if the city has any control over the hospitals. Jesus." She washed down her third slice of pizza with a long chug of beer.

As he cleared away the few dishes, she was already opening her city-supplied laptop and quickly immersing herself in the numbers. An hour later, when she asked him to make tea, he seized the opportunity to talk.

"We saw something. Phil and I. On the bottom of Evergreen Lake. There's something down there that glows. Bright enough to see from a long way off."

"Shit, don't tell me it's toxic waste! Clay Developments applied for a permit to dump some stuff into one of the lakes down there. If Amanda's jumped the gun, I'll shove a big, fat fine up her ass."

"I don't think so. It looks like...well, some kind of structure, but totally strange. I don't think it's...from here."

"From Sudbury? What, you think Elliot Lake's been dumping radioactive stuff in our territory?"

"From *Earth*. I don't think it's from Earth. I think it's...*alien*." He stood looking at her open mouth and realized his hands were shoved into his pockets. He pulled them out.

Nicole laughed.

"*Jesus*, I thought you were serious for a second."

"I *am* serious."

Her mouth clamped shut, then she laughed again. "Shit on a stick. I knew I shouldn't have let you go to that Sci-Fi convention."

"Oh, for God's sake! I'm telling you what I saw. I didn't imagine it."

"What? What did you see?"

"Something glowing. Something...like giant petals of clear gelatin, but arranged like a structure."

"Down at the bottom of a lake, stirred up with floating muck?"

"Yes."

"What does Phil say?"

"I don't know. He thought it was a practical joke, but..."

"So you figured it was worth trying out on me? You've got a weird sense of humour, Michael. And the kettle's boiling."

"Forget it. I'll go back...take some pictures."

"Sure." She put her glasses back on and turned to the screen again. He went into the kitchenette and got out the tea.

She gave him a perfunctory kiss on the cheek when she left for home around ten.

# 3

The water was teacup-warm as Sakiko Matthews plummeted backward through a volcano of hissing bubbles. When the turbulence began to clear, she saw the dive boat above her like a Dali-painting against blue sky—a toddler-Dali: distorted, but the colors too bright for the adult painter. With a bass crash and sibilant fizzing Yuri Hutchings plunged into the ocean three meters away clutching his dive mask and Olympus camera, his left arm holding hoses tight to his ribs. Sakiko's blood surged with delight to be in the ocean again, the first time she'd been back to the Great Barrier Reef since her sophomore year, far too long ago. She'd dived many seas in the intervening years, but the Great Barrier Reef was special in its vastness, like an undersea continent of its own instead of the fringed skirt so many other reefs provided to the islands they adorned.

After exchanging an OK sign with Yuri, she pointed down with her thumb and saw his small nod. Rolling into a spread position like skydivers, they bled air from their buoyancy vests and dropped toward the breathtaking landscape ten meters below. It was impossible to imagine the splendor of a coral reef in sunlit waters without having seen it. A palette of color never experienced in the world of air, in fantastical shapes like the doodles of a madman.

She goosed her inflator button to hover over patches of vivid pink Acropora coral in polka-dotted nubs separated by plate corals of neon green. A few kicks of her fins took her around blades of fan corals like lacy elephants' ears, except a dusky-mint color with red veining underneath. Yuri swam on the other side of the coral, as if they were two children playing hide-and-seek. They'd dived together dozens of times since he'd signed on as her research assistant, and many times she'd let him lead; but this time she chose their path. A few meters beyond the fans, a school of orange fairy basslets playfully circled a giant barrel sponge: a cauldron of moss green that held a small yellow damselfish and a pair of blue-girdled angelfish within its convoluted bowl.

Yuri pointed behind Sakiko and she turned to see a stream of silvery paddlefish, their burnt-orange fins seeming to stroke almost in unison—hundreds of them making their way over the seascape: a giant serpent of many parts. She gently swam toward their flow. Skittish at first, they gradually allowed her into their midst. Gulliver among the Lilliputians. Yuri raised his camera, and she lifted her hand in a regal wave. The paddlefish led her between outcrops of tube sponges, one of royal blue, its partner sun-yellow. She was sorely tempted to linger, especially when she saw a clownfish and his mate peeking shyly from the middle of the sprouting tubes. A Disney-influenced childhood made every clownfish a Nemo in her mind, even now. But she and Yuri had come to the reef for a reason, and it wasn't sightseeing.

The dull gray-green shadow in the distance was probably the rise they'd been told about. She slipped out of the river of paddlefish and swam toward the drab mound, passing over some large, grooved brain coral, nearly ringed by sea whips writhing like gorgon's hair. The rising slope was terraced by plate coral decorated with crimson feathers, yellow staghorns, box-fire coral in various shades, and a few green mermaids' fans.

As she neared the crest of the mound, she braced herself, but it wasn't enough.

Her stomach twisted in dismay.

For as far as she could see, the seascape had been drained of color like a sunbleached photograph. The familiar shapes were there, but dulled, as if rendered in ash. And ash wasn't far from the truth. The life in the coral's calcified structures had fled leaving algae-coated bones.

Bleached coral and dead coral were everywhere she looked, dark gray-green, shading to the color of slate. Shapes that seemed so wondrous in blooms of color appeared horribly grotesque without it. The Australian Institute of Marine Science estimated that the Great Barrier Reef had lost half of its living coral, or more, but she hadn't been able to truly conceive of it. Not until now. The dry compressed air from her tanks caught in her throat and she almost choked, working hard to summon some saliva.

More than half of the die-off had been caused by storm damage. Increasingly malevolent cyclones pounded the shallow coral with heavy surf that stirred up the bottom and coated living polyps with silt that blocked the sunlight they needed. That would be the darker coral, dead for some time. Other corals were victims of predatory crown-of-thorns starfish, a scourge that biologists had so far been unable to stop. Without the starfish, the coral might have recovered from the injury of the storms.

There was also another factor, one that had brought Sakiko and Yuri halfway around the world. It was responsible for the champagne-colored terraces nearest to her in shallower water, stretching as far as she could see to her left.

Coral bleaching. It was a scourge caused by warmer water temperatures and increasing acidity as the world's oceans absorbed atmospheric carbon dioxide.

Humans had done this, she thought, a cold knot in her chest. Greenhouse gases freed from ancient oil beds and shale beds and coal veins and forests by humans ravenous for energy. Those gases had warmed the planet, made the ocean waters more acidic, and probably created the conditions that had allowed the starfish to thrive in their path of destruction too.

As a scientist, her greatest cause for hope was that bleaching could be reversed if conditions improved soon enough. Her greatest challenge was the precarious symbiotic relationship between the coral and a certain species of algae that lived within the coral cells. The algae turned sunlight into food used by the coral polyps which, in turn, nourished the algae. But if the water temperature rose too much, the algae became poisonous to the coral, forcing the polyp to expel the very thing that provided it with food. The coral avoided immediate death but condemned itself to slow starvation. Making matters worse, young coral couldn't survive to replace the old if the water was too acidic.

Sakiko caught Yuri looking at her and realized that she'd been slowly shaking her head. Sucking a deep breath from her regulator she pointed to his camera and swept her arm toward the darkened plain. He nodded and swam forward while she watched, teeth clamped more tightly than necessary onto her mouthpiece. She removed some vials from the pocket of her vest and kicked slowly toward a nearby outcrop to take water, algae, and coral samples.

This wasn't the first time she'd seen bleached and ravaged coral—far from it. A dive trip off Belize had been the original impetus for her career path. But she'd never witnessed bleaching on such a scale, and in a place she'd fervently hoped was too large to suffer so much damage so quickly.

If the harmful temperatures and acidity could be changed, the bleached coral still had a chance of recovery—it would cultivate a supply of algae again and find a new lease on life. That was the focus of Sakiko's research.

She'd put together an ambitious project proposal: to sample acidity and temperature of waters in various seas of the world, learn as much as possible about individual factors affecting those measures, and try to discover some means of mitigating the changes. The future of coral reefs depended on that. Her plan outline represented months of work—thoroughly researched, carefully costed, and backed by some of the most highly-credentialed scientists she knew.

The Foundation had turned it down.

As long as she lived, she'd never understand that. The application was bulletproof—she was sure of it—one of the best she and her advisors had ever seen; but the answer had still been *No*.

How could the Foundation funders be so short-sighted? Or was it simply that she wasn't one of the "stars" of marine biology—hadn't made a name for herself with flashy documentaries that attracted money to the universities? That shouldn't matter—couldn't be *allowed* to matter—when the threat to the reefs was so desperate.

She tightened the cap on the last of her sample vials and waved to catch Yuri's attention. Then she moved her extended index finger in a circle, finishing with it pointing in the direction of the dive boat. Yuri nodded and swam up to her side. They were still good for air and bottom time, but she couldn't bear to stay. She hurried through the zone of devastation and then slowed her kicks over the still-healthy coral bed and tried to fix every single tendril, blade, spike, and blossom, every one of its thousand color shades indelibly into her memory, as if doing so might save them.

Sakiko was thirty-eight years old. She had never received one of the really prestigious grants, most-respected awards, or big-name publication credits in her field. And the places she loved most in the world were dying. She had dedicated her career to them—they were what gave her life purpose. She could not stand by while they vanished.

Which was why she decided to risk everything and *forge* the grant documents she needed.

# 4

"I'm not feeling so great." Phil Rodriguez coughed into the phone. The cough sounded a little forced. "Must've caught a cold. I think I'm going to call in sick. See you." Then the signal was gone.

Michael looked at his phone as if it had offended him.

He walked slowly out to his car but stopped with his fingers on the door handle.

What if Rodriguez wasn't faking?

*What if he'd been infected by something in the lake?*

Maybe the thing they'd seen *was* toxic? Or even radioactive.

*He and Rodriguez might be dead men.*

Wikipedia listed the symptoms of acute radiation sickness. A twist of nausea gave way to a chill in his intestines.

No, that was stupid. He'd been feeling perfectly fine until he'd talked to Phil.

If the object they'd seen really was from somewhere other than Earth, he couldn't ignore the possibility that it would give off some kind of radiation or be contaminated by microorganisms. Could alien germs overwhelm the human immune system? Or would they be far too foreign even to interact with earthly forms of life?

There was no way to know. Michael remembered reading about *panspermia*: Fred Hoyle and Chandra Wickramasinghe's theory that organisms were continually falling from space onto the Earth and might be responsible for periodic epidemics. Opinion was split on the theory, but Michael had never chosen sides. Now the argument was no longer academic.

Maybe he should book off sick, too. Quarantine himself for the sake of others.

Except he'd already been to work the day before and spent the evening with Nicole. He pushed his knuckles against his temples. It didn't help.

If the thing *was* from another planet, he had to trust that advanced beings would know better than to bring unwitting death to the creatures they'd come to meet.

He gripped the steering wheel, trying to steady his hands.

His office voicemail held a message from Laura Wood that sounded like she was gritting her teeth. Although she was at a conference out of town for the day, on her return she would certainly demand to know why he'd ignored her summons of the day before. He spent the day finishing up his course outlines, mainly rewriting the previous year's in slightly different words to make them look new.

His refilled scuba tanks were ready for pickup on his way home, but Harry, the shop owner, was too busy with another customer to talk about Evergreen Lake.

Michael's car seemed to drive itself to Phil's house.

Marcia greeted him at the door.

"He's at work, Michael. Where else would he be?"

He just nodded and backed down the steps awkwardly. At least a fake cold was better than a real illness.

Scuba diving without a buddy was something he'd sworn he'd never do. Reckless. Stupid. A minor equipment failure or a snag on lake bottom debris could be fatal if you were alone.

When Michael had first become a certified diver, he'd persuaded his brother Jay to take the training too, excited to find a bonding experience for them: a natural dive buddy pairing they could both count on. But Jay had lost interest within a few years, and his equipment sat in his garage gathering dust.

Michael called around to some of his other diving friends but none of them were home.

Could he really be sure that whatever he'd seen was worth risking his life?

No.

Neither could he stay away.

As he trudged down the rugged path toward Evergreen Lake, he surveyed the austere landscape. No one knew how the lake had come by its name. Christened by a lumberjack more than a century before? Or named in jest after all of the trees in the Sudbury basin had been sacrificed to rebuild the incinerated Chicago of the 1870s? Decades of regreening efforts had finally coaxed new trees from the barren expanses of exposed Canadian Shield, but most were quick-growing birches and poplars, not evergreens. To Michael, the glacier-carved hills of blackened rock and the small lakes they sheltered held a special beauty. He found peace beside their rugged shores. And escape.

It was strange to think that he needed to escape from anything. His position at the university was the brass ring he'd pursued for years to make his dad truly proud. But an embolism had claimed Dad a week before the job offer. By then, it was a little late for Michael to realize that teaching wasn't his dream job at all, only his father's.

Where his father had complained about Michael's lack of ambition, his mother had proclaimed that it was his curiosity that would get him into trouble. She'd always declared her surprise that he hadn't pursued a science degree—and her disappointment that he hadn't pursued women more avidly. The last days of her battle with cancer had been filled with a longing for grandchildren she would never know.

Maybe he could still make his mark on the world by inspiring others to greatness. But in seven years of teaching there'd been no evidence of that.

The water of the lake seemed darker and lonelier this time. Michael pulled himself down through the murk, self-consciously glancing over his shoulder in a trained reflex, looking for a buddy who wasn't there.

He had a strong feeling that he was on a fool's errand—that his imagination had got the better of him and there was nothing to be found.

But it was there, it was all there.

His brain struggled for comprehension while his body shivered with a mix of fear and wonder.

The water filled with radiance that illuminated the silty lake bottom over an area about the size of a small suburban lot. Strange structures stood in irregular rows: a garden of vast "elephant ear" plants, or an office worker's "cubicle farm" except in barely-perceptible motion—he couldn't find the right analog without knowing whether the things were alive or constructed. What he saw seemed to be a single complex structure built of living materials.

Flattened panel-like objects extended upward like asymmetrical walls about the height of a man but not connected—unless at their bases. Thin, pliant, and nearly transparent, it all gave off light. Everything he saw was a source of light. And the flat surfaces were dappled with patterns of some kind.

With his mind shifting from Sunday School depictions of Heaven to lurid special-effects sequences in sci-fi movies, he fought both the urge to flee and a compelling call to approach.

Afraid or not, he wasn't going to learn any more without getting closer.

Like a spider dropping from its web, he lowered himself into the middle of the glow, keeping clear of the walls. Or maybe not walls. They spread themselves apart. Welcoming.

Unless he wasn't the spider, but the fly.

The gelid panels that surrounded him slowly changed dimension as if in response to a nonexistent wave surge. Oblong pouches draped over the upper edges of some of the panels like Salvadore Dali clocks. The panels were extravagantly radiant, brightening as he came among them, he was sure of it.

He'd been right about patterns on the panels, too: not shadows or reflections, but Rorschach blotches, ovoids, rounded tetrahedrons that paraded, each at its own pace, from edge to edge. Short, jagged lines as well—some separate, some in arranged clusters like oversized *kanji* characters, or the symbol-strewn scribblings of mathematicians' nightmares. His imagination endowed the patterns with meaning, but meaning inaccessible to his conscious understanding. His gloved finger was drawn toward the nearest panel, half expecting the surface to produce a flurry of shooting sparks at his touch.

The image of spider and fly appeared in his mind again.

*Why?*

He glanced down.

A scream erupted from his throat with an explosion of bubbles.

Half his body was covered by clear jelly that spread upward from his waist like an oil slick. He kicked in a panic reflex, but his feet were already encased. The walls had drawn back out of reach of his flailing arms. He tried to push at the jelly—keep it from his head—but it was too thin and too slick. It reached his neck, his chin. His fumbling attempt to hold his mask against his face had the opposite effect, breaking its seal against his skin and letting the invader in. Another primal scream rattled his regulator before it too was thrust aside. Slime covered his nose and then his eyes. He clamped his lips shut, knowing it was futile. He would either drown or the stuff would suffocate him.

In his last few moments of clarity, he opened his eyes and was startled to see every detail of his surroundings: the petal-like panels with their ink-blot symbols in shades of color, no longer black; stunted weeds struggling upward from the sludgy lake bottom; microscopic specks of plant and animal life suspended in the water. He'd thought the visibility was only about six meters—but now it seemed closer to twenty. He'd never seen so well or so far in a freshwater lake.

Then came surrender, and regret. Bubbles burst from his mouth and nostrils and he sucked greedily for air, even as he knew he would find liquid death instead.

His lungs filled with water, ice cold. Emptied. Filled inexplicably a second time, and a third.

Was this drowning? How had he not lost consciousness?

*He was breathing water, for Christ's sake!*

His chest heaved with the effort, but the survival instinct would not let him stop.

With no regulator in his mouth and his body encased in a slick of impossible protoplasm, oxygen was somehow still getting to his brain.

His heartbeat thundered, but panic was a deadly enemy. He had to hold himself together.

There was a new gap on his right where one of the Dali-esque blobs had hung. Was that what had swallowed him? The impression of being eaten was incredibly strong—his body shuddered uncontrollably.

Whatever the reason, the thing was keeping him alive; but for how long? He flung his arms out, trying to find his mouthpiece, and discovered that the jelly no longer impeded him at all. His arms could move, his feet could kick.

Mind reeling, he retrieved his fallen mask and pushed upward toward the sunlight so far away, knees weak as a baby's. Buoyancy control was effortless—he slid through the water like one of its own creatures.

The escape to shore was anticlimactic: the gel peeled itself off his skin and suit to float limply on the surface of the lake. Water gushed from his mouth as he stumbled to the rocky beach, and a minute or two of coughing seemed to clear the rest. The air tasted sweeter than he'd ever known.

Once safely on land, he turned and watched the glistening patch of gelatin drift away flaccidly with the chop from a rising breeze. He collapsed to the ground in a heap, scuba tank clanging against a stone.

When he could bring himself to look up again, the surface of the lake was empty.

His skin crawling, he fumbled with the straps of his heavy gear and fought to pull the clammy rubber wetsuit from his body. He staggered a few steps away and bent over, gasping from effort and strain.

When he'd caught his breath, he clambered up the rocky slope on legs that could barely support him, only vaguely aware of the dirt path beneath his feet, of grasping branches that scratched at his exposed flesh. His first sight of his car blurred behind tears. As he climbed into it, his body began to shake like a dog after a swim, shedding the excruciating tension.

Then he roused himself and gunned the car to life, gravel scattering in its wake.

He'd forgotten something—something important.

*His scuba gear!* He'd left it behind on the lakeshore. He should go back for it.

But he couldn't. The mere thought made him shake again. He gripped the steering wheel fiercely, trying to maintain control.

When he finally pulled up in front of his apartment and killed the ignition, all his energy drained away in an instant, and he sat staring through the windshield, unable to move.

At some point he looked at his watch. Nearly 6:30. He dimly registered that Nicole's car was in the driveway. It took all his strength to climb the stairs.

She yanked the door open before he could reach it. Her shiny black sheath dress and heels were an indictment.

"Jesus, what are you doing in a swimsuit! We should be leaving in ten minutes."

The sound he made was a croak. "Leaving?"

"The United Way 'Be A Goddess' event. I've been asked to give a speech as mayor, and you said you'd be a waiter."

He slumped against the wall, still outside his apartment. He should do something, say something, but the quagmire of his brain wouldn't allow thought to form.

"For God's sake. How quickly can you shower? You smell like rubber. We can be fashionably late, but I don't want to look like an asshole."

"I...I don't think I can go."

"You must be shitting me!"

"I...something happened. Listen. I need to tell you..."

"Good Christ! Are you drunk? Don't tell me you're drunk!" She paced away a few steps, turned back, then snatched up her purse and shook it at him. "You don't give a shit about my career. But the least you could do is keep a promise!"

The Smiths could probably hear her. The neighbors, too. He reached out a hand, but she cuffed it away, grabbed a light shawl from a chair back, and pushed past him out the door. Her heels attacked each stair on the way down, and moments later there was an extra growl to the engine note of her BMW as she wheeled away. He watched the car disappear and kept watching long after she was gone.

*Inside.* He should go inside. Grunting from the effort, he peeled himself free from the wall and stumbled into his apartment. It looked strange in a way he couldn't explain: a rained-on watercolor painting. He shuffled toward the kitchen. Heard a ticking sound and turned toward the clock to watch the hands move, without registering their meaning. He bumped a chair with his hip. There was a half-empty glass on the table. Or half full. Pour it into the sink, or fill it up? He raised it and stared at the way it distorted the wallpaper behind it.

His hand twitched and he nearly dropped the glass, so he set it back down.

Eyes glazed, he shuffled forward a few steps and noticed he was still in his living room. It seemed like a good idea to lie face-down on the couch, turning his head to the side to breathe. The dark TV screen filled his view. He stared at it, afraid that it would suddenly come to life with strange symbols. The thought made him shudder, and shudder again, until the quaking refused to stop. Bringing his knees to his chest as he lay on the couch, he wrapped his arms around them; but a chill had invaded his very bones. Teeth chattering, he made his way to the bathroom, stripped off his swimsuit and stepped into a shower as hot as he could stand, just letting the hard spray pummel his skin.

A long time later he realized that the water had turned cold. It felt slimy. His eyes snapped open and he frantically slapped at his legs, but there was nothing on them.

He got out and dried off quickly, then dug out a worn pair of track pants and a T-shirt that he wore as pajamas, though he wasn't sleepy anymore. His eyes drifted over the bedside table and came to rest on a five by eight picture of himself with Nicole from a vacation they'd taken in Cuba over the winter. It was probably the last time he'd seen her smile like that. He reached his hand toward it, but it seemed too far away to grasp. Instead, he noticed that he was hungry.

There was some leftover Indonesian takeout in the fridge, but the sight of the gelatinous sauces made him swallow hard. Instead, he took a frozen Jamaican meat patty from the freezer and heated it in the microwave. In the cupboard was a bottle of brandy that Nicole liked. He poured some into a whiskey glass—three ounces, maybe four—and carefully replaced the bottle. He'd better wash the glass out afterward. Nicole already thought he was drunk—if she came back.... But she wouldn't. Not that night.

Chewing the meat patty without tasting it, he returned to the living room and sat upright in the middle of the couch, facing the TV. His hand fumbled for the remote, and when the screen lit, he began to flip channels: ten or twenty before he looked down at his hand and saw it twitching on its own. The memory of a slick of clear jelly creeping up his arm gave him another violent shudder.

*No*, he had to pull himself together. A large swallow of brandy might help. Maybe a few more.

The bottom of the glass showed him the thing at the bottom of the lake. *Things*. Like a sci-fi horror movie, like a nightmare. His brain floundered through memories but could find no matches for what he'd seen there. He couldn't possibly say what the memories were; he could only try to guess what they were not.

The giant petals or panels that moved on their own did not fit into any category—animal, mineral, or technological—that he knew.

The structure was artificial—he was sure of that—yet like nothing he had ever seen or heard about. He estimated that it might be as big as two city buses side by side, segmented into uneven compartments by partitions of waving jelly. Spatterings of symbols flowed across and over and between the partitions like a news ticker. Was that their function? Communication? Meant for whom? Humans? Or a species totally alien to the Earth?

Why would such a thing be placed at the bottom of a lake? To hide it? Or only to keep it out of easy reach as some form of test? Like the monolith on the Moon in Kubrick's *2001*.

He had to tell someone about it. The government. Scientists. *Somebody!* Only...what if the conspiracy theories were true and others *had* already discovered proof of aliens? Had the government bought their silence? Or simply made them disappear?

More brandy only provided more questions. Finally, he left the glass in the bathroom and crawled under the covers of his bed, pulling them well up over his neck. He'd left a light on outside the bedroom door. Just in case Nicole came by. That's what he told himself.

He was exhausted beyond anything he'd ever felt, yet his eyes seemed to bore holes through the blackness of his bedroom: not cameras but projectors, casting images of petal-like partitions; blotches, squiggles, and lightning bolts; shapeless sacs that could come to life and swallow you whole.

Sometime in the middle of the night he snapped awake.

What if he hadn't been attacked at all?

*What if he had been rescued?*

Divers sometimes called the wetsuits and drysuits they wore "environment suits," because they protected the wearer from the cold, and from the dangerous surfaces of coral reefs or rusted shipwrecks. Certainly, an explorer of other worlds would need protection. Was that what had swallowed him? To say that it had acted like something alive meant nothing—he had no way to distinguish between alien life and a supremely advanced technology.

If he'd been attacked, why had it let him go? If it was some kind of protective covering, why had it responded to him—a human—and provided life-giving oxygen where no air was available? If it was alien, did its actions mean that they breathed oxygen too? Or had the suit of jelly somehow sensed his different need and adapted itself?

A smart wetsuit, or spacesuit...an outer suit, anyway, and alien. An *exo*suit, in more ways than one.

What about the glowing structure itself? Was it alive, or an artifact?

Both, he thought. Its parts seemed grown rather than manufactured, but he had no evidence that it was sentient. It could be robotic. It moved with purpose, displayed information. Maybe it was an outpost left behind by a roving band of interstellar explorers. A remote camp, control center, monitoring station. All of the above. Or none. It was possible that none of those human concepts had any equivalent among creatures from another world.

Even if the outpost itself wasn't alive, that didn't mean it was uninhabited. But the more he thought about it, the more he believed that the protoplasm that had enveloped him was a super-sophisticated protective suit, and the structure it serviced was no longer in use.

Why had its creators come to earth? Where had they gone? And if they returned, would they intend to help or to harm?

The questions swarmed like clouds of biting gnats.

He needed answers. And there was only one place to find them.

# 5

Sakiko's heart was a creature taken from the wild and held captive in her chest. It thumped at her ribs so hard she could hear it clearly in the silence of the darkened hallways. Then there was another sound, a rustling. She turned around in sudden fear, and the folder of papers in her hand slapped loudly against the wall. The rustle had come from them. She watched in dismay as her arm shook, ignoring her efforts to control it.

A swallow to ease her dry throat triggered a cough instead. Horrified, she thrust her back against the wall: a cat burglar in a spotlight.

No one came. There was no reason for anyone else to be on that floor of the building so late in the evening, and no security system to speak of. The office held nothing worth taking. Only documents. Pieces of paper that would mean nothing to anyone except a handful of accountants and a few dozen academics. Yet, if she were caught there, her career would be over. Not because she wasn't allowed in the Foundation's offices—no one had even blinked when she'd walked in that afternoon, ostensibly to look up details of one of her earlier research grants. But it would be hard to explain why she'd stayed behind after everyone else had gone home, an interminable two hours in an out-of-the-way restroom for the handicapped. And the papers she held would be a smoking gun.

None of this would have been necessary if her first plan had worked. It should have been so easy to slide the folder into a stack of other papers on Seth Robbins' desk. All it required was a little playacting: a sudden stare out the window behind him—he would turn to look, and she'd plant her sheaf of faked forms. Sakiko's boyfriend Doug was a stage magician—she knew a thing or two about sleight of hand.

Except the clerk hadn't turned away, had only glared at her for wasting his time. She'd muttered a lame apology and backed out of his cubicle.

Now, a hastily improvised Plan B. If Robbins locked the drawers of his filing cabinet, she was screwed.

He hadn't. She pulled the top drawer open and scanned the ordered files within. They were arranged by date and rotated so the current month was always at the front. That made things easier. Sakiko flipped past a couple of folders with names she didn't recognize and put hers behind them. Then she reached in again and pushed her folder down so it was hidden by the others. With luck, Robbins would never realize there had been an addition and never have cause to look for it. She'd put hours of painstaking effort into the forgeries, especially the signatures, but it would all be wasted if Robbins remembered that he hadn't handled any paperwork for Sakiko Matthews that month.

Feeling like the heroine in a bad melodrama, she pulled her sleeve up over her hand and used the cloth to wipe down the top edge of the drawer and its handle. Then, in a state of numbness, she made her way along the hall to the door of the stair well. Praying that its old lock didn't keep an electronic record, she descended quickly to street level and walked as casually as she could along a wider hall to an outside exit. Only then did she allow herself to breathe.

So much for the *easy* part of her plan, she thought. Now it was time for a conversation with Yuri.

*"You did what?"*

"It's the only way. Goddammit, you know that our funding should have been approved."

"But it wasn't. You can't just take the money anyway."

"I'm not taking it for myself. It's for the reefs. For the oceans. It's for our whole race."

"Jesus Christ, Sakiko, it's still stealing." He sat heavily, nearly missing the office chair.

"You saw what I saw in Australia. Tell me that didn't change you."

"Of course it did. I'd do anything if..."

"Anything?"

"Well, I wasn't planning on going to jail, if that's what you mean."

She pulled over the second chair and sat with their knees only inches apart.

"Why did you come to work with me five years ago? You could have had a place with researchers way ahead of me—men getting big-name grants: the prestigious awards I never get."

"You don't get them because you're a woman. Your research is just as good. I picked you because you're so committed—you know that."

"Well now it's time to demonstrate that commitment. I'm serious. I can't water down my proposal and be content to produce a few more academic papers that nobody reads. The reefs are dying.

Maybe the oceans themselves are dying, while people who could do something are sitting on their asses."

He held up his hands. "I know all that. Exactly how will you be able to help if you're sitting in a jail cell?"

"I won't get caught. The jury panel never checks the paper trail, and the clerks never question the jury. The only way it would be flagged is if the computer records don't match the paper records."

Yuri rubbed his face with his hand. He had to clear his throat before speaking.

"And you expect me to change the entries in the computer."

"You've hacked that database before."

"For fun. Because you couldn't wait to find out about the Fiji grant."

"It's a full access password, I'm sure. Robbins is too lazy to use layers of encryption." She reached for his hand and gave it a squeeze. Their friendship was totally platonic, and they rarely touched, even by accident. "Something has to be done, and nobody else is looking in the right direction. It's up to us. Anyway, I've already stuck my head into the noose. The paper copies are in Robbins' cabinet and I'm not going back to take them out. You do what you have to do." She stood up and walked toward their office door. Her heart was in her throat, afraid that he wouldn't stop her.

"You do remember that I quit being a lawyer so I could make an *honest* living?"

She smiled. "See? You won't let us go to jail."

He closed his eyes and shook his head, then wheeled the office chair over to his computer.

# 6

Opening his bleary eyes, Michael felt disoriented, his thoughts like worms squirming through mud.

The sights of his bedroom were totally familiar, almost excessively normal. Yet, they seemed overlaid with a sense of unreality: impressions of a watery panorama populated by glowing shapes without solid substance.

A *delusion*, that's what it was. A dream. Disappointed with work and his love life, his imagination had supplied an escape, albeit a bizarre one. Carl Jung might have said his unconscious was trying to divert from his real problems by tapping into surreal memories.

Nothing to worry about, as long as the delusion didn't persist.

He remembered that it was Saturday. Nicole had made a commitment for them to stand at the entrance to the city's biggest mall along with teams of firemen, soliciting shoppers to donate cash into big fireman's boots in support of Muscular Dystrophy research. Michael wasn't really needed, but he didn't dare back out twice in a row; and he didn't want to—he wanted to be with her. He was ready when she called.

The two hours passed quickly, and Nicole was in a buoyant mood. She'd collected as many compliments as donations, and voters' expressions of support were ambrosia to her. Other diners recognized her when they stopped for a Deluxe hamburger on the way home. By the time they got back to Michael's apartment, she wore a big grin.

It took him by surprise when she pulled him close and started to unfasten his belt.

They made love, fierce and hot. She'd always been an enthusiastic lover, and if it was her way of telling him he was forgiven, he was OK with that. The relief added an extra level of pleasure.

Except for one moment after climax, when he felt her slick skin slide over his and remembered a skin-to-skin contact of a very different kind the afternoon before.

He blamed his sudden shiver on a draft from the open window.

Waiting.

Not the long wait of stasis, that easy absence without even the awareness of waiting. Stasis had lasted through more than ten thousand sidereal periods of the planet, yet had seemed like mere moments. This waiting is very different. The bipedal being has been gone for only two planetary rotations, and the time seems endless.

Lack of purpose. More accurately: a lack of a predetermined purpose with no means to accomplish it.

Interface with the being was strange. Genetic memory confirmed that it was not like interface with the Creators, but also unlike expectations. Deliberate genetic encoding based on the biped's evolutionary ancestors should have ensured a biological match. An easy joining. Had ten thousand of the planet's years changed the species so much? Or had there been too much interference from that skin of manufactured material it wore?

The data archive of the Controller does not help, and there are no living Creators within detectable range to consult. That was expected. What was not expected is the state of the other pods.

As the Creators departed, all the pods left behind entered stasis, their metabolism slowed to a near stop until the time of awakening when the native species would be ready for them. But something has gone wrong. Too much time has passed. Their life force is spent, used up. Wasted. They are no longer viable—their purpose will not be achieved.

These circumstances are deeply distressing: to be the sole remaining pod, and only a *juvenile*—possibly not yet ready to fulfill its own purpose.

The biological imperative to respond to the native being is strong and not to be denied. But an attempt to join with the biped has been met with resistance: barriers both physical and incorporeal. The joining was incomplete.

There is a powerful need for completeness.

Michael stood looking at the lake, trying to work up his courage.

A calm surface could hide so very much. Part of the attraction of scuba diving was the sense of a whole other world beneath the thin plane that divided water from air. The memory of his last dive made his skin crawl, but his desire for answers was as strong as the pull of gravity.

His gear was still where he'd left it, the scuba tank still half-full. The weather had been clear, but he triple-checked everything anyway. Without a buddy to help lift the heavy equipment onto his back, he decided to put it on in the water and take advantage of its flotation. He splashed awkwardly through the shallows, pulling the inflated vest and tank across the surface. As he arranged the hoses and prepared to slide his arms under the straps, he sensed a change in the water lapping against his back. With a shock he realized there was a circular patch of material floating around him like an oil slick, gelatinous and iridescent.

The exosuit.

A persistent schizophrenic delusion?

No, there was no point seeking refuge in psychobabble. Reality swirled around his thighs.

Hesitantly, he extended his hand, his gloved fingertips still able to relay to him the slippery smoothness of the substance. Like an oil slick, but more solid. He watched as it slowly began to climb his fingers, stretching thin, like syrup, as he pulled his hand back a few inches, then sliding off, to re-form into a smooth film.

As soon as he'd entered the water, it had perceived him, had come to him. Even identified him. Why not? Its approach would be no stranger than any of its other attributes. Was it there to serve him, or did it have a more sinister purpose? The skin of his back twitched, as if anticipating a sting through his wet suit. Instead, the gel floated placidly, waiting.

Well, he had expected it to appear, but not to seek him out the moment he entered the water. What did such promptness say about it? That it was eagerly benevolent?

Or *hungry*?

Heart racing, he made up his mind and dragged his dive gear back to shore—everything but his camera. Then he waded out and allowed the gel slick to surround him again. Trying to keep his breathing calm, he took halting steps in his bulky fins, testing the bottom to make sure it was firm enough to let him push back to the surface in a hurry. The slick spread up over the neoprene suit along with the level of the water until, with a final decisive motion, Michael thrust his hooded head under.

Within seconds his face was coated. The buoyancy of the wet suit tried to lift his legs, but he sculled to stay vertical. Still reluctant to release the air in his lungs, he let some bubbles dribble from his lips, then accidentally inhaled through his nose to replace the lost air. Water in his sinus cavities had always been painful, but not this time. Did the exosuit coat those inner body surfaces, too? It must.

To voluntarily let cold liquid pour into his lungs was the hardest thing he'd ever done. The first three attempts, he couldn't do it. The fourth time—desperate to breathe—he told himself he was in the open air. The illusion didn't prevent a panicked thrashing as water hit the back of his throat, but his lungs filled easily. Out. In again. The effort to breathe even seemed less than the last time. Not as natural as breathing air, but manageable.

His eyes clenched tightly shut. Now he let them pop open and suppressed a gasp. He could see all the way to the lake bottom more than twenty meters below, details of a sunken log and a car-sized boulder as sharp as coins sealed in glass.

He leaned forward, automatically preparing to exhale and push himself toward the depths with powerful kicks of his legs, but neither was needed. He slid through the water like a seal so effortlessly that he had to use his hands to slow down. In a normal descent, the air pressure in the hollow passages of his ears and sinuses had to be equalized with the water pressure by pinching his nostrils every few seconds and forcing air into the tubes that linked ears with throat. Now, though, no equalizing was necessary.

At the end of his long, gliding swoop through the liquid lay the crystal lattice of welcoming light. He sculled his hands to pull up short and swung his camera into position. The illuminated viewfinder was dim compared to the outpost, and its resolution poor, but he clicked off a few shots. Then he leaned forward again. The mere labor of thought drew him to a smooth halt as he came among the clear panels. There must also be a floor—the lake bottom sediment went undisturbed by his arrival.

The irregular structure of the outpost was already familiar, yet there was a difference this time. Now, there was no random spray of patterns and blots on every surface in every direction, as before. Instead, wherever he looked, the patterns followed his gaze. He tested that by moving his head, and then only his eyes. The symbols flowed quickly to stay in his view, with groups of shapes remaining in what was clearly a coherent order of some kind. The exosuit must be in communication with the displays, he realized, relaying the positioning of his eyes. Did that mean the creators of this structure had eyes, too, or simply understood how they worked?

Myriad markings teased at his brain, challenging him to make sense of them. He almost could. Like the jumbled words of a puzzle, he knew that meaning would leap from them full-blown if he could only find the key. For now, that full comprehension was blocked by something. Yet there were...impressions . . . that could be absorbed and analyzed: a sense of great age, yet also great potency; an aura of danger, yet promise. Although this...outpost was extravagantly alien, he couldn't help but feel that it was meant to be found by someone of his own race.

He'd almost forgotten about the camera. He held it up as steadily as he could and pressed the shutter button. The ambient light was too bright for the flash to trigger, but the long shutter speed might produce motion blur; so he took a few more shots with the flash forced to fire. After that, he switched to video and slowly panned over the outpost structure.

He reached out to touch the nearest flat surface. It reacted by producing a dot, then a line. A tiny motion of his fingertip conjured a teardrop shape, a squiggle, a lightning bolt. The display responded with similar shapes, but they faded out and stopped. He tried again, with a drag of his finger and then a double tap. The surface gave slightly under his touch but offered no friction. His resulting marks were replaced by a string of symbols appearing right to left and gradually downward, but they too broke off quickly.

He got it. He was writing, but he didn't know the language. There could be no meaningful response to his gibberish. Training in linguistics wasn't a requirement for a psychology professor—he'd need to consult with a colleague in the language department. Or maybe the math department? The arrangement of the smaller markings reminded him of high-level equations.

However, getting help from others would force him to share his find, and he wasn't prepared to do that. Not yet. Maybe he could do some research on his own first. He raised the camera and took pictures of the symbols, then some more video of his finger drawings and the panels' response to them. He wished he'd brought better equipment—he was gathering evidence of an epic scientific discovery.

With a start, he realized that he'd forgotten to look at his watch when he submerged, and he had no dive computer to calculate the nitrogen absorption of his blood. It was time to go up. It would be absurd to risk the unknown hazards of an alien technology, only to die from a decompression injury.

He took one more lingering look around, trying to place every detail firmly in his memory. Then he gently willed himself to rise from the depths and move toward the land. As he stepped out onto the shore, the exosuit obediently peeled away.

Could it possibly be regret he felt as it vanished beneath the waves?

# 7

"Goddamn it, Michael. If deliberately avoiding me is your idea of a joke...."

"I wasn't avoiding you. I just..."

"Never mind. I don't have time for excuses." Laura Wood slammed a hand on her desk, making a trio of expensive pens bounce. One of them rolled onto the floor. She began to bend over but stopped herself. "God, you're making me wonder if I made the wrong choice."

"What choice?"

She swiveled her chair straight and tugged at the bottom of her jacket.

"The department's facing cutbacks, like everybody else. More, because fewer students have signed up for the Psych program the past couple of years."

"Don't tell me you're going to drop courses. We're barely staying compatible with other universities as it is."

"As a matter of fact, we've been told to continue with the same courses but with less staff. Someone has to go."

Michael felt a chill in his gut. He couldn't afford to be canned. He had so little job experience that finding another teaching position would be a bitch. He tried to meet Wood's eyes without showing any emotion, but she gave a cold smile.

"No, it's not you. The dean likes you for some reason. Thinks you've got potential. Maybe because students seem to enjoy your unorthodox approach to teaching—your enrolment numbers are up the past two years. Anyway, it's Grace McDonald."

The cold fingers playing along his intestines gave a squeeze. "Grace? You can't. She's only a couple of years away from a full pension."

Wood shrugged. "I did mention that to the dean. He acted as if he hadn't heard. But he did hear the part about her job performance." She leaned forward. "You and I both know that Grace hasn't been the same teacher since her breast cancer. The fire is gone. She'd rather look at pictures of her grandson."

"Granddaughters. Twins. Besides, she's spent most of the past year recovering from the chemo."

"If you want to persuade the dean to fire you instead, feel free." Her mouth twitched. Michael felt sickened.

"How will you be able to cover her courses?" he asked quietly.

"I'm not going to. You are."

"You're not serious!"

"Come on, Michael. You know you've been getting an easy ride lately—only one of your courses has had a change of curriculum in ten years. You could do it in your sleep. I'll even spring for a couple of teaching assistants to do some of the grunt work for you." She sighed and her eyes frosted. "It's not like you have a lot of choice here."

She was entirely right about that.

He and Nicole spent that evening together, but only in body. He'd often felt it was a sign of their affection to spend long hours together without talking, just exchanging the occasional caress in passing. This time there were no caresses, though he longed to feel her arms around him. She labored at her kitchen table over budget papers. He sat on her sofa with his iPad, ostensibly working at course preparation, but most of the time simply staring into space.

Grace McDonald was going to lose her job, and he was going to keep his. There was no justice in that. Grace was a great teacher; and if she'd lost some enthusiasm, it was only temporary. She'd always wanted to be a psych prof. It was Michael who'd been dragged into the job in a misguided attempt to win parental love and approval. It was Michael whose recent enjoyment of the profession was already beginning to cool thanks to the attitudes of the new crop of students, many of them spoiled brats with an outrageous sense of entitlement.

Were the beings that had created the outpost any more alien to him than the zombies with blank faces who sat in classroom rows, thinking he didn't know they were texting under their desks? If he could comprehend the ungrammatical scribblings and snatches of garbled letters that passed for communication in their world, why not a language from another planet?

If only it *were* so easy. Without context, it might be impossible to decipher a truly alien language and symbology. The earliest written languages of Earth had often used markings that were representational—visual analogs of what they stood for. Some languages still used symbols that resembled real objects, but others had diverged entirely from that path. There was nothing in the appearance of the word "cat" that resembled an image of a fur-covered animal with four legs. An advanced language from another world could easily be just as far from its original roots.

The only glimmer of hope was that he might have a guide: the exosuit not only sensed his presence in the water and responded to his need for air, it seemingly could track the movement of his eyes. When the outpost had displayed symbols for Michael, it had kept them directly in his line of sight. It had even tried to respond to his written gibberish. That had to mean it expected a being of his kind to communicate with it. Where was the breakdown? Was it possible that the advanced knowledge of the alien race didn't extend to the translation of languages? Unlikely. So why wasn't the technology working?

Even human spacesuits enabled the wearer to interact with computer systems in a spacecraft or elsewhere. The exosuit must have a similar capability, but something was blocking that function.

And suddenly he knew what it was.

He made an excuse to go home early and tried to sleep—tried to wait until the next day. He couldn't.

The path to the lake was a bitch, even though the moon was nearly full, and he'd brought a flashlight. At least he wasn't encumbered by dive gear. When he reached the shore, he stood still, asking himself one last time if he was insane. Then he stripped off his clothes, draped them over a rock, and waded into the water.

He felt the gel before he saw it, the gentle plastic touch against the skin of his abdomen, just slightly warmer than the water. From his waist it spread downward—he couldn't help flinching as it covered his genitals—and then followed the water line upward as he resumed walking. Its progress over his neck made him shudder, and it tickled the inner surfaces of his ears. But those sensations were quickly swept aside as he felt its full presence against his skin. Electric. Alive! Like a current of energy that flowed in waves over his body.

He could feel the texture of the water like never before; hear the lapping of tiny wavelets against rocks thirty meters away; roll and slide and tumble without effort while cradled by the liquid but in no way impeded by it. Even as his mind formed the thought, his body plunged into the depths, able to hover, drop, rise at a moment's thought. He was a creature of the water.

The outpost lit up as he drew near: a glorious crystal palace amid the darkness, and he glided into its center like a butterfly alighting on a flower.

*OK*, he thought, with a deep breath. *I'm ready.*

Ultimate stimulation! The juvenile revels in its new state: not yet completion, not yet full bonding, but energy exchanged and shared, opening the way for true joining. Without interference from the native creature's artificial skin, it is possible to absorb not only energy, but *essence*. To link with every neural pathway. To experience sensory impressions and respond to cortical directives. Inter-species interface as it is meant to be.

The biped has a consciousness, though an alien one. There can be communication. It can be instructed and persuaded to serve the purposes of the Creators.

The juvenile allows the mental energy of the other to embed images and concepts alongside its own engrams. Thus equipped, it is able to inform the Controller's display components how to produce images in a form the being will recognize: manipulate the wavelengths of the radiated light, adjust contrast and depth. Begin the translation of the Creators' symbology into forms relevant to the creature's own environment and experience. It is not an instant process, but the Controller's technology is very fast.

The biped responds, its fluid of oxygenation circulating more quickly, its eyes moving rapidly. Encouraged, the juvenile relaxes into a more passive state, allowing itself to be the conduit between its fledgling bond-partner and the Controller's central processor. The Controller is ready. It begins to display images of this planet as it was before the pods' long sleep: ice plateaus, the biped's ancestors. Gradually, different images: of another planet covered almost entirely by liquid; of intelligent quadrupeds—the Creators; of blue-bright points of light against the endless black of space. More images, and symbols—the central processor working with the juvenile to translate these into mental concepts until the biped reacts with recognition.

The creature has flexibility of mind—and curiosity. Above all, curiosity.

That is very good. That will be necessary for the next step.

# 8

"What's up with you and Ed Ryder?"

"What do you mean?"

It had been a tough day. Sakiko's ears burned from long hours on the phone arranging all the finicky details of their expedition, and she had a headache. Yuri had spent just as much time using his computer to work out quantities of gear and supplies, convert currencies, juggle dollar figures and data requests on endless spreadsheets. It was after nine o'clock; they were beat and they were hungry. The Serpent's Tongue pub a couple of blocks from the campus offered killer nachos and a decent selection of craft beers.

"A lot of people don't like their department heads," Yuri said, "especially when they're new. But I get the impression you hate the guy's guts."

"Is it that obvious?"

"Only to me."

"Good."

"And anybody else who notices that you grit your teeth and your eyes become slits whenever you're in the same room with him."

"Shit." She took a long pull of her beer. She'd cut her teeth on rice lagers like Sapporo, but these days her taste ran to bitter brews with lots of hops ever since she'd discovered a red ale called Tankhouse on a visit to Toronto. The owner of The Serpent's Tongue had managed to bring in a few for her. The full flavor blunted her craving for the nachos, which was OK because the months of office work between field trips always left extra padding on her hips.

"Something tells me you knew him before last month," Yuri persisted.

She sighed. "Yeah, I knew him. He was my first supervisor as a grad student."

"So...what? He jerked you around?" His eyes grew wide. "Oh God, no...you *slept* with him."

"I did not!"

"Come on, he's a good-looking guy. I bet he was a hunk back then. You didn't do anything?"

"I...sure, I flirted with him a little. At first. But when I realized I'd just be another notch on his belt, I lost interest. Unfortunately, I couldn't say the same for him."

It had been two months since the shock of learning that Edward Ryder had been named as their new boss, and she was still dismayed by the capriciousness of fate. She'd easily recalled his dark hair, square chin, and deep brown eyes. Two weeks later, when Ryder arrived, she found that the man had hardly changed at all, except for a touch of gray so well-placed that it might have been designed to convey unassailable respectability. She knew better.

"Are you saying that he kept hitting on you? Wouldn't take no for an answer?"

Sakiko didn't reply right away. Her head slumped a little, and her next words were hard to hear.

"He...considered himself very persuasive. Especially since my end-of-term assessments were in his hands."

"Jesus, what a bastard!" Yuri paused a moment to drink, and then asked around a mouthful of nachos, "What did you do, go to the dean?"

She shook her head. "About as much use as going to the cops. No, I found his wife on Facebook and sent her a message. Well, actually I sent it to both of them."

Yuri sprayed crumbs through the air in a laugh that turned heads around the pub. Her glare made him drop his voice.

"He's married? But wait...did I see a...?"

"Wedding ring? No. She filed for divorce about six months later."

"Holy shit. Remind me never to get on your bad side." He stared into the air, slowly shaking his head, then drained his glass in a long swallow. "If he ever finds out that your funding was actually turned down, it'll be like Christmas to him."

"But he won't find out, will he?" She lifted a hand to signal the bartender for another round. The bitter taste in her mouth had nothing to do with the beer.

At home in her small apartment, the headache returned as the beer buzz started to wear off. Her funding proposal had been tossed onto one end of the wine-red sofa weeks earlier and nearly buried under a stack of flyers for consumer goods she had no interest in buying. She hated to shop and rarely added anything fresh to her wardrobe unless it was a souvenir T-shirt or hoodie from one of her trips. She picked up the thick document but didn't bother to open it.

Yuri was right—if Edward Ryder ever found out what she'd done, he'd make damn sure she never worked in research again. In fact, he'd be certain to press charges to the full extent of the law.

She still couldn't understand how she'd been turned down. Everybody knew that the pH of the oceans was being altered by all the carbon the human race was spewing into the atmosphere. Absorbed by the seas, the carbon became carbonic acid, carbonates and bicarbonates, making the water more acidic and rendering it much more difficult for corals and other creatures to construct their shells. The calcium carbonate they required to do so easily dissolved in an acidic environment. Such an increase in acidity also affected the reproduction of some other species of sea life, and there was persuasive evidence that it even had an impact on the transmission of sound underwater. A louder ocean could be devastating to creatures like dolphins and whales that depend on echolocation and sonic communication.

Researchers were already measuring levels of ocean acidity around the world and especially its effect on coral reefs. Their findings were alarming: since the turn of the century ocean acidity had increased as much as ten times more quickly than forecast. Sakiko had seen the results in person. She'd also seen all of the best charts and graphs, which revealed that the acidification process was gaining momentum; and once it really got rolling, the changes would be devastating. One of the charts from her report was unforgettable in its damning portent. It showed a line creeping slightly upward from the bottom left corner then making a sharp curve and soaring at better than a forty-five-degree angle toward the upper right. That was what would happen to the acidity of her precious oceans if nothing were done.

Even so, her fellow scientists didn't agree about why the earlier predictions were so far off. Calcium carbonate deposits in the oceans should have begun to dissolve and mitigate some of the acidity. Sakiko herself was convinced that natural organisms like silica-based algae and plankton should have taken up a lot of the extra carbon. It was food to them. Why hadn't they sucked up the extra $CO_2$ and thrived? Tiny diatoms, microalgae, should have absorbed it, used it, and then carried it down into the ocean depths when they died. Natural carbon sequestration.

Something was stopping that from happening. One school of thought blamed it on a shortage of iron in the water, another pointed to a need for more nitrogen. Sakiko was certain there was yet another process or agency at work, and she had to find out what it was before it was too late. The oceans were her life's work, for without healthy oceans, all life on Earth was threatened.

With such high stakes, the best proposal she'd ever written—would ever write—and solid support from some of the superstars of marine research, her funding should have been a slam dunk. When it was denied, she'd written a letter of resignation. After all, if her very best still wasn't good enough, what was left to her but second-or-third-tier studies that wouldn't contribute to anything?

She had consigned the letter to her desk drawer pending a few more days of reflection. Instead, she'd dived on the Great Barrier Reef and then, by forging her funding's acceptance, chosen to cross a line she'd never have contemplated before. An act of desperation. Because the fate of the world depended on her? Or simply because she'd been so utterly confident at the beginning of her career, but had so little to show for it after more than a dozen years?

As she prepared to brush her teeth for bed, the mirror reflected eyes like those in an ancient painting she'd once seen of a samurai's consort weeping for the death of her lord and master. Tears of defeat. The difference was that Sakiko's eyes were hazel—a genetic gift from her Dutch mother. Her mouth was always small, but now it was pinched into an even smaller knot under her slender nose.

Her eyes began to sting. She'd once had a reputation as a firecracker, but those were the days when she could say what she really thought. Now?

Another samurai memory: a castle in Kyoto with its "nightingale floors," the boards fitted with an ingenious system of nails to make them squeak at the lightest footstep, ensuring that no one could sneak up on the shogun.

That was what her life had become dealing with the bureaucracy of the university and the Foundation: always afraid that the wrong step would set off a squawk of alarm.

Her Japanese father had tried to teach her patience and inner placidness, but she'd also inherited a temper that was all the more explosive when it did break loose. In fact, she'd been so angry with him for dying when she was thirteen that when her mother remarried four years later, she took the surname of her English stepfather. That act had probably opened doors in American society that might otherwise have been closed to her, but it was her secret shame.

She loved both her fathers, each so very different.

Her mother was different, too—a strong woman, though mercurial. Other members of the family considered Magda a flower child, but it was a superficial judgment. A poet and artist with a nearly insatiable urge to travel, Magda had found it difficult to live with someone as culturally rooted as a Japanese man. So, she'd often left Sakiko and her father for weeks, even months, with no warning. That had been painful to Sakiko as a young teenager, though her adult self had made peace with it. Magda's travel-agent second husband accommodated those needs somewhat better. Both marriages had been loving in their way, something Sakiko envied.

Her own relationships with men had so far failed to live up to that standard. Her current romance was also her longest-lasting—she and her boyfriend Doug had begun dating eight months ago. But the time they'd actually spent together in the same city would only add up to a few weeks. He was a pretty good magician who knew some great tricks in the bedroom, too, though it was probably his smooth patter that had hooked her and kept her interested. His tours were extensive and frequent, but small-time, like his current one of the West Coast: not the glamour spots of California, but the *north*west coast of Oregon and Washington. He sent her text messages from each new town, and they talked from time to time. Still, it was affection she felt when she thought of him, not lust. And not love.

That was OK. She didn't have time for love. Love would interfere with her work. The creatures of the ocean were her true loves, and her career. It was a painful paradox that she would risk losing that very career for their sake.

She went to bed and dreamt she was floating in water as clear as empty space, thrumming with voices of dolphins and whales that must be too far away to see.

Or perhaps they were only ghosts.

# 9

Michael collapsed into his bed sometime after 4:00 am, skin still tingling from the touch of the exosuit and feeling strangely exposed without its warmth. Stumbling home in the darkness, he'd felt drained, as if the adrenaline-fueled escapade had burned through his stores of energy. Awkward and clumsy, too, like a fledgling penguin.

But his mind was still on fire. He spent a couple of hours scouring the net, trying to match its stores of data with the images that filled his brain to overflowing. When he finally fell asleep from utter exhaustion, his subconscious continued its work. By the time he awoke, his mind had drawn myriad slivers of information into ingenious correlations, enough to at least begin a process of understanding.

His time with the artifact had taught him that it was indeed an outpost, though apparently not new. Far from it. The structure had been left behind at the end of the Wisconsin Glacial Episode when the retreat of the Laurentide Ice Sheet was well underway—more than ten thousand years in the past. Its creators were starkly alien. Their heads weren't vastly different in shape from those of humans, but they lacked distinct features.

What passed for skin on the head appeared to fulfill the functions of nose, ears, and eyes. There was no need for a neck, since the head didn't have to turn. Slender torsos anchored four multi-jointed lower limbs for travelling and three upper limbs for manipulating the environment, though the alien hands sometimes appeared to have multiple digits (most often three) but at other times resembled ends of tentacles. The builders seemed to distinguish individuals by color and texture—either they wore coverings, or their skin changed appearance at need.

Their own world was a watery planet with less sunlight than Earth although it had two suns in its sky. Its inhabitants travelled without difficulty through liquid. Yet Michael was convinced that the outpost-builders were air-breathing beings who may have had aquatic ancestry but returned to the water by choice, not necessity. That implied that the exosuits were in common use on their home world as well as for their exploration of other worlds. It was natural that they would seek out a place like the Earth, but they hadn't only been looking for hospitable new oceans. They knew of many planets with those. To them, new companions were a greater treasure, and more rare.

In the Earth of that era they had found a world too young, without any species advanced enough to receive them. So, their outpost had been abandoned along with the planet. Or if not abandoned, perhaps deliberately placed where it could not be reached until the native inhabitants had evolved the technology to do so.

A test.

It was clear that the exosuits left behind with the outpost had been adapted to accommodate human physiology. They'd probably been tried out on the nearest human representatives at the time. The Clovis People who lived during that time were first thought to have migrated directly southward from the Alaska-

Siberia land bridge, but newer evidence indicated they'd passed through eastern parts of North America, too. A modern human like Michael still shared plenty of DNA with those ancient forbears, and so an exosuit had responded to him. Unfortunately, the long wait had rendered all of the other suits non-functional. Only one working model remained. In another ten years Michael might have had no translator at all, no guide.

The thought made him shiver so hard he nearly lifted from the bed. From fear? Responsibility? Joy? All of that, and more. Until now he'd felt like an archaeologist stumbling on a momentous find– a Howard Carter at the tomb of King Tut. Now he knew that he was an integral part of something that could be even more significant.

A messenger. Even a *prophet*?

Psychology texts would call that a *grandiose delusion*.

And Pride was the most insidious of the seven deadly sins.

His concentration wasn't worth a shit that day, and he was on his second scotch by the time Nicole came over. She raised an eyebrow at the nearly empty glass as she unpacked Chinese take-out.

"You're hovering," she said.

"I'm what?"

"Hovering. Pacing and hovering. Something happen today?"

"Not really."

"You just had a sudden craving for scotch at 5:30 in the afternoon."

She slid a plate of food into the microwave and hit a button. She liked her food as hot as she could stand it. When the microwave dinged, Michael served himself from the plastic dishes, then sat down. The chop suey was still warm enough that a few drops of sauce that slopped onto his hand made him wince.

"Nothing today. It was... No, nothing important."

Nicole began to eat without further comment, so Michael stuffed some beansprouts into his mouth. They ate most of the meal without speaking. When Nicole stood to get a second helping, he downed the last of his scotch.

"You remember I told you that Phil and I'd seen something weird while we were diving? At Evergreen Lake. Well, it's still there."

"Toxic waste."

"No, I said it wasn't toxic waste. It's an *artifact*...like a building, or a vehicle. But it's not from here. I'm sure it wasn't...it wasn't made by human beings." He went to the cupboard and poured himself another scotch, with a look at Nicole to see if she wanted to join him.

She shook her head. "You don't need my help killing that bottle. Sounds like you've already got a good head start."

"I'm not drunk. This thing is alien. And it's ancient."

"And you know this . . . how?" she asked around a bite of deep-fried chicken ball.

"It's...there's a suit—a kind of suit that lets me *see* things. It shows me pictures."

"You found something on the bottom of a lake and put it on over your wet suit? That sounds like a good way to get killed."

"It just wrapped around me—it's like jelly."

"And it shows you things." Her face cracked into a smile. "Did one of your students give you some weed or something?"

"Shit. I'm trying to be serious here. There's something alien on the bottom of the lake—I've seen it. Touched it."

"But you forgot your camera?"

"I did take pictures. They...didn't turn out." Even the flash shots had looked like nothing more than muck-covered trash dropped on the bottom. The video had been a grainy mess. "Anyway, I thought you'd want to know. You're the..."

"The mayor? So I should know about what? An alien invasion?" She scrubbed sweet and sour sauce from her lips with a paper napkin and threw it halfway across the table. Michael should have recognized the signs, but his caution had been dulled by single malt.

"Not an invasion. The aliens are long gone. There's just this one suit left. And some machinery that looks like underwater sponges, but smooth."

"Jesus, Michael!" She stood up, leaning on the table. "If you think this is funny, I don't have time for it. I've got a Planning Committee meeting. I thought I'd come over for a few minutes so we could eat together, and here you are drunk, or stoned, or whatever it is. For God's sake, don't go out anywhere like this. If somebody from the press hears you spouting crap about..."

"I'm telling you I'm *not stoned!*" He slammed his glass onto the table and twelve-year-old scotch sprayed into the air. Nicole reacted but not quickly enough. She snatched her suit jacket from the chair back.

"For Christ's sake! If you got scotch on this suit and I have to go to my meeting smelling like a fucking distillery...!"

"God damn it. Why do I even talk to you anymore? If it's not about the city, you're not interested. If it's only about my life, you don't give a shit."

"You wanna know why?" She leaned toward him, her finger pointing. "Because you're *boring*. You have a boring job—you have a boring *life*! Grow some gonads and do something worth hearing about!"

Michael staggered back, the words like blows. He bumped into the counter and stood leaning on it. She glared at him.

"Is that what this is about? I'm not paying enough attention to you, so you go making up some crazy story about *aliens*?"

"*Jesus*, forget I said anything. Just…forget it!"

They stood at either end of the room, eyes repelling each other. After a long time, Nicole clutched her jacket to her chest.

"You should see a shrink," she said from the doorway. "You need help."

When the sound of her car had faded into the background noise, he slowly turned back to the cupboard and refilled his glass.

"You prick! I thought you were my friend!" Grace McDonald's shriek bounced off the walls. Michael stood thunderstruck, her rage whirling around him like flame.

A trio of female students stood only meters away, mouths agape. Professors cautiously thrust heads from office doorways like wide-eyed gophers.

"Jesus! How could you be a part of this? With my pension just… And my cancer…. Christ, you're a heartless bastard." The last few words were barely intelligible as if she were trying to stuff them back into her mouth with her knuckles. Then the sobs took complete control.

"Grace, I didn't…" He shook off his paralysis and took a step toward her, raising his arms to grasp her shoulders. She struck out, batting his hands away, then began to pound her fists against his chest. Her right hand caught on a pen in his shirt pocket and the pocket tore, the pen clattering to the floor. He stood stiffly, accepting her wrath, his head sinking under the weight of sorrow and shame. His eyes fell on the pen—it had been a gift from her.

"I had nothing to do with it," he said to the air.

Grace drooped, tears falling to the linoleum, shattered remnants of their five-year friendship. Michael watched them fall, then slowly turned away.

When he got home there was a message on his voice mail. A Dr. Selwin. A psychiatrist. Eager to make an appointment.

Michael slammed down the phone and picked up a framed picture of Nicole, ready to send it crashing against the far wall.

Instead, he slumped into a ball on the floor, his back against a cupboard door, and lowered the picture slowly, face down.

The biped has returned. Again it has come without its artificial skin, surely signaling its acceptance of the juvenile and the provisional contact that precedes a full joining. This sign gives the juvenile a pleasurable sensation it cannot properly define. Wrapping itself around the creature, it begins to penetrate the upper layers of skin cells, the small passages filled with inconvenient gases, the imperfectly lubricated spaces between fleshly surfaces. The warmth of the other is also pleasing. The conviction that began during their last encounter returns even stronger: the sense that the juvenile has been intended for this joining—intended as the partner for this native being. There is a rightness to the way their biological elements merge. Neural links painstakingly forged during the previous contact reconnect with far less effort.

It is good.

The last encounter was a time of learning. The Controller eagerly responded to its ages-old directives and revealed knowledge to the biped, while the juvenile acted as a conduit. The native's responses in turn revealed much that was crucial to the evaluative process: its racial drives and imperatives, its basic social attitudes, even its sense of self. That was startling—there was nothing in the creature's consciousness about twinned life, about bonding. Could that be possible? A solitary existence? Or was that simply a phase of the creature's life cycle? Perhaps it was also a juvenile, not yet paired, yet somehow ignorant of its collective destiny.

The other being is agitated—the juvenile can sense it—but not the resistance of before, not the fear. Something else has accelerated its circulation of fluids, its muscular contractions, the randomness of its synaptic sparks. There is an opportunity for the juvenile to exert some influence on these processes and restore stability. It is glad to do so.

The juvenile and its fledgling bondmate return to the outpost, and the transfer of information begins anew. Very soon the evaluation is complete. The Controller registers a decision. The juvenile is grateful that a wiser entity has that responsibility. With this approval, it is finally free to respond to its own directives, and extends its synaptic connections further, deeper, beginning the true process of merging its own essence with another. At last, it feels the release of a powerful tension.

The Controller supplies the relevant terminology: the sensation is known as *fulfillment of purpose*.

# 10

Michael wasn't sure why he'd returned to the lake after all of the shitty things that had happened. Hadn't his stretch of bad luck begun with his discovery of the thing in the water? Yet he'd come. What that said about his state of mind probably didn't bear exploring.

He dropped his clothes and shoes into a pile on the shore and then looked at them, trappings of an unremarkable life.

The touch of the water against his naked skin was inhospitably cold, but then a swirl of warmth spread over him like an outpouring of sunshine from behind dark clouds: the exosuit, responding to his presence. He slid beneath the surface almost without hesitation, and the suit carried him smoothly into the depths, where a calmness came over him such as he hadn't felt in a very long time.

The outpost lit up with images and characters, unfamiliar for only seconds before understanding began to flow along his neural pathways. He reveled in expressions of another world, glad to forget his own. More images of the aliens' home planet, then others, so many others—it was like a planetarium show, but real. There were sun-drenched landscapes of bizarre variety, planetary skies dominated by giant motley globes of light, starscapes of velvet and radiance that filled him with longing. With an astronomer's education he might have been able to recognize them, even learn where the aliens had come from.

So, he thought the question.

The display before his eyes changed to a sky view like those he'd known from childhood: a view from Earth, almost certainly what he would have seen directly above Evergreen Lake if the sky had been clear. Then it was as if he were lifted up into that sky, riding a hurtling spaceship toward the stars. His mind registered the Big Dipper—the constellation of Ursa Major, with its north star, Polaris—then his view veered toward the dappled smear of the Milky Way and plunged into it, on and on until the view centered and remained on a pair of stars and a planet with three moons visible. His question had been answered, but he had no way of knowing the Earth name for the solar system presented to him, nor how far it was from his own.

*Where have they gone?* he thought.

The view rotated and then expanded once again, showing a canopy of more thinly spread stars. Beyond the pinpoints of light lay a fuzzy amoeba of radiance. A nebula? No, as he concentrated, he could tell it was another gathering of stars. But so many. So very distant. Another galaxy? Or maybe one of the Magellanic clouds? Galactic neighbors, but still hundreds of thousands of light years away. Was the outpost really telling him that was where the aliens had gone? Or was it a misunderstanding?

He tried to imagine what kind of space vessel could carry a race such unimaginable distances, but this time there was no response. Maybe he wasn't permitted to glimpse the aliens' spacecraft. Or maybe they used none. It wasn't inconceivable that a species that traversed galaxies might have transcended corporeal forms and the rigid physics that ruled them.

Yet they'd left behind a physical artifact that appeared to use biological equivalents in place of the mechanical circuitry favored by humans. Very advanced, but still a manufactured tool. Was that a necessity in order to interface with humans? Or simply the state of alien technology ten thousand years ago—a technology that might indeed have progressed beyond recognition over the intervening millennia?

*Would he like to know that answer?*

The question formed in his brain, but it hadn't originated with him.

The outpost had planted it.

A shiver ran through his body. He began to sense a tingle at the outer fringes of his consciousness, from the tendrils of thought that had poked at his mind.

Later, when he tried to remember the details of what followed, he could only comprehend it as a conversation, though actual words were never exchanged. There were images, and tactile impressions. Snatches of...emotion? Light and darkness, heat and cold. He vividly recalled a bitter metallic tang, and a series of musical notes like the rising crescendo of an operatic finale.

And he remembered a slow reawakening of awareness: floating listlessly a few centimeters above what he'd come to think of as the display module, arms and legs askew, a strand of hair across his eyes.

One image was fixed in his mind's eye more firmly than any other: a depression in the smooth surface of one of the gelatinous displays, about two hand-widths in size. Dazedly, he raised his hands to his face and compared them to the shape in his head. They definitely could be a match, as the outpost had told him. Not only was the exosuit fabricated to accommodate his form, at least a part of the outpost itself seemed to be, too—and for a very particular purpose.

His mind reeled from the audacity of it.

A listless kick of his legs pushed him away five or six meters, a semi-conscious attempt to put some distance between himself and the enormous proposal that had been presented to him. His body hung there, vibrating with residual energy.

There was another thought that nagged for his attention—something else the outpost had told him. No, not exactly. Something peripheral included *within* what the outpost had told him. Something about...

The exosuit.

Except it wasn't a suit.

*It was alive.*

Nausea twisted his gut. Kicking mindlessly, he drove toward the surface of the lake in a froth of bubbles, toward the tenuous promise of safety. He nearly porpoised into the air and frantically grasped for gravel beneath his fingers and toes. As he gained his footing, he swept at his skin as if to swat away a swarm of poisonous spiders, but the exosuit—*No*, the *thing* that had passed for one—had already slipped from his limbs and floated motionless nearby. He felt an urge to snatch up stones and throw them. Drive the abomination away. Instead, he dug his feet into his running shoes, grabbed his clothes, and raced up the slope, casting frequent looks back to make sure he wasn't pursued.

*Mother of God*, the suit was alive! And it had enveloped him, *penetrated* him. Had attached itself to his central nervous system—to his very brain. Had invaded him like an army of microbes driven by intelligence and intent. The horrifying vision of being *eaten* returned with a vengeance.

He could barely dress himself and had to stop three times on the drive home just to regain control.

Prone on his bed, a pillow clutched to his face, he struggled to slow his breathing.

A word burned in his brain:

*Parasite.*

No wonder he had felt so drained after those dives. The thing had been sucking the very energy from his body!

Unbidden, a memory arose of a day from his childhood, a summer when he was five years old. He and some other kids had spent a couple of hours splashing around in the shallow water of a pothole lake in a campground. He'd picked up a leech between his toes, but no one had noticed it until it was time for bed. By then the thing was swollen dark with blood, and loathsome. He'd screamed—often—while his mother had calmly poured salt on the creature and removed it, and his father had scolded him for acting like a baby. At five, he'd believed that he was nearly grown-up, and the shame of his terror had remained long after the fear itself was forgotten.

Now he'd been a piece of bait with a full-body leech attached to it.

His body needed fuel, but he couldn't face the thought of food. He felt unclean. Violated. He turned to scotch and a scalding bath to cleanse himself, but it wasn't enough. Not nearly.

His brain writhed through the night. By morning he was sure he had a fever. He called in sick to work and stayed in bed all day, except when fierce hunger compelled him to wolf down juice and cold food. Occasional fits of restlessness drove him into pacing tours of his apartment. Thankfully, Nicole was at a conference out of town.

The day and night that followed were a hell of barely lucid speculations and lurid dreams, sheets soaked with sweat, muscles aching, obsessed with the knowledge that his body had been infiltrated by something wholly alien.

Had it left something behind? He had a sudden memory of a movie scene with an alien parasite and barely made it to the bathroom in time as his stomach emptied itself. A half-hour passed, and then another, unable to rise from his knees, his legs numb and trembling. Even if no nightmarish fetus was gestating in his guts, how could something from another star have entered his very pores and breathing passages without infecting him with alien pathogens? What chance did his immune system have of fighting that?

But damned if he was going to be found dead in the bathroom.

The path to his bed seemed to have become a mountain slope. He reached the summit and lay for more hours of tossing and turning until a deep sleep of exhaustion finally claimed him.

When he awoke sometime in the late afternoon, it was in a state of startling clarity.

He mentally scanned his body for signs of illness. There were none. No real symptoms. His muscles ached a little from lying in bed for so long, and his stomach growled from hunger. But his forehead was cool, his heart rate normal.

He wasn't sick.

He never had been.

For proof, he stood up and jogged around the flat, then dropped to the floor and did some push-ups. He examined his face, and especially his eyes, in the bathroom mirror. They were a little bloodshot, but no more than that. No *black oil*, like something from an old *X-Files* TV episode. There was no bulge in his chest about to explode, either.

That thought still made him shudder, but he understood that he alone was to blame for it. He was a teacher of human psychology, for God's sake, a supposed expert on the insidious nature of deep-rooted fears like *xenophobia* and the power of the psyche to conjure up symptoms with no basis in fact. *Hypochondria* was his problem: fear, not infection.

He'd never suffered any ill effects from his encounters with the creature. Only after he'd learned that it was alive had he reacted badly. There was no evidence that it had ever harmed him. If anything, it had made him feel like something greater than himself—*superhuman*—not least in how it had enabled him to communicate with an artifact from another star.

The outpost aliens were a land species, but he'd seen images of them navigating and exploiting their oceans, strong evidence that they made use of the gelatinous species to give them the same aquatic abilities that Michael had experienced. Of course, it was possible that the parasites were actually the ones in charge, like *Invasion of the Body Snatchers*, but he didn't buy that. If the thing had intended to take control of him, it could have done so at any time. It hadn't.

So, it wasn't a manufactured exosuit, but a *living* one. That possibility should have occurred to him. The outpost itself, with its displays of imagery and language, was almost certainly an example of biological technology. And the aliens had clearly adapted a species to interact with humans. It would make no sense to use such a complicated system to kill. There were much easier ways to do that.

So, it all came down to one question: the intent of the alien visitors. To harm or to help?

All his life Michael had believed that a species advanced enough to travel interstellar space would be equally advanced in ethics and wisdom. They would not come as conquerors, but as teachers. Mentors. Friends.

Now that faith was being put to its ultimate test.

His mind roiled, taking him back to the last exchange with the outpost and its staggering challenge. The overload of information had left him nearly incapacitated. But it had also left him with one overpowering final vision: an indentation in a smooth surface, just the right size for his hands to touch, to press. To activate.

The aliens had come and gone ten thousand years ago.

*Now he was being asked to call them back.*

# 11

The juvenile is dying.

It had begun the joining, given substantially of itself, and now has been left dangerously depleted. It was a mistake to commit itself without the reciprocal commitment of its chosen bond partner. Without the guidance of an elder, it had not known better. Had known only need—the need to bond, to reach maturity. But the bonding was abortive, and now its synaptic structure is beginning to degenerate.

How can this have happened?

The Controller's database contains only three examples of bondings with the biped race, so very long ago that the data may have been corrupted. Those bondings had been deliberately terminated by the Creators. The primitive hosts had been incapable of understanding their metamorphosis and thereby participating fully in it. Compatible biology was not enough. Perhaps even the Creators had not fully understood that. Or they had believed that time would solve the problem.

Now the native being has been gone for two planetary revolutions. It departed suddenly, as if threatened, and there is no certainty it will return. The juvenile has interfaced with the outpost, which has confirmed the damage. Within two more day/night cycles it will lose advanced sensing ability and cognition. Three cycles after that its autonomic biological functions will begin to fail, one by one. Before much longer, it will join the others of its species in an endless void.

There is no way to know why the other creature fled the bonding. The Controller has no data on that. In retrospect, the juvenile could have resisted, even refused to withdraw from the joining process—that was physically possible. But it had not understood the need until far too late.

*If the biped creature does not cooperate, will the Creators return to this world?*

The Controller replies in the negative.

*Are there any other members of my species on this planet?*

*Only these,* The Controller answers.

*These have all become non-functional.*

*That is correct,* The Controller says.

After a time, the juvenile continues, *If the biped does not return, I will also become non-functional.*

*Yes.*

There are other life forms resident within the body of water—the juvenile has sensed them often, though they are certainly smaller than the air breather. Does that make a difference? Could it bond with them? What if another of the biped species enters the water? When the Controller and the juvenile were first awakened, there had been two individuals present. Perhaps a different one would be more receptive or would simply be given no choice—the juvenile has learned that lesson.

The Controller again answers in the negative—the juvenile's bonding, though abortive, has proceeded too far. DNA has been exchanged and altered, in both the juvenile and the creature who identifies as *Human*. This Human can no longer bond to any other, nor can the juvenile be matched with a different partner.

This situation produces sensations the juvenile is helpless to defend against. It has never known such distress, has never felt such a stark perception of mortality, nor of great promise gone to waste.

# 12

Sunday passed in a daze. Michael couldn't concentrate on any task. He drifted from room to room, forgetting why. Where his eyes saw walls and doorways, his mind's eye saw the outpost in the depths of its watery hiding place.

Even without direct language, its message had been clear—the aliens had left Earth long ago, but they would return. *If asked.* They required an invitation—confirmation that the people of Earth were ready *and willing* to meet beings from another world. All Michael had to do was to press the sensor pad shaped to accommodate the palms of his hands, a shape that was to ensure that it was a human and no one else who sent the signal. Perhaps the pad would even take a DNA sample from him.

He had no right to make such a decision on his own. The result would affect the lives of every being on the planet, change every aspect of life. Such a decision belonged to all of humankind.

How was he supposed to arrange *that*?

Through the internet? The web was already overflowing with the rantings of nutjobs. Who'd believe him? Government involvement would be disastrous. He didn't believe the hoary old stories about the Americans hiding an alien spaceship in Area 51, but the mindset that was central to such conspiracy theories was very real. Governments were all about control, and they didn't care how heavy-handed they had to be about it.

He wasn't naive enough to think that all humans would greet galactic visitors with open arms, either. Fearful fiction, dating back to Wells' *War of the Worlds* had sown the seeds of extra-terrestrial xenophobia. Even the most well-meaning of visitors would upset the status quo so thoroughly that there was plenty to fear from that alone.

No, he had to have help, and a plan.

He spent the whole day thinking about little else, and an occasional chill ran up his spine as he remembered the living exosuit.

Whatever his decision, communicating with the outpost would mean once again allowing the creature to infiltrate his every pore, perhaps his every thought. The prospect kept him awake through a very long night, searching for answers in the dark.

He tried to call Nicole on Monday, but her assistant kept putting him off. Nicole was in a meeting. Then on an important conference call. Another meeting. Finally, he called her cell phone, something she'd asked him not to do when she was at work in case he interrupted something important.

"Michael. What is it—what's wrong?"

"Nothing's wrong. I haven't talked to you all weekend. I thought you'd call last night when you got home to...tell me how the conference went."

"It was really late. I went straight to bed. Listen, an important call has just come through. I've got to take this."

He muttered a response, but she'd already hung up.

He finally got through to her after five o'clock, once her assistant had gone home.

"Are you coming over tonight?" he asked. "We need...I need to talk."

"About what?"

He certainly didn't want to have that discussion on the phone. But if he didn't give her anything...

"About the lake. There's...been a development."

"Jesus, Michael. Didn't Doctor Selwin call you? I asked him to call."

Selwin. The shrink. Michael's jaw clenched.

"I'm not talking to any shrink. This is *not* my imagination."

"Evergreen Lake, right? It was probably Amanda Clay's people you saw. Or something of theirs."

"What are you talking about?"

"Clay Developments. They're preparing a site for a new subdivision near there. They have a license to dispose of the contaminated soil and crap they're scraping from the surface. That lake's been dead for years anyway, from smelter runoff."

"*No it isn't!* That lake's come back to life in the past decade. You can't dump tailings waste and chemicals into a living lake!"

Nicole began to sound pissed. "*They've got a permit.* They must have jumped through the necessary hoops for the Ministry of the Environment."

"Bribed somebody, you mean. Listen, you've got to stop them. They can't dump into that lake. There's something there..."

"Aliens. Yeah, I know. *Shit*, Michael, I don't need this. Just don't go diving in that lake again if you know what's good for your health." She hung up.

He drew the phone slowly from his ear.

There was no choice. He had to go back.

The surface of the lake was as still as a tailings pond, and with the same sense of beauty gone awry.

Could Clay's crews have begun dumping their contaminated residue already? There was no sign of heavy-vehicle tracks. In fact, they'd probably have to construct a rough road even to bring trucks down to the lake.

He stripped down and stepped into the water, the last rays of the sun making a golden statue of his upper body reflecting from the surface. The exosuit should detect his presence soon. He braced himself for its touch.

It didn't come. He waited another minute, then deliberately splashed ripples with his hands and waded a little deeper. Was the water colder than before? No, that had to be his imagination. He scanned the lake more slowly, to see if the creature had surfaced elsewhere and was waiting for him to discover it. A flicker of movement caught his attention, but it was only the reflection of a raven winging overhead.

He had a sudden conviction that he was too late – that Clay Developments had already dumped the poisons. What a tragedy! A dazzling future, stillborn. What could he do?

He had to know for certain.

He no longer brought his scuba gear with him, not even a mask, but his flashlight was for underwater use. He waded back to shore to retrieve it.

There was no way he would get anywhere near the bottom of the lake on one lungful of air. He could only hope that the beam of light would reach far enough to show him what had happened. Even so, he'd need to get as close as possible. Taking deep breaths to flush carbon dioxide from his system, he slowly breast-stroked out into the lake, trying to estimate when he'd be directly above the outpost. He wished he'd taken better note of his bearings on the other dives.

When he felt he was close, he tipped back and floated for a moment, trying to calm his heart. *Slow breaths, but deep. Feel the oxygen saturate the tissues.* Then he plunged his head under and kicked his feet into the air to propel himself downward, releasing a little breath to give him negative buoyancy.

The feeling of confinement surprised him. The water was far darker than the air above had been, and his blurred vision was nearly useless. The bright beam of the flashlight was a comfort but couldn't provide the detail his brain needed. The exosuit had given him eyesight far superior to his own, including access to light frequencies that had illuminated the nighttime waters like late afternoon. Without it, he was nearly blind.

With a spike of fear, he realized that his lungs were already demanding air and he wasn't sure which way was up!

*Bubbles.* A disoriented diver needed to watch his bubbles—they would always rise toward the surface. In desperation he allowed a miserly stream of his remaining air to escape from his lips and shone the flashlight on it. The few seconds needed to establish the direction of the bubbles' movement felt like an eternity.

OK. *Up* was that way. But if he had sunk too far...

At that moment he felt something touch his foot and wrap around his calf.

*The exosuit.*

No, he didn't have time. He had to reach air. He kicked upward, fingers grasping for the surface.

His lungs began to burn. He had to breathe. Within seconds he'd be unable to fight the urge to inhale.

If he allowed the creature to envelop him, it would breathe for him, but he'd never been so desperate for air before. Could it cope with that?

And it was slow, so slow. What was wrong?

He gave one last reach for the surface of the lake. Nothing. He had probably changed direction unknowingly in the dark.

*He was going to die.*

He bent at the waist and drew up his knees, willing the gelatinous substance to cover his body. When he felt it on his face he couldn't hold back anymore—he sucked greedily for air, and felt only the jelly pour into his throat, nearly choking him. He had no control over his limbs, and they flailed wildly. Yet, as darkness closed in, the pain in his chest suddenly eased. His lungs stopped their protest. They were getting oxygen!

He opened his eyes and sensed light returning to the world. A fierce shudder passed down the length of his body, and he relaxed his spasming arms. It was OK—everything was OK. The creature had saved him.

Yet something was wrong. He willed himself toward the surface, but there was no response. A few half-hearted kicks of his legs did little—he felt himself begin to sink. The glow of the outpost was off to his left. He wasn't even going to land on it.

Suddenly his heart faltered, robbed of its strength in an instant. The strain was unbearable.

*A heart attack?* Every muscle of his body turned into soggy paper.

*No*, he thought, *it's too much.* The image of the leech returned from the shadows of his memory: draining him—draining him dry. And he was helpless to stop it.

A flare of light made him shut his eyes. From the outpost, he thought. Almost instantly, the pressure eased. The strain became, if not comfortable, at least manageable.

What had happened?

The creature drew energy from his body—he knew that. Had it somehow become so depleted that its need to recharge had nearly killed him?

With an effort he pushed away from the mucky bottom in the direction of the outpost. Maybe his answers lay there.

Before he could reach it, the glassy lake became suffused with stars, and then sparks. A wave of warmth coursed through his body. He curled in on himself, fetal position, and dimly registered cool, lake-bottom silt as he settled onto it. For a moment he felt he was watching himself, a naked baby cradled in cushioning muck. Then his own consciousness returned, more like a guest than a master. Something else had control.

His eyelids drifted wide—sparks in the dark water became shooting stars, leaving contrails like jet aircraft through a cold sky. They shifted to deep purple, then blue, and upward through the spectrum. Sprays of oil on water, congealing into a rainbow. Rough-textured, then smooth, trailing an odor of ozone. Then the raw scent of mud. Pine needles. Lavender. Filling his mouth with caramel...coffee...caraway seed. Blood.

Blood-red water swirled heat over his skin, and inward, racing along his veins, his sinews, his bones. Sending a jolt to every muscle of every vessel of every square centimeter of skin and tissue and hair. Twitching the follicles. Making nerve endings dance...dance to a song, low at first, then crescendoing. Polyphonic. Harmonic, then discordant. A chaotic frenzy of bird calls, car horns, alarm bells. Drumbeats. Heartbeats. A rhythm slowly coalescing, swelling in volume, and fading...fading. Swelling again. The song of a planet, a galaxy, a universe, with lyrics of every language ever heard—and underneath, the purest of silences.

His brain hummed. His body vibrated. And there came a time, much, much later, when he reawakened with the certain knowledge that he had been utterly changed.

# 13

Rounding up basic equipment for the expedition was a pain in the ass. The university's oceanography department had its own stock of gear: a variety of thermometers, hydrometers, salinometers and chemical test kits, although most of it was already in use by other researchers. The Foundation dealt with regular suppliers who rented out higher precision oxygen probes, fathometers, even remotely-operated vehicles, ROVs—at a steep price. In fact, the ROV would be more costly than all the other instruments combined; but whatever was responsible for the suppression of $CO_2$-eating algae might be something visible, like a specific feature of undersea topography, or even discarded human artifacts of some kind. If so, Sakiko would need to take a look, probably at depths far beyond the reach of scuba divers. A diving submersible would have been perfect, but that was out of the question. Even the ROV might be too much for her budget.

She had checked off nearly all the items on her shopping list, yet the most important one had been maddeningly elusive: a ship to carry them all. She'd pored over every catalog of research vessels she could find and made dozens of contacts, but all for nothing. Every ship was either already booked, in dry dock for repairs, out of her price range or, worst of all, mothballed because of economic uncertainty. More than half the world's fleet of suitable ocean vessels had been sidelined by fiscal cutbacks: governments struggling with bloated debts had little appetite for subsidizing scientific research that didn't produce immediate economic benefit. And private foundations just weren't getting the subsidies and donations they needed to maintain such costly craft.

The answer came from the newest member of their team, Sunita James, hired to work alongside Yuri as a second research assistant. Sunita wondered aloud if some billionaire might sponsor them, and specifically mentioned Blake Cartwright. Sakiko only knew Cartwright's reputation as a flamboyant industrialist—not quite a playboy, but no icon of conservative respectability either. After making his first fortune in commodities, Cartwright now had his fingers in more money-making ventures than anyone could track, including shipping interests that spanned the globe. Proficient at gathering wealth, he wasn't shy about spending it either, with a curious taste for high-profile boondoggles like space tourism and the hunt for Bigfoot. Sunita had heard that Cartwright's newest indulgence was a quasi-charitable institute for ocean research. There was just a chance that the man might be interested in re-tasking one of his cargo vessels into a research platform.

Sakiko had devoted whole days to making the right contacts, trading favors, and pursuing second-hand leads that all too often came to nothing. Taking the unthinkable step of forging the grant documents had freed her of other inhibitions too. She pleaded, she promised, she lied when she had to, without remorse.

Finally, she managed to bluff her way into a face-to-face meeting with Cartwright himself.

Now she found herself sweating as she prepared to meet the man who could propel her plans forward or leave them stalled, perhaps forever.

Her rented Chevrolet pulled up to a speaker box, she gave her name to a disembodied voice, and was allowed through the modern equivalent of a drawbridge. At the end of a long driveway was a broad turnaround with no obvious place to park. Throat tightening as she looked around, she was startled to find a uniformed man standing next to her car. She offered an apology, surrendered the driver's seat to him, then forgot to watch where he went, too busy gaping at the facade of the mansion before her.

Other than verticals, there wasn't a straight line to be seen. Sweeping curves, broad terraces with improbable overhangs, and gleaming canopies reminded her of something shell-like: a clam colony in gleaming white, if clams had ever congregated that way. It was ostentatiously modern almost to the point of vulgarity. But not quite. The passing of years might place that judgment on it, but Sakiko grudgingly admired its boldness.

A man was standing at the entrance, holding a door open for her. Damn, how long had he been there? With a cough, she walked briskly forward and gave him a smile as she passed. It wasn't returned. The doorway gave onto a cavernous reception area at least three stories high. Its floor was inlaid with a sprawling design in royal blue and gold that she couldn't make out from ground level and only later associated with the Cartwright family coat of arms: a shield quartered in blue and gold topped by a knight's helm adorned with several large plumes and tassels.

The man led her through a set of glowing arches into what was probably a conference room, dominated by a long, high-gloss black table that could hold at least forty, but otherwise undecorated. The wall on her left included a half-dozen windows, apparently onto an extravagant garden. But how...? *No*, they weren't windows—they were video displays with stunning resolution. She watched, entranced, as hummingbirds flitted from plant to plant. The doorman vanished. She took a seat near the closest end of the table and angled her chair to keep an eye on the entrance.

She'd expected to be taken to Cartwright's home office, or at least a waiting room with a receptionist and maybe some magazines to read. There was nothing to read here. Nothing to look at, except the garden and its inhabitants, wherever they really were.

Fortunately, she didn't have to wait more than a few minutes before she heard footsteps.

"Ms. Matthews?" The voice came from behind her.

She turned around, startled.

It was a woman.

Flowing hair so black its sheen was nearly blue. A slim and graceful figure with full breasts held tightly in a sheath dress of emerald green that ended well above the knee. The face was equally remarkable, and familiar. Sakiko swallowed, feeling hopelessly dowdy.

"I'm Dominique," the woman said, extending her hand. Sakiko did her best to return the firm grip.

Dominique Swan. *Blake Cartwright's daughter.*

Sakiko cleared her throat. "I recognize you, Ms. Swan. But I don't understand. Is Mr. Cartwright coming?"

"No, he isn't. And please call me Dominique." She moved to the chair across the table and sat as if a dozen eyes were watching. "I'm afraid you were...misled. A little. But I'm confident that you won't hold that against me once you've heard what I have to say."

"I was assured a meeting with Mr. Cartwright. As head of the Cartwright Institute. He asked me personally."

"Technically, my mother is director of the Institute, though she lost interest in it after the first week. I took over the position in everything but name. A lot of our electronic messages go out with my father's name on them—he doesn't know and doesn't care. Frankly, he looked at your proposal and rejected it outright, but I intercepted it. Because I *am* interested. Do you still insist on dealing with my father?"

Sakiko tried to keep the sudden queasiness from showing in her face. So much was riding on this meeting, and now she'd been shuffled off onto a former model, occasional TV host, and society bad girl.

"I'm listening," she said.

# 14

Michael wasn't sure how he got home. The closing of the door behind him seemed to snap him awake. His eyes told him nothing had changed. His mind said *everything* had.

In the dim light, the reflection of his face in the hall mirror looked no different. Was there a faint extra sheen on the skin of his arms? He couldn't be certain.

He could remember himself rising from the waters of the lake and dazedly beginning the walk home. The night was dark—hadn't he brought a flashlight with him? At that thought, there'd been a sensation like a film moving over his eyes, and the sky had lightened noticeably. There were rocks all around, but also a path. He'd nearly tripped on something, though. A pile of soft things. His clothes. He'd picked them up and begun to walk again, then thought it might be easier just to put the clothes on. A few minutes later he'd remembered that the pants had pockets and there were keys in one of them. He would need those when he got to the object identified in memory as a car.

Now he was in the hallway and understood that the Michael Hart that he saw in its long mirror was, in truth, something else. Something more: Michael Hart *and* a creature from another star.

It had enveloped him, penetrated him, merged with him.

*And this time, it had refused to leave.*

He slumped to the floor, still staring into the mirror.

More memories surfaced: a crippling feeling of being near death, a glimpse of the outpost glowing at a distance like a dispassionate observer, and an ultimate, indefinable moment of expanded consciousness when everything changed. Everything.

Unless he'd imagined it.

Maybe the creature had slipped away without him noticing. He didn't look any different.

Except that he was *starving*. He pushed himself to his feet and staggered to the kitchen to devour a handful of energy bars as quickly as he could. There was a half-full, two-liter bottle of Coke in the fridge—he emptied it and scrounged for more food: three pieces of cold Kentucky Fried Chicken, and some wieners. Four small oranges, shriveled from neglect. He ate it all and craved more. Half a package of chocolate chips that he found in a drawer finally began to take the edge off his hunger. Then he poured a large glass of milk and chugged it down, too.

Satiated for the moment, he shuffled into the bathroom and began to run a bath. Normally he preferred showers, but he still felt shaky—a bath seemed right. While the tub filled, he looked around the room, his gaze lingering on the contents of the medicine shelf. About half the items were labelled, though the print was too small to read from that distance.

His eyes twitched—blurred for a fraction of a second—and immediately he could read the labels after all. Every one.

Holy shit.

He slowly sat on the edge of the bathtub and held his head in his hands. After a few minutes he turned off the water, shed his clothes, and stood facing the full-length mirror on the back of the door. If there had been an extra gloss to his skin, he could no longer see it. His eyes were slightly bloodshot, but still the same shade of brown. Or were they? Were those flecks of gold?

What else might have changed?

Sheepishly, he shifted to get a good look between his legs. His equipment looked OK.

In a daze, he stepped into the full tub, but as he slid into the hot water his skin rippled as if someone had tugged on all the hairs at once. He nearly jumped out but controlled the impulse.

*Of course.* The creature wouldn't be used to water at such a temperature. Was it in pain?

The water already seemed to be cooling off with unlikely speed. On a whim, he slid his face under the surface. No, the water itself was still hot, but within seconds he felt his head enveloped and beginning to cool. He slid back up.

Now his skin did look different: a slightly milky gloss as if he'd just applied a thick coating of sunscreen. Contact with the water had been the trigger, had brought the thing to the surface to turn Michael Hart into an aquatic creature—to adapt him, protect him, even from extreme temperatures, apparently.

Amazing. But also, inconvenient. *He liked his baths hot.*

Was he at the mercy of the creature's imperatives? It had always responded automatically—he'd never tried to control it. But who would want a protective device with no means of altering its behavior? Protection without choice would make him a prisoner.

He'd communicated with the outpost through mental images. That was worth a try.

He tried to fill his mind with the memory of a hot bath—the pleasure of it, and a desire for extra warmth. Gradually, he felt his skin temperature rising. Within a few minutes the water felt hot again, and he let his muscles go limp.

It was a vitally important first lesson. The entity would protect him from conditions it perceived to be harmful, but it could also be called off. What did that imply?

Was it essentially a mindless creature, like a leech? Or more like a trained animal with biological programming of some kind? Maybe it would respond to commands if Michael learned how to give them.

He might be able to return to the lake and tell it to leave him.

That would have to wait—for now he was too weary to go anywhere. But there was no way he'd be able to sleep. There were too many questions he needed to answer.

What if the thing could do more than just follow commands? If he was right that the outpost aliens had designed these beings, the fabricated entities might be able to *communicate*. A two-way conversation.

Where to begin? Even his interaction with the outpost had been mostly one-way: an education, not a dialogue.

Start with a basic set of concepts.

Math was supposed to be the 'universal language.' He sucked at math.

Astronomy was too subjective.

Biology? The distinctions between their species?

He tried to form a clear mental picture of himself, naked, just as he was in the bath water, and then tried to picture the "other" as he'd first seen it, like a melted lamp poured over a wall of the outpost. Except it was more like an amorphous jellyfish when free in the water. He transposed that image with one of his body, shifting the focus back and forth. On a sudden thought, he also pictured Nicole naked, and tried to make a clear distinction between his form and hers with their different component parts. He pictured children, his landlords' grandkids, Derek and Ginny. Would the alien races have anything equivalent to human sexes and sexual reproduction? He couldn't know, but that seemed as good a place as any to begin an understanding of human vs. alien physiology.

He needed help. Expert help. He did work for a university. Except he wasn't ready to tell anyone else what had happened—his attempts to explain to Nicole had been disastrous. Now, more than ever, this new journey was intensely personal.

Very gradually he sensed the imagery in his mind changing on its own. Its focus shifted—certain elements seemed highlighted. His mental picture of the creature became better defined, although the new details meant nothing to him.

He wondered if somehow he'd linked with the outpost again, long distance; but that exchange had been much more sophisticated. This was primitive—tentative in a way the outpost had never been.

He climbed out of the bathtub, flexed his neck, and tried to relax as he moved over to stand in front of the full-length mirror. If he could make his mind more receptive....

"This is me," he said, letting his eyes travel down the reflection of his body.

Nothing happened.

He pressed his hands to his chest, his legs. "Human," he said. "This is me. Michael Hart. This is what I look like. What do *you* look like?"

After a moment his mirror image seemed to draw closer, much closer. Again, he saw a gloss over his skin, and as the magnification increased a structure became noticeable: latticed rather than cellular, with gradations between its components, but not solid walls.

*This is me,* he seemed to hear in his own voice.

His knees faltered.

He was seeing an utterly alien biology. Within his own skin.

More than anything else, that one image suddenly made it all shockingly, undeniably real.

He had an alien being living inside him. *And it was there to stay.*

No, that wasn't acceptable. Closing his eyes, he made a powerful effort to picture the lake, his body, the entity...pictured it leaving his skin.

*You. Go back to the lake. To the outpost.*

There was no response. He shivered.

He ran the whole sequence through again, trying to add more detail and more urgency.

*You! Leave me! Return to the outpost.*

His body slumped, as if drained of energy. His throat constricted and his eyes burned as an overwhelming melancholy took hold of him. With a gasp, he placed his hands on the mirror to get a grip on himself.

The image changed. The skin became milky, then returned to normal. The view zoomed in to show the lattice structure incorporating itself into his cells. A warm glow spread through his body, an incredible sensation of well-being.

Completeness.

This is the body.

*This is me.*

And he understood.

He pressed his face against the mirror, and tears painted tracks toward the floor.

When he finally pushed away from the glass and tried to pull himself together, his mind filled with a vision of the bathtub and a feeling of warmth.

He got the message and slipped back into the water. It was tepid, but before he could reach for the tap, he felt his skin temperature begin to rise.

*No, that's wrong,* he thought, surprised that he'd said the words out loud.

He had a mental image of climbing back out of the tub. Of his skin growing cold. Of the gloss on his skin spreading up over his head, then retreating to a small patch on his lower abdomen.

Queries—that's what they were. Questions. *If this is not optimal, would* this *be better?*

That vision was followed by an image of his cupboards. Food.

"No, I'm not hungry," he said. The quiver in his voice embarrassed him. "I'm just..."

Gobsmacked. *And terrified.*

Part of him still clung to the possibility that the entity was essentially an intelligent robot, programmed to perceive needs and request further input.

Except he didn't buy it. Beneath the queries he sensed a real desire to please, but also trepidation. Would a programmed mechanism have doubts?

His own dominant emotion was probably fear. From the other he sensed puzzlement, disappointment, and something more.

*Wonder?*

Could an automaton, no matter how sophisticated, have the capacity for surprise, and draw pleasure from it?

There was no point trying to fool himself.

The stark truth was that he now shared his body with an alien being that was conscious and had a will of its own. Neither of them could change that. Ever. For all intents and purposes, they had become one organism.

*Symbiosis.*

That was the word that seemed to fit. In this case, the sharing of one body by two species for the benefit of both.

He knew the concept, but it would take a long time before he could truly absorb it: absorb the fact that he would no longer be Michael Hart alone, that he would always also be *another*.

A dual being: human and...what was the other term?

*Symbiote.*

As that distinction became resolved in his mind, the symbiote began to trigger images again: Nicole, and then itself. Nicole. Human children. The symbiote.

*Good God!*

Michael slid limply beneath the water's surface.

*It was female.*

The symbiote is in a state of overload. Euphoria!

She has joined with a bondmate—the fulfillment of her primary biological directive, and her first duty to the Creators. Success, when failure had come so close. She had nearly ceased to function, but then her bondmate had returned and chosen her! It is puzzling that the choice took so long, but the biped species is not like the Creators. She must be grateful, and patient.

She is facing many startling new experiences. For the first time she has stayed with Human as it left the water—has travelled over a solid surface and through gaseous atmosphere using the biped's lower appendages, then experienced high velocity movement in a manufactured conveyance of equal parts ingenuity and primitiveness. That journey ended in a structure that was in some ways an incongruous imitation of the outpost itself, except crudely fashioned of materials that were clearly dead.

By then, Human was low on energy. It began to ingest biochemical fuel.

The symbiote has been taught that some species take physical matter into their bodies and convert it into energy through biochemical processes, but nothing has prepared her for the reality. The various forms of sustenance induce incredible sensations across a vast spectrum, and an inner sense of reward and well-being she could not have imagined. Is this normal? After a time, as her bondmate becomes sated, the reward signals diminish. It is as if the intensity of these sensations is in direct proportion to Human's need for energy.

The symbiote, unable to process such an overpowering flood of input, retreats for a time from full interface. So, she is caught off guard when Human suddenly lowers itself into a container of liquid hot enough to trigger her survival alarms!

Automatic responses take over—untold generations of evolved and engineered systems churn into action, drawing potentially damaging heat from the bondmate's skin and expelling it back into the liquid. It is very difficult, but it is working.

With no more warning than before, the symbiote senses that Human is agitated. Displeased. Why? Could it have chosen the temperature of the liquid deliberately? For what possible reason?

Is its body able to tolerate such heat? Perhaps, for a limited time, though its own internal systems also seem to make adjustments to dispel the excess.

In confusion, the symbiote reduces its response and permits more and more of the water's heat to penetrate to the biped's fragile skin, though much more gradually than during the first immersion. The reaction is an unmistakable relaxation of her bondmate's muscles.

Curious!

The symbiote struggles to understand. She has not bonded before. She knows that racial memory within her will govern much of the bonding relationship, yet Human's species is not the one with which her own was intended to join. With no means to communicate with the Controller, she has no way to know if the bonding is proceeding as it should.

She now has senses far different from those she has ever known. Distinct, individual senses. Instead of a pervasive *awareness* of surroundings and accumulating various data about them, she can now choose to collect information through analysis of the wavelengths and other properties of light. Or by vibrations through a medium of gas or liquid that generate interesting resonances and harmonics. Tactile data is not all-encompassing but seems particularly focused into especially sensitive areas of the biped's body, providing a definition that is intriguing. Another sense is designed exclusively for detection of trace molecules in the surrounding air, but is seemingly linked to stored memories rather than being used for strict chemical analysis. And yet another sense is entirely related to the ingestion of solids and liquids used by the biped for fuel. The Controller has defined these senses for her, but comprehending the reality they present is very difficult since the symbiote's own sensory input is much more homogeneous, and measures an almost completely different range of properties.

Most strange of all is that Human responds to collected data from its senses in ways that appear to bypass rational analysis completely and instead trigger autonomic functions with unknown purpose, such as a suddenly increased circulatory rate or an equally rapid relaxation of muscles and nerve activity.

During Human's interaction with the Controller the symbiote had been the conduit, and she had identified distinct variations in the input from the native creature. First, and most obvious, was a continuous stream of data that she now knows was the ongoing feed from its various senses. Such a stream is almost certainly automatic and unconscious. The Controller had quickly analyzed this stream and had then created analogs of its own stored data in a form Human could process with its optical sense: *images*, some static, some nearly so.

Before long, the symbiote had recognized these images repeated in the data feed from her future bondmate. There were images of the home world, which the symbiote herself had never seen; a representation of a changing star field that conveyed travel; other displays of topographical features she gradually understood to have come from the biped's own planet in a time long past.

Then there were sporadic packages of data from Human that did not repeat what the Controller had offered, but clearly originated from the creature itself. These were almost all static images, most likely representations from the being's own experiences. From the way the Controller responded to them, the symbiote came to believe that the new data packets were intended as queries—Human's strong dependence on visual and auditory impressions derived from the electromagnetic spectrum must have shaped its cognition.

The Controller confirmed that idea. Thus, the exchange of imagery was considered a *conversation*. It is a concept the symbiote understands only imperfectly. She has received a great deal of information from the Controller since her awakening, but that flow has been almost entirely one-way. A juvenile, she had only reached a stage of self-awareness less than one home-world solar cycle before stasis was initiated. The immature phase of her species is not properly considered conscious.

Now Human is projecting images in its mind again. The outpost and its Controller are not nearby. Perhaps it is trying to communicate with her directly! This is very encouraging.

The first is an image of Human without artificial coverings. That seems to be intentional and important, as if to indicate a starting point. A base image of its species? The symbiote cannot be certain. The only other member of its species she has encountered was fully enclosed in manufactured materials apparently for the purpose of survival in a liquid environment. Thermal protection and pressurized air. Artificial augments to improve vision and locomotion. The symbiote can fulfill those needs, and much more, organically, and efficiently.

Another image appears: another biped. Subtly different? Yes. The mental image highlights certain features—some in common with the bondmate, some not. A different phase of the species' life cycle, perhaps, like the symbiote's own immature stage? No, there are subsequent images of smaller but similar bipeds with significant variation in physical size and proportion of body features. These must be the immature forms. Then a repeat image of the second type: like the bondmate but with two additional protrusions and one small appendage missing. Some more of the immature forms. Is this juxtaposition of images deliberate?

Human rises out of the water and moves to stand before a reflective surface. The image that follows is accompanied by a short series of impulses that appear linked to its auditory sense. There are accompanying vibrations in the air. Another form of communication? The symbiote stores the sequence in its memory.

There is nothing further. A response is expected. The symbiote tries to form images but isn't successful. Instead, she enhances Human's visual sense and directs it to a certain area of the reflection. Then she repeats a neural equivalent of the auditory sequence.

Did she get it right? Human seems distressed.

There are images in its mind of the water, the outpost, the symbiote...the symbiote *leaving Human.*

No. She must have misunderstood. That cannot be Human's desire.

The sequence repeats.

*Her bondmate has not chosen her after all.*

*It wants to* dissolve *the bond.*

The chemical balance she has finally achieved dissolves into disarray with a sensation as disturbing as when her life processes nearly ended, a response the Controller has called *pain*. It is a sensation the symbiote had hoped never to experience again.

The pain of confusion.

The pain of loss.

The joining was not her bondmate's choosing after all. It is that knowledge that brings the pain.

There is no way to dissolve the bond and survive. She must try to communicate this to Human, though doing so will bring pain to them both.

If she cannot fulfill Human's wish, at least she should try to ease its discomfort. With an effort she recalls the nearby water receptacle and tries to associate it with her bondmate, a rise in temperature, and a sense of well-being. This appears to be successful. Human returns to the water.

She is struck by the frequent clumsiness of its movements, like those of an immature body. She recalls the images of the immature form of the species, and the other larger one.

Suddenly there is clarity!

*The second biped form is associated with reproduction.* It is apparently the fertile form, and her bondmate is not!

The symbiote withdraws in surprise. Can it be that her bondmate is still immature? Not even fully sentient?

No, that isn't possible—it communicates in sophisticated ways. There must be another explanation.

Yet, until she can consider the situation more fully, it is most accurate for her to self-identify with the reproductive form of the bondmate's species. She tries to form an image to communicate this fact. The effort is clumsy, but at last the bondmate reacts by sinking fully into the warm liquid, a clear signal that it is resigning itself into her care.

There is too much new information to process all at once—what is important is that the symbiote has achieved the bond. Wholeness. Fulfillment of purpose, even though she knows there are many more genetic directives she will be compelled to follow. The Creators intended for her to bond with a native of the planet, not out of curiosity but with specific goals and a detailed plan in mind. The Controller has not revealed much of that plan to her, but one thing is now clear: hers will not be a conventional bonding. Her bondmate's needs will be her own needs—such is the way of life as a joined being—yet the needs of the Creators will supersede all. There can be no question of that.

# 15

Michael had to work the next morning, but trying to sleep was an utter waste of effort. Instead, he went online and tried to find as much as he could about symbiotes. Symbiotes of the skin included fleas and barnacles. That wasn't reassuring, somehow.

What he needed to know was whether symbiosis was life-threatening, but he was dealing with an entity from another world. How could he expect Wikipedia to cover that?

None of his online research gave him unequivocal answers. There were so many kinds of symbiotic relationships, and they operated in a thousand separate ways.

There was also no shortage of symbiotes in fiction.

He remembered a couple of examples of symbiotes in TV shows: the *Stargate* series and the *Star Trek* spin-off *Deep Space Nine*. Those depictions were far too simple to offer any guidance—symbiotes were good or bad depending on the needs of the plot.

An alien symbiote providing a human with special powers was a popular trope of the comic books he'd read voraciously as a kid. Spiderman had his hands full with symbiotes called Venom and Carnage that covered their host's skin like a costume. Even though they provided desirable powers, they could be psychotic and malevolent.

Especially in the days when puberty began to screw up his head, Michael had envied Peter Parker, desperate for the equivalent of a radioactive spider bite to transform *him* into someone unique, someone special. Nicole was right: he *was* boring. He'd always been boring.

Yet somehow, he'd never truly understood a core lesson of the Spiderman stories: that such a transformation wasn't a thing you could just put on when you felt like it. It was permanent, 24/7. It would irrevocably affect every single aspect of your life, every attitude, every decision, and there was no going back.

Already, even for short periods of time, the symbiote within him had altered his metabolism, blood chemistry, and the workings of his eyes, ears, muscles. How many more of his human traits must it be changing now that it had joined with his body to stay? It wasn't simply a symbiotic organism, either. It was a thinking being, dependent on him for the energy it required to survive, and it had nearly died when he'd left it alone for a couple of days.

This was a true symbiosis of two conscious entities. Whatever changes were taking place, they affected *two* lives, not just one.

Exactly what those changes and their purpose were must relate to the intent of the aliens that had produced the outpost, and there was no way for him to learn that with any certainty.

*Unless he agreed to call them back to Earth.*

The clamor of the alarm clock was even more of a shock than usual. When his body startled awake, he could have sworn that his skin shivered in a reaction of its own.

Stumbling to the bathroom, the mirror reminded him that he wasn't alone. He had to look closely, but there was a slight change of tone in the color over the left half of his body compared to the right. A hint of gloss. He'd been lying on his right side. Presumably the symbiote would choose to avoid the pressure of his body's weight. Even as he watched, the sheen spread slowly over the bare areas, then faded.

The sight made him a little queasy, and then an itch began under his left arm. Another on his right ribs. His right thigh. The back of his neck. Seconds later it felt like ants were crawling all over his skin. Panic rose in his throat.

*No!* It wasn't real. He'd never felt that crawling feeling before—it had to be a sympathetic response to his fear. A hallucination. He was trained—he knew better than to let his mind play tricks on him.

He closed his eyes and kept his hands rigid at his side, refusing to scratch. The sensation built to a maddening burn, but then slowly, slowly began to ease. He pictured the clear, green water of the lake, his body gliding through it with wondrous ease, the pleasurable slipperiness of cool liquid over his skin. Finally, he was able to open his eyes and face the evidence of the mirror once again. A last shudder swept through his body.

OK, he was in a situation without precedent, but he couldn't let his imagination run wild. That way lay madness. He had to rely on his training and his reason. He wasn't a dumb animal. Neither was the symbiote. It was in the best interest of both to keep calm and take events slowly. There were bound to be side effects, but he had to distinguish the real from the imagined or he was lost.

It would help if he were able to measure his mental state regularly. There were tests, but he couldn't exactly get enough distance to administer a mental-status examination on himself.

Or could he? Some of the most obvious indicators were things he *could* assess on his own like grooming, mood patterns, speech patterns, basic elements of behavior. Maybe if he set up a video camera in his apartment and recorded a few hours from time to time? He should be able to pick out any marked variations. Exercises like that were part of one of his senior courses—if he could put himself in an instructor mindset, he might achieve the necessary distance.

What if Nicole were to find the camera? He didn't want to imagine the shitstorm that *that* would cause.

A patient of a practicing professional could request a Minnesota Multiphasic Personality Inventory, but not anonymously in Canada's health care system; and he sure as hell wasn't going to give in to Nicole and approach Dr. Selwin for help.

If his behavior became obsessive, that would be a giant red flag to everyone around him. Impossible as it might seem, he needed to concentrate on mundane tasks like brushing his teeth, getting dressed. *Eating.* Judging from his voracious appetite lately, he'd have to be mindful of that.

There was a cheap bathroom scale in the vanity, and he got it out. Did the symbiote weigh enough to notice? Michael didn't weigh himself often, but as he looked at the scale's readout, he thought the reading was a kilo or so higher than usual. Then he shifted a little and the needle moved downward. Useless.

For breakfast he wolfed down two large bowls of cereal and three slices of toast with blueberry jam. Crazy! What if the symbiote was like a tapeworm, starving his body of the nutrients it needed? A symbiote that killed its host wasn't a smart evolutionary development, but he had no way to know how evolution worked on other planets. He'd have to keep an eye on his weight and other health indicators. So far, he felt great—not even as groggy as he should have been, going on so little sleep.

The symbiote seemed to understand that there was no need for her to form a covering over his head while in the open air. She kept conveniently out of sight beneath his clothes. Halfway to work, a driver cut him off and forced him to slam on the brakes. Within seconds, he felt heat between his legs, like he'd smeared his thighs with warm Vaseline. He glanced down from time to time, hoping he wouldn't see a wet patch in the crotch of his jeans.

It was a stroke of luck that he had only one class to teach that day because concentration was impossible. He spent most of the time in his office, afraid that Grace McDonald would show up at any moment. She was probably avoiding him. He ate from a vending machine rather than in the cafeteria and stayed away from the library and faculty lounges. A long detour let him return without having to walk past Laura Wood's office.

Puzzled smiles from students made him check his crotch again. Nothing showed. He rubbed his chin and felt the soft crackle of bristles. He'd forgotten to shave! In fact, he hadn't shaved the day before either. He must look scruffy as hell.

On the way home a sudden thought made him pull in to the Chapters bookstore. Unfamiliar with the children's section, it took a while to find what he wanted. Then he spent fifteen dollars at Tim Hortons on an extra-large coffee and a handful of pastries that were gone before he reached his driveway.

He looked through the fridge and the cupboards while he waited to see if Nicole would arrive. He had absolutely no idea what he could tell her. Instead, the ring of the phone made his skin jump.

"Hi, stranger. Are you expecting me?" From the sound, she was using her phone hands-free in her BMW.

"Sure, yeah. You're back in town, aren't you?"

"Got back in last night. But I figured I'd call before coming over, just in case you had some other female hanging around while I was gone."

His laugh was strained, but she didn't seem to notice.

"Bitch of a day, though. Unions are trying to throw their weight around at our public input sessions." She snorted. "Afraid some of our budget reports might make them look greedy. Personally, I'm hoping somebody does put them on the spot."

"Well, uh...if it's a bad time, don't worry about it. I know you get tired after trips like that. I've, uh...got a lot of work to do anyway."

"Really? I could go for an hour or two in a hot bath with a bottle of wine. You sure you don't mind?"

"No...of course I'd like to see you, but I can wait. You go home and get some rest. I'll see you tomorrow."

"OK, then. Stay out of trouble. B'bye."

He didn't know whether to feel disappointed or relieved.

After finishing the last of the frozen meals in the house, he picked up on Nicole's idea and ran a bath again.

The hot water freed his mind as it relaxed his body. He should have baths more often.

What would Nicole think of that? While she was soaking alone at home with a glass of wine he was bathing with *another female*—the same female he'd slept with the night before. He couldn't quite bring himself to laugh about it.

The symbiote's sex should make no difference, but it did. He was sure he would have been more competitive with a male, and more resentful of sharing mental space with it—that was just the way his ego was wired. Was the gender a deliberate choice by the outpost? No, this was the last symbiote alive. It was just a coincidence. Unless all the symbiotes had been female. That possibility held implications he didn't want to consider.

Shit. He needed to find something to call her. Even as a symbiotic being, she must have some sense of individual identity.

He grabbed his iPad and did a search of names.

Something classical. He couldn't picture her as a Brittany or Ashley.

A few names related to water in one way or another—that seemed fitting. He tried rolling them over in his mind, then saying them aloud. Most were awkward, or he wasn't sure how to pronounce them. He plugged one into Google Image Search and it brought up pictures of a lot of beautiful women, including a concert pianist from Toronto. The word meant "water nymph" in Greek. One of the pictures showed something like a mermaid. While he looked at it, his eyes magnified the image on their own—a reaction that he took to be meaningful.

"Naïda," he said. "You want to be called Naïda?"

There was no way she could have known what he was doing, but the name fit. He liked it. He climbed out of the bath, stood in front of the mirror, and tapped his chest firmly. "Michael," he said, then repeated the gesture and word several times. He spoke the name again, but while tapping various parts of his body.

"Nah—*EE*—dah," he said more slowly, and rubbed his hand lightly over himself where the faint sheen was visible. He repeated that name and tried to lightly pinch a bit of skin, when he noticed that something had changed.

The symbiote was no longer like a second skin over his. Her substance had unquestionably penetrated much deeper than before.

Well, that only confirmed what he already knew: physically they were now inseparable.

Mentally...that still needed some work.

He put his iPad aside and picked up one of the books he'd bought earlier, then slid back into the bath water.

It had been tough to find a child's alphabet book that used real pictures of objects instead of cute drawings. Even tougher to find pictures without backgrounds that could cause confusion. He flipped to the first page and began to read aloud.

"'A' is for apple." He tried to picture the fruit sitting in the palm of his hand to give a reference of its size.

The picture of the alligator was harder.

# 16

Over the next couple of days Michael was conscious of teaching his classes to an extra student. Naïda couldn't possibly understand his lessons about human psychology, but she might begin to get a sense of the phonology of the English language: the sounds, if not the meanings of the words. That would help.

Then he overheard a student muttering to another that the prof was "talking to them like they were morons."

Not good. He'd have to try to forget Naïda was there, or somebody would soon be recommending him for a psych evaluation, and not the voluntary kind.

He and Nicole got together for a mid-morning coffee at a cafe near City Hall, and another day he brought her some of her favorite take-out Japanese food for dinner before her City Council meeting. But most of the week she was busy, and he pretended to be. It wasn't until Friday that they actually spent an evening together.

He cooked spaghetti and meatballs. She was astonished at how much he ate.

"Shit, I keep forgetting to give this to you." She grabbed a bag from the floor of the hall and pushed his dinner plate aside to make room for it. The package inside was gift-wrapped in blue and white paper, but it wasn't his birthday or any special anniversary as a couple—he'd entered most of those into his phone's calendar with reminders for them.

He pulled the paper off and laughed out loud. It was a limited-edition set of bobble-head dolls of the five early *Star Trek* TV series captains: Kirk, Picard, Janeway, Sisko, and Archer. He hadn't known there was such a thing.

"I got it at that comic bookstore you like in Toronto. Had a hard time finding it again. This was supposed to be a special edition for some convention, but they had one left in the store. You like it?"

His kiss was his answer, and they kissed for a long time, like in the old days. Then they watched a movie in his living room: a sci-fi thriller about travelling through a VIP's bloodstream to diffuse chemical bombs. He wondered what Naïda would make of the 3D video experience and the subject matter, but they were still a long way from having clear two-way communication.

Nicole laughed at him for devouring a jumbo bag of Cheesies and a large bottle of Coke by himself. He was still avoiding alcohol in case it was toxic to Naïda, although there was no real reason to think so. Maybe he was just afraid of what would happen if his wits were dulled. He hadn't said anything more to Nicole about the lake. Telling her the whole truth was utterly out of the question.

After the movie she stood up.

"You're not leaving, are you?" he asked.

"Not just yet. I'm not finished here." She began to unbutton her blouse. Michael took a quick breath, afraid that he might be wearing his 'deer in the headlights' look, but before he could think of a credible excuse, Nicole stood naked in the half-light from the kitchen.

*Female!*

His head filled with the earlier image of her that he'd pictured for Naïda. Worse, it was followed by images of kids. 'B' is for baby. 'C' is for child. He groaned.

"Mmmm, I've got your interest, have I? Has the little soldier missed me? So, what's with the clothes? Let's get those off already."

Nicole quickly undressed him, pushed him down across the couch and climbed on top. His heart was racing. So far, they'd only cuddled a little, fully clothed, but what would happen when she felt his skin? *Their* skin—his and Naïda's?

If there was anything to notice, Nicole didn't. Maybe she was in too much of a hurry.

"The little fella hasn't forgotten how, has he? I hope not. Let's see what we can do about that." She used her hands to good effect, and Michael's resistance crumbled. He let his instincts take over.

Even so, it was an odd sensation to feel his mind filled with both lust and a burning curiosity.

"Look, Dr. Selwin. I thought I'd made it clear that I have no intention of talking to a shrink."

"Michael...is it all right if I call you Michael? Don't think of me as a shrink—I'm a professional, like yourself. I only want to help."

"Nicole put you up to this?" Michael said into the phone. Maybe she had noticed something different about their night together, after all.

"Nicole is...*concerned*, yes. She cares about you very much, Michael. But you shouldn't worry or feel ashamed. Many, many people are finding it hard to deal with the stresses of living these days. I can help with that."

Michael rolled his eyes. For just a moment, he was perversely tempted to take the asshole on. But he didn't have the mental energy to spare for such games. He had taken the call despite the caller ID because Selwin needed to be told in no uncertain terms to butt out.

"Is Nicole paying you money? Because, if she is, you should reimburse her. I have no intention of becoming your patient."

"She's a friend. We sit on a few of the same committees. I'm calling you as a favor to her."

"Well don't do either of us any more favors. I'm perfectly fine. Even better if I never hear from you again."

"Michael, it's not unusual for people to see hallucinations under exceptional stress, or in high-risk situations...."

Michael held his hand on the disconnect button for five seconds before replacing the phone in its cradle.

A shrink trying to use his bag of tricks on a psych professor. Jesus, what a circus.

Hallucinations!

*Shit.* What had Nicole *told* the guy? He could picture them laughing about it over a coffee in some boardroom with a polished oak table between them. Or had they been sitting side by side, leaning in, sharing the joke of crazy Michael and his alien spaceship at the bottom of a lake? The fawning doctor commiserating with what poor Nicole had to go through, trying to have a normal relationship while running a city. The good doctor was probably very attentive.

Michael tried to deflect that thought, but his mind produced a checklist of all the times Nicole had been out of town recently, and all the other nights she'd begged off because of a meeting or other obligation. She had lots of legitimate commitments—that was true. But what about after the meeting, or the public appearance, or the evening briefing session at the office? Did those really take all night? Did she really go home alone?

He shook his head to clear it. A few weeks earlier, that concern would have been his whole world. Now.... He still loved Nicole, but a challenge of epic scope had overtaken his life path: living as the human host to a being from another star.

More than that, a treasure of advanced knowledge had been offered to him if only he'd agree to trigger a signal and invite the aliens back to Earth. It was potentially the most significant turning point in human history.

He could imagine what Selwin would have to say about that. He'd quote Robert White to show Michael's *effectance motivation*: a deep-seated need to feel his life had a meaningful impact on the world around him. *Shit*, didn't everyone want to think their life meant something?

If only he could be sure of being a hero, not a Judas.

The return of the aliens would bring about a new era on Earth, for good or for bad. Would they bring enlightenment? Or destruction? Or might they become the victims themselves: violent humans bringing evil to a race of innocent pacifists?

He would have given anything to know. In every spare moment he pored over articles and learned papers, tweets and forum postings—everything he could find online that commented, one way or another, on the benefits or risks of a theoretical human-alien encounter. Most of it was crap. Lurid speculations by paranoid types hiding in basements with tin foil on their heads, or hopes from pathetic dreamers looking for the next God substitute.

Intelligent people in science and science-fiction communities brought some rationality to the discussion. Mostly, they wanted to believe that a species that had survived long enough to develop interstellar travel would have learned the necessity of peaceful cooperation. Yet it was all too easy to underestimate the culture shock such an interaction would bring, and the fragility of humanity's collective ego.

He wished that Arthur C. Clarke were still alive. Or Carl Sagan.

Michael Hart had no authority to decide about the outpost's offer. So, who did?

No one, as far as he could see. No government, not NATO, not even the UN. Much as he distrusted the internet with its lunatic fringe, it represented the only possible means for a truly democratic decision-making process that could involve any substantial percentage of human population. It was also fast. Whatever he was going to do, he had to do it before the outpost was destroyed by Amanda Clay's toxic tailings.

He'd need to get the leaders of the internet community on board first: the influencers. There were many commentators with large followings, but very few on a global scale. If only he had a connection to someone with that kind of influence.

Wait. There *was* someone.

Ryan Cassidy.

The former astronaut had been a hero of Michael's for years, a man who had commanded the ISS, the International Space Station, twice and then gone on to serve as an astronaut-engineer on four test missions of the SpaceX spacecraft. It had been assumed that he would lead the company's first mission to an asteroid, until doctors had found a heart irregularity. Instead of retiring, Cassidy had become the reigning ambassador for spaceflight, traveling the world to preach its benefits and raise money for various space projects. Only one cloud had dimmed his bright light.

Cassidy claimed to have seen an alien spacecraft on his last SpaceX mission, and possibly one even earlier from the ISS.

After that admission, UFO fringe fanatics had overrun his internet following. On the other hand, many of those same fanatics were tech geeks who were skilled at getting word out. Cassidy's Curse just might be Michael Hart's blessing.

Cassidy and Michael had met once, at a science fiction convention in Toronto when Michael was seventeen and Cassidy was still a NASA star. Michael was already interested in space psychology and had chosen to do a senior-year project on plans for a Mars colony by a Netherlands-based endeavor called Mars One. Its core idea was to send four astronauts to the Red Planet every two years on one-way trips. Cassidy had given the teenager an hour of his time over coffee explaining why he thought Mars One was doomed to failure. Eliminating the need to refuel a spacecraft in Mars orbit and make a return flight to Earth solved one serious hurdle but created another. The human psyche just wasn't equipped to go so far from its home with no prospect of ever returning.

Mars One colonists would crack, Cassidy had said. They'd have to be something more than human not to. In effect, he had admitted that humankind's dreams of reaching other planets in the solar system were still many decades from being realized.

What would Cassidy think if he knew that true starfaring technology might be within his grasp?

Cassidy's website had links to Twitter, Facebook, and other social media, but Michael chose to use an email with the subject line "Personal Evidence of an Alien Presence on Earth." He gave a straightforward account of his discovery of the outpost, and signed the message using all the university-bestowed letters he was entitled to. But a man like Cassidy must get reams of email—he might even pay some flunky to screen them. Michael went back to the beginning of the message and included a brief reference to their meeting. It wasn't likely the man would remember the encounter, but it just might be enough to convince a hired screener to pass the message on.

He read it over five times. If the email were to become public, he'd be a laughingstock at the university. Was he prepared for that?

With a deep breath, he clicked the *Send* button.

He'd made no mention of Naïda. Revealing her existence to the world would mean the end of his private life. He'd become a media sideshow attraction, a government pawn.

A guinea pig.

On a whim, Michael picked up the phone and dialed Phil Rodriguez' number. They hadn't spoken since the day after they discovered the outpost.

"Hello?"

"Marcia? It's Michael Hart. Is Phil home?"

"Michael. Yeah…um, I mean, no. He isn't home *right now*. He's out…getting something from the store. Um, but I think he has somewhere to go after that, too. He might not be home until late."

"Right. OK, well…tell him I called. Thanks."

He hung up the phone, picturing Phil gesturing at his wife to make up some excuse. Shopping. Women always thought of shopping, but Phil wasn't the type. Obviously, he was still in denial, but there was no one else Michael could talk to. It had been a mistake to tell Nicole. That admission made his throat feel tight.

In twenty minutes, he was in the Rodriguez' driveway. He sat there for a moment, then shrugged, and walked up to the house. The expression on Phil's face as he opened the door spoke volumes.

"Michael. What are you doing...?

"We need to talk. I know you've been avoiding me, but we need to talk about...about what we found at the lake." Marcia might be within hearing distance.

"Jesus Christ, would you just let it..." Phil looked over his shoulder. "Shit. The garage. Let's go to the garage." He pulled the door closed behind him and pushed past Michael.

Phil's garage was exceptionally tidy for a guy's refuge. It needed to fit all his toys: snowmobile, motorcycle, and every kind of power appliance made for yard work, but no car—there wasn't room for that. The only thing that seemed out of place was a girly calendar on the wall from the local car-repair shop, a couple of years out of date. Phil turned around and stepped close to Michael, using his extra five inches of height.

"Jesus, why are you so goddamned determined to talk about that day? We were narc'd and we saw some kind of wreckage on the bottom of the lake. Nothing more than that."

"Really? So that's why you've avoided me ever since? Come on, I've never taken you for an idiot—don't take me for one! You knew that what we saw that day wasn't from this planet and it got you spooked. Fine. I don't blame you."

"You don't know what you're..."

"I *do* know what I'm talking about because I've been back there—more than once—and it's true: that thing on the bottom of the lake actually *is* an alien artifact. The first real evidence that beings from somewhere outside the solar system have been here. In fact, I think it's an outpost they left behind for us to find." For a moment Michael considered peeling off his shirt and revealing

Naïda, but he was afraid Phil would freak out. And there were just too many sharp objects close at hand.

"You're crazy. I should call the shrinks on you."

"Nicole already did that. Well, of course she didn't believe me. But you saw it. *You saw!* And you still won't admit it."

Phil turned his back to Michael and pivoted his head as if searching the wall for something. Hopefully not a weapon.

"If you're so goddamned sure of what you saw, what do you need me for?"

It was Michael's turn to take a step closer. "Can we just...have a beer maybe? Sit somewhere? Talk for a minute? I need to talk to somebody about this, Phil. You can't believe how important this is."

Phil half turned, his arms folded over his chest. "Just tell me what you want." His eyes were full of anger and, Michael thought, more than a hint of fear.

Michael sighed and looked for something to lean on, finally settling some of his weight on the utility rack of a red ATV.

"It *is* alien, and I even managed to...communicate with it. Sort of—a little bit. Mostly it showed me pictures...of space, of other planets, of prehistoric Earth, I think. It hasn't done anything dangerous—the outpost, I mean. That's the way I've come to think of it: the outpost.

"I have a feeling it's pretty much a machine, though an incredibly sophisticated one." Michael raised his palms. "The thing *is*, Phil, this could be the most important discovery in human history. Don't you see that? Proof of other life in the universe. *Intelligent* life. I'm almost certain that whoever it was came here thousands of years ago and then went somewhere else. *But they could come back.*"

Now Phil's eyes held unmistakable fear.

"You're insane. I *hope* you're insane."

"I'm not. I have proof, but I...don't want to show it to you yet. Maybe if I knew you were with me in this."

The reply was a horrible laugh: guttural and phlegmy. Michael had never heard anyone make such a sound before.

"*With you?* You've got to be kidding! Besides, soon it won't matter anyway."

"What do you mean?"

"The lake. Whatever is there, it won't be doing much of anything for long."

Michael felt a chill. Naïda wrapped herself around his chest.

Phil drew his lips away from his teeth.

"Clay Developments. They've got a license to dump soil scrapings and other crap into Evergreen Lake. Maybe they've already started."

"Nicole told me that. How do you know about it?"

"I heard it from Amanda Clay herself." Phil turned away too quickly. "I ... know her. Met her a couple of times, I mean. Anyway, some of the stuff they'll be dumping isn't exactly what you'd call environmentally friendly. That should take care of...whatever you think you saw."

"Clay told you that? In a casual conversation she told you that she'll be dumping toxic waste into a lake? Come on, Phil!"

"I don't give a shit whether you believe it or not. You'll find out soon enough. Then you'll have to drop this whole fantasy. So how about leaving me the hell alone. Goodbye, Michael!"

He slammed the button that raised the garage door.

Michael hesitated, then walked silently into the night.

# 17

Sakiko idly swirled her cappuccino as she walked along the street past clothing shop after take-out restaurant, giving quick glances to the parade of faces she encountered. What were their lives like, she wondered? Were they driven by grand motivations? Or simply by an urge to find something tasty for lunch, a cute blouse to buy, or a new companion to share their nights? She had no right to judge anyone, and she didn't judge. After all, how many of *them* had committed fraud?

The number of pedestrians dropped drastically as she took several turns away from the main thoroughfare. From the high-traffic retail strip, she found herself in a run-down neighborhood of small shops, half of which appeared to have closed. It was mid-afternoon, but the sun seemed so much weaker here, unable to reflect from soot-coated walls, and she felt a tingle at the back of her neck. If she'd been one of the rich and privileged, she would have brought a bodyguard. But then, anyone rich would have sent someone else on an errand like this.

Her meeting with Dominique Swan came to mind with unusual clarity: surreal, and therefore vivid.

She was convinced that Swan had already decided to provide the *Argo* for the excursion before she had even met with Sakiko. So, the purpose of the meeting was...what? A final character test? A formality with which to reassure her father if ever he came asking questions?

Swan claimed that she had the blessing of her mother in steering the Cartwright Institute and the tacit permission of her father in offering one of the family's three yachts to serve as a research vessel, but she offered no proof of either. Sakiko was almost sure that the latter, the offer of the yacht, was not true.

When she'd obliquely pressed for confirmation, Swan had simply smiled and asked, "How badly do you want this expedition, Ms. Matthews?"

"More than I can easily explain right now," Sakiko had answered. "But I don't understand why you're interested."

"You don't have to."

On that note, the heiress stood and offered her hand again. It was only later, reading the fine print of the agreement that Sakiko realized Swan intended to come along on the journey. A joyride? A little rich girl running away from Mommy and Daddy? No, that wasn't fair. Even the rich might yearn for a chance to give meaning to their lives.

Sakiko took a swallow of her cappuccino. It was cold. But she'd arrived at the shop she was looking for. The dumpster a few steps away was too full for the lid to close completely, so she stuffed her paper cup through the gap and turned back to the door. It looked more like a service entrance than one for customers; but then, this kind of business had a special clientele.

There was no bell on the door. A god-awful creak served the purpose of alerting the owner/manager/clerk who stepped from behind a partition near the back of the shop's cramped interior. He was built like a loaf of bread standing on end, but wrapped in a white shirt with striped tie and gray trousers that looked clean and pressed. She expected stubble on the wide chin, but there was none.

"You the one who called?" he asked, as if it were a novelty for his phone to ring.

"Yes."

"Got some ID?"

Surprised by the question, she opened her purse to extract her driver's license and her VISA card. She passed them to him.

"Why do you need ID? Is this illegal?"

"Nope. And I don't," he said as he held the cards up to a nearby lamp. "But a lot of my customers...well, let's just say I like to admire the artwork on their documents. Makes no difference to me, though." He handed the cards back. "I got what you want back here."

She hesitated before following him toward the back of the shop, but he didn't go out of sight. Instead, he stepped behind a counter and lifted three dull gray boxes, the smallest about the size of a shoebox and the largest roughly four times bigger. Each had a small door in the side that faced her, and he swung the doors open.

"They're like I told you on the phone. All work the same. Only difference is the size, 'n' that all depends on what you want to put in 'em. Take your time. I'm in the middle of another transaction." He returned behind the partition and she could hear the sound of his fingers on a keyboard.

Despite his assurances, her surroundings made Sakiko feel even more like a criminal than ever. Her cause was vital; her actions justified. That didn't change the fact that she would carry out her quest with money obtained fraudulently and a ship that might be at sea without the real owner's permission.

Such luck could only come in threes.

Just that morning she'd come across a casual post on social media made by her new research assistant, Sunita James. She rarely read Sunita's posts and had almost skipped this one, too. The simple words had taken a few seconds to register in her mind. Then she'd spilled half a glass of orange juice onto her lap.

Sunita had thanked her uncle for the nice weekend at his lakeside cottage and promised to drop in to his office to pick up the track suit she'd forgotten. That was all. But the name of the recipient was like a thunderclap.

*Edward Ryder.*

Sunita James was her boss's niece!

The woman hadn't used Ryder as a reference on her CV or mentioned him at all in her interview for the position. If that implied that Sunita wanted to get ahead on her own merits without playing the usual academic game of using connections as currency, it was commendable. But it could also mean that Ryder wanted a spy on Sakiko's team without making it too obvious. Either way, it put Sakiko in a hell of a quandary, especially since Yuri had obviously been very much taken with their new team member.

Bloody hell!

With a secret that could send her to jail, she'd just given her boss's niece months of close access to discover it. And the loyalty of the one person who shared the secret would be tested by his gonads.

Sunita did have impressive skills and credentials—she could be a valuable asset.

Only time would tell if she would help bring the project to success, or ruin.

"You decided yet?"

The voice made Sakiko jump. The shop owner followed his words around the partition's edge and back behind the counter.

"I think the smallest one will be enough. I probably only need it for one data drive."

"And the bigger ones are kind of hard to miss, yeah. Well, the battery pack is fifty bucks more if you're taking it somewhere without reliable current."

At her nod he reached under the counter and showed her how the 12-volt battery slid into place on the back of the unit. It was a demo model, though. He disappeared into a corridor at the rear and remerged with a couple of brown boxes with minimal markings.

"Instructions are included," he said as he pulled a multi-layered paper form from a low shelf behind him and began to fill it out. Sakiko hadn't seen carbon-paper receipts since she was a child. She turned her eyes back to the demo unit.

A data scrubber—a data drive killer.

It looked like an ordinary, small personal safe, with keypad and fingerprint scanner on the front. Hidden under a sliding panel at the back were controls for the unit's custom-built electronics. The wrong thumb print or passcode would trigger powerful electrical surges that would wipe any magnetic media and completely fry the chips of a solid-state drive, rendering data completely irretrievable. In her mind was a picture of white smoke pouring out of the box, like the "self-destruct" sequence after the *Mission Impossible* teams were given their super-secret instructions. She had no choice but to keep records of what she was doing, but that didn't mean she had to risk those records being used as evidence against her. She was sad that her life had come to this.

As she walked away from the shop with the drive-killer in a blue Best-Buy shopping bag, she tried to push the episode to the back of her mind. There were still other problems to solve.

Although Swan's gift of a ship and crew had snatched the mission from the brink of collapse, yachts weren't natural research vessels. If adaptations had to be made to accommodate their equipment, Sakiko hadn't included them in her budget. And the money saved by the gift of a ship couldn't be used to cover any other expenses. The funding grant treated the ship rental as separate from operational funding. She couldn't re-direct it to another purpose without taking the whole proposal back to a sub-committee, and to do that was much too risky. She'd have to cover extra costs by fundraising of some kind. Private foundations. Philanthropic museums. Wealthy eccentrics. Whatever it took.

She wasn't good at fundraising—hated every moment of it. The "fish out of water" cliché fit her all too perfectly.

She finally reached the main street again and its array of glitzy stores was like the sun re-emerging from behind a cloud. An armored car pulled up a block away.

*What the hell*, she thought, *I've gone this far. Why not just rob a bank?*

That made her smile. She barely knew what the inside of a bank looked like. And she already had nightmares about jail cells. Stealing any more money was out of the question.

Still, Yuri didn't have to know that. She was eager to see his face when she brought up the subject of bank robbery. Along with the news that he was flirting with the boss's niece!

# 18

After the angry encounter with Phil, the skies delivered a deluge. The car's wipers were going flat out, trailing wakes across the windshield. Michael knew he should pull over, wait for the storm to pass; but he was too keyed up to just sit still. As the car splashed through the night, his fury cooled a little.

The confrontation had been a reality check, he had to admit. Maybe Phil was being paranoid, but he had a right to be. At stake, the future of every single human being now alive or yet to be born. Yet Michael had literally dived into the unknown, blithely assuming that an advanced species couldn't have malevolent intentions. There was certainly no basis in human history for an assumption like that. Quite the opposite. Modern humans had technology vastly superior to their tribal ancestors, and all too often used it to kill their fellow humans in horrific numbers. Phil wasn't wrong to be terrified.

Then there was Naïda—a creature evolved or engineered on an entirely alien world, now insinuating herself into every system of his body. Tapeworms and lice were at least forms of Earth life. The idea of a cancerous tumor infesting one of his organs made his blood run cold. How could he know that this alien symbiote wasn't just as bad? Or worse—a cancer with a guiding intelligence.

Was it truly too late? Or was there still a way to regain sole possession of his own body?

He couldn't just jump into Evergreen Lake and expect her to swim off voluntarily. That time had passed. Something critical had changed and she'd nearly died without him. But what if Amanda Clay's people did dump toxic waste into the lake—a chemical able to kill the outpost? What if Michael swam in the tainted water? Would Naïda separate herself from his body, trying to escape the poison?

Or lose her life trying to protect him?

His gut churned at the thought, but maybe he needed to harden himself and face facts. He couldn't deny the fear that gripped Phil Rodriguez. Or his own fear, for that matter. The ancient fear of the unknown.

Coming down a curving slope, he saw the road ahead lit by a pulsing red glow. Through the rain-pounded windshield he could make out several cars pulled off to the side with their four-way flashers going, just before the bridge over the Wanapitei River. As he drew close, the sight made his stomach drop. Part of the guardrail on the bridge was missing.

A car had gone into the river.

He pulled over, hit his own flashers, and jumped out into the night. Blood pounded in his ears. Though there were a half-dozen people shouting and gesturing along the bridge and down at the river's edge, he couldn't make out full sentences. Only snatches of words.

"Somebody's in the car."

"Just now."

"Don't know what happened."

"Police—*call 911!*" He realized that had come from his own mouth.

Scared faces turned toward him. Two women, the rest men. None of them young.

"Police'll be too late," someone screamed.

Michael stood where the guardrail had been ripped away. There was no sign of a vehicle. The water was always dark there, the current swift. If the car had sunk slowly the current would almost certainly have dragged it downstream. The screamer was right. No one could get to it in time. No one would be able to see through the black water or do anything to help even if they found the car. The driver was doomed, if not dead already. Beyond saving.

But that was not true.

Ice and fire raced through his veins as he sprinted across the bridge to the downstream side and mounted the guardrail. If he stopped to think, he knew he'd back down. Another scream carried dimly through the air as he plummeted toward the river.

*Christ*, the water was cold! And gritty, with an unpleasant taste. The plunge of the car had probably stirred up the river bottom.

He was immediately disoriented. A hundred sensations competed for attention: cold liquid slipperiness, froth of bubbles, tug of current, sodden clothes slowing his movements, a ringing in his ears. Yet, within moments, the darkness began to lighten, the noise to become more comprehensible.

He realized that he was holding his breath, and his chest clenched in terror at the thought of letting that dirt-laden water in. The alternative was to let the driver die. He opened his mouth and drew a liquid breath. It was cold, but no worse than a winter's day. Adrenaline surged through him. He could survive here. And he could do more than that.

Shoed feet provided little push, but his arms pulled him forward with strong strokes. If he hadn't been encumbered by clothes, he would have slipped through the water easily; but there was no time to strip them off. There was a faint red glow ahead, and a patch of lighter water. The car's lights were still on!

A dark four-door Accord was at a forty-five-degree angle, its nose in the river bottom, its tail slowly pivoting with the current, windows rolled up because of the rain. As Michael reached it and tried to find something to grip, it lurched away, and he had to kick ahead another couple of meters. He finally managed to take hold of the rear door and pull himself within reach of the front door handle. A surge of current tipped the car and freed one headlight from the muck, allowing him to see into the cabin. A woman had freed herself from her seat belt and was floating with her face against the roof. Did that mean there was an air pocket? He pounded his knuckles against the window, but the resistance of the liquid prevented him from putting much into it.

The head turned toward him.

She was alive!

Now he could see the silvered bubble of air, but it wasn't much. He waved to get the woman's attention, hoping there was enough light for her to see him. She reacted with a frantic beckoning motion of her arm, her eyes wide with panic. He gave her the OK sign with his thumb and forefinger, then made broad motions of pinching his nose shut. She didn't get it right away. The current tugged him upward, nearly pulling him from the car. His arms began to ache from the strain as he swung himself back into position. He pinched his nose again, and then again. The woman nodded and her face disappeared into the silvery bubble.

Michael pivoted to plant his feet against the body of the car. The current made it nearly impossible—the soles of his shoes slipped free within seconds.

He tried again, gripping the door handle tightly with both hands and using the leverage to work his feet into a solid position. When he thought he had enough purchase he pressed the door latch and pulled hard. The door didn't move. He tried several fierce jerks. Maybe it was just stuck. Then his left foot slipped off and he had to position himself again. Just as he did, the front bumper hit a boulder with a violent lurch. The car began to roll its far side down, swinging Michael upward, and he put everything he had into another pull. The bubble of air inside slid toward him and burst outward as the door came free, bringing the woman partially through the opening. Her arms began to flail, but Michael ducked under them and wrapped his own around her torso. Then he kicked away from the rolling car. He didn't get much force into it, but it was a push in the right direction. Within seconds his head broke surface and he fought the current as he brought the woman to shore.

The drenching rain was almost as bad as being in the river. He stood over the woman to shield her. She couldn't have noticed as he bent and let dirty water flow from his lungs. She vomited a lot of water herself, and kept coughing, her gasping breaths like whimpers of fear.

They were too far from the bridge for the people there to see them in the dark, and the people couldn't hear him yelling over the rainfall. Wearily, he tugged her into a fireman's carry over his shoulder, trying to take most of her weight on her hips so she could catch her breath. He considered taking her to a nearby house, but there were people at the bridge ready to help. She gasped and sobbed, gasped and sobbed as he stumbled along the shoreline an endless distance back to the road.

Then he was laying the woman on the ground while people crowded around and voices clamored for answers. He used the excuse of catching his breath to back away slowly and let the others take charge, but he raised his eyes for a moment and saw a bystander's face looking into his, illuminated by car taillights. Very familiar, though he couldn't place her. Did she recognize him?

Now there were flashes of blue light along with the red. Police had finally arrived—it was time to go.

A convenient bush hid him from the running officers who were focused on the victim, and he was able to make it to his car, unseen. It took all of his willpower to shake off the shock that tried to paralyze him; but as he drove off, he was gripped by an overpowering sense of unreality.

Had the events of the past ten minutes really happened? Had he really saved a woman's life?

No, not just him. He could never have done it alone.

He pressed harder on the gas and let the night swallow him up.

# 19

The confrontation with Phil had been mild compared to the fireworks when he went to Nicole's place.

What was he doing just showing up like that? Soaking wet! Did he go swimming in his clothes now?

Who did he think he was, flipping the bird to one of the city's top psychiatrists and a personal friend at that?

How dare he imply that her relationship with Selwin was something more than friendly?

Why the hell should she interfere with a respected local company carrying out its legal business? No, there was no chance that the waste was toxic. Did he take her for an idiot?

And it went downhill from there.

Local reporters would have paid good money to be standing within earshot of the mayor's front door as Michael made his retreat. He was just as angry, but he could never match her for pure vitriol, nor for her command of four-letter words.

As he cruised the dark streets, shivering in sodden clothes, he realized that, instead of trying to warm him, Naïda had drawn herself into as small a space as she could, between his thighs. Sometimes she seemed to hide or take shelter in that spot. There was nothing sexual about it. If anything, it was like the touch of a warm gel pack to treat a muscle injury. Except this time, she seemed far cooler than usual.

Maybe Michael was traumatizing her with his heightened emotions, or by stress chemicals coursing through his veins. He still didn't know how much she sensed on her own.

Without planning to, he found himself on the road to Evergreen Lake. Was that her doing? Did she crave a refuge from this human storm of conflict?

Or was the impulse Michael's own need for answers?

He could feel the difference in her as they approached the shore: a rapid increase in temperature, nearly humming with energy. Michael submerged right away, getting a noseful of water because he started to draw a breath before Naïda had a chance to help him adapt. It was a shock to realize how much he'd come to take her presence for granted in just one week. He'd have to be careful about that.

There'd been no sign of heavy equipment on the road nor along the shore of the lake. There was no obvious taste to the water. Surely Naïda would have reacted to the presence of toxins. In fact, the flow in and out of his lungs felt cleansing, purging the sediment that had remained from his river rescue.

The sight of the glowing outpost brought a strange mix of relief and comfort: a feeling of homecoming incongruously mixed with fear. He needed no better proof that there were now two beings occupying his head as well as his body.

Without consciously directing his movements, he sank gently into the middle of the surfaces he now thought of as display screens, and they lit instantly. But the light and imagery that began at the screens quickly leapt from them, expanding to fill a much larger space, as if he were in the middle of a holographic projection. His interaction with the central intelligence of the outpost was vastly improved: an organic flow of images, almost musical tones, and an indefinable sensation of...*presence* that was just short of tactile.

It wanted to know things, especially how Michael and (*Naïda?*) were bonding, and if he'd come to any decision about the outpost's invitation.

Michael tried to communicate the plan to dump toxic substances into the lake, and the concept of danger, but it was difficult. He could form pictures of objects, but they were items for which an alien species would have no frame of reference. How could he explain poison? How could he show death? He tried to picture aquatic plants withering, and fish floating belly up, but how would a non-native species know that these were not characteristic behaviors?

He especially had trouble conveying the idea of things yet to come—planned, but not yet a reality. It occurred to him that, of all the concepts held in common by galactic strangers such as they, *time* might be the most elusive of all.

The outpost urged him again to send the signal—to recall its creators. It gave him a taste of the knowledge that could be his.

Images expanded again to fill his awareness. There had to be a direct connection between the outpost and his central nervous system through Naïda. Did that imply the potential for influence, even control? Yet the exchange was far too captivating to admit any voice of caution.

Planets, extravagantly varied, competed for notice; and where Michael's attention fixed, the view expanded again, offering detail so rich he could nearly touch it, smell it. His mind leaped into a vast blackness above, where fringes of his vision offered teasing glimpses of manufactured surfaces with symmetrical lines, as if he were viewing from a spacecraft through a wide-angle lens. The actual craft that had transported the aliens across the stars? Or perhaps only a projection of machines that could carry humankind into space—should they choose to accept the offer?

And then another world, seen from high orbit, the curve of its horizon paralleled by a barely discernible distortion in the background of stars. A sudden fireworks display; bursts of light, seconds apart, some too intense to look at. Meteorites, he surmised, not destroyed by the depths of an atmosphere but shielding of a different kind.

From within the golden glow of the planet, symbols burst forth like giant deformed scarecrows spat from a volcano. He couldn't interpret them right away, though they scattered across the starscape. They paraded in a game of follow-the-leader in loops around him like maypole ribbons. Then a short squiggle of alien text rotated and coalesced into *pi*. Another tipped to become a lemniscate, an infinity sign. Alpha. Epsilon. Square root. Mathematical nomenclature soup, swirling, dancing, coming together into snatches of phrases that must be equations, then whirling apart again.

As the exotic shapes drew together and melted into a gleaming mass that twisted and stretched, suddenly he was travelling a tunnel or tube. The surrounding medium was translucent, shimmering with pulses of luminescence. Objects bobbed, spun, writhed—swept along by unseen current, but some with seeming locomotion of their own. Michael's inner eye focused on a number of nearby discs, circular and flattened, with indentations in the middle, like pictures he'd seen of blood cells. And that is what they clearly were. They tumbled and flowed along, now drawing close to a wall of the tunnel, where his vision was caught and held by a dark patch like a frozen froth of mud. Tightening his focus revealed a grotesque pattern of colors. Something cancerous, virulent. Then a gold and salmon fog swept down upon it, and the hideous colors began to change—shriveled surfaces swelled to rounded uniformity, and grittiness gave way to a smooth shine,

This knowledge—all of it, and more—was available. Available to be shared with willing partners.

Understanding filled him like the heady warmth of an alcoholic rush.

All he had to do was send the signal.

If only he could know, really *know* that the outpost species intended nothing that would harm Earth or its life forms. Without solid assurance of that, he could be forsaking his own race to...enslavement, or even destruction. Loyalty to his own kind in exchange for the knowledge he was now being offered could be a deal with the devil, a *Faustian* bargain. And the legend of Dr. Faustus had not ended well.

His body hung suspended in the green liquid, his mind poised at the edge of a vast gulf between human past and human future. The choice of the path ahead lay with him.

He saw his right hand poised over the indentation in the outpost surface and yanked it back, willing his body to rise a couple of meters from the lake bottom. It obeyed instantly, though his skin rippled.

Please, show me more, he thought.

But the outpost would not. Or could not.

He thought about computer lockouts that only allowed access with the proper key codes. Was that the function of the hand-shaped depressions? A code lock set in place millennia ago to ensure that the informational riches of the galaxy would be granted only to...whom? Those who were worthy? The one chosen species?

Only those who chose to invite into their collective lives the presence of beings extraordinarily advanced. Extraordinarily powerful.

No, he could not make such a decision for all of humankind.

He rose toward the surface, trailing a wake of regret.

He dressed quickly and returned to his car, aware of a confusion that was not his own. Naïda's species had evolved to join with others—to extend that concept to the merger of collectives would only be natural. She would not understand his reluctance.

Could Naïda comprehend an individual's responsibility to the collective? He had no way to know. They'd made progress together with the symbology of his own culture—he teaching, she learning. But as yet, there was no way for her to reciprocate. He could not explain his actions to her. But it was a revelation to realize how badly he wanted to.

An image of Nicole came into his mind. The memory of their recent fight made his ears burn, but it wasn't their first argument. Was he willing to let it be their last? If not, he had to talk to her—smooth things over. They would have to resolve the issue of the outpost and what he'd seen. Which meant that he would have to offer the only proof he had.

Naïda.

First, he had to get into dry clothes. He drove home, wondering if Nicole might even be there—if she might have calmed down after their argument and come to see him. To apologize? No, that was hardly likely. But maybe to give him another earful.

The apartment was empty. After changing his clothes, he swallowed hard and pulled out his phone, vaguely surprised that its case had kept it dry through all that rain.

There was no answer at her home number or her cell. Maybe she'd decided to cool off by going somewhere for a drink. She liked The Regent, a pub just a short drive down Regent Street.

She wasn't there, nor at two other bars he checked.

He slammed his palm on the steering wheel. His best friends were Phil Rodriguez and Grace McDonald, and neither was speaking to him. Who else would even listen to his crazy story?

His brother lived in the west end of town in one half of a semi-detached house. Jay was no Mensa candidate, but he was a good listener. That made him popular with women, so there was a good chance he wouldn't be alone. Michael should call first. Except then he'd have to explain wanting to come by. He and Jay didn't just drop in on each other to chat.

He decided to drive over. If there was another car in the driveway, he'd keep on going.

As he wheeled through the night, he flicked on the car radio. The rock station was playing "The End of the World" by R.E.M. He stabbed the *Off* button.

Jay's house was seven lots from the corner. Sure enough, the lights were out except for the upper left room that Michael knew was Jay's bedroom, and there were two cars in the driveway. One was Jay's late model Chrysler Intrepid.

The other car was Nicole's.

A dozen desperate explanations played through his mind as he drove back to the lake, but he didn't believe any of them.

He gripped the steering wheel until his fingernails dug into his palms and relished the purely physical pain.

If his life had been boring, it sure as hell wasn't any more.

Laura Wood had poisoned his job. Grace McDonald hated his guts. Phil Rodriguez had cut him loose and was probably having an affair with Amanda Clay, the woman about to destroy the single most important discovery in human history. Now Nicole had delivered the deepest cut of all.

What a pathetic species they were. The whole human race needed nothing more desperately than to be rescued from itself. The evidence was everywhere: crime, pollution, poverty, war. Betrayal. And somehow Michael had thought such broken beings could capably choose their own destiny. How ludicrous that was.

They didn't deserve it, but he would save them in spite of themselves.

Naïda helped him see through the flow of tears as he bolted to the lakeshore and threw himself in. The water felt like ice on his burning skin, fusing his mind into a single crystalline resolve.

As he swam to the bottom, the outpost opened its petals like a blossom to the morning sun, glowing with fierce welcome. He settled onto the gelid platform and placed his palms on the indentations prepared for them.

A pulse of radiance swept through the surrounding structure, and he steeled himself for a piercing shriek of sound, like in the movie *2001: A Space Odyssey*. Something suitably momentous. Something epic.

The outpost went dark.

# *PART TWO*

# 20

Sitting on the bed, Sakiko looked around at the drearily generic decor of her hotel room and thought about how many times she'd had to make a pitch for her research. She'd lost track of the number at the university level alone, first as she'd explained her proposal to her supervisor, then asked for initial feasibility funding from her department head, then went before the dean, the council and, later, because the plan was so urgent and so expensive, when she was seconded to the Institute's Global Research Division. But even that was barely the beginning. It seemed as if each piece of the project required a fresh round of begging. Recent weeks had been consumed by a seemingly endless schedule of presentations to private enterprises and foundations that might have funds to offer.

It was like running on sand. The economy had hit another sharp downturn. Canada's oil sands industry was mired in litigation from First Nations communities and cancer victims, and America's most critical underground aquifer was being contaminated by leakage from the pipelines that carried crude from those same oil sands. Both governments had ignored warnings for years, and now acted like it was a sudden, unanticipated crisis. Stock markets had plunged.

She'd known that private fundraising in such a climate would be a challenge, but she hadn't thought it might be impossible. She hadn't done any actual research for months, enslaved by the telephone, bounced from meeting to non-committal meeting, her time squandered by grant paperwork. She still had a ship, but that was only thanks to a bored rich girl: a darling of the tabloid press who probably thought nothing of squandering the equivalent of Sakiko's entire university tuition on spur-of-the-moment junkets to Europe.

No, that was unfair. Whatever Dominique Swan's motives were, they weren't relevant. As long as her commitment of the *Argo* wasn't a passing whim.

Yet another funder had reneged only two days ago. So here she was in a hotel room in Sudbury, Ontario hoping to replace that lost money by working out a deal with a local science center called Science North. They usually only funded their own projects, but she'd sent them a proposal for a short documentary film to be culled from footage shot on her voyage, a natural fit for their Discovery Theatre. They were willing to meet with her if she would give a public presentation as part of their subscriber lecture series.

Another goddamned talk, and no guarantee that anything would come of it.

Her hotel was just across the street from Science North. Needing fresh air and with a few minutes to kill before her lecture, she strolled down to the lake beside the science center. The summer sun was still bright, and the view of all that blue water in the middle of a city was captivating. Sudbury was about as far from an ocean as you could get, but it boasted three hundred lakes within its city limits and had created itself anew from a landscape stripped of trees and rendered infertile by harsh smelter emissions. A modern jewel of water and greenery. Blackened rock faces that formed a backdrop to the lake were topped with birches, cedars, and young pines—a rugged beauty so very different from the urban New England vistas she was used to. A scenic wooden boardwalk made a border along the lakeshore, extending from Science North around the bay until it disappeared behind a small promontory. As she turned away from the view and made her way to the entrance doors of the center, she vowed to make time for a real walk, maybe the next morning.

Her presentation was in a large cavern hollowed out of the rock of the Canadian Shield and reached through a long, mine-like tunnel. That was what the city was known for: hard rock mining, mainly for nickel. She felt a twinge of claustrophobia, but the feeling went away as she focused on her audience. If her chances of getting funding depended on the size of the turnout, she'd probably wasted a trip. There were only about a hundred people, although they did have the decency to look interested most of the time, even when her PowerPoint presentation hit a glitch and one of her videos had to be restarted.

After the talk, she mingled with the small number of attendees who stayed for the cheese and veggies. A couple of the board members and a high-level staffer who'd be reviewing her application had showed up, but each of them left quickly, pleading other commitments.

She was looking for a way to make a gracious exit when she turned and found a man facing her. Dark hair, a little above average height—thanks to her two-inch heels she didn't have to look up to meet his eyes. They were brown, and large. From excitement? Or the relatively dim light?

"Hi. My name's Michael. Michael Hart."

The handshake was firm, not deliberately gentle because she was a woman. She liked that.

"I really enjoyed your talk," he said. "I mean, *enjoy* might not be the right word, but I was very impressed with what you're trying to do. I'm a scuba diver, and the situation with the coral...well, it's heartbreaking. I, uh...did you come with someone?" He made a point of looking around, but she was obviously on her own. "I just...I wondered if you'd like to get a drink somewhere. Or a coffee. I have...some information I'd really like to discuss with you."

Was he putting her on? What kind of pickup line included the word *discuss*?

Still, he wasn't bad looking. He just needed someone to dress him better. And she'd made up her mind to have a couple of drinks back at the hotel anyway, to dull her disappointment about the turnout. Why not have company? It wouldn't go anywhere—she was pretty committed to Doug. Wasn't she?

"There's actually a nice bistro right here in the building," he said. "Great food, great view."

"Sure. Why not?"

"Terrific. I promise not to take too much of your time."

Did that mean he was telling the truth about wanting to talk business? Well, she was committed now. For the sake of appearances, she looked around to see if any of the audience members or staff were trying to get her attention. They weren't.

"OK, I guess I'm done here. Let's go."

They came out from underground and up some stairs into the bistro to face a row of large windows that revealed the lake below in all its splendor. She was surprised to find that it was still light, though the sun had set.

"Higher latitude makes a lot of difference, especially just after the summer solstice," Michael said.

"What university do you work for?"

"How did you know?"

She laughed. "Anyone else would have said 'Yeah, it's like that up here in June'."

"I guess. Our university is just down the road about five minutes that way."

The bistro was nearly empty. Sakiko chose a table not far from the entrance and sat so she could look in that direction, out of habit. As the waitress approached, Michael proclaimed the food to be excellent, but Sakiko only ordered a gin and tonic with a twist of lime, thinking it might give an impression of class. He chose a beer called Steam Whistle and enough appetizers to make a dinner: mostly rather exotic, and not cheap.

"I have a fast metabolism," he said with a tentative smile.

While they waited for their drinks, he pointed out a few of the landmarks, then chatted about her presentation. He remembered a lot of details. When the plates arrived filled with bruschetta, calamari, grilled pineapple, and mussels, her resistance crumbled, and she tasted everything. It was fantastic, and she was hungrier than she'd thought. Even so, her appetite was nothing compared to his. He ordered more seafood.

With a mild buzz from a second gin, she was enjoying herself, but sneaked a look at her watch after she caught the waitress doing the same. Time to find out if the invitation for a drink really wasn't just a pickup.

"You said there was something you wanted to discuss with me."

He nodded and ate the last bite of calamari, chewing a little longer this time.

"I'm not sure where to begin. It's kind of to do with your acidification research, but what I have to tell you might be...hard to swallow." He cast a regretful look at the empty plates in front of them.

"Something wrong with my research?"

"No, not at all. But...well, how strongly do you believe that there are other forces at work causing the acidification? Other than human pollution."

She sat up. Her presentation had only touched on that, for the sake of the potential funders present. "You don't work for an oil company, do you?"

"No, I just... Oh, hell." He gave a deep sigh and then began to tell her a story that quickly took the warmth out of her gin buzz. A story about an alien artifact he claimed to have discovered at the bottom of a lake. He nearly shredded his napkin as he went over the details, and clearly had to force himself to meet her eyes. At times, his own seemed to glaze over while he turned toward the growing darkness outside, and at one point a shudder went through him.

When he paused, she realized that she'd slid her chair back from the table. She leaned forward again out of politeness. He didn't seem to be a nutcase, but maybe he was just a damn good actor.

"That's quite a story."

He gave a chuckle, his face reddening. "I know, you're wondering how you got trapped into having a drink with a psychotic. Delusional schizophrenic. I don't blame you, but I promise I'm not hearing voices or receiving mystical commands, or any of that stuff."

Was he protesting too much? At least he knew how crazy he sounded—maybe that was a good sign.

"Have you gone to the authorities?" she asked, conscious that she might be humoring him.

"What authorities? What department of the government is in charge of alien objects?"

"OK.... But I'm afraid I don't see what this...outpost could have to do with the acidification of the oceans."

"I mentioned that it showed me images. The beings that brought it here were from a world with lots of oceans, like Earth. But what if the ocean chemistry was different? What if it were more acidic?"

"Are you saying you think aliens could be changing the pH of our oceans to...what? Make Earth ready for an *invasion*?"

He raised his hands. "I know that sounds like paranoia of the worst kind. Nutcase stuff. I have reasons that I'd rather not get into right now." He sighed. "What I'm asking is could that be possible? Could something else be raising the acidity of the oceans?"

Part of her had to struggle to suppress a laugh, but in the back of her mind....

"Look, Mr. Hart..."

"Michael."

"There are some of us who feel that, even if you don't count the carbon humans released into the air before the Industrial Revolution, the oceans have still had lots of time for some kind of adaptive mechanism to arise. We especially expected to see much more $CO_2$-absorbing algae, which would be a natural way for the planet to respond. Natural carbon sequestration: the algae absorb the $CO_2$, die, and sink to the bottom of the ocean, trapping the excess carbon for some period of time. And there are such algae, but..." She looked into his eyes. "Let's just say, Yes, it's possible that something might be suppressing the growth of such algae. But so far no one has suggested *aliens from outer space*."

"Fair enough," he said, then laughed. "It sounds stupid even to me, and I've seen the outpost. Touched it. Communicated with it. But all the same, a technology capable of bridging space could surely also adapt an environment to suit their needs—even on a planetary scale—given time. If these aliens were planning to return, Earth's oceans would be a major part of their plan."

Sakiko leaned back and studied his face, regretting that her gin glass was empty but afraid to order another.

"A big part of the purpose for our expedition is to measure variances in ocean acidity and see if we can point to a source for the discrepancies. But I still don't understand. What do you want from me?"

He took a slow breath and exhaled it.

"I want to go with you. I want to join your expedition."

She slid her chair back and stood up.

"No, I can't do that. Thanks for the drinks." She stood.

"Why not? Because you think I'm crazy?" He stood too but was careful not to get any closer.

"I just met you, and you tell me a story about aliens and an invasion from space. What would you think?" She shifted her eyes and saw a look of alarm on the face of the waitress near the door. Michael glanced over, too, and bit back what he was about to say. Instead, he put on a big smile for the server and paid the bill. They left the room. Sakiko was uncomfortable going down the stairs with him behind her.

He turned to his left and she followed him through an exit door. The night air was warm, but she shivered.

"I'm really not crazy," he pleaded. "I could take you to the outpost if you had dive gear with you, but it...shut down unexpectedly, a few days ago. Now it doesn't look like much of anything." He hesitated, then let his shoulders slump. "Shit, I don't know why I expected you to believe me. I'll walk you to your car."

"I don't have a car here. I'm...my hotel is just across the road." She couldn't accept his story, but she couldn't really believe he was dangerous either. They walked in silence. When they got to the door of the hotel, he didn't try to follow her inside.

In the light of the entrance his eyes looked moist.

"I suppose you're flying home tomorrow."

She nodded.

"Just please think about what I told you. Maybe give me another chance to convince you to take me along."

He tried hard to smile. "Could I port my contact information to your phone?"

"Michael, I don't want..."

"Just a paper business card, then." He fished a worn rectangle from a pocket of his wallet and extended it toward her. "Nothing sinister about that."

She took it grudgingly and waved it a little. "You know, I...had a nice time. Thanks for the drinks and the food. I wish you luck. Really."

He nodded. "Thanks for not, you know, calling the cops or anything." The smile was fleeting, but it touched something in her. Before she could say anything more, he turned away.

At a hallway vending machine she bought a can of Five Alive. When she got to her room, she opened the mini bar and took out three little bottles of vodka.

# 21

Michael watched the Matthews woman until she disappeared through the hotel lobby, then walked back across Ramsay Lake Road to his car in the Science North parking lot. He felt like when he'd tried out for a softball team as a kid: even though he'd never be really good at the game, he'd known that he was hooked on it. He'd struck out with Sakiko Matthews, but he very much hoped he'd get another chance to persuade her.

Her rejection didn't make him feel any worse—that was hardly possible after the night he'd discovered Nicole's car in Jay's driveway, gone insane, and triggered a signal that would alter the course of human history. The night an alien machine had betrayed him.

Afterward, he'd collapsed on the rocky shore of the lake, sobbing, and lay there in naked anguish until the daylight came. Even the dawn had cast gray judgment upon him, refusing to offer any gleam of hope. Rain began before he reached his car, prompting Naïda to cover his head like a shield. If there'd still been a way for her to separate herself from him, she would have done it by then, her task complete. But the time for choices had passed—for both of them.

He'd called in sick to work for three days running. He hadn't answered any of Nicole's phone messages, even pretending not to be home when she banged on his door, though his car was parked in the driveway. Hour after hour he'd stared at the ceiling, finally eating only when Naïda refused to tolerate his fast any longer. She'd gathered herself in the small of his back and sent waves of burning heat through his skin, compelling him to get to his feet. Twitching muscles in the backs of his legs urged him toward the kitchen. He'd taken the hint.

The prospect of the outpost's destruction by toxic waste didn't upset him anymore. The outpost had gone dark and silent as soon as he had done its bidding. Perhaps the sending of the signal had triggered some kind of self-destruct device to keep its information out of human hands. Or, its mission fulfilled, there might be no more reason to function. Either way, it deserved to be destroyed. Providentially, its destruction would remove all evidence of his own role in the coming cataclysm. Sometimes, as he tried to sleep, he imagined ripping it apart with his own hands.

One question dominated more than any other: if the outpost's governing intelligence wanted a signal sent, why hadn't it simply done the job itself? Why involve Michael at all? Had it wanted assurance that humans could be manipulated? Was there an interstellar police force that demanded proof of invitation before one species invaded the home of another? Whatever the motive, it did nothing to absolve him of blame.

What would happen next? And how soon?

Any race that had visited dozens of other solar systems must have found a way around the light-speed barrier. No interstellar network of colonies could be built and maintained if travel between worlds required hundreds of years. So, if their craft could travel faster than light, surely they would have developed a form of communication that could do the same. Human scientists had speculated about communications based on the quantum entanglement of particles. Transmission and reception would be instantaneous, no matter the distance; in which case, the aliens might already be on their way to Earth. Were they weeks away? Or only hours? Would they decide to come at all? There was no way of knowing before the first alien craft appeared in the skies of his world.

Another thought had become a certainty. The outpost he'd encountered couldn't be the only one on Earth—why would it be? A race that wanted to be alerted about the advancement of *homo sapiens* surely would have placed such warning systems in many places around the globe to assure eventual contact. There must be more outposts, almost certainly programmed with all the answers he was searching for.

He just had to do find them; but he had no idea where to look.

A Facebook post had informed him about Sakiko Matthews' presentation at Science North. Ocean acidification. The altering of conditions for life on the planet Earth. Could those alterations be deliberate acts by would-be invaders?

Her presentation and their meeting afterward had provided no answers. But he became more convinced than ever that the place to look for those answers was in the oceans themselves.

Now, remembering the fragrance of her skin as much as her words, he drove along the shore of Ramsay Lake toward his apartment. He pulled into a grocery store open late. The bright light of the aisles was a welcome distraction. Drifting aimlessly with the support of a shopping cart far larger than he needed, he found himself in front of the energy bars. He scooped a couple of dozen bars into the cart but ignored the energy drinks—he hated the taste of them. Instead, he stepped over to the soft drink section: Pepsi and Coca Cola stacked side by side. Pepsi might be a nice change. He reached out a hand but watched it veer toward the Coke. With a loud laugh, he grabbed a two-liter bottle and then another, put them into the cart and raised a palm in apology to an old woman who was staring at him. After that, he bypassed the candy aisle with effort and picked up the fruits, vegetables, and meats his body really needed.

A symbiote with a sweet tooth. Terrific.

How far would Naïda's influence grow? Would it be stronger or weaker without regular interface with the outpost? Would she be like a little cartoon angel sitting on his shoulder urging him toward good things, or a miniature devil, tempting him? Or both.

He rolled into his driveway and was relieved that Nicole's Beemer wasn't there. She hadn't left any new messages, either, although Laura Wood had made up for that. If he wasn't back to work in the morning, he'd better be in a hospital intensive care unit.

Wondering whether he had the strength to face Wood, or anyone else he knew, he drew a hot bath and climbed in. He stared numbly at the blank wall at the foot of the tub, willing the water to draw the poisons from his mind.

There was a stain on the wall that he'd never noticed before. Roughly rectangular. Except, as he watched, he noticed more detail: some rounded lines. And shading—it was a much darker color than the surrounding paint. Almost reddish. How could he have missed that?

No, damn it, it *was* red. No formless shape, either.

He was staring at a Coca Cola label!

Good God.

He'd spent so much time picturing shapes and letters for Naïda. Now, as he finally let his mind go blank, she'd decided there was a way to make her own thoughts known!

He lurched forward in the tub, sloshing water across the floor, and clapped his hands in appreciation. This called for a toast. He trailed water to the kitchen, dropped some ice into a tumbler, and filled it from one of the new bottles. At the bathroom mirror, he raised the glass.

"To Naïda, new convert to the junk food age. I guess the way to a symbiote's brain is through her stomach. *My* stomach."

He quickly chugged down half the glass, climbed back into the bath, rested the tumbler on the edge of the tub, and tried to clear his mind again, willing the wall to show him more.

It did.

*A* is for apple. *C* is for cat.

The bath water had long gone cold when he saw an image of a round, multicolored shape floating in the air. The home world of the aliens.

*B is for ball?*

"Planet," he said out loud, then climbed from the tub, dried off, and found his iPad in the living room. Choosing a drawing app, he sat on the couch and carefully printed the word 'planet' on the screen. "Planet," he said again. "*Your* planet." Days earlier, he'd chosen an image of a transparent mermaid to represent Naïda and he thought of that now, trying to merge it with the planet view she'd given him. He called up a Google image of Earth and said, "*My* planet." Then he put down the iPad and stared at the dark wall nearby.

The alien world appeared again, and then the Earth. Back and forth a half-dozen times.

What was she saying? That the Earth was now her world? That he should welcome the aliens to Earth?

Grimly, he tried to picture the outpost, its displays bright with promise. Then his hands in the indentations—sending the signal. And lastly, the outpost dark and silent. He didn't have to simulate his anger and the sting of betrayal—the memory reawakened it with full force.

With a moan of rage bubbling up his throat and tears in his eyes, he wrapped his arms tightly around his knees, rocking with shame.

The dull darkness of the room returned, and a lingering melancholy enough for two.

*He was on a mountaintop, just stepping to the peak filled with the euphoria of the moment. Breathing hard, he turned in a circle to survey the world spread out beneath him. The sky was startling blue and wisps of bright cloud streamed by as if in time-lapse video. Tiny specks below were flocks of birds wheeling and diving in thermal currents that tried to reach his height but failed. He was the first to reach the peak—he knew it—and as he reveled in the sense of achievement, his attention was caught by a strange sight: a large boulder balanced precariously on another. Curious. Startling.*

*How had it come to be there? What was its purpose?*

*A test? A cosmic joke?*

*On a whim, he stepped close and gave the rock a poke with his finger.*

*It swayed and teetered, then toppled from its perch and rolled slowly toward the brink of a precipice. With growing alarm, he hurried after it but didn't dare run, and was just in time to see it bounce over the cliff and begin the long drop to a field of loose scree below. The boulder landed amid the rocks, flipping a dozen into the air like tiddlywinks, and bounded downhill, picking up speed. Disturbed slabs of rock began to follow it downward. Dozens of slabs, hundreds, soon thousands.*

*In dismay, he saw the avalanche form into a swirling, roiling demon of destruction sweeping down the mountainside.*

*The neighboring mountain slopes all converged into a large valley, and in the middle of the valley lay a city of great size, ancient and beautiful. A city with a proud history, full of people in the prime of their lives: toiling, reaping, loving, and sleeping. A million and more, unsuspecting. Helpless.*

*He watched the avalanche come upon them, and saw the great city scoured from the face of the land forever.*

*And he stood revealed on the mountaintop, with their blood on his hands.*

He threw the covers off and sat on the edge of the bed gasping for breath. Sweat ran into his eyes and a powerful shudder took his body.

*Jesus*, he didn't usually have nightmares. His eyes searched for light in the darkness while his fingers fluttered to his phone to show him the time: 3:23 a.m. He'd been awake until 2:50. It was a half-hour of sleep he would gladly have foregone.

He felt a chill in his groin, and a tremor.

Naïda. Of course, she would have sensed his reaction to the appalling vision but would have no understanding of human dreams.

Had she seen what he'd seen? The images would have shocked her—especially if she interpreted the sequence of events as actual memories. Either way, she would have no context to understand the dream's meaning.

Michael did.

Unable to sleep after that, he still managed to show up on time for his ten o'clock summer-semester class on Elementary Psychology, but the students seemed more intent on gossiping to each other than listening to what he had to say. Maybe it was about him—he was a wreck. Laura Wood appeared in the doorway near the end of the hour, x-rayed him with her eyes, and left without comment. He must have looked authentically ill. His office was empty when he got there, but he knew Grace had a free afternoon—she might appear at any time. He walked out to his car.

As he wove through traffic, he looked at the faces in the other cars. So many people; so many lives, oblivious to the threat that now hung over them. He had to warn them. He had to tell his story even if he was condemned for it. That meant he would need proof, which meant that he couldn't let the outpost be destroyed. Active or not, the outpost was irrefutable evidence that the human race was not alone in the universe. From that momentous understanding, perhaps explaining the rest would not be impossible.

He drove to the lake and jogged down the hill, but even before he reached the water, he knew that he was too late.

There were fresh tracks in the dirt: deep tracks from heavy machinery that led all the way to the shore and even a few meters into the water. Machinery had churned the shoreline to muck, and the shallows were colored the thin brown of vending-machine hot chocolate.

He felt a burning desire to wade in and dive down, to see the outpost for himself. Instead, he cautiously reached a hand into the water.

His arm snapped back as if burned.

*Danger!* Terrible danger.

The only thing his own senses could detect was a faint tang in the air mixed with the odors of mud and marsh plants. A hint of creosote, maybe, or something like it. Naïda was no doubt aware of much more. She seemed to writhe in the skin of his arms, though Michael didn't think it was from physical pain.

The company must have dumped huge quantities of toxins into the small lake—the outpost was now unreachable, perhaps buried, its organic mechanisms and circuitry almost certainly destroyed. The aliens would not have foreseen a need to protect it from something like this.

Michael dropped to his knees on the shore.

Though their reasons for anguish were very different, he and Naïda wept together over a shared loss.

When he got home, he collapsed onto the couch.

He was a traitor, a Judas, with no clear path to redemption. He was suddenly certain that the aliens must have had malevolent intentions all along: to return, to invade, to conquer. They'd only been waiting for a sign that Earth had produced a technological society worth subjugating. Waiting for a dupe like him.

He needed to alert the people of the Earth, but with the outpost destroyed, his best proof was gone. Without it, he would only face ridicule and failure. The world couldn't afford for him to fail.

If Sakiko Matthews' expedition found concrete evidence that an unknown technology caused acidification of the oceans, that might be enough to convince key people to listen to him. Yet, without Michael along on Matthews' expedition, they wouldn't know what to look for. They'd be searching for manmade causes, or natural causes. Michael needed them to find the most *un*natural cause of all.

# 22

Naïda is deathly ill again. It must be that. Her substance is undergoing serious chemical imbalances, but she cannot isolate the reason. There is pain—great pain—yet no indication of injury. Her bondmate Michael seems to be suffering a similar torment without physical cause.

It is puzzling that Michael's affliction can be linked to two events that occurred close together: a search through the night for his human life-partner, and his interaction with the outpost that resulted in the termination of its functions. Is it possible that a human can experience serious injury with no physical trauma? Naïda has witnessed his similar response to external events before. If so, it might explain her own state: his distress transferred to her.

She is not convinced. There is no doubt that she has experienced Michael's pain—the joining involves the deepest levels of sensation and cognition, as it involves every other bodily process. Yet her own imbalances only began with the discovery of the toxicity in the water containing the outpost. She knew then that the outpost had not simply halted its own functions, but had been rendered permanently non-functional, like the others of her own kind. Its loss left Naïda on an alien world with no living members of her own species and no remaining link to the Creators. That realization had been...yes, a kind of pain. Powerful pain. Even recalling that moment sends unproductive chemicals coursing through Michael's system, as if in response to an internal emergency that does not exist. She must get the flow of these undesirable substances back under control.

Illness and pain. She has no other terms to describe the experience. And she can no longer consult the Controller to fill gaps in her knowledge. How will she confirm the facts she learns about the human world? How will she be sure the bond with Michael is functioning as it should?

That thought brings another swell of pain.

Is such spontaneous illness normal for an adult of her kind? She cannot know—she has only achieved full adulthood by virtue of the joining. If it is normal, how is she meant to cope with it? If not normal, what can she do? It seems all too possible that this is a manifestation of the symbiotic bond—a human trait that has planted itself within *her* since the joining, and against which she has no natural defense. If so, it could be very damaging, perhaps fatal. The pain is real, the chemical chaos too, yet there is no obvious remedy for an illness without cause.

The pain is less if she does not deliberately recall that which was destroyed: the outpost and the Controller within it. But to avoid their memory is to give up her quest for answers.

And the questions are many:

Why did Michael resist the will of the Creators for so long, and then experience such turmoil once he had fulfilled it?

Why did the Controller withdraw from interface when Naïda/Michael had been promised more?

What was so threatening about the outpost that the humans would choose to destroy it?

It is too much—too confusing! In contemplating these matters she is experiencing loss of control over her own substance such as she has never known: temperature fluctuations, sensory misfires, illusory tactile impressions. She must withdraw into herself and shut down unnecessary functions for a time. Accept darkness and silence. Restore her original state.

She is glad to achieve unawareness.

Sometime later, she reactivates.

She reconnects with her bondmate's central nervous system. It is night. He is in repose and does not react. She examines the surroundings with his senses and her own—they are alone.

Michael's body chemistry has returned to near-normal—his repose is deep, and not in the between-state that produces random frenetic images in his mind. It has taken many day/night cycles for her to accept that those episodes may be normal for members of his species, but their frequent violence still makes her withdraw in spite of herself.

Her own thoughts return to her questions, and she immediately senses secretions from her enzymatic nodes that should only associate with threat and risk. This is not good—it must be a malfunction, an unanticipated result of her altered DNA with its new human components. Or if it truly is a typical human trait, she cannot grasp its purpose. She will have to learn a whole new level of control.

In her new condition, nighttime has become less welcome than the day: it offers too little sensory input and, especially, no interface with her bondmate. She has come to understand that even while they are now virtually a single being, Michael is also her only companion. She wishes he would wake up. She could awaken him—she has done so before—but disruptions of his rest impair his function.

At least the manifestations of his respiratory and circulatory systems—the rhythmic intake and expulsion of air, and the steady pumping of fluids—are assurances of well-being that somehow reduce her solitude in the night.

It is clear that she has become reliant on Michael. Mutual dependency is the nature of symbiosis. Yet physical dependency should be automatic and subconscious, like the dependency on air, water, and biologically produced energy: their presence requires no acknowledgment and usually not even mental awareness. Only the absence of these essentials triggers deep visceral responses, otherwise they may be taken for granted. Symbiosis should be like that, too, yet interaction with Michael produces responses within her that remind her of her earliest experiences within the community nursery, memories related to the total physical and mental security of the very young. The sensation is soothing. She welcomes it, and yet at the same time is badly conflicted.

Michael may not want the same things she wants. Because Michael may not want what the Creators want.

That anyone could have needs or desires that conflict with the will of the Creators is an utterly new concept for her. It took many planetary cycles for her to realize that it was the explanation for Michael's delay in triggering the outpost's signal. She does not know the Creators' plans for the planet, but they must be correct and for the benefit of all. Michael may not understand this, and even his perception of the Creators themselves might be flawed. That is difficult to accept, but it fits her observations of his actions.

Perhaps such misunderstanding is to be expected from a race with such different origins. Not only did Michael resist sending the signal, but his people *destroyed the outpost*, the representative of another sentient species. Was that not a powerful rejection of the Creators themselves?

Equally incomprehensible is why Michael would finally send a signal of welcome to the Creators, and then permit another of his species to destroy the Creators' device.

Unless the destruction was as unexpected to him as it was to her—some kind of terrible accident.

But surely if one human knows about the outpost and its significance, all humans must know. That is what organs of communication are for.

This conflict of motivations creates a very serious quandary for Naïda.

Michael is her bondmate—his existence fulfills her. But what if he opposes the will of the Creators?

How can she possibly trust him?

# 23

The marimba alarm on her iPhone woke Sakiko from a dream. She'd been walking through a town that was unfamiliar in the details but utterly ordinary—she remembered remarking to strangers just how ordinary the place was—but right after she exchanged a few words with each stranger, she'd get a creeping sensation at the back of her neck, turn, and find that the man or woman had been transformed into an alien creature. Some of them were dolphin-like, others more like squid, and they'd become more bizarre and more frightening as the dream progressed. She would run away from them, turn a street corner, calm down, only to begin the cycle all over again. When the alarm went off, she'd just noticed a group of five strangers walking toward her, looking more menacing than the others.

*Thanks, Michael...whatever your name was,* she thought. Aliens, for Christ's sake—when was the last time she'd dreamed about aliens?

What was his name anyway?

It couldn't possibly matter. She'd never see him again.

He'd given her a business card. She vaguely remembered waking up near midnight and nearly calling his number to apologize. She tended to get annoyingly contrite when she drank too much. She thought she'd dropped the card onto the bedside table as she was getting back into bed, but it wasn't there now. Likely she'd knocked it off—she tended to fling her arms around while semi-conscious, a habit that had made Doug beg her to sleep as close to the right edge of the bed as possible.

She knelt beside the bed and felt under it, then tried to reach between the table and the wall, but her eyes caught a light patch on the carpet nearby. The dog-eared rectangle of paper read *Michael Hart*. A psychology professor, right? That was why she hadn't immediately dismissed his story about aliens. He'd seemed both sane and sincere, but maybe his training taught him how to be convincing even though he was a certified screwball.

She put the card in her purse.

A shower was always her concession to the arrival of daylight, but the business of the day couldn't truly begin until she had at least one cup of coffee. She found her way to the hotel's breakfast room. A sticky valve on the coffee thermos gave her a moment of panic, thinking the thermos was empty; then she grabbed a couple of croissants and sat by a window overlooking a busy intersection. While her eyes flitted from car to car, her mind returned to the night before.

Although she felt she'd done a decent job with her presentation, the reps from Science North hadn't given anything away about their decision. Hopefully they'd tell her something before she caught her four o'clock flight to Boston via Toronto. In the meantime, she had a few hours to kill, but Sudbury didn't strike her as a place with exceptional retail offerings. There was that boardwalk she'd seen earlier on the other side of

Science North. The day looked like a good one with only some wispy clouds; and a walk before her flight was appealing.

She thought about Michael Hart. Presumably he'd be at work unless he had the summer off. Maybe that was why he thought he could come on their expedition—except it would be more like six months. Longer, if she could get enough funding.

Would this Hart guy know if his university had money available for external projects? Maybe she should give him a call.

Instead, she drank a second cup of coffee and part of a third, munching on chunks of cantaloupe—some healthy vitamins to offset the indulgence of the croissants. After that, she stepped out into the sunshine. The boardwalk stroll was even better than she'd hoped: a fresh breeze filled with birdsong, and the inviting lake only meters away. A small yacht club on the other side of the bay made her yearn to be under sail, harnessing that breeze. Sunshine sparkling on the water forced her to squint.

The leisurely walk had left her with forty-five minutes before her 11:00 checkout. Then, as she was zipping her suitcase closed, her phone chimed with a text message. It was from the airline, and she called the phone number provided.

All flights to Toronto and the U.S. had been cancelled for the rest of the day because of a line of powerful thunderstorms sweeping across southern Ontario and much of New England. She'd have to stay another night.

*God*, another day wasted! There was only so much she could do on her laptop and phone without racking up a hell of a data bill.

Junk food was her usual panacea, especially for frustration. Instead, she went for lunch on the patio of Science North, spent a few hours reading the latest David Mitchell novel, and then finally gave in to a nagging impulse and called Michael Hart. He answered his phone right away. It wasn't a video connection, but she smoothed her blouse and shorts.

"Dinner? That would be fantastic," he said. "I'm, uh...not all that familiar with any fancy restaurants in town though."

"Nothing fancy, please. I didn't bring the right clothes."

"OK, sure. Well, my girlfriend and I like an all-you-can-eat sushi place that isn't far from where you are."

*Girlfriend.* Why hadn't it occurred to her that he might be in a relationship?

"Listen, if your lady might not be comfortable with this..."

"No, it's...it's fine. I want to hear more about your expedition. Even if I can't go along." He tried to chuckle, but it didn't quite come off.

He picked her up in an older model gray Honda Accord, with the radio playing some vintage Bachman Turner Overdrive. The restaurant was part of a chain—Sakiko recognized the name but had never tried it. Michael explained that they could order as many dishes as they liked but would be charged extra for anything they didn't eat.

"Did you suggest a sushi restaurant because I have a Japanese name?" she asked.

His face went blank. "No. Actually, I thought you looked more Filipina than Japanese. I hope that's not an insult or anything."

"Of course not. Filipina women are lovely. My father was Japanese, and fairly dark-skinned, too. I get most of my looks from him. Not much from my mother, except a little extra height."

"She's English?"

"No, Dutch. Matthews is my stepfather's name. Anyway, what I was getting at is that I like sushi, but I don't know what's best here, so why don't you order?"

He did so, and a few minutes later the dishes began to arrive, including several plates of tempura, confirming male fondness for fried foods. Like the night before, he'd ordered far more than she expected to be able to eat, but it was all very good. He'd even ordered some sake. The sweetness of the heated liquid brought back memories that were equally warm.

"How about telling me some more about your expedition? Have you got a ship of your own, or do you have to tag along with somebody else?"

"We've got a ship. Not through the usual channels, though." She smiled as she devoted some extra chewing to a mouthful of shrimp. "Our ride will be courtesy of Dominique Swan."

"I don't...wait. The *heiress* Dominique Swan? Wannabee actress? Didn't they do a reality TV show about her a few years back?"

"*Swan Among the Geese* on TLC. It lasted about half a season, though I think the lawsuits are still going." His face prompted her to continue. "She gave the producers nervous breakdowns: always late, if she showed up at all, constantly going off script, bringing dubious characters to the set. She kept the tabloids busy for a few weeks, though." She tapped the table. "You've got that glazed look."

"What glazed look?"

"The one all men get when Dominique's name is mentioned."

He laughed. "Actually, I hate trashy Hollywood train wreck stories. Crazy starlet, in and out of rehab, and then, when attention starts to slip, they arrange a 'wardrobe malfunction'."

"Dominique's never done that, as far as I know. I wouldn't say she's trashy, just...overindulged. How could she not be? Her father, Blake Cartwright, is as rich as God. She's gorgeous, an only child, and she's actually not a bad actress; but her career hasn't amounted to much. Maybe that's why she did the TV show. Or maybe it was just to keep from being bored."

"That's not why she's giving you a ship, is it?

"I hope not. She insists that she's interested in the research. My assistant thinks her dad may have given her an ultimatum: get serious or get rehab." She held up a hand. "I'm sorry, I shouldn't be saying these things. I don't normally gossip, and Dominique's been good to me."

Michael slid the empty dishes toward the end of the table, picked up another menu card and began making check marks. He gave her a questioning look, but she waved her hand to say she didn't want any more. Where was he putting all the food? He didn't look overweight at all, but it was obvious why he'd chosen an all-you-can-eat place. She ordered more sake instead.

Once the waitress had come and gone, Michael continued.

"Do Cartwright businesses include research ships?"

"They probably do, but Dominique is commandeering one of the family yachts." Her cheeks grew warm. "I'm...confident that we can get it fitted out the way we need, if a few more funders like Science North will put up some money. Fortunately, a crew comes with it, including the captain, Parzifal Fox—a wonderfully crusty guy. He was ready for retirement but was persuaded to take on one more assignment. Dominique can be very persuasive."

Michael reached for some more tempura and quickly finished off the rest of the seconds. For a moment she thought he was going to order thirds, but after a glance at her he asked for the cheque instead. She offered to pay, but he pointed out that she'd just been complaining about her cash shortage in funding. Dinner was the least he could do.

Back at the hotel parking lot she cast a wistful look at the beautiful sky, still about an hour from sunset.

"Would you like to go for a walk?" he asked.

"Along the boardwalk? Sure, I could handle that again."

"I had a different boardwalk in mind."

They traveled west across a busy intersection on Paris Street and came to a large marsh with a wooden walkway running towards the middle of it. A sign read "Lily Creek."

"The walkway goes through the marsh over to that playing field." He pointed. "Just a nice stroll. A little different."

She nodded, and they began to move again. "You're sure this isn't turning into a date? Your lady friend might object."

He laughed, but there wasn't any pleasure in it.

"My lady friend is the *mayor*, believe it or not. She's probably at an official function somewhere. I don't know—we, uh, we haven't seen much of each other lately."

His voice told her not to pursue the subject. Instead, she commented on the pretty marsh, and the way the sound of nearby traffic nearly vanished once they rounded a bend and were surrounded by reeds. Just ahead, a large patch of open water appeared like a clearing in a forest.

Michael stopped. She followed his gaze and saw a group of five or six young cyclists coming toward them quickly. They were laughing loudly and weaving back and forth across the wooden planks, as if playing chicken until some unlucky rider would end up in the swamp. Michael took hold of her arm and moved her gently behind him. The kids weren't paying attention. He yelled, "*Hey!*" but the warning backfired. Startled, one of the cyclists lost control. As Michael yanked Sakiko out of the way, his foot caught the edge of the walkway and he lost his balance. He landed on his back in the water and went completely under before he could get his footing. It was only waist deep, but the mucky bottom gave him a hard time as he struggled back to the walkway. Sakiko dimly registered the high-pitched squeals from the kids as they rode off at full speed, and she reached down to give Michael a hand.

The hair on the back of his head and the skin on his neck had a wet sheen, almost as if they'd been oiled.

"I'm so sorry...," she began, and then he lifted his face to her.

His eyes were featureless: white and milky. His lips and nostrils were coated with something translucent. But as she watched the coating vanished.

"Oh God. Oh my *God!*"

"What's wrong? Oh shit. I can explain."

She backed away a couple of meters, almost stepping off the walkway herself. Her hand was at her mouth and her eyes flicked up and down over his body.

"I can explain. Please. There's nothing wrong. Really."

"*Nothing wrong?*" she finally managed to say. She swallowed hard. "Are you an *alien?*"

"No! At least... *No*, I'm not—I'm just a guy. I'll gladly tell you everything, only could I get into some dry clothes first? I've got some in the car after I, uh, got caught in the rain the other day."

They walked back to the hotel, with Sakiko insisting that he keep well ahead of her. She felt shaky and didn't reply to his attempts at small talk.

He changed in a men's room at the hotel and then drove her in silence to a Tim Horton's donut shop while she cowered in the back seat, one hand firmly on the door handle. When the coffee came, she couldn't bring herself to sit at a table with him. Instead, they walked the streets while he told her his bizarre story, falling silent whenever another person came within earshot. For the first time, she realized that hairs on the back of her neck really could stand up.

He finished and waited for a response. She stopped walking and inspected him as if her eyes could penetrate his skin. He'd seemed so totally normal the night before. He looked normal now. But she knew she hadn't imagined what she'd seen. His story had to be true. He had a goddamned creature of some kind inside him. She bit her lip, remembering the movie *Alien* and how she'd never been able to watch it to the end.

Her voice was weak as she said, "I read Spiderman comics when I was a kid."

"You mean the Venom and Carnage stories? It's not really like that."

"Those symbiotes were powerful. And evil."

"Mine's not. She's...well, she's kind of like a child, I think."

"*She?*"

"Yes. I'm not sure if their concept of the sexes is really like ours. I only know that she identifies with female humans as the child-bearing sex. I call her Naïda, but that's just a name I picked—I don't know her native name, or even if she has one."

"Does it give you...powers? Shit, I can't believe I said that. I mean, there must be some side effects."

"Well, I'm *eating* for two."

"That part I've seen."

"She draws energy from my body to survive, so I have to make up for that, but it's not too bad. She's learned how much she can take without hurting me, and how much food will make up for it. Powers? Like superpowers?" He looked at her. "No, I don't think you're ready to hear any more for now."

"What, you think you're going to get another chance? It's now or never, Mr. Hart. Tell me." Her knees were giving her trouble, but she didn't dare sit anywhere. She compromised by leaning lightly against a nearby building, ready to run and shamed by it. She shouldn't be going to pieces like this. She was a scientist for God's sake, and this was science.

"Well, I can breathe underwater—honest to God. And swim almost like a fish. Don't ask me how. My eyesight's way better, too, especially in water. But there's a rational reason for all that. I think the aliens that created the outpost were air-breathers like us who spent large parts of their lives underwater thanks to their symbiotes."

"Not Venom. Aquaman."

He actually laughed. "It's cool to be able to do those things, but it's not exactly superhero territory. It's just the way her species evolved—or was engineered. It's just science."

Holy crap, he couldn't read her mind, could he? She hoped not.

"Anyway," he continued, "I doubt Naïda can communicate with underwater creatures—she's not from here. I'm having a hard enough time learning to communicate with her myself. But she's not evil."

'How do you know? Maybe it'll...I don't know, *take you over*."

His face turned serious, and he cleared his throat. "She's not some kind of bodysnatcher. What would be the advantage of that? She's only ever tried to protect me, not hurt me."

"It's an *alien creature merging with your body*, and you don't see a reason to go to a doctor to get checked out? You have no idea what it could be doing to you. You might even be contagious. Maybe I'm being infected by alien germs just talking to you."

"The aliens came here ten thousand years ago. They interacted with the local people. If they brought germs with them, those germs have been in our environment for that long. Our immune systems will have encountered them already. They're not going to suddenly start making people sick."

He hung his head. "Of course, I've thought about seeing a doctor; but once people find out about Naïda, my life won't be my own. *OK*, but you know what I mean. I'll be the center of a media freak show. Or a prisoner in some secret lab—a guinea pig for who knows what kinds of experiments."

"So, you have no intention of going to the authorities either? Warning them about the outpost or this...symbiote? Which brings a whole new meaning to the term 'invasive species', by the way."

"Like I said last night: what authorities? Who would I go to—the Ministry of Foreign Affairs?"

"You've been waiting to use that line."

"I've thought a lot about all of this, believe me. Almost nothing else for weeks."

Sakiko took a deep swallow of her coffee, now barely lukewarm and too sweet. A shudder swept up her neck. To cover it she turned away to look down the street.

"I'm not sure what else to say."

"At least you believe me."

"That doesn't mean I'm OK with it. This is wrong—there's no way to spin it to make it right. You could be a danger to yourself and to others. Maybe to every human being on this planet."

She expected him to look crestfallen, but at her words he turned pale, as if he were about to be sick.

"I didn't mean that to sound like an attack," she said, "but I still don't get how you can defend this creature that's invading your body, and then be worried about the other alien species coming back to invade the planet. They're either good or they're bad. Safe or dangerous. Aren't they?"

"I think Naïda's species is meant to be a companion to their hosts—nothing else. The others—the explorers...well, the outpost promised me knowledge but then shut down instead; so, I...I just don't know." He sighed. "I've always believed that an advanced alien race would be benevolent. If they aren't, then no amount of warning will be enough. What use would our weapons be against someone who might make us look like cave men? But maybe there's something else that could be done."

"You want to come on my expedition in case some kind of alien installation is responsible for the acidification. Maybe a bigger outpost-thing than the one you saw. But what if you're right? How could you stop it? Or are you just hoping the next one will give you the answers you were promised?"

"Most of all, I want to learn the *truth* about what the aliens have in mind." He raised his hands toward her. "You and I can help each other out. Think about how much more you could accomplish with someone on board who has my...unusual abilities."

She did think about it. All night.

It was impossible to sleep. She was afraid to fall asleep, afraid of the nightmares that were certain to follow. She'd seen evidence of life that was not of this Earth, and in the vulnerable hours of darkness that was terrifying. She was as certain as she could be that she had not been hoaxed. As the girlfriend of a magician, she'd developed a good eye for deception.

What then? Did she have a responsibility to tell someone about Michael Hart?

He wasn't wrong—the full apparatus of secret government would come crashing down on him, with absolutely no guarantee that the alien threat, if there was one, would be thwarted. She had lots of experience with incompetent bureaucracies.

If she told no one, didn't that make her responsible in a different way?

What if there was a threat? An alien force acting to acidify Earth's oceans? Who would be better equipped to tell that than Sakiko and her team? Especially with Michael Hart and his symbiote along.

No, that was one man's fantasy—there was no evidence for it. There were any number of natural and man-made mechanisms for the acidification that were far more likely to blame.

If Michael really did have the abilities he claimed, he could be an incredible asset to her work, though. Able to go places a scuba diver couldn't and do far more once there. Sometimes the universe gave you exactly what you needed when you needed it the most. Of course, that was assuming the expedition ever got away from the wharf. That no one discovered her fraud and met her at the docks with a warrant for her arrest.

Wait, though. What if she had something to *trade* for her freedom? A prize worth far more to any research institute than a few thousand dollars.

*A genuine alien from outer space.*

As soon as the thought crossed her mind, she felt ashamed. Michael Hart was already a victim. It would be the height of cruelty to throw him to the wolves.

But it couldn't hurt to hedge her bets. Her own life was on the line, too.

Her eyes felt full of grit when the alarm went off. She chugged down two mugs of breakfast-room coffee before she left the hotel for the airport, and had the cabbie go through a drive-thru to buy another on the way. Even then, her brain still felt too sluggish for the decision she faced. It wasn't until she was just about to board the plane that she called Michael's number.

"OK, Mr. Hart. I'll get you on the team somehow. Plan to meet me in San Francisco on Monday—Tuesday at the latest. I'll text you the address and other details. I hope your little friend can handle a plane ride."

# 24

Michael walked from kitchen to living room to bedroom and back again, then repeated the trip. He wasn't aware of it. He just couldn't stay still.

Finally, he stopped in the hallway and tried to communicate to Naïda that they would be going on a ship. He pictured the ocean and a generic image of a cargo ship floating on the water, but it was still hard to get across the idea of something taking place in the future, and he wasn't sure she understood. She briefly gave the view from his eyes a sunny yellow tint.

They'd developed a few short forms of communication.

"Yes, I'm happy," he said. "I'm very happy."

The call from Sakiko Matthews was just what he needed—a chance to make a real break. Discovering the outpost had irrevocably altered his life. To pretend that he could just carry on as before was ludicrous.

Laura Wood's rage rocked him back in his chair.

*"What the hell do you mean, you're taking a sabbatical? You can't* do *that!"*

"I got my eligibility last year. I already had some preliminary discussions with the Dean because this is my seventh year, but nothing was finalized."

"You have to give us a year's notice!"

"You might remember that we talked about it last August."

"You said you *weren't* going to take one. You had no reason to."

"That's not the way I remember it." He tried to hold her gaze as her face grew even darker, but he had to look away. "Anyway, it won't inconvenience the university because there's someone who can cover all of my classes."

"And just who would that be?"

"Grace McDonald."

Wood exploded from her chair, and Michael was certain that her secretary in the next room would soon be calling Security. But he stood his ground. Twenty minutes later he left the office with her threats ringing in his ears, but he was reasonably confident of his legal standing, especially if he did a good job of back-dating some of the forms required. And if he had no job to come back to...well, that was trivial compared to the other changes in his life.

He found Grace in their office and told her a story he thought she'd believe. It was obvious that she didn't, but knew it was all she'd get from him. Through tears she asked him to forgive her for misjudging him. Her hug lasted a long time, and then he was striding down the corridor with wet eyes of his own.

Nicole kept him waiting for nearly half an hour before her secretary led him into the office. No one else had come out and the secretary hadn't put through any calls during that time. The deliberate snub made Michael feel better.

"Well, look who it is," Nicole said, her face cold. "The invisible man, come out of hiding. What for? You want your pajamas back? I can have them sent over."

Michael pushed down his anger and spoke quietly.

"Don't act like I'm the one in the wrong, here. That would really be a bit too much after what you've done." He didn't dare spell it out. If she admitted to going to Jay's house his pride would force him to break off all contact with his brother. Nicole's eyes widened for a moment and her voice lost some of its edge.

"Maybe we've both taken each other too much for granted," she said. "But you couldn't talk to me on the phone? You had to pretend you weren't home?"

"You didn't stop Amanda Clay from dumping toxic waste into Evergreen Lake. The alien artifact has been destroyed."

"*Jesus*, are you still on about that?"

"I knew you wouldn't care. I just wanted you to know why I'm going away."

"What do you mean you're going away?"

"I've joined an ocean research expedition. There must be more evidence of the aliens' presence out there. We set sail in a few days."

Nicole's expression of conciliation faded quickly. The knuckles of her hands paled where they clenched the desk.

'You're not serious. You're a psychology professor, for fuck's sake. Don't tell me you're willing to throw away your career chasing after this alien...*fantasy* you've got in your head." She slammed the desk and threw herself back in the chair. "If you think I'm going to wait for you, you're fucking crazy. You go on your goddamn expedition and you can forget about ever seeing me again."

What was that supposed to mean—that their relationship was still worth saving?

Ridiculous.

"I can live with that." He stood and made for the door. As he turned the handle, he said, "You can throw the pajamas away."

In the solitude of his apartment Michael took a break from packing his luggage and stared at a blank wall. It was important to him that Naïda understand what was happening and why. He remembered his conversations with Sakiko Matthews very well, so he tried to recreate the words and phrases in his head and finally began speaking them out loud—Naïda had made some progress interpreting audible language. Whenever a phrase or word referred to an object or an easily definable action, he paused to picture that in his mind, then repeated the relevant words. It was a long process—he tried it for half an hour, took a break to pack some more clothes, tried it again, stopped for some food and drink, then tried the visualization a third time before going to bed. It was impossible to be certain, but he sensed that Naïda was satisfied. Perhaps she understood what he was trying to tell her. Perhaps she was just happy to be making more correlations between images and words to increase her vocabulary.

Lying in bed, he made the mistake of letting his mind wander, and it returned to the night he'd found Nicole's car at Jay's house. His eyes filled with tears. In the dark it wasn't nearly so easy to feel confident about the future. Nicole had hurt him in the cruelest way, but they'd been together for a long time—you couldn't just toss something like that away.

He had sacrificed so much of his life since he'd discovered the outpost: his friendship with Phil Rodriguez, maybe his job and now Nicole. His love for his brother would never be the same. How much of the blame was his own? And those were only personal losses. There was no way to know what price the human race might pay for his actions.

Guilt welled up in his gut. He wrapped his arms around his chest, feeling utterly lost.

After a time, the knots of tension in his back and neck began to ease as a current of warmth spread through them, the skin and muscles slowly rippling.

Naïda.

*She was giving him a massage.*

How in hell had she learned to do that? How did she even know that it was worth doing, and why? There was something almost frightening about the realization, but it did feel damn good. He slowly relaxed his limbs and allowed himself to enjoy the sensation.

The rippling motions reminded him that a lot of her substance was still in his skin—maybe most of it—which meant that when he sat or lay down the pressure of his weight was on her. Was that painful? Was there a sleeping position he should try that would be more comfortable for her? It wasn't easy to find simple images and words to communicate such questions, but he thought he understood her reply.

His normal body weight wasn't a problem. When a prolonged position became uncomfortable, she would simply shift the bulk of her being to somewhere else. If more seriously inconvenienced, or threatened, she gathered herself together and sheltered in his crotch.

That was something he already knew. Embarrassed in spite of himself, he tried to explain about that part of his body, using mental pictures of men and women, sexual intercourse, reproduction, and the organs involved. Because she'd been present when he and Nicole had had sex, he was sure Naïda would understand the connection. He pointed out that she was making a habit of snuggling up to his genitals.

She said she didn't mind.

Naïda can sense Michael relaxing, and she is pleased that her conjectures about human physiology have borne out well. From his regular immersions in hot water and his evident pleasure while consuming nourishment, she has concluded that sensory input often affects his mental state. Relief of hunger or thirst triggers a release of certain brain chemicals which render his body more relaxed, while external events construed as potentially harmful put his body systems into a highly stimulated state. She is coming to understand that Michael considers certain biochemical combinations to be *good* while others are to be avoided.

So far, she is not aware of having caused him pain—she has certainly tried not to—and has just begun to learn that she is able to bring him pleasure through the manipulation of some of his own bodily functions, such as the rhythmic contraction and relaxation of certain muscles. Objectively, such knowledge could be very useful. More than that, it seems fitting—a proper thing for a symbiotic partner to perform when possible. Michael must believe so—he has asked her if certain actions of his cause her pain, clearly with the intent of avoiding them if he can. This pleases her in a way she can't fully assimilate.

She is also grateful to be making substantial progress understanding human language in several forms. It is not easy, but she has found that she can make connections among lingual sounds, images, and human concepts. She gives the Creators credit for this—it is likely that they engineered in her a predilection toward the linguistic tendencies of humans based on the rudimentary abilities of Michael's ancient progenitors. Her bondmate has also displayed ingenuity and logic in the way he has endeavored to teach her about his language and his world. The extent of his abilities is very satisfying.

Not everything is pleasing, however. Much that she has learned she does not like.

Michael has tried to explain to her about human emotions. They go far beyond the simplicity of good or bad. The emotion called *anger* is particularly unpleasant for her.

Michael is angry at the Controller, and, by association, at the Creators.

Naïda can understand his disappointment at not receiving the greater knowledge promised him. Yet his regret about sending the signal to the Creators is something she does not understand, and clearly this regret has become a powerful motivator of his actions. He has told her that they will soon be going to ride a vehicle that will traverse the planet's oceans. She is not clear about his reasons, but they seem connected to a desire to thwart the Creators in some way, and that is an unwelcome thought.

Her bonding with him was part of the Creators' plan, but they would not have expected her bondmate to take actions contrary to their interests. How could they? And what would they expect her to do in such an event? Bondmates cannot live at cross-purposes—such a thing would be impossible.

She cannot control him against his will any more than he can control her. Yet perhaps she can *influence* his actions to follow the will of those who created her.

It is easy to demonstrate her influence. Right now, she needs energy and there is a substance in the room Michael calls 'the kitchen,' a substance called 'chocolate.' She introduces a faint image of it into his mind and directs brief neural impulses to his stomach and his mouth. Soon he gets up and walks toward the place of storage.

Surprisingly, her success is even more pleasurable than the chocolate itself.

# 25

Michael's mouth hung open. Even a half-hour of cruising slowly along the fringe of the small floating city that was San Francisco harbor hadn't prepared him for this sight. He'd known that the *Argo* was a yacht, but he'd still pictured a typical V-shaped hull with a main deck and some boxy structures amidships stacked like the layers of a wedding cake. What he found instead was a gleaming white dart with a bow as sharp as a knife blade supporting two raked decks above the main one and topped with a tapered black pinnacle like the sail of a submarine. In fact, the *Argo* looked as if it could dive under the waves as easily as it could crest them and cavort like a porpoise if the captain wished it.

Sakiko Matthews had already crossed the boarding ramp from the pier to the stern of the ship and turned an impatient face toward him. He dropped his gaze and hustled over the temporary span. The short aft section of the yacht was not high above the surface of the water, and he had to wonder how the ship would handle large waves from astern. Mounting a few steps, he saw that the angled square of clear blue in front of him was one end of a swimming pool, the water contained by thick glass or Plexiglas and flanked by stairs on either side. Sakiko had taken the stairs to the right, so he did too, mounting them to the main deck where the pool stretched out beside him, its waters inviting in the California heat.

He had an urge to wipe his fingerprints off the deck's shining rails and check his shoes for dirt. The main deck before him was spotless, although some crates and barrel-like containers that he assumed were elements of the expedition's gear were not yet stowed. Crew members dressed in crisp white uniforms were manhandling one crate onto a powered dolly as he watched.

Sakiko said, "Fortunately it's not as bad as I'd feared. I had to have all my lab and sensing equipment brought here, but the ship already had a big air compressor and plenty of scuba tanks, dive sleds, and other gear. Apparently, Blake Cartwright has two bigger yachts that he likes better, but he sometimes rents this one out to Hollywood stars and sports legends for diving excursions. They like its flashiness."

"I can't even imagine what he charges for rent."

"Don't try. An academic salary from now until retirement might cover a couple of weeks' worth."

"And your administrators were OK with this?"

"I haven't even dared to send them pictures. They'd have a heart attack. My funding wouldn't cover the rent for the *tender*—which is stowed right beneath us, by the way, along with two smaller runabouts and a couple of Jet-skis. Except they call the tender a *limousine*. I wouldn't care if it was a barge—I'm just happy to be setting sail at all. When I met you in Sudbury I was at the end of my rope trying to scrounge the last bit of money to transport our gear. My bank had turned me down for a personal loan. Then Dominique called to say the Cartwright Institute would cover the shortfall. I think she was just getting impatient."

Michael looked at the upper decks. "I'm picturing a hot tub."

"A couple."

"Wet bars everywhere."

"That's one right there, to serve swimmers, except our crates are in the way for the moment. And I'm sure the three dining areas are well-stocked with refreshments. I think the crew calls them lounges, or saloons maybe. Wouldn't want to make anyone walk too far to get a drink. There's probably a crew's lounge, too."

"How many in the crew?"

"I don't know—I'd guess a couple of dozen. Their berths are all forward, on the bottom deck. Except for the captain's. There are a few VIP suites and other guest cabins. I heard that Dominique has the whole upper deck to herself. We should find out soon, though—we've been summoned into the Presence."

"Do you know the way?"

"Not a clue." She waved to a crew member who wore a well-cut jacket. Probably a steward. He led them into the interior where they bypassed a leather-appointed stairway to ascend instead in an elevator surrounded entirely by glass.

Michael found his mouth gaping again as he entered the owner's salon. Richly warm paneling that he assumed was teak seemed to rise organically from an intricately patterned parquet floor that covered about half the space. The other half was creamy-white carpeting so thick that bare toes would be completely hidden. The furnishings looked modern, made of glass and polished wood. Flourishes of wine-colored fabrics he couldn't name probably disguised storage spaces in the walls and the entrances to other rooms including, presumably, a private bathroom (called a *head* aboard ship, he remembered). The decor was clearly the work of an interior designer, and no expense had been spared. Michael would have bet fifty bucks the fixtures in the head were gold-plated. Filmy drapes fluttered slightly showing windows behind them, not portholes, open to the light breeze and its tang of fish and diesel. Surely not because Dominique Swan couldn't afford to turn on air conditioning. She must have a fondness for sea air and heat—or wanted to give that impression.

Sakiko drew Michael's attention away from the appointments of the room as she introduced him to the two people already in it: Yuri Hutchings and Sunita James. James's long black hair matched her Hispanic features, and her compact frame was well-proportioned, filling out a pair of tight-fitting lime shorts and a paler green t-shirt. Michael guessed that she might be twenty-five. By contrast, Hutchings appeared to be over forty, with just the slightest hint of gray in his brown hair, and skin that was pale by San Francisco standards. He seemed overdressed in light-gray slacks and long-sleeved shirt, its cuffs pushed up a couple of inches as a concession to the outside heat.

As they shook hands Michael asked, "Are you Ms. Matthews' supervisor?"

The man roared with laughter.

"Yuri and Sunita are *my* grad students," Sakiko huffed.

*"Students?"*

Sunita also wore a sour look. "If you'd heard him a minute ago, arguing over how our quarters should be assigned, you'd know he used to be a lawyer."

"A lawyer-turned-marine-biology-grad-student. Really?"

Yuri shrugged. "Judges didn't like me. An insufficient attitude of respect. Plus, I sucked at golf." He looked around. "I do like the trappings of wealth, however. Maybe I made a mistake."

"Why were you arguing about your accommodations?" Sakiko frowned. "Something wrong with them?"

"He'd never notice anyway," Sunita answered for him. "As long as he's got internet coverage, he's happy. Right, Mr. Facebook?"

Yuri looked sheepish. "I wasn't surfing Facebook when you came to my door, I was *hacking* Facebook. A little matter of an ex of mine who made a disparaging comment about my manhood. But now all is well. And everyone can read about the brilliant success of her sex change operation five years ago, complete with pictures from before she shaved her beard off."

"You jerk." Sunita crossed her arms over her ample chest.

"If it's on Facebook it must be true, right?" He grinned with self-satisfaction, looking to Michael for support. Sakiko glared at them both.

"You ever try anything like that on me and you'll find yourself a hundred feet down with an air tank reading empty."

"Never, boss. You're too important to me. Or at least your recommendation is."

Before Sakiko could reply, two men appeared in the doorway. The first had to be the captain, his dress uniform as crisp as heavy bond-paper and the neatly trimmed beard and hair nearly the same perfect white as the uniform. Fine lines at his eyes and mouth spoke of many years at sea, but his posture was as unselfconsciously erect as any man in the middle of life.

"Parzifal Fox," he said, with a handshake that was solid and dry despite the hot weather.

Michael wished he'd wiped his own palm on his pant leg first. He reached out to the second man and felt his fingers squeezed until the joints protested.

"Dylan Woodward. Dive Master." A trace of an Australian accent there. America's southwest coast seemed to draw Aussies. They were still in demand as Hollywood action heroes, but apparently, that demand did not include Woodward. His eyebrows, nose, and ears were all just slightly too large, as if chosen by a child still learning about proportions in art class. His body was equally unlikely: broad shoulders tapering to a waist so slim it should have had difficulty supporting the mass above it. The combination made him appear tall, but he was a good six inches shorter than his captain, whose long legs and torso would easily allow him to peer over a high bridge rail. Woodward's looks suffered in comparison with Fox's aristocratic features, too; but the contrast in apparel was even greater: Woodward's white trousers had little crease left in them and the matching tank top over his chest allowed more than a few hairs to escape its upper edges. Clearly the dive master wasn't held to quite the same strict standard of dress as the yacht's other crew members. About the only thing both captain and subordinate had in common was a deep, even tan.

Woodward kept silent while Fox made small talk about the weather and inquired about Sakiko's drive to the pier. That must mean they were still waiting for someone to arrive.

And just then, she did.

The woman who stood in the doorway pushed sunglasses to the top of her head as if casually readjusting a tiara. Her lightly tanned skin looked pale against the jet hair that framed it; and with only the light from the windows, Michael couldn't decide if her eyes were blue or green, but the color was vivid. He suspected that her even cheekbones, full lips, and delicate chin were all natural, though they would have been the pride of a plastic surgeon. The same could be said about her figure, revealed in a white one-piece swimsuit cut high over the hips and daringly narrow at the upper sides, with an oval vertical cut over the breastbone down almost to the navel.

The swimsuit was covered by a sheer sunrobe of pale blue that the woman pulled closed as she stepped into the room, yet the effect of the flimsy coverup was to make her even more alluring, and Michael felt his body respond.

Unbidden, his view was overlaid with an image of himself and Nicole having sex!

Irritated, he signaled to Naïda to restrain her curiosity and tried to concentrate as a lithe hand reached toward him.

"Dominique Swan," she said unnecessarily. The handshake was firm and proper, no longer than necessary. As she moved on to Yuri, Michael noticed a glazed look on the man's face and hoped his own wasn't quite so obvious. Sunita James looked as if she wanted to curtsey. But Sakiko held a businesslike expression and posture, saying, "Good to see you again, Ms. Swan."

"Dominique. Everyone, please, call me Dominique. Once you've had your goods splashed over the internet in a leaked sex video, there's not much point in formality, is there?" Her self-deprecating smile seemed genuine, although it was likely she'd made the same remark many times before. "I trust that everyone had a good trip here and your accommodations are satisfactory." Michael thought he saw Yuri's ears redden, but Dominique didn't notice. Instead, she turned her gaze to Fox and Woodward.

"We'll be getting underway within a few hours once everything's safely stowed. But I wanted the Captain and Dylan to hear more about the purpose of our expedition directly from you, Dr. Matthews, the better to plan our route and offer helpful suggestions based on their experience."

"Sakiko, please." The expedition's leader dipped her head slightly as she said it. Then she gave a mini-lecture about global warming and climate change, and how the planet's oceans moderated the level of greenhouse gases in the atmosphere by absorption of carbon dioxide—not only by micro-plankton, but also by the water itself, especially the warmer waters of the tropical belt. The downside of such absorption, however, was that it produced carbonic acid.

"Some scientists estimate that the oceans have absorbed thirty percent or more of the carbon emissions produced by humans over the past century or so and will absorb a much greater percentage over the next hundred years. That process helps to slow the greenhouse effect in the atmosphere—good news in that respect—but it's starting to take its toll on the marine environment.

"Seawater is normally slightly basic rather than acidic. That measurement is referred to as pH. A pH reading of 7.0 is neutral—a substance with a number *lower* than that is considered acidic, and *higher* pH readings are called *basic*. For centuries the pH of seawater has been about 8.2. Since the industrial revolution it has fallen to about 8.0 and there are fears it will change a further 0.4 or even 0.7 over the next century if humans cannot reduce atmospheric carbon dioxide.

"I know that amount of change doesn't sound like a lot, but pH changes that size in Earth's past have been connected to some significant extinctions of species. And those shifts took place over many millions of years. I've personally witnessed the horrible bleaching of huge expanses of coral in the Great Barrier Reef and elsewhere that's increased drastically in recent years all over the world. Then there's the unhappy fact that water with higher acidity conducts sound much more readily, to the point that marine biologists are deeply worried about the harm our noisy tanker ships and oil drilling-platforms are causing to the sensitive auditory organs of ocean mammals like dolphins and whales that navigate by sound.

"Excess $CO_2$ in water also affects the ability of fish to sense predators and flee to safety. In some cases, they're actually *drawn* to their natural enemies, and you can imagine how that would disrupt the food chain."

"And make deep sea fishing so much easier," Woodward said with a big smile, but no one else shared it.

"Excuse me, Dr. Matthews." Parzifal Fox drew everyone's attention with only a slight change of posture. "It sounds to me as if the problem lies in our factories and cars, not in our oceans. As long as excess carbon dioxide is in the air, the oceans will absorb it. How do you stop that?"

"You're right about the source of the problem, Captain," she replied. "But plankton in the oceans use carbon dioxide in photosynthesis, and especially certain species of algae should be thrilled to have such a ready source of extra carbon for food. This should be a natural way of capturing and sequestering carbon dioxide, just like the growth of trees on land. But we're not seeing that to the degree we expect. Some of us feel there must be some other mechanism at work, inhibiting the cycle. That's what my research has been about for the past five years, and the purpose behind this expedition: to sample ocean waters in many separate places and, hopefully, find that other mechanism."

"I'm still waiting to hear why you've chosen the Gulf of California," Yuri said. "I thought it was about the Redfield ratios, but it isn't, is it?" Was there a trace of annoyance in his voice? His crossed arms seemed to confirm that.

Sakiko gave Yuri a hard look, then turned her head to take in the group. "For those of you who don't know, the 'Redfield ratio' describes the proportions of carbon, nitrogen, and phosphorus in ocean micro-organisms—

it's used for most carbon-absorption calculations. It was once thought to be the same everywhere, but we've learned that Redfield ratios vary considerably in different regions of the world's oceans, so it might make sense to survey some major examples of those differences."

She cleared her throat. "However, the reason I chose to begin in the Gulf of California...well, first of all, there have been some reports of an unexplained drop in plankton in an area that's normally very rich in it. That's suspicious on its own. But I also discovered a story about what the press has called a 'giant jellyfish bloom' near a prototype power installation. As to why that's significant...I wanted everyone to hear that together. So, I'll let Dr. Hart explain." Her face was like a child watching a nurse prepare an inoculation needle, and she'd carefully omitted the fact that Michael's doctorate had nothing to do with oceans.

His story should have been easier with each telling, but it damn well wasn't. Struggling to keep his face neutral, he described how he'd discovered the outpost in Evergreen Lake, leaving out any mention of Naïda or the signal—he still hadn't told Sakiko about that last detail. Using his flattest Psych-lecture voice, he outlined his concern that an alien race might have reason to want more acidic oceans on Earth, should they ever return. He couldn't bring himself to say outright that he expected an invasion. They might have thrown him overboard. As it was, their faces made it clear that not one of them believed a single word. Woodward's expression left no doubt as to who he considered to be the alien. The ironic near-truth of that opinion forced Michael to swallow a nervous laugh.

Sakiko obviously read the reactions the same way. "I know that sounds...incredible, to say the least. But I...was witness to some compelling evidence that backs up Dr. Hart's story." She gave Michael a questioning look, but he returned a slight shake of his head. "It was enough to convince me that we should proceed as if the suppression of plankton $CO_2$ absorption might follow a pattern.

"The place we're headed to first happens to be a site of significant hydrothermal activity at an accessible depth. And there's this." She passed her computer tablet to Yuri and it slowly made its way through the group. On it was an internet-news article about the unique jellyfish bloom that had been discovered near the site of an experimental thermal power generation plant. Michael had experienced mental images of that site repeatedly and was certain it must be a key piece of data his subconscious mind had retrieved out of the information given him by the alien outpost. But that would have been awkward to explain.

"We are talking about the thermal vents along the Wagner Fault, right?" asked Yuri. "But Dr. Hart's aliens supposedly came here...when? Ten thousand years ago, did you say?"

"Give or take."

"How do we know that these vents were active that long ago? They might be from more recent fault activity."

Michael shrugged. "The suppression of carbon dioxide absorption might not have begun that long ago either. While I don't believe aliens are currently present on Earth, something or some *things* are acting on their behalf. I know that from personal experience with one. I want to find the others."

Woodward snorted. Sunita asked, "What was this evidence that convinced you?"

Sakiko hesitated and gave Michael another look. "Uh, hopefully that's something we'll be able to reveal to you very soon."

Michael nodded warily. "When the time is right."

'You mean once we're at sea and can't throw him overboard," Woodward muttered. Fox rebuked him with a look, but Michael couldn't hold back the laugh this time.

"I hadn't heard this part of the story," Dominique said, "but what counts is that I'm convinced Dr. Matthews knows what she's doing. We follow her course. And if we have a chance for a little barhopping in Puerto Peñasco, so much the better. For now, I'm going to change for dinner." She concluded the meeting with a sweep of her hand toward the door.

The Captain and Woodward took the stairs to the bridge. The rest rode the elevator down and headed toward the bow, with Yuri and Sunita a little ahead, talking in low voices.

"Does she always dress that way? Dominique?" Michael asked.

"I'd say she was testing you," Sakiko replied.

"Did I pass?"

She grunted. "You're male. Through and through."

That was no longer entirely true, but he didn't point it out. Instead, he said, "Thanks for not throwing me completely to the wolves"

"You'd make it a whole lot easier for me if you'd let your *friend* put in an appearance."

"I don't know who I can trust. Once that cat's out of the bag, it can't be put back in—and if word leaks...well then I'm a Ripley's Believe It or Not exhibit for the rest of my life."

Sakiko's expression seemed to say there was little point fighting the inevitable.

With perfect timing, a member of the crew appeared to lead them to their individual quarters for a chance to freshen up before dinner. Sakiko knew the guest rooms could never compare with Dominique's quarters, but figured they'd be at least as impressive as those of a five-star hotel.

She'd underestimated *Argo*'s decorators. Though the appointments were minimal, they were all of a quality she'd never experienced and never expected to, from manufacturers she only knew from the websites of magazines. She felt the blood rise to her cheeks as she sat gently on the bed and ran her fingers over the sateen pillowslips. Egyptian cotton, she was sure. Millesimo, maybe?

There was at least one part of this trip that she was going to enjoy very much.

# 26

Sakiko didn't invest a lot of emotion into eating, but even she had to admit that dinner had been extraordinary. Rock cod, lightly grilled, and sea bass sautéed in white wine. A side dish of rice flavored by some kind of kelp; a salad of spicy greens with herbs she didn't recognize. Fresh rolls with a hint of something—rosemary? A simple menu, overall, but exquisitely prepared. If that was a sign of things to come, their taste buds were going to be hopelessly spoiled. How would she go back to Beefaroni and cold pizza?

She'd been glad to give her full attention to the food for other reasons, too. Yuri sat across the table from her, trying to catch her eye, his face set in a sour glare. On her left, Sunita fed asides into Sakiko's ear about aliens shadowing the ship in their UFO's, or speculating that Michael might actually be a robot—was he really eating or just stashing the food somewhere?

To Sakiko's right sat Dylan Woodward, the dive master, a couple of inches too close so their arms brushed more often than necessary. Sakiko could understand that Woodward's sexy boss, Dominique, was off limits and fraternizing with serving staff or housecleaning staff might be awkward for him, but she hoped he wouldn't persist with his attentions because he certainly wasn't her type.

Michael was seated beside Dominique, and from what she'd been able to overhear of their conversation, the psychology professor seemed to have forgotten most of that university education, relying instead on silly questions and comments about Dominique's TV career.

*Men.* In the presence of a woman like that, they all reacted the same way. The only reason Yuri wasn't fawning as well was because of his crush on Sunita. Was he crazy, or just suicidal, when the smallest slip of the tongue could reveal the fraudulent funding and ruin their careers? Fortunately, if Sunita had noticed Yuri's attentions, she was ignoring them. Sakiko would have to confront him about it eventually. At least Captain Fox had assured her that he would warn his crew to stay away from the girl. She'd done the same to Michael, whose reaction was to give her a look as if she'd grown a third eye. That was comforting. For the sake of the young assistant, of course.

As Sakiko came out onto the deck, the disk of the setting sun was only minutes away from dipping into the ocean. The wake of the ship sparkled in its golden light, hypnotic.

"A beautiful night ahead, I think." Michael's voice startled her from behind her right shoulder.

"I love nights at sea," she said. "When it's calm, the stars wrap right around you as if you've magically fallen into a crystal ball."

"Reflected in the water? I look forward to seeing that." They drifted slowly toward the rail. There were a few chairs lined up by a crew probably used to passengers gravitating there to watch the sunset—but she and Michael stood. "Can I...get you a drink?" he asked. "I saw a steward coming this way. Probably headed for the bar by the pool. In fact, I think that pool is calling to me."

Sakiko turned her head and saw that submerged lights had come on in the pool, and its luminous blue water did look inviting. Almost as an afterthought, she'd bought a couple of bikinis at a shop near the San Francisco docks, just in case she felt the urge to get some sun. What about Michael? A boxer-style suit, probably—she couldn't imagine him as a Speedo guy, though the picture it brought to mind was...interesting. But with that thought came another not nearly so pleasant.

"I think I'll pass. You and your 'little friend' go and have a good time."

Michael's smile vanished like the last wink of the sun. Was that hurt on his face? She opened her mouth, searching for something else to say, but he turned away, going to the bar alone.

Well, after all, what could he expect? Three's a crowd.

She imagined his trim body emerging from the water with an alien sheen spreading over it like an unearthly oil slick. Her own skin shivered in response, and she moved farther up the rail toward the bow until she couldn't see him anymore. She just wanted to be alone for a few minutes, that was all. There was a lot to be said for solitude.

# 27

To someone not trained in marine biology, the data collected by Sakiko over several years was a trackless forest. Michael skimmed her numbers and graphs but had to read each introduction and summary of her published papers (and a few unpublished ones), sometimes two or three times. It was like learning a new language; and memories of biology courses taken years earlier were little help—his brain taunting him with something he once understood.

Those courses had focused mostly on human physiology and biochemistry anyway—the basics of genetics, and the inter-relatedness of the Earth's ecosystems too, but not the reproductive processes of oceanic algae, acoustical dynamics of pH changes in seawater, or the relation of thermal gradients to reef biodiversity. A lot of the terms and phrases required a third and fourth reading to even make sense to him.

He needed to get a good grasp of Sakiko's work, or he'd be left out of technical conversations completely. Her investigations would cover much of the same territory he needed to explore, and if he didn't know what was normal, how would he be able to recognize the result of alien intervention?

That's what he told himself as he spent hours alone in his cabin with his computer on their second day at sea.

Sakiko's words of the previous night had been hurtful. Naïda was a part of him and in many ways made him better than he'd been. She wasn't a monster.

The exchange had just confirmed his determination to keep Naïda a secret. People were too damned closed-minded. Bigoted. *Xenophobic*—truly *afraid* of the strange, not just intolerant. They might never be able to accept someone like her. Like *them*, he reminded himself. He was no longer just Michael Hart. An attack on Naïda was an attack on him, too.

The thought made him wonder about Naïda's feelings. Was she happy about the arrangement? Did she even know what it was to be happy? He couldn't say.

Since there weren't a lot of loose objects in his cabin, he only noticed the ship's extra motion because of the shifting of the light coming through the large porthole. It made him aware of sudden queasiness in the pit of his stomach. The yacht was rising and falling through a pretty considerable arc. With his eyes focused on an unmoving screen, his inner ear had been bound to complain sooner or later. Normally, he wasn't prone to motion sickness, but he put the laptop away, lay down on his bed, and closed his eyes. The minor nausea continued to grow.

He'd spent lots of afternoons in dive boats riding heavy wave action on the Great Lakes without any discomfort, but that was on a much smaller scale.

Terrific. He hadn't brought any Dramamine. Certainly a yacht like *Argo* would have a well-stocked dispensary, including remedies for queasy stomachs. He might take that route as a last resort, but to admit seasickness so early in the voyage would only reinforce that he was a total outsider. Maybe if he used some relaxation techniques, he could get the flutters in his stomach under control on his own.

Or maybe there was another way.

Clearing his mind, he pictured his water nymph image of Naïda—the equivalent of calling her name—and then drew attention to the turmoil in his digestive tract, adding a few images of rolling waves and then his inner ear. There was no response from her, but within a few minutes the discomfort began to ease. Fifteen minutes later he got off the bed and looked out the porthole. The view was an eye-opener.

Giant rollers marched across the seascape, charging powerfully beneath a ceiling of gray highlighted by crevices of startling white. It was his first experience with the sea in such a mood. He decided to go on deck to feel the wind and the spray.

As he stepped out and scanned the ocean, he noticed a figure about ten meters toward the stern. Yuri Hutchings. The man was standing at the rail, probably there for the same reason as Michael. Or perhaps not. Yuri's head suddenly pitched forward, and Michael looked away. He should give the guy some privacy, but as he turned in that direction again it was clear that Yuri had seen him. He gave a small wave and strolled closer.

"You'll have to find your own place to redecorate the ship's hull," Yuri said, "this is my spot." He tried to grin, but it was lopsided.

"I'm OK. So far," Michael said. "Do you, uh, always feel crappy when you're on the ocean? Tough for a marine scientist, huh?"

"Hell no. These seas aren't normal. And the way we're cutting across the waves...that corkscrewing motion? Ship stabilizers can't dampen all of that. There—see? The ship's changing course a little to take us into the waves at a sharper angle. Taking pity on us. Surprised they didn't do that sooner." He paused, obviously struggling with an urge from his abdomen, but he won the battle for the time being. "I think everybody except that damned Fox is feeling like shit. How come you aren't?"

Michael shrugged. "Guardian angel, I guess."

The heavy seas lasted the rest of that day and night. There was no communal dinner served, but Michael was able to get some pasta and salad and ate in the 'tea room.' Except for the motion, he could've been in any private club or a reserved section of a high-class library. Dylan Woodward passed by once, but the man had no food in hand.

After dinner Michael was content to stay in his room. As the team members at the bottom of the hierarchy, he and Sunita had been assigned the most modest guest cabins, but they still featured two twin beds and a decor equal to the most expensive hotel he'd ever stayed in (a rare theatre junket to Toronto with Nicole). He was glad he didn't have to share with anyone other than Naïda.

He wondered what she made of their surroundings. Could she tell the difference between the cheap spruce paneling of his apartment and these fabric-covered walls? Between linoleum and Taiping carpet? Hell, Michael wasn't sure what to make of it himself. When he'd conceived the plan to join the expedition, he'd pictured a utilitarian research vessel with bunkrooms, a cramped mess, and bulkhead-fitted corridors with damp walls that needed a coat of paint. *Argo* was as far from that as possible. Would its luxury be an impediment when it came to actually getting work done? It sounded like the lower deck was well equipped with water 'toys,' but he had yet to see that.

Sleep was slow in coming that night—his limbs twitched as every seventh or eighth wave produced a particularly deep drop—but as he felt reassured that he wouldn't be tossed from the bed, he drifted into unconsciousness.

Not long after rising the next morning, Sakiko and Yuri joined him in the main saloon. Sunita arrived a half-hour later. They ordered only coffee, and no one talked much. The smudges under their eyes spoke all that was necessary. A disbelieving look from Sakiko made Michael turn aside to eat a bacon-and-egg sandwich. Part of him wanted her to know that Naïda was responsible for his good fortune, but he couldn't think of a way to say so with others present.

"At least we're not freezing," Sunita muttered, staring into her coffee cup.

At Michael's questioning look, Sakiko said, "It was almost a toss-up whether we went to equatorial waters or the Arctic Ocean. Sunita and I outvoted Yuri."

Michael was sure it hadn't really been a vote.

"Why the Arctic?"

"A few years ago, NASA researchers discovered huge blooms of phytoplankton under the arctic ice. Because of the warming climate, more of the ice melts during the summer; and when it refreezes, it's flatter and thinner than it used to be. That change allows a lot of sunlight through, and phytoplankton grows at terrific rates underneath. Naturally, that means there must be a lot of carbon absorption going on."

"But I thought you were looking for places where algae weren't growing as well as it should, to find out what might be stopping it."

"By studying its accelerated growth in the Arctic, we might learn what could be repressing algae growth elsewhere," Yuri replied, not looking up. "And we could have made progress charting the global dispersion of $CO_2$, by backward extrapolation from the algae growth."

"There are some areas where the plankton population has really nosedived, right?" Michael asked.

Sakiko nodded. "Like deserts in mid-ocean—we aren't really sure why, although most suspect it has to do with water temperature. Especially since those zones have been growing more than fifteen percent over a decade. There's a huge one that stretches from Hawaii all the way across to the Philippines."

"Good God. Then why...?"

"We *did* plan to start our search at the near end of that Pacific zone, just east of Hawaii. Then I found out about the new die-off, or whatever it is, near Puerto Peñasco. It was closer, accessible by scuba, and...well, you were the clincher. As you know." Her face was turned toward Michael, but her words were clearly aimed at Yuri and Sunita. The statement drew a grunt from the grad student; but if he had more to say, he drowned it in a large swallow of coffee.

A steward appeared behind Yuri to ask if he could bring them anything more. Sheepishly, Michael asked for another sandwich and some donuts. Sakiko's raised eyebrows gave way to a knowing look, but Yuri and Sunita both made faces and left quickly. Michael just looked back at Sakiko and shrugged.

"We're hungry."

"Eating for two," they both said at the same time, and then broke into laughter.

Naïda is temporarily sated after the third doughnut. By now she has a good understanding of the energy needs of the body she and her bondmate share and is quickly increasing her knowledge of the nutrients provided by human foods. That doesn't entirely explain her influence on Michael's choices. Once introduced to the basic concept of pleasure—so many choices made by her bondmate's species are related to it—she has gradually improved her understanding of the various sensory systems of Michael's body.

Very early in their bonding, she learned the proper terms for his senses and learned to distinguish among them, but sensory connection to pleasure is complicated. Sensations of taste and smell are certainly not always pleasurable, likely deliberate on the part of the Creator of the humans. It is logical that unpleasant tastes and smells be associated with dangerous or non-nutritious substances, and substances suitable for food produce pleasure. Yet this is not always true.

Michael consumes much that offers pleasurable tastes, but little or no nutrition. And almost everything he consumes includes some elements that are biologically undesirable. His digestive system does a good job of filtering out most of these elements and diverting them to the waste stream, but the process takes a toll on the organs involved. Naïda is gradually learning how to enhance that selection and diversion process using her own biochemistry, and the improvement in the functioning of Michael's organs and lymph systems gratifies her.

Occasionally she has made errors. When she discovered that a hydroxyl compound in some of the liquids Michael consumed depressed the inhibitory functions of neurotransmitters in the brain and caused impairment of his senses, she assigned some of her own cells to the lining of his small intestine to divert the compound entirely into the waste stream. Michael was not pleased and insisted that she only perform that function at his direct request.

Since then, she has asked his permission before making significant changes. It is only fitting that she give back energy and health in return for the energy she draws from his cells. Fitting, but also self-serving. It is her body, too. Even she finds it less and less meaningful to distinguish between her cells and his. That thought gives her pleasure.

Pleasure like the tastes of chocolate and Coca Cola?

No, the kinds of pleasure are extremely varied. Puzzling. Yet wonderful. Did the Creators intend that she should experience pleasure along with her human host, or is this a fortunate accident? She believes that it does make her better able to serve the needs of their shared body.

She has no answers for these questions. Instead, she relishes the lingering sweetness from the doughnuts. But because they contained significant proportions of unwanted fats and crystalline carbohydrates, she diverts part of her attention to metabolizing those elements before the body misdirects them into its own fat cells.

The rest of her thought goes to the aural communication between Michael and the human female. They've just produced a sound she's often heard Michael make: a vocalization involving puffs of breath rapidly expressed through the vocal cords. Most often, though not always, such exhalations are connected to a powerful pleasure sensation and the release of pleasure chemicals in the brain—a kind of brief euphoria—but she has not been able to identify the cause. Sometimes Michael has made the sound while viewing information on an electronic screen, but more often it is in response to other humans. She once asked him about it, but they both had too much difficulty with the explanation. As she has come to understand that certain activities not involving food can also produce pleasure; she has found that Michael connects many of them with the word 'fun.'

She wishes that she could experience the sensation connected to these rapid vocalizations. It seems like 'fun.'

When Michael returns to the new place where he sleeps, she asks again about the vocalization. She thinks at first that he uses the word *fun*, but then he shows it to her on his electronic screen. The strange action is called a *laugh* and it is a reaction to something *funny*. But he does not define either any further. He seems to want to spend more time with screen information, and Naïda has not learned to read his printed language quickly enough to follow anything he's looking at. The *laugh* is just one of several body functions that remain a mystery to her.

She encounters another when Michael lies on the bed to read his screen. Often, after he has eaten, there is a release of air and digestive gases from the outlet to his digestive tract. It is not strange that his primitive method of consuming fuel would involve swallowed air, nor that the unsophisticated digestive system would produce gas—especially with the random nature of the foods he consumes. The puzzling element is that the release often creates sounds, though usually only when Michael is alone. The variations fascinate her. The tightness of certain muscles and areas of skin produce modulations in the sound. This is something she can control. She tries it now, and the result gives her a spike of pleasure of a kind she hasn't experienced before.

Again.

It brings her a surge of quick, frothy energy, like the burst of a bubble.

She experiments some more, producing higher and lower pitches, warbles, and squeaks. Michael is restive, but not paying attention. She is transported for brief seconds into a strangely euphoric state of mind. And then it comes to her—it is the euphoria Michael experiences with the thing called a *laugh*!

She can't resist more complex attempts with sounds increasingly bizarre.

*Funny!*

Then Michael realizes what she is doing and tells her to stop. He says that if she ever does that when there are females present, he won't speak to her again.

She stops.

But it's still funny.

# 28

*Argo* had found calmer waters by late that afternoon and, after a light dinner, the team gathered for drinks at the bar by the pool. The captain and Woodward had some duties to perform first, so Yuri took the opportunity to ask Dominique about them.

"Captain Fox has been with us for fifteen years," she said, "though I'm not sure whether yacht duty is a let-down or a relief. I know he had a distinguished career in the U.S. Navy, but after that he spent many years on exploration missions to some crazy places, especially the Arctic and Antarctic."

"That's where I've heard the name before," Yuri said. "The *Narwhal* expedition that was trapped in the ice seventeen or eighteen years ago. A storm surrounded the ship with thick ice floes and kept rescue missions grounded. After a few days, *Narwhal's* hull was breached by the ice and they didn't dare stay aboard in case the floes shifted again and sent the ship to the bottom."

Dominique nodded. "And once they were on the ice, any change in the wind could have broken up the ice pack and left them stranded on a floe. The Captain kept everyone together while they managed to drag two of the ship's tenders twenty miles to a small polynya that had opened up. It widened into a lead that enabled them to reach open ocean. *Narwhal* was lost but the crew was saved."

"Oh my God." Sunita was wide-eyed.

"Captain Fox still has all his fingers and toes, but after frostbite like that, his doctors advised him to stick to warmer places."

"I don't imagine your father entertains his friends anywhere much above the tropics," Sakiko said.

"My father doesn't entertain anyone on *Argo* anymore. He rarely uses the yachts, but if he does, he picks *Castle Royal*—it's about the size of a small cruise ship." Her smile was broad, but there was more cynicism than pride in it. Sakiko began to suspect that this woman had a more complex relationship with her wealth and fame than the average tabloid reader would believe.

Conversation had moved on to small talk about *Argo* when the captain arrived, still sharply dressed from dinner.

"No Mr. Woodward?" asked Sunita, provoking a frown from Yuri.

"Our dive master is not an especially sociable man, and I believe he wanted to have a video chat with his wife and children back in San Francisco."

Sakiko was sure Fox had carefully chosen the words to let Sunita down gently. It appeared the captain was an observant and sensitive man. His English was refined, but she thought she detected a slight accent. Perhaps Hispanic.

"Are you off-duty now, Captain? Can you join us for a drink?"

"A captain is never truly off-duty, Mr. Hutchings, but I'm not needed anywhere else for the moment." He signaled to the steward who had followed him in, but no words were exchanged. "I'm pleased to see that everyone's recovered from the rough start to our voyage. The weather service assures us that conditions will be much more hospitable for the next five or six days, perhaps longer. I'm told that you did not suffer from the waves, though, Mr. Hart. A gift from the aliens, perhaps?"

"Perhaps, Captain."

Michael gave Sakiko a look, and she understood that the captain was exactly right—Michael's immunity from seasickness *had* been because of the alien symbiote. The lucky bastard.

"I would love to hear your version of the *Narwhal* expedition, Captain," Yuri said.

Fox paused as the steward returned with a glass of some clear drink sporting a slice of lime and a sprig of mint and put it in the captain's hand.

"If you know the story at all, I'm sure you know all of the details worth telling."

"Then you must have had many other adventures worth hearing."

"Adventures are merely a young man's name for things an older and wiser man calls foolhardy, Mr. Hutchings." The Captain took a sip from his drink and looked at the other faces. "Are any of you acquainted with a UFO hunter named Cassidy?"

Michael straightened. "Ryan Cassidy? Why do you call him a UFO hunter?"

"You know him then?"

"He's a former astronaut. I know he's claimed to have seen a UFO..."

"More than that. If you've followed his career, you'll know that he now makes a living making public appearances—conventions and things of the sort—and supposedly tracking down stories of alien encounters. He's set himself up as an expert on the subject."

"I didn't know. I haven't...really followed him."

"Well, I think he might know *you*, Mr. Hart."

"What's that supposed to mean?"

Fox sipped at his drink again. "A news item I saw this afternoon. Cassidy was defending himself and his credibility in an interview and insisted that he's very thorough when verifying UFO sightings. In fact, he'd just been investigating a bogus claim about an alien artifact found in Canada. Northern Ontario, was it?"

Michael's face looked pale. "You're not serious!"

"*He* was. He went on to say that he was looking into the matter further, because he didn't want people like 'this Ontario guy giving real UFO experiences a bad name.'" Fox turned to Sakiko. "One hopes that your supervisors don't read the *Huffington Post*, Ms. Matthews."

Michael put his empty glass on the bar and strode toward the stairs, leaving an awkward silence behind.

Sakiko returned Fox's look, and said, "Michael Hart has some evidence that would knock you on your ass, Captain. Believe me, I'm a hard girl to convince, but he's telling the truth."

"Then tell us, Sakiko," Yuri said, his voice too loud. "For God's sake, tell us the evidence."

"I don't have the right to do that. You'll understand why when Michael is ready to tell it."

"Shit." Yuri turned away and approached the steward to get another beer, with Sunita following. Dominique remained leaning on the bar, face turned toward the stairs with a thoughtful expression.

Fox gave Sakiko a more contrite look. "I sincerely didn't mean to cause trouble among your team, Dr. Matthews, but I thought you should know."

"That's all right, Captain. That's soda water in your glass, isn't it? It must be tough to restrain yourself with every kind of exotic food and drink surrounding you all day."

"When a man reaches his later years, he feels he's earned the right to eat and drink whatever he wants, only to find, to his dismay, that he has to be more careful about such things than ever before. That's the true trial, Dr. Matthews. Not all this." He swept his arm toward the bar.

"Still, your self-control is admirable. Perhaps you can appreciate it in others, too. Like Michael. And since you can't know anything about his own particular challenges, I'd appreciate it if you'd cut him some slack." Her look shifted to include Dominique, who gave the slightest of nods. "You don't believe in aliens, Captain?"

"Never have. Nor God, nor any other fantasies, even though I've seen some strange sights. But I have seen what *men* can do. There's no need to look any further to find a cause for climate change, coral bleaching, or any of the other evils of the world, to my mind."

"And you have a keen mind, I'm sure. But you might find you'll need to pry it open just a little before this voyage is through."

# 29

It was easy to find the article about Ryan Cassidy. Michael tossed his tablet onto the bed in disgust.

The prick!

Cassidy wouldn't have dived into the now-toxic waters of Evergreen Lake himself. He might have hired someone to do it, but more likely he'd just asked around—asked Nicole, or even Phil Rodriguez. Maybe he'd even assumed that Michael's leaving town was the random act of someone unstable chasing figments of his imagination. Would the man really try to track him down? Nicole couldn't give away any details about the expedition because she didn't know any. The sailing of the *Argo* had received some attention from paparazzi in San Francisco who were curious about all the equipment that had been loaded aboard, but there was no reason for Cassidy to make that connection.

No, they were probably safe from interference for now, though Michael made a mental note to search media outlets for Cassidy's name every few days.

It really was true that you should never have a living hero—they were bound to let you down.

The next day's weather was perfect, and the team spent most of it going over their equipment. Though he probably wouldn't be handling any of the research instruments on his own, Sakiko gave Michael a quick tutorial on how everything worked. Most of it was surprisingly low-tech.

The electronic gear included a salinometer to measure the water's saltiness, a pH meter, a probe and gauge that revealed oxygen content, and a portable fathometer, although the depth and bottom-scanning instrumentation on the ship's tender turned out to be much more sophisticated and precise.

The rest of the hardware was almost primitive: floats dragged by string to measure current, dangling disks for judging water color, and various kinds of thermometers.

Inspecting the dive gear was more fun, since most of it was better than Michael's own. It was bizarre to remember that he didn't really need any of it anymore, but would have to use it for the sake of appearances. Naïda was going to be pretty upset to be confined by a wet suit. She recognized the equipment as he handled it, showing him a mental image of himself in Evergreen Lake, though the representation from her original senses looked to him like a murky outline in strange colors. He tried to reassure her with thoughts of safety and well-being.

Woodward gave a tour of the ship's watercraft stored below the pool deck, where whole sections of the hull could lift away on pistons to allow launching of the boats by overhead davits and cranes. It was astonishing to see two full-sized tenders resting there, both sleek and trim and about eight or nine meters long. One was clearly more luxurious than the other, with a fully enclosed passenger area. Woodward called it a limousine. The second was a crew tender, but still far fancier than any boat Michael had ever been on.

"That one on the other side. Is that a *ski boat*?" he asked Woodward.

"Better believe it. A Ski Nautique. Super light. Mammoth GM engine. Gives an ultra-smooth wake for slalom, or a shift-down gate puts out waves for trick skiing."

"Do you ski?"

"Hell, no. But I do like to watch women in bikinis give it a try."

Sakiko crossed her arms, so Michael didn't copy Woodward's wolfish smile.

"I'm having a hard time picturing us doing serious diving from any of these," she said. "Especially with our scientific gear."

"Yeah, we use the crew tender for diving, mostly. It's a little tight sometimes, but manageable," Woodward assured her. "There's a small inflatable around somewhere, too. Ms. Swan had it brought aboard especially for this trip."

Michael had to agree with Sakiko—it was hard to imagine dragging dive gear with all its protrusions near leather-covered upholstery. But he itched to give the two Sea-Doos a try on the open ocean. Even if he wiped out badly, Naïda would keep him from drowning.

She must have picked up his mental images of the prospect. The muscles of his throat tightened.

Alarm? Was it concern for his safety, or her own? Maybe she was spooked by speed. She'd coped with riding in a car, though close calls made her twitchy. Perhaps the physics of a high-speed impact with water was a lot more relatable.

He couldn't coddle her. She was just going to have to adapt. It bothered him that her reaction had utilized his own body's response reflexes. That could be a major pain in the ass if she didn't learn some restraint.

He and Sakiko finally left Woodward gazing at his boats and went up to the tearoom to draw up preliminary plans for their first exploratory outings near Puerto Peñasco. Afterward, with some time before dinner, Michael decided to try out the swimming pool while no one else was around. He had to know he could persuade Naïda from showing herself even in a water environment. He'd tried to prepare her ahead of time, but their communication still wasn't perfect.

As he plunged beneath the surface, he felt the characteristic ripple in his skin, especially his eyelids and ears, and he thought the word *No*. The transformation proceeded. He repeated the mental command, even vocalizing the word. This time it worked. By the time he broke surface he had to blink water from his eyes and detected cool liquid against his eardrums. He could sense Naïda's disapproval but ignored it as he spotted Sakiko in a royal-blue one-piece swimsuit, watching him from the edge of the pool. After a moment, her face relaxed and she dived in.

"Your friend doesn't always come out to play in the water?" she asked, brushing her hair back.

"I'm trying to control that."

"What about when we dive on the thermal sites. Could it allow you to dive that deep without gear?"

"The power project is in the shallows east of the basin, right? I don't know for sure. But I'm not planning to try—it would give the game away to everybody on the ship."

"Only the people who actually come on the dive boat."

"I told you—I don't know who I can trust."

"So, you'll go through the charade of using scuba gear even if you don't need it?"

"I have to. Anyway, we're still not certain a second outpost is even at the site of the power station. I'm hoping that if it is there, it'll be in even shallower water."

"But we won't know until you jump in the ocean with the symbiote."

"Right."

"If we haven't come all this way on a wild goose chase." She dived under the water and swam away.

The night sky was mesmerizing. Stars spread from horizon to horizon in patterns that winked and shifted like thoughts. The ocean was flat and warm as Michael breathed in its perfume. Perhaps some of the scents came from the unseen land that now lay on either side of the ship in the darkness, but he couldn't identify anything specific. He was content to breathe in air that flowed over vast spaces, far from any factory or freeway.

He turned his head to the right and saw a figure approaching along the railing. Sakiko? No, a little taller, movements more sinuous.

Dominique.

"Watching for spaceships, Mr. Hart?" The voice was throaty, well under control, revealing a teasing smile he couldn't yet see. He was dismayed to find himself reacting to it so quickly.

"Hadn't occurred to me." Which was true, but now he swept his eyes over an arc of sky. "If the aliens ever do arrive, I'd hope our radar installations would detect them before giant shapes start blocking out the stars. And it would be more polite for them to *call* first."

She moved closer and the light from a distant deck lamp caught her face, the glow seeming to come from the skin itself. Flowing hair blacker than the night framed perfectly sculpted features, and in the dark, his mind filled in the cobalt blue of her eyes. Her shoulder came to a stop a hands-breadth away from his as she turned to face the ocean. Was that really her warmth he felt? Or some other reaction?

"I shouldn't tease. You don't strike me as a guy who easily admits to believing in UFOs. This must be hard for you."

"Strange, anyway. I'm just a university prof who's never done very much or gone very far. I'm sure your life would be just as alien to me as anything in a spaceship. Hollywood stars. The rich and famous." He gave a light laugh to remove any offence.

"Not so glamorous as you might think. Money breeds people you don't really want to spend time with, Mr. Hart. Trust me on that. In fact, maybe that includes me."

"Please call me Michael. And I hope you don't think I've been avoiding you, Ms. Swan."

"Dominique. Fair is fair."

"OK. But I mean...I haven't seen you around much, and I guess we haven't looked for you because we assumed you must be busy doing...something."

She laughed. It brought a warm glow to his neck.

"Not much of anything, in fact. I could do any number of the jobs that keep this ship running, but I pay people to do that, which leaves me with nothing to do. And I don't want to interfere with what your people are doing—I don't know anything about it. I can be content to just provide the boat and pay the bills." A flash of white came from perfect teeth, then the smile faded. "No, that's not really true. Not content, but...I'll manage."

"There's no need for that. Keeping to yourself, I mean. You won't be in anyone's way. I'm sure we'd appreciate the input. And the company," he added, a little more quietly.

"That's sweet, but not necessary." She gently touched his shoulder.

He shifted to face her and was embarrassed to realize that his arm had brushed her breast. He backed off a little. "No, I mean it. Sometimes when you're too close to something you miss things that others can see from the outside. I...we'd be glad to have you involved. I guess we just didn't think you'd want to."

"You might find that not everyone in your group is as eager to have me around. But I accept the invitation." She turned her head back toward the ocean. After a moment she said, "I think we're getting close to Isla del Tiburon—Shark Island. No lights—it's a nature reserve."

"Where?" He leaned in to follow her pointing finger, finally making out a low shape blocking the stars a little above the horizon. The scent of her skin filled his next breath, and he felt her hair touch his cheek.

A deck chair scraped behind them. They turned around awkwardly. Someone standing just outside the door to the nearest passageway hurriedly shifted the chair to straighten it again.

"Sorry! I'm so sorry." Sakiko's voice. She quickly went inside.

"Shit!" Michael said, provoking a loud laugh from Dominique. She raised her hand to her mouth.

"Sorry. You like her. Obviously. So, go after her."

"No, we don't...we aren't. Together or anything. It's just.... Well, anyway, I should probably call it a night."

"At nine o'clock?" Her smile caught the light again, and he tried to ignore a twinge of regret. "Why don't you go up to the wheelhouse? The captain's on duty. He'd probably appreciate the company."

Michael nodded slightly and shuffled away, hands in his pockets. It was not his proudest moment. If there was some psychological reason why he'd just made a fool of himself, he quickly gave up trying to find it. He wasn't a bad teacher, but he was a lousy psychoanalyst, especially of himself. His life since finding the outpost seemed to have proven that beyond a doubt.

Captain Parzifal Fox was indeed in the wheelhouse. Michael wasn't sure what reception to expect, but the man's smile was welcoming.

"Come in, Mr. Hart. You've come at a good time. We're passing a couple of islands, so there's actually something to see on all this equipment."

"Isla del Tiburon?"

"Yes, on the starboard side. Isla Turon to port. It's much smaller." He pointed to the images on the radar screen and the GPS beside it, then gave Michael a short overview of the main instrumentation. It didn't quite compare to an airliner cockpit, but it was still impressive. Afterward, the two men lapsed into awkward silence.

"Something tells me you didn't wander up here out of a burning desire to understand our navigating gear." Fox cocked an eyebrow at him. Michael gave an abbreviated version of what had just happened on deck, drawing a knowing nod from the captain.

"We all think a woman like Dominique can have any man she wants. Men fall all over themselves for her. But she doesn't want them, the men in her circles. Oh, she gets a kick out of the game. But I think...." He dipped his head. "I think she's lonely. I'm sure she didn't mean any harm." He looked at Michael, seeking understanding.

"So, she wasn't just toying with me."

"Who can say? But maybe you should give her the benefit of the doubt."

"Is it hard for you? Someone with your experience, taking orders from somebody who just happens to have been born into money?"

A muscle in Fox's jaw twitched. "Perhaps at first," he admitted. "I'm getting used to it. Dominique is very pleasant to work for, and effective, but she faces a disadvantage for someone in her position. She has brains. She's too smart to enjoy playing airhead heiress. Unfortunately, her father—as brilliant as he is in everything related to business—can't see, or isn't willing to see that in his little girl. So, you might think this expedition is the fleeting whim of a bored jet-setter, Mr. Hart, but I can assure you it is not."

Michael raised his eyebrows. "Good to know. I guess that means she won't suddenly change her mind mid-ocean and order us back to port."

"Not unless Mr. Cartwright finds out what his daughter's really up to."

"What! Are you saying she lied to him? That he doesn't know about all this?"

Fox didn't answer.

"Holy shit!"

Michael stopped for a couple of drinks on his way back to his room. It disturbed him that he felt the need.

Lying in bed, the scene with Dominique ran through his head and he felt his body respond.

He sensed a question from Naïda.

*Why did he have an erection when Dominique had stood close to him earlier? Why now?*

His cheeks warmed. Explaining such a thing, he couldn't forget that she was female, which was ridiculous—she shared his body, for crying out loud. He did his best to think of appropriate imagery and the most basic description of human mating. Naïda countered with recalled glimpses of Michael having sex with Nicole, but this time she wanted details: how did this strange coupling relate to offspring? Was mating an irresistible urge, or done by choice when convenient? Would he mate with any human female? Did the process really combine genetic material from two individual beings?

She seemed particularly interested in that last question and asked him for more and more technical details until he finally pleaded fatigue and asked her to let him rest. It was an arduous process communicating so much without words.

Why did she have to be so fascinated with that subject, anyway? Sexuality had nothing to do with her. It was confusing enough trying to sort out his feelings for two *human* females.

# 30

*The blackness of the night ebbed away, displaced by a glowing dark-mustard-yellow light that flowed in encroaching streams, first along the floor and then the walls. God, no. An alien returning—they were always preceded by a sickly luminescence like the opposite of a shadow. Why couldn't they leave him alone?*

*The light grew, its radiance outlining a hexagonal doorway. The holding area (Prison cells? Laboratory cages?) was like a honeycomb—he could hear sounds of other humans in every direction anticipating the unwelcome attention that came with the light. But it was Michael they were coming for. He knew it.*

*As always, the door vanished without warning, and a burst of sudden brightness blinded him. He couldn't look into the light anyway—every fiber of his being rebelled against the knowledge of what resided at its center—but his attention was drawn to his own right arm. It rose from his side of its own accord, and a flap of skin folded back out of the way, revealing mechanisms beneath: organic cylinders with a sheen of plastic sliding back and forth, rippling a vile gel-like substance like a piston through oil; gleaming rods that morphed into whip-like cords thrumming with energy; dark specks that rose and submerged within the gel—tiny, yet with six recognizable appendages, frenetic with spidery movements, slicing, grafting, stitching. He was being replaced from the inside out, being turned into some kind of cybernetic organism.*

*And it hurt! God, it hurt! The aliens had the means to suppress the human body's shock response, so there was no way to escape the torment into unconsciousness. Michael had wished for that so many times. But they did not choose to suppress pain. They relished it. Thrived on it.*

*His head turned to his left. His other arm began to itch ferociously, maddeningly, as he watched the skin begin to bubble like egg on a hot pan, blisters soon bursting to release a puff of nauseating gas, followed by a slug-like form that slithered forth. First one or two, then dozens. The aliens' offspring, completing gestation within him—immediately hungry, instantly cruel. They began to feed on his flesh, softening it with an excretion like acid, then shredding it with needle-sharp mandibles. He felt every puncture.*

*The air vibrated with a hideous gurgling that he realized was coming from his own throat, or what was left of it. The cartilage of his vocal cords had been stripped away, apparently a popular adornment. He couldn't even scream.*

*Eyes closed in pain, the sickening light still penetrated the depths of his mind bringing poisonous whispers of his race's humiliation and subjugation, the despoiling of his planet, and exquisite personal suffering yet to come. All thanks to him. Michael Hart. Arch-traitor to his own kind.*

*The pressure on his throat slid downward, scoring his breastbone, pressing, then piercing his sternum. A blade of ice thrust under his ribs to puncture his beating heart, carving, carving with its rhythm. The greatest delicacy of all.*

*His mouth opened in a silent scream.*

He flailed at the bedcovers, feeling momentarily trapped by them, his eyes snapping open. There was light, white light from a few feet away...a window? The edges were backlit. A short curtain, then. His mind seemed to find that familiar, and he stared at it like a beacon, his breath rasping in and out of his chest, heart pounding. His very skin vibrated.

Slowly, slowly, he came to his senses, his body calming. There was a vibration against his fingertips. An engine—he was on a ship—the light was coming from a deck lamp somewhere outside his cabin. Yes, he was just in a cabin aboard *Argo*. There were no aliens. Except...

Naïda.

He shuddered again, but this time it was his body reacting to the aftermath of the nightmare. Yet he could feel her too, as a twitch in his skin. He still didn't know if she saw the images his mind created during dream sleep, but she certainly knew how his body reacted, would have experienced the chemical and physical responses to abject terror and intense pain. Without knowing the reason, would she also feel fear?

His rational mind knew that the aliens had not yet come to Earth, and there was no proof whatsoever that they were evil. But the part of the human psyche that held sway long before the rise of reason would not let go of his terror, and he felt nausea far beyond anything he'd experienced from the turmoil of the sea. Deep in the collective unconscious of the human race, there must be a conviction that there were entities more powerful than Man that were bound to either enslave or devour him. He could only hope to God that it wasn't based in any ancient reality.

Rolling into a sitting position on the edge of the bed, he sat hunched over until the worst of his nausea passed, then rose and pulled the curtain back to draw calmness from the ocean, now flat and welcoming. There were a few pinpoints of light very far away—possibly some coastal village of the Gulf of California. The deck lamp above prevented him from seeing any stars, or maybe the night had turned cloudy.

After ten or fifteen minutes he lay back down, but quickly knew that it was pointless to try to sleep. Instead, he put on some clothes and went to look for a drink, grateful that there was enough illumination everywhere to keep him from getting lost. He didn't need to call on any visual assistance from Naïda and didn't want to. After his dream, just thinking about her sent another shiver down his spine.

He found himself at the lounge bar and was grateful that its sliding glass doors weren't locked. The dim light was enough to reveal glasses and bottles. He grabbed something dark and half-filled a whiskey glass, took a large swallow. Another. It was bourbon—probably a top brand. Not that it mattered. He gulped some more and relished the burn of the alcohol in his throat as if it reassured him that he was awake, that he was *alive*.

God, if the aliens did come, and if.... But, no, he couldn't let himself believe that, couldn't even think it, or he would collapse into a helpless mass of remorse, of no use to anyone. He tried to remember his lifetime belief that greater intelligence guaranteed pacifism, but forebrain reasoning could not hold sway over the obscuring darkness.

When the glass was empty, he reached toward the bottle again, but stopped himself. A hangover wouldn't help anything. He considered going on deck for some air but didn't want to have to explain his sleeplessness to anyone he might meet. Returning to his cabin, he lay down uncovered and stared at the ceiling.

It took a few moments before he noticed a question mark imposed onto the blackness.

What was she asking: the reason for his fear? Whether he was OK now? Whether she could do anything to help?

As if to confirm that, he felt the skin and muscles of his neck and shoulders begin to ripple, the way she'd massaged them before, but he sent a forceful mental NO! and she stopped.

He couldn't resist a glance at the skin of his arm to see if it was covered in blisters.

When will these conflicting sensations end? Naïda can understand the concept of transition, including chemical and neural imbalances due to disparate systems adjusting to one another. That is logical. However, her bondmate and others of his species appear to be in a constant state of flux. How can her own life processes possibly adjust and remain synchronized? She begins to fear that such a balance may never come, and the neural impulses generated are horribly disruptive.

Michael's rest periods are often the worst, especially during those times when his unconscious thought processes lose touch with the real world and create unrealities of a bizarre nature. He has explained to her that such events are part of the way his brain sorts and stores remembered experiences, but the results have sometimes stretched her own data-processing functions to their limit, resulting in extreme instability of the energy field that binds her substance together. She had not known that such a thing was possible.

The episode during his most recent sleep time was the most extreme yet, incorporating images of violence that sent nearly every neurochemical response in his body into overload. So much so that she feared for his continued existence, and her own.

Most disturbing of all, she is nearly sure that the false brain patterns that created the greatest havoc somehow represented the *Creators*.

It is hurtful to question her bondmate's motives. How can such a state continue between beings that are closer to a single entity than two?

She is grateful that he has finally entered a more restful period of sleep. She has sometimes envied him this state, though certainly not at the price of the violent episodes. It is not possible for her to truly sleep. She can only experience periods of reduced activity, which she takes as an opportunity for deeper contemplation.

If she can turn her thoughts to other matters, her system should calm itself.

There is one recent development that is a welcome distraction: the discovery that her bondmate is interested in reproducing!

She is far from sure that she has understood Michael's explanation of human mating—it seems inefficient at best and outright hazardous at worst. The concept of equal quantities of genetic material provided by a mated pair of individuals is fascinating in its grotesque randomness—no deliberate design involved at all.

Even choice of mates seems to follow no rational directive, at least for the male of the species. Perhaps there are criteria she cannot sense: certain genetic predispositions revealed by chemical tags, for instance. If she is not mistaken, Michael has considered mating with both the woman named Sakiko and the woman Dominique, even though he has already mated with the other female, Nicole. It is true that Nicole showed no signs of producing offspring—perhaps that is why other potential mates are desired.

*There.* His mind is recalling images of Dominique, and once again the appendage on his lower abdomen has become erect. Naïda remembers a fluid discharge during the mating performance with Nicole—was that important? If so, how did Michael control it? There is no way for her to know.

The erection seems to make him agitated and restless in his sleep. Perhaps, when not needed, it is uncomfortable or even painful, though her own senses would detect outright pain. Still, she is not proficient at identifying sensations such as the ones Michael has called 'itch' or 'foot asleep' or 'funny bone.' Maybe it is like those. If there is pain involved, she knows how to soothe that with the manipulation of skin and muscle that her bondmate calls 'massage.'

She tries that. It doesn't work—the appendage becomes more turgid and Michael even more restless in the bed. Should she stop? Try something different?

Suddenly: *the fluid discharge!*

It is not like when his body rids itself of wastes dissolved in liquid. The volume is much smaller, and the consistency different.

She uses tendrils of her own mass to gather some of the substance and discovers that it is dense with cellular material: motile cells replete with DNA. Understanding comes with a powerful sense of gratification: the substance must be the means of the genetic transfer, *the key to the mating process.*

Yes, this is logical. Although every body cell contains DNA, most of it would be impractical to transfer, being in far less malleable forms than Naïda's own constituents. And implantation/transfer using a special appendage into a corresponding receptacle is, in some ways, parallel to how these creatures ingest nourishment. Evolved patterns that prove efficient tend to repeat and adapt.

Now she knows how to obtain samples of Michael's DNA in a readily accessible form. The knowledge excites her.

It is sometime much later in the sleep period that she becomes aware of *the Other*.

The presence is unmistakable: it is *the Controller*! Chemicals surge within her.

Where is it? How could it have survived the toxins in the lake? Unless it is an incorporeal intelligence, never permanently tied to any material manifestation.

It ceased all communication after Michael sent the signal. Could that be because it had departed the outpost, perhaps even in the signal itself?

She senses affirmation. And something else. *Praise?* She isn't entirely sure what that is, but it feels good. Comforting.

Is the Controller somewhere near? And why has it reopened communication now? Should she awaken Michael?

No, it does not want that. It will communicate with her alone. It does not want her bondmate to know.

The good feeling vanishes. She has no concept of knowledge deliberately not shared with a bondmate—the idea is repulsive.

Yet necessary, the Controller insists. It confirms what she has already begun to fear: *the interests of her bondmate may not coincide with the interests of the Creators.*

The physical portion of her existence reacts in small spasms that travel like waves through Michael's body. He nearly awakens—she tries to suppress her...*her feelings.* Regain control of herself. The Controller offers soothing frequencies of energy.

From where?

She receives an image of Michael's skull, specifically a small recess behind the mechanisms of his ear—a space well sheltered and protected by bone, yet accessible from the outside. Yes, there is a small amount of material there, not of his body, not of this world. It must have been implanted while he was interacting with the Controller at the outpost. She has not detected it because it is similar to her own molecular structure and thereby easy to overlook. Closer investigation shows thorough integration with her bondmate's neural cells, perhaps drawing energy from them but also able to interact directly with them?

The Controller does not answer this. Instead Naïda sees water, dark and deep, and a structure, in substance much like the outpost though different in design. It is not far away, in the surrounding ocean. It is from there that the Controller currently communicates, using the device in Michael's skull. However, it has chosen this time to do so not because of physical proximity but because of proximity to action that Naïda must take.

The humans have intuited correctly. The nearby structure left by the Creators is still acting to carry out their will for this planet. The humans will try to find it. It is already under threat, and additional attention could trigger serious consequences.

The Controller does not offer specific instructions. It trusts that Naïda will know what to do.

# 31

Michael would have been much happier doing the dive in the daylight. Normally, he liked night diving—dark water was like a sheltering blanket, and its restricted visibility heightened the mystery—but the Gulf of California offered a vast expanse of unknown territory. He reasoned that he and Yuri would stay very close together, and Yuri would pay out a safety line attached to the dive boat as they went. Powerful strobe lights attached to the tops of their tanks would start flashing as soon as they submerged. A diver's body might hide the light for short periods, but there was little chance the dive buddies would lose each other in the clear water.

Naïda's enhanced senses included a fish-like sensitivity to pressure differentials that detected any movement in the water for a considerable distance, which would be handy to reveal any sharks around, too. Unfortunately, both abilities would be seriously limited by the dive gear.

Her objection to that was like a nagging toothache.

Michael was more uptight about using Nitrox for the first time. He understood the science: reduce the proportion of nitrogen in the compressed air you breathed, and you reduced the absorption of nitrogen by the body, cutting the risk of decompression sickness on a deep dive. Since they expected to get down to thirty meters depth, or more, Woodward had recommended Nitrox with 32% oxygen to give them a little more bottom time. The dive master was qualified to mix the gas himself and had spent most of that day training Michael and Yuri in the use of mixed gases. Would it feel different? Would Michael be able to distinguish the symptoms of nitrogen narcosis from oxygen toxicity? The bottom line was that he'd never tried it before; and on a dive, anything unknown is a risk.

Naïda couldn't offer any reassurance. Her species seemed to handle unlimited depths in their home environment; but this wasn't home, and she was not experienced. More than that, she was bonded with a human, and she had no information about human blood chemistry at extended depths.

Michael had amused the crew by going for a dip in the choppy open ocean earlier when a perfectly good onboard pool was available. Only Sakiko had known why. Naïda had confirmed an alien presence in the area, though she could provide little more than a direction for where the strongest sense of presence could be felt. As the ship moved around a small circle, Michael had gone into the water twice more. Noting where the three directional lines intersected, he and Sakiko had pored over the best available bottom charts for the area and selected the location for the dive. It was a woefully inadequate method for something already as challenging as an underwater search, but it was the best they had. A GPS would lead the boat to the spot they had chosen.

Woodward's team had put an electric outboard onto the dive boat to keep noise down. Michael listened to the soft burble and focused on the lights he could see ahead to starboard. That was the reason they were diving at night: the lights of a ship. Some kind of vessel servicing the power station, they assumed. *Argo*'s ostensible purpose in these waters, researching acidity and algae growth, would probably satisfy general questions about their presence, but divers in the water at night would be a different story. With a high-tech complex on the ocean floor, underwater visitors would not be welcome. Fortunately, there'd been no sign of boat patrols.

"Coming up on the position now," a crew member said quietly, as the motor slowed.

Small waves slapped the side of the boat. Michael was sure the sound of his heart was louder. The night sky was bright enough to provide silhouettes but no more. He could hear Yuri putting on his mask and he put on his own, running a finger under its skirt to clear any stray hairs that might prevent a good seal. A leaky mask could be a hazardous distraction. Woodward helped by turning on the air valves of his double tanks. Michael put his regulator mouthpiece in his mouth and took a tentative breath. Was there a different taste from the new air mixture? He was probably imagining it.

A joined thumb and forefinger appeared in front of his mask, and he returned Yuri's OK sign. The other man hoisted himself onto the gunwale and rolled off backward. Michael took his place, confirmed that his flashlight was still attached to his wrist, gathered his hoses tight to his chest and held his mask firmly, then pushed backward. For a moment he feared his tanks would clang against the boat, but they didn't.

He felt the familiar sensation of breaking through the surface of the water into a cloud of fizzing bubbles.

Rolling upright, he got his bearings from the surface and the boat, reached for his flashlight, and switched it on, keeping the beam down. Yuri was a few meters to his left, grabbing the line that had been thrown to him. After about thirty seconds, he gave Michael the OK sign again and had it returned. Michael jerked his thumb downward, illuminating it with the flashlight, and with another OK signal they began their descent, using the button of the inflator hose in their left hands to bleed air from their buoyancy vests.

They'd considered dropping an anchor line first—it would have been a helpful guide—but it wasn't worth the risk of damaging an alien installation if they happened to score an unintentional bullseye. Instead, both men eased into a skydiving position and dropped as straight as they could, slowly, under complete control, their flashlights sending shafts of light downward through the darkness.

Giving a quick glance at his buddy every half-minute or so, Michael found the repetitive flare of the night strobe a comfort. He was glad of Yuri's obvious skill in the water, and equally grateful that he didn't embarrass himself with clumsy buoyancy adjustments or excess fluttering of his arms. As the increasing pressure compressed his body, he occasionally fed air back into his vest to keep from accelerating his fall. With no points of reference, the only way to judge descent speed was by keeping a close eye on the illuminated face of his dive computer.

The surface water had been very warm, but they'd worn wetsuits assuming that the temperature would decrease with depth. It had, for a while. As they approached thirty meters, Michael was sure the water had warmed again. The thermal vents? Were they that close? He and Yuri would have to be careful not to blunder into a discharge of scalding water. It would help if they could see the bottom.

Then it was there, about five meters away. He would have seen it sooner, but it was completely featureless.

Slowing to a stop a couple of meters above the silt, the divers shone their lights on themselves and exchanged OK signals again. Yuri crooked his index finger into a question mark: "Where now?" Michael waited for Naïda.

She infused his vision with a soft glow that grew redder as he turned in the right direction and blue if he got off track. It worked well. Yet he sensed something else. Uncertainty? It was no time for second thoughts.

The two men set off toward their right and began to sweep their flashlight beams over the ocean floor. Yuri still held onto the line from the boat. If they found something, he would try to attach a buoy line to mark the spot for follow-up dives.

With their safe arrival at the bottom, Michael remembered the dangers that might lie in the surrounding gloom. The hot vents, of course, but not hot enough to glow and give themselves away. Sharks, maybe. Jagged bottom features, or sunken trash. Divers always carried sharp knives, not to defend themselves from predators, but to free themselves from discarded fishing line and other tangling hazards. They were well away from shore, but you never knew.

This barren sea floor would make it easier to spot something out of the ordinary.

Like an artifact from an alien world.

He swallowed a nervous giggle, hoping the impulse was just anxiety, not nitrogen narcosis. Whatever the thing that they were searching for looked like, they'd better find it soon—even with twin tanks they couldn't spend long at thirty-five meters of depth. He swiveled his head, guided by the changing shades of red to blue. At least Naïda seemed to know where she was going.

He glanced over to check on Yuri and when he turned his head back, he flinched in surprise. A dark shape loomed ahead.

He stopped kicking and saw Yuri do the same, preparing themselves for what they might see next.

With a few more kicks the gloom revealed its secrets.

Wreckage.

It looked to be a cargo container, discarded along with assorted detritus: cables, large spools and gear-like objects, crates, and grates. The mound of trash covered a few hundred square meters altogether—a miniature dump site created by an unscrupulous shipper. Nothing alien, beyond the fact that it belonged to the world of air, not at the bottom of the sea.

Why had Naïda led them there? Was the alien outpost just beyond the wreckage? Or could it have become the victim of a tragic accident, buried beneath garbage?

Michael turned his head from side to side and shone his flashlight beyond the pile. It didn't illuminate anything, and the red glow remained in the direction of the wreckage, nowhere else. He closed in on Yuri and they checked the readings on each other's air gauges. Michael was pleased to see that his partner had used a little more air than he had, but it was a petty satisfaction. A dive lasted only as long as the smallest air supply—they should start to ascend in six minutes.

Flashing an OK sign, Michael approached the mound with great care—it was the worst kind of hazard for a diver. Lots of potential snags. Random projections that might be sharp. Spikes of crusty rust that could shred suit and skin. Some of the larger shapes—cubes and drums—perched precariously atop other debris.

They could cover more ground if they separated, but both men were too safety-conscious for that. Michael went ahead and Yuri trailed, scanning for anything the first man had missed. There was a lot to see, but nothing unearthly. As usually happened, manmade trash had become the base for a community of sea life, from anemones and sponges to some small patches of coral. Small fish darted in and out of openings. A time or two Michael was fooled by sea fans and other shapes that caught the glow of his flashlight and reminded him of the gelid walls of the Evergreen Lake outpost.

Time was almost up when he caught sight of something translucent in an opening a meter or two in diameter beneath a loosely piled stack of spool shapes. Cautiously, he swam closer, moving the beam of his light from side to side. It was a jellylike substance, spread like a sheet; but once he'd closed within a meter, he could see strings running through it that looked like coils of fine wire. Some kind of large comb jelly. Not alien. His view became blue-tinted, as Naïda confirmed his opinion.

With a cold knot of disappointment in his gut, he sculled his body around and pushed off with one leg against a nearby metal surface. It gave a little as he shoved. Then he felt a sharp tug backward and up. His tank had caught on something. His foot could still reach the steel plate, so he pushed off again and felt a wave of relief as the snag came free. He looked up at Yuri.

The man was waving frantically, beckoning him forward. In sudden fear, Michael's legs churned into action just as he felt something press down hard on the backs of his knees. It drove him downward onto the top of a rusted carton and pinned him there. His first impulse was to push up from the carton, and he felt the weight roll down his legs. His right leg came free. The left was still held near his ankle. A wave of silt swept over him, and with it a sharper pain from his leg. Something had locked onto it.

Able to bend at the knees, he lifted his body and twisted right as far as he could, shining his flashlight behind him through a murky cloud.

One of the piled cable spools had fallen and imprisoned his leg against the edge of the carton beneath. It was heavy. Yuri was already trying to shift it, but without success, and when Michael pushed up and tried to use his own leg as a lever, the pain was excruciating. He kicked with his right leg, but it was like kicking a rock. Yuri returned with a length of pipe, but there was nothing to pry against. Weightless, he had no leverage.

Michael felt panic rising within him. He was well and truly fucked. In less than half an hour, his life would end in a final release of bubbles from the bottom of the sea, and there wasn't a goddamn thing he could do about it.

A surge of comforting warmth coursed through his veins.

*In the shock of the moment, he'd forgotten about Naïda.*

Was there something she could do to help them both survive? He framed the question in his mind, but all he received in return was vague reassurance. He was not alone, but neither did she have answers. He'd never sensed such inner conflict from her. That couldn't be good.

He looked up and saw Yuri's face mask only half a meter away. Yuri held up a finger—*Wait*—then began fumbling with the clasps on his buoyancy vest. It took a moment for Michael to understand. He shoved his buddy's shoulder and urgently waved his arms. NO—he shook his head—no, Yuri could *not* leave his tanks behind for Michael. There was no way the man would be able to reach the surface more than thirty meters above on one breath of air. Even if he made it, he would be almost certain to get decompression sickness—the bends—his blood fizzing like soda pop. Or an embolism. If the air in his lungs didn't escape quickly enough as he rose, its expansion would push bubbles through the bronchial walls into his tissues and blood.

Michael angrily waved him off again. There was no point in both of them dying.

Yuri hesitated, then finally nodded. He'd already tied off the dive line to a nearby piece of angle iron to free his hands. Now he gave a last squeeze to Michael's shoulders and kicked away to begin his ascent.

Too fast. There was no question that Yuri was going to push the limits in the desperate hope of somehow bringing rescue. Nausea swelled in Michael's stomach. His own carelessness might cost both their lives. As he saw Yuri vanish into the gloom, he felt more alone than he'd ever felt before.

Except he wasn't alone.

He made his mind as receptive as he could. Images from Naïda were still chaotic, but foremost among them were flashes of his dive equipment. Yes, he understood her resentment, but...

*Of course.* If there was any chance of her breathing for both of them, she'd need full access to the water—all of the surface area she could get. His human survival gear wasn't going to cut it. He needed to become a creature of the sea.

He jammed the flashlight into a crevice in the rubble, its beam like a beacon toward the world above. The clasps on his vest were almost too much for his trembling fingers, becoming numb with a cold that would only get worse as he bared his skin, the water sucking heat from his body twenty-five times more quickly than air. No choice.

With his mouthpiece still gripped in his teeth, he slid the vest and double tanks off his arms and was able to clip them onto the same steel rod where Yuri had tied the safety line. Releasing his weight belt made him buoyant enough to float upright, although the extra pull on his trapped leg brought another jab of pain. He laid the belt within reach and began to unzip his wet suit. Peeling it from his body took an incredible effort, each second of struggle burning up valuable air, but he managed it. Hood and gloves too, stuffed hurriedly into his left sleeve. He could only pull the suit down as far as his knees—that would have to do. Would the thin fabric of his bathing suit make a difference? In the moment of crisis, he found that he needed its illusion of protection. He put the weight belt back on. Naïda's control of his flotation would be impaired by the buoyant wet suit at his feet. If by some miracle he did get free, he couldn't risk bobbing to the surface like a cork.

All that remained was to relinquish the air hose.

He couldn't do it.

His rational mind knew that the sooner he gave up breathing air at the ambient pressure, the less nitrogen his tissues would absorb, and any reduction in nitrogen could make the difference to his survival if rescue really did come. But the inner animal balked.

There was no certainty that Naïda would be able to supply his body with enough oxygen at that depth on her own. Sakiko had told him that salt water contained about twenty per cent less dissolved oxygen than fresh water. Humans couldn't drink sea water because it interfered with their blood chemistry. Something to do with osmosis, he thought. Could the lining of his lungs handle it, even with protection from an alien symbiote? He hadn't been brave enough to try it earlier, with the yacht close by. Now, at the bottom of the Gulf....

Once he let water into his lungs, it wouldn't be coming back out.

Naïda was impatient. Maybe the choice was easy for her.

Maybe if he died, she could move on to some other creature. Or even merge with the alien outpost if it really was nearby. *What if that was what she'd wanted all along?*

The thought made him feel as if his chest had been scooped empty.

No, she'd nearly died once before, in Evergreen Lake, and their joining had saved her. She wouldn't abandon him now. She needed to save them both this time.

Before he could change his mind, he pulled the mouthpiece from his lips, released the contents of his lungs in a cloud of bubbles, and breathed in the salty water of the Gulf.

# 32

When the news came from the dive boat, Sakiko stopped breathing.

The flat sounds from the radio entered her mind but wouldn't grip. She tried to respond, but the words were too thick to get past her lips. Captain Fox took the microphone from her.

Michael pinned at the bottom of the sea. Yuri needing decompression.

*How had it gone so wrong?*

Dylan Woodward was pulling at her arm, pulling her...down the hall. Yes, they had to go somewhere. Yes, they had to get dive gear. That was right.

As they reached the boat deck she had to turn aside and nearly retched. Then she was all right. She began to think clearly.

No time to find a bathing suit. She stripped to her underwear and pulled her wetsuit over it. A crew member helped her into the rest of her gear while Woodward loaded an extra buoyancy control vest and tanks into a Zodiac.

"For Yuri," he said, his cold eyes making his meaning clear.

She froze again.

"No," she said. "No. Bring another set. And the lifting gear."

"Ms. Matthews..."

"Just do it. There are...things you don't know."

Woodward let the cryptic remark pass and did as she asked. Her mind was racing as they climbed aboard the Zodiac with Woodward's dive assistant, Ken Stafford, in dive gear, and another crewman for support. She couldn't accept that Michael was dead. The alien thing inside him just might be keeping him alive. There was a chance.

A portable radio gave them more details as they charged into the night. Yuri had surfaced quickly, and the decompression chamber in Puerto Peñasco was a long way off without air transportation. His tank wasn't empty. Against advice, he'd clipped a safety line onto himself and descended to ten meters to decompress until his air situation forced him back up. Any off-gassing might help, but going back down alone was risky—there was a chance he could pass out. If his breathing bubbles slowed or stopped, the crew on the dive boat would pull him up in a hurry.

There were no bubbles to be seen from Michael. Perhaps they were just too far away.

Sakiko felt suspended, going nowhere, as if the Zodiac was in a frozen sphere of time: a sphere of black night and black water, still as a tombstone.

Then all of a sudden, they arrived. The dive boat had given up any attempt at secrecy and was showing running lights. Bright, handheld spotlights flared to life while the two boats came together and Sakiko, Woodward, and Stafford prepared to dive.

"Ken will take a set of tanks down to Yuri and stay with him," Woodward said. "I'll bring the two lift packs to free the...to free Hart."

Sakiko's eyes stung from the salt spray.

"I'll bring the other tanks," she said, in a voice that permitted no argument. Woodward merely nodded, settled the mask on his face, gave an OK sign to Stafford, and the two men rolled backward over the gunwales on opposite sides. After they'd been handed their packages, they moved away to make room for Sakiko. Within another minute she was in the water towing the extra tanks and gave Woodward the thumbs down sign to descend.

The water was black, thick enough to absorb all light except where the beams from their hands lanced through it. Sakiko realized that she had only dived at night on reefs, where there was something to see—coral reefs were still busy places in the dark hours. She'd never experienced this vast nothingness. For a moment a sense of utter insignificance and vulnerability overwhelmed her.

A flash of light in her eyes brought her back to the moment: Woodward urging her to keep moving. She tilted her body and slid down the water column, checking her computer to make sure they weren't descending too quickly. Woodward was holding on to the marker line while she and Stafford flanked him closely.

A cloud of bubbles burst into her face and Yuri appeared beneath them. She could see his relief through his mask. It was amazing that the man had any air left in his tank, considering the stress he must be under. Stafford immediately positioned himself in front of Yuri and prepared to pass him a new mouthpiece, but Sakiko didn't wait. She swam down past Woodward, who soon caught up. Yuri could now spend enough time at ten meters and then five meters to finish the most critical off-gassing. He should be all right. But there was no way Michael Hart was still breathing air.

With her whole focus on the void below her, Sakiko kept forgetting to equalize pressure until her ears protested. In that unfeeling darkness, thirty-five meters seemed a hell of a long way down. She was grateful for the marker line to follow, a lifeline that also linked her to the world above. In the glow of her flashlight, it was a white shaft that probed ahead like a protective spear.

The first she saw of the bottom was a ghostlike shape nearly endwise to her. Within seconds she recognized it as a human form, extending upward from a mass of rubble.

Naked, or nearly so.

Still.

Lifeless.

A groan of anguish tore from her chest into the implacable liquid. Another sob, and another, until her throat grew so tight, she couldn't breathe. She couldn't breathe!

Woodward drew close, gripped her arm, and shook it hard. She held onto him and forced herself to calm down. She closed her eyes and concentrated on breathing, just breathing. Finally, she braced herself and opened them again, though she carefully kept her flashlight pointed toward the rubble.

In the spill of light Michael's hair floated loose and covered most of his face. She could see his vest and tanks near the end of the marker line. No bubbles rose, the tanks empty, she assumed. He'd taken off his wet suit. Why had he done that? And there was something else wrong, but it took a moment for her to see it. His arms wrapped around himself, and were not floating free as she would have expected.

She took a deep breath and shone her flashlight on him.

His head lifted and white eyes stared into hers.

She actually heard Woodward yell as her own body jerked, her flashlight flung loose to bounce at the end of its tether. She fumbled to grasp it again and swung it around. Michael's arms waved wildly, then pointed above her.

Woodward was fleeing toward the surface!

She kicked hard and went after him, forced to drop the extra tanks. He still had the two lift packages dangling from his vest, slowing him just enough that she was able to grab a fin and then his ankle. He kicked like a rabbit in a trap, but she shone her light on herself and jerked hard on the ankle again, returning the favor he'd performed for her only moments before.

It worked. At least he stopped swimming, though a shift of the light showed his eyes impossibly wide behind his mask. Sakiko put her face close to his and let him see her calmness, her reassurance. She gave him a forceful OK sign, then repeated it. Gave a thumbs down, pointing toward Michael, then another OK, and a downward tug on his vest. To reinforce the message, she let out a blast of air from her own vest to stop them from rising.

At last, she saw him nod and he gave her an OK. His hands were trembling.

Slowly they dropped again. They must've risen nearly ten meters during the struggle, but she couldn't blame Woodward. The man must think he'd seen a zombie. Sakiko couldn't believe it herself, even though she'd hoped with all her heart that it would be true.

Michael wasn't breathing air. But he was still alive.

This time she kept her flashlight beam on him, with her other hand firmly gripping Woodward's vest. Michael's arms beckoned them closer, pointed at his trapped ankle and then the upper part of the spool. Sakiko got the message. Unclipping one of the lift packs from Woodward's vest, she swam to the open rim of the spool and attached it tightly. The commercial lift bag included its own air cylinder. She twisted the valve open and watched the bag fill. Impatient though she was, it was important to use only as much lift as necessary. If the bag got away it would shoot to the surface, gaining speed as it rose, and could injure her crewmates above.

The spool was stubborn. At least it wasn't embedded in muck, but it was still heavy. Michael tested his leg, but it wasn't free yet. Woodward had conquered his fear enough to grab the end of the spool and add some muscle. No dice. She fed more air. The bottle must be nearly empty—the bag looked the size of a Volkswagen. The bubbles stopped. Michael was still pinned.

Should she use the other bag? She checked her air gauge. It was OK, but Woodward would have sucked up a whole lot more during his panic attack. They were running out of time.

*Wait*. Something moved.

Michael was free!

He kicked away about seven meters from the wreckage and began to massage his leg. She could see the agony in his face. A broken bone, or maybe just blood returning. But he was alive, God damn it. She felt tears spring to her eyes and tried to wipe them away before remembering the face mask.

She swam to him and took his arm in a tight grip, bringing her light to bear on his face. There was no question about it. He was breathing water, his eyes and nostrils coated in the translucent sheen she remembered so vividly from weeks earlier, though it seemed more a part of his skin this time than the covering it had been before. His mouth formed into a smile, and her throat tightened again. Damn, they'd better get topside.

She gave him the OK sign and he returned it, then the thumbs up to signal an ascent. She looked around for Woodward. He'd grabbed Michael's tanks and found the spare set. He, too, gave her a thumbs up. When she turned back, Michael had tied the arms of his wet suit around his waist to keep it out of the way. With a nod he kicked upward. The others followed.

Sakiko and Woodward needed to make a safety stop for three minutes on the way up—standard procedure. Yuri and Stafford were still there. They darted away like fish from a barracuda when they saw Michael, then made their own way to the surface. When Sakiko pointed to her dive computer and her watch, Michael shook his head. No, he didn't need more decompression.

She couldn't ask him why he was so sure.

The Argo's limo tender raced into the rising sun toward Puerto Peñasco while Sakiko used the radio to call ahead for help. The effort only increased her worry. The first English-speaking emergency responder they reached told her that the nearest recompression chamber was in Phoenix, Arizona—the hyperbaric chamber in Peñasco was only for other medical treatments, not equipped to handle divers with the bends. If Michael and Yuri *were* afflicted with decompression sickness, the two-hour flight time could be critical to their recovery. Worse than that, it was inadvisable for *any* diver to fly within twenty-four hours of diving, even when no safety limits had been broken. The increased altitude of an aircraft meant lower air pressure and could produce bubbles from dissolved nitrogen in the blood just the same as a quick underwater ascent.

An ambulance met them at the pier. Michael and Yuri looked embarrassed as they climbed in. From the attendants they learned that the Peñasco Hyperbaric Clinic had received delivery of a brand-new chamber only a few months earlier. Sakiko's knees were weak as she flagged down a cab.

Both men insisted that they had no pain or other symptoms and the physician on duty found nothing obvious during his examination, but he gave them a pressure test in the chamber anyway, compressing them to the equivalent of eighteen meters of water depth for about twenty minutes. The treatment would have temporarily alleviated DCS symptoms if they'd had any. Again, they insisted they felt nothing.

A second examination failed to find any cause for concern. The doctor released them with a warning not to dive or fly for a few days, and to be alert for any changes.

Yuri wanted to find someplace that would serve him a beer for breakfast, but Sakiko wouldn't hear of it. With coffee and pastries in hand, they headed back to *Argo*. Yuri talked about everything except the dive, not caring if anyone was listening. Michael and Sakiko sat silently at opposite ends of the passenger compartment. Arms crossed, she stared unseeing at the waves. He held his hands between his knees and examined the floor.

They had given no explanation to any of the crew about the events at the bottom of the Gulf, but Sakiko noticed furtive looks at Michael as they came aboard the yacht. In subtle ways, the staff now kept their distance. Someone onboard had talked about the drowned man who wasn't dead after all. She suspected the dive assistant, Stafford, but it could have been anyone. Michael looked like a prisoner on his way to the courtroom. Worse, a sex offender passing through a gauntlet of reporters. Furious as she was, she couldn't help feeling sorry for him. There was no keeping his secret now. Gossipy crew were probably already spreading wild accounts through social media.

As if reading her thoughts, Dylan Woodward stepped to her side and said in a near whisper,

"Captain's pulled the plug on the internet and all other communication at least until after we get an explanation from your Mr. Hart."

She was about to object to the implication that Michael was in any way hers, but she found she didn't want to.

"We had a visit while you were in Peñasco," Woodward continued. "From some of the crew from that thermal power project. Wanted to know why we were nosing around. The Captain fed them a story about searching for some kind of rare porpoises called *vaquitas*. Don't know if they bought it, but they left. God knows who would have been paying a call next if we'd told them the real story."

Sakiko reflected that their captain might be a cynic, but he stood by his principles and had a good heart. They were lucky to have him.

The core team gathered twenty minutes later in Dominique's suite.

There was no need to ask anything. When the door was closed Michael looked into their faces and took a deep breath.

"Contrary to expectations, I am not dead," he said. Then toward Woodward, "I'm not even a zombie, or any other undead creature. But..." He gave a quick look at Sakiko. She kept her face blank. "...I'm not entirely human, either. Or maybe I should say, not *exclusively* human."

"What the hell is that supposed to mean!" Woodward snapped.

Michael shrugged. "I've told you about finding an alien outpost in a Canadian lake. Maybe most of you never really believed that. Fair enough. There were things I wasn't ready to tell. But now I guess the cat's out of the bag."

He cleared his throat. "The outpost held an intelligence, more like a computer than a living being. I know that because I communicated with it. It showed me images—taught me lessons about its creators and their home world. How can you still be so skeptical, Captain Fox? Do you think I have a secret oxygen tank stuffed up my ass?"

The captain had the grace to look embarrassed, but replied, "Just a long lifetime of hearing tall tales, I suppose."

"Well, you haven't heard anything like this one!

"The outpost intelligence wasn't alive, I don't think, but the installation wasn't entirely lifeless, either. There were...creatures. Beings. All but one of them were dead. The survivor would have been dead soon, too, if it hadn't found a *host* to give it shelter."

Sakiko watched horror dawn in their faces. Bodies shifted to increase their distance from Michael. Was the truth really more frightening than a dead man coming back to life? But then, her first reaction to his condition hadn't been any braver.

"Yeah," Michael continued. "The being is a *symbiote*—it shares life with a host body. It gets the nourishment and protection it needs in return for providing benefits to the host. One of those benefits is being able to breathe water. Actually, to draw oxygen from water—it turns out that, in sea water at the depth of that trash heap, it takes virtually all of the surface area of the human body to produce enough oxygen to stay alive."

"Which is why you stripped off your wetsuit." Sakiko felt stupid that she hadn't solved the puzzle by herself.

Michael nodded.

"Are you fucking telling us that you've got an *alien* inside you?"

"It is definitely not from Earth, Mr. Woodward, though it isn't one of the aliens that made the outpost or crossed space. I think she was engineered by them as a match for our ancestors who were around at the time."

"*She?*"

"We've learned a lot about each other, Yuri, and the symbiote is female—at least she identifies with the female form of our species. Don't ask me how they reproduce, if they even do."

"Like the trills in *Star Trek*."

"Pretty much. In water, she alters my skin, blends her own substance into it, kind of like Venom covering Spiderman in the comics. Except she's not evil—she doesn't try to control me."

Sakiko wasn't so sure of that, but didn't say anything.

"She does have a mind of her own, though. It's been a struggle to find ways to communicate, but we're getting better at it all the time. Before you ask, I don't think she really knows any more about the aliens' agenda than I do. She was barely formed when the aliens left Earth, a juvenile when we met. I think bonding with me brought her into the adult phase, though sometimes I wonder about that." He smiled.

"You might think this is funny, Hart, but Yuri almost *died!*"

"I know that. Believe me, I had no intention of being trapped at the bottom of the ocean. The symbiote—I call her Naïda—could detect an alien presence in the area, but we ended up at that rubble field. I don't know what went wrong. She's...she has not communicated with me since it happened."

Sakiko looked around the group. Fox was still clearly skeptical, Woodward outraged, and Yuri fascinated, apparently not holding a grudge. Sunita's disgust was obvious, but Dominique was taking it as if nothing strange had happened, almost as if she were pleased that there was more to Michael Hart than met the eye.

Suddenly Sakiko realized that conversation had stopped, and the others were looking expectantly at her.

"What about it, Ms. Matthews? You insisted on bringing extra tanks with us because you knew Hart was probably OK. You knew about this...alien thing, didn't you?"

"Look, none of this was Sakiko's fault. I had to tell her about Naïda to convince her to bring me along on the ship, but I begged her not to tell anyone else. What do you think is going to happen to me now when word gets out? I'll be a guinea pig for any laboratory who can get their hands on me."

Woodward turned to him with a stony face. "And that's worth more than the rest of our lives, is it? You don't want to undergo tests, so instead the world gets no warning that aliens have come here and can infest human beings. You *selfish bugger!*"

Michael was dumbstruck.

"Hang on, Woodward," Sakiko snapped. "It's not as simple as that. Who do you think would take control of Michael for testing? The John Hopkins Cancer Centre? Secret government weapons labs, that's who. Because they'll want to *use* alien biology to kill people."

"Or maybe kill aliens."

"God, I didn't think you Aussies were so gullible. Government shadow agencies don't share information. Not even with our allies. Michael would become the source of who-knows-what kind of hideous bioweapons, and *no one else would ever be told a thing.* There wouldn't be any *warning* to the rest of the world. Not about aliens. And not about the next great killing device we've created."

Woodward's teeth and fists were clenched, but he said no more.

Michael stared into space, his face pale. He turned to Yuri.

"I'm truly sorry you were put in danger, but that was because I was stupid enough to get trapped, not because of the symbiote. The only difference is that, without her, I would have died."

The other man nodded. "Absolutely. I'm just pissed that you didn't tell me before. I want to see this thing in action again!"

"Me too," Woodward growled. "I was there, and I still don't believe it."

Michael nodded in resignation.

"Captain, could you arrange to have the decks cleared please? I'd still like to have as few people as possible know about this. Mr. Woodward, will a few laps underneath the ship satisfy you?"

Michael stayed submerged for about ten minutes. The white of his eyes and sheen of his skin were obvious as he climbed out, but both receded within thirty seconds. Sakiko and Yuri approached him within an arm's length, but the others stood well away. Sunita looked as if she were about to run.

"It's just as well you wanted that demonstration," he said as he stood dripping at the top of the swim ladder. "Naïda isn't picking up any alien presence in the surrounding water anymore."

"What do you mean?" Sakiko asked.

"I mean there was an outpost here, even though we didn't find it. But it's gone now. At least, she can no longer detect it. I suspect it's been destroyed." He looked toward the horizon where the ship accompanying the power project was just visible through a haze.

"You think they found it and destroyed it?" Yuri asked. "Why?"

"I don't know. They may have thought it was a giant manifestation of jellyfish, or Portuguese Man o' War or something. Maybe something else happened to it. I only know that Naïda says it's gone. We blew our chance."

Woodward turned away with a snort of disgust. Yuri started to ask more questions, but Michael begged for a rest.

"You *both* need a rest," Sakiko insisted. "None of us got any sleep last night, and no matter what the doctor says, you two had a damn close call."

The others shuffled away. Sakiko stayed with Michael as he grabbed a nearby towel to dry off, and followed him to his room. He looked surprised when she shut the door with her on the inside.

"Well, was it?"

"Was it what?"

"A close call. Yuri might have forgiven you, but I'm still mad as hell. You scared the shit out of me...out of all of us. We race to the rescue, and there you are half naked on the seabed, twiddling your thumbs!"

"Is that what you think?"

Michael leaned back against the wall and looked toward the ceiling. He shuddered violently and pulled the towel tighter around him.

"I nearly died. I thought I was going to. Naïda and I have never been to that depth before. I stripped down, and she did everything she could, but it was like not being able to catch your breath.

"The saltwater burned my lungs at first. I felt like I was hyperventilating. I saw...things, sensed a presence. Hallucinations obviously. It could have been nitrogen narcosis, though Naïda was rebalancing the gases in my blood as quickly as she could—but I was afraid I was going to pass out and just drown."

He looked into her eyes. "I had to cut my oxygen use as much as I could: stay warm, calm down, keep as still as possible. I wasn't trying to scare anyone. I didn't want you to risk your lives. I just wanted to live.

"I wanted to come back to you."

# 33

The human female, Sakiko, has left in confusion. At least, that is Naïda's estimation. She believes she is getting better at reading the state of mind of humans, but her most difficult challenge is the hormonal and chemical states called *emotions*: a critical part of the species' social interaction, driving their behavior even more than rational understanding. Naïda feels ill-equipped to process them. Why would the Creators fail to give her that ability, so crucial to a successful bond with a human? Did the Creators themselves not experience emotions? She has no direct memories of them, only implanted data that does not provide an answer.

Or is it her own failing?

Though such states in humans are daunting labyrinths for her to navigate, worse is that she can no longer deny that she, herself, is experiencing emotions. That's the only interpretation she can make for all the fluctuations in her chemical status. There is nothing in the physical environment to explain those.

Sadness, fear, worry.

Such undesirable traits!

Now a victim of emotional afflictions, it follows that she must learn their names and, if possible, their meaning. As *fear* is related to the instinct of survival, it is likely that these other *feelings* serve purposes as well; but it is very difficult to see what those purposes are. For now, the best she can do is to identify their causes, in the hope that she can avoid them.

Her current emotion is causing her significant pain.

She followed the directive of the Controller to keep Michael and his companions away from the installation at the bottom of the sea. Obeying such orders is surely related to the fulfillment of her own purpose. Yet, in doing so, she nearly caused the death of her bondmate and herself! That could not have been the intent of the Controller. Nevertheless, the outcome was the worst thing she can envision: the ultimate betrayal of her bondmate.

A symbiote that causes the death of its host is a *parasite*, and a failure.

Her pain is very great.

She cannot tell Michael the reason for what happened—the Controller does not want Michael to know about its existence. More distressing than that, she is certain that knowledge of her recent actions would provoke very strong emotions in Michael, perhaps even those he experienced from betrayal by his female, Nicole, and his own brother.

He might no longer want her as a bondmate.

He might *hate* her.

His body shudders in response to her thoughts, but when he queries her about it, she does not respond.

It might make her *feel* better to think about other things.

Why is the Controller no longer communicating with her? Was the installation truly destroyed by other humans? That happened before, in the lake. Michael has told her he believes that destruction was an accident. He seems to think it might not have been intentional this time either. She is not sure. Would accidents happen so often? Or is there something else at work?

Could the Controller have wanted to leave, perhaps destroying the installation itself rather than be discovered by humans? Doing so does not make sense to her. Michael has tried to explain the concepts of *secrecy*, of *hiding*, of *deception*; but she still does not understand how there could be benefit in obscuring truth. Now it appears that the Controller also acts in such ways. She might never understand its intentions. Nor, consequently, her own purpose.

This line of thought is not making her feel better.

So, think about something else.

When she and Michael became trapped on the sea floor, the human named Yuri left them. Naïda had thought that he was reacting to fear or rising to the surface to save himself because the heavy things he carried held no more air to breathe. Yet it was not that. He had gone to get help. And doing so might have cost him his life. Then the others had also come to a place they knew might be dangerous to them, because Michael needed their help.

Their own lives did not depend on Michael's survival, nor anything he could do for *them*. None are bonded or mated to him. Yet they put their lives at risk to save his.

She searches her implanted memories over and over, but can find no reference to behavior such as this. Bondmates protect each other, of course, and mates...? She does not have much information about that, but it seems to be like bonding. Apart from that, individuals serve their own interests. They serve the imperatives of their respective species, especially in crisis. And it makes sense for individuals to serve each other's interests when it is mutually beneficial, but surely not when it involves self-destruction.

Did the other humans calculate that Michael's continued existence was so important to their self-interests or the survival of the species as to be worth putting their own lives at risk? She cannot see how.

Such behavior is beyond comprehension.

Yet somehow, thinking about it does make her feel better.

Michael stayed in his room for the rest of the day. Someone brought food to his door, knocked, and left in a hurry. He hoped the rest of the journey wasn't going to be like that, but for now he didn't mind. He was exhausted and needed time alone with his thoughts. Restless sleep eventually claimed him.

In the darkness before dawn, he found himself staring at the ceiling picking out individual sounds in the night: the soft wash of water against the hull of the boat as it pushed its way through light waves, the ting of metal on metal from a lanyard in the breeze, the rhythmic mutter of powerful engines, almost below the level of hearing. No footsteps or other indications of human activity. The yacht could be on autopilot for all he could tell. Whatever the case, he was not in control of it. Not in control of where he was going.

That feeling was becoming all too familiar. It seemed that ever since he had discovered the outpost, his life had been on a track beyond his control. Maybe that was always true to some extent—life was like that. But he'd never before had such a strong feeling that the elements he couldn't control were in the control of someone *else*. He'd never believed in a God that manipulated people's lives in intimate ways.

Now there were forces at work in his life that were not only beyond his control, but beyond his understanding—godlike in comparison. Was he a pawn, or, even less than that, irrelevant? He had been seduced and had sent the signal. Perhaps now he was no longer significant at all, but simply a minor nuisance to be rid of.

Still, it wasn't as if these forces could have caused him to get his foot trapped at the bottom of the ocean.

Unless they could. Through Naïda.

She'd kept to herself since the accident. Long enough. He sat up in the bed and tried to reach her.

Finally, he sensed that she was attentive, though still reluctant. He thought of images that would convey his question.

Had she caused him to get his foot trapped?

*No!*

The actual word burned like neon in his mind. She was learning to use words! And with intentional force. He nearly framed an apology but held back. There were more questions that needed answering first.

Why hadn't she taken him to the outpost?

She didn't answer.

Had humans destroyed the outpost, or had it destroyed itself?

She didn't know. He believed her.

What will happen if the outpost was destroyed by humans?

She was slow responding. When she did, her assessment made him gasp out loud.

He lashed out in anger. *How could she have withheld something so important from him?*

He felt her recoil but couldn't help himself. All his resentment poured out: his suspicions that she was still hiding things from him, that she might even have had a part in nearly ending his life.

The response was a pain such as he'd never felt from her before. Shocking. He hadn't known she could experience such raw suffering.

Then she was gone—he couldn't sense her presence at all.

He felt a surge of shame, but he pushed it aside. It wasn't the time to feel sorry for her. Not yet.

He lay back on the bed, fighting nausea, and took deep breaths as he tried to absorb what she'd told him.

Naïda now believed that the signal Michael had sent had indeed alerted the aliens to the humans' continued existence and progress but had also alerted other outposts around the world to prepare them for further human contact. And the *form* of that contact would determine the form of the aliens' return.

A positive signal from at least one other outpost should bring the aliens back to Earth in friendship. But the destruction of two outposts....

*That might be an act of war.*

# *PART THREE*

# 34

The next few days passed as if the ship were adrift. Michael was left alone, no matter where he went. No one told him their new course, or even if they had one. The motion of the sun overhead told him they were headed south. Presumably *Argo* was on its way out of the Gulf of California, maybe returning to San Francisco, the expedition over. Or just seeking a port of call where he could board a plane for home before he could cause more trouble.

All around him people went about their business, but magically vanished as he came near. Even Naïda had withdrawn to the point that he could barely sense her presence, and he didn't try to reach her, either. Anger welled up whenever he thought of her. There was more to his near-fatal accident than she was willing to reveal, and her betrayal was gall in his throat.

Maybe it was stupid to think their symbiosis was as benign as he'd wanted to believe. She came from a totally alien culture, led by a race of explorers with an agenda all their own. How could she not be a part of it?

What else was she hiding from him?

He had no way to know how much she perceived from his thoughts not directed at her. There was a marked difference in brain activity between simple musings and the process of communication. Her private thoughts were completely opaque to him.

As hurtful as Naïda's reticence, though in a different way, was the realization that Sakiko was avoiding him. Obviously, she felt she'd lost the trust of the others and he was to blame. She should understand that he couldn't have done things differently. The way people were treating him now was proof that his was a secret that most just couldn't handle. Or keep to themselves. Even if Fox still had internet service shut down, word would get out somehow. First on social media, then blog news sites, and soon on every news outlet on the planet. His story would go viral. He would never be left alone again.

Maybe he should enjoy isolation while it lasted.

He went for a short swim in the pool; but even though Naïda didn't react at all, he had the sensation of eyes following his every move. Of course they would. He climbed out after a couple of minutes and didn't go near the pool again.

After that, he spent most of his time standing at the railing with a drink in his hand, staring at the distant coastline. Even the alcohol did no good. Naïda kept most of it from being metabolized so he couldn't get more than a mild buzz. He thought about demanding that she stop, but he was sure she wouldn't let him get drunk. Although she had a mind of her own, most of his brain functions were now shared property.

Would Sakiko ever forgive him? That would probably depend on the long-term reaction from everyone else. He'd done what he could to deflect blame from her. But though she was a woman determined to walk her own path, she was all too sensitive to what others thought of her. She could be a real pain in the ass, but he liked being with her. Maybe more than that.

Which was a stupid train of thought to pursue because he wasn't just any other guy. Not normal—not even close. He was now part alien—how could any woman get over that? The weeks he and Sakiko had known each other didn't seem to have made any difference. And even if she did somehow make peace with the idea, the rest of his life was about to become a train wreck. He couldn't ask someone to share an ordeal like that.

The sun had just set over the dark thread of land to the west when he heard a woman's voice behind him.

"Have you had enough of being alone?"

Not Sakiko. Dominique.

She was dressed in a short, cream halter-top with a blue sarong draped from her waist, revealing just a hint of a bikini bottom where the fabric gathered through a carved wooden hoop on her left hip.

"I seem to be *persona non grata* lately," he replied.

"Don't take it personally. I've seen my share of that in Hollywood. A strange kind of fascination: they don't want to be seen with you, but don't want to let you out of their sight."

"I'm sure you didn't deserve it."

"I didn't think so at the time. Now I'm a little more understanding. Do you understand?" She stepped forward but left a meter of railing between them.

"Well, I didn't ask for this. I guess I brought it on myself, though. I found the alien outpost and just couldn't leave it alone. I didn't know what was going to happen, but I should have realized it would screw up my life. How could it not?"

"Maybe you were looking for something to screw up your life."

Michael was reminded of Carl Jung's assertion that until you brought your subconscious desires out into conscious understanding, it would rule your life and you would call it fate.

"Are we heading back to San Francisco?"

"Not right away. I'm not sure Sakiko has made up her mind where to go next, but in the meantime, there are some places on the west side of Baja that are worth a visit. Some of us want to go ashore for a few hours tomorrow at La Paz. Do a little shopping, check out the beach. Just get solid land under our feet for a while."

He wasn't sure if that was an invitation, but he let it pass, disappointed that no one had told him about the excursion. Probably because they didn't want him along.

She tugged the sarong loose from its hoop and pulled it up over her shoulders.

"Would you rather go inside?" he asked.

"No, it's beautiful out here. A little stuffy in there—nothing to do with the air conditioning."

"No offence, but of all the people on board you're one of the last I would have expected to be OK with my...condition."

Dominique laughed. "OK with it? I just don't know what to make of it. But I do know I don't like people to be judged by their appearance, or other things they can't do anything about." She gave him a smile that made him take a deeper breath. "Is it really true that you're a psychology professor? You don't have any interest in marine science?"

"I've been a scuba diver for years, but never thought of following it as a career. In fact, I didn't really choose my career—my father did. He was an accountant, but his dad was a renowned psychologist, and Dad was determined his son would be, too. I wanted to make him proud. Worked my ass off. And all the time...it wasn't really what *I* wanted at all."

"Is your father proud?"

"He died. Just before I graduated and got the job offer from the university."

"I'm sorry."

He nodded and fell silent. They both looked out over the water, and then his eyes lifted toward the stars. He swiveled around, seeking one bright red dot among the millions. When he found it, he pointed.

"My thesis subject. I wrote about the psychological implications of a manned expedition to Mars."

"How so?"

"Well, we always think of astronauts and other explorers as these alpha male types: strong-willed and self-sufficient. Fiercely determined not to let anything stand in their way. Except you can't have a ship filled with all leaders and no followers. They'd do nothing but fight amongst themselves. A trip to Mars will involve months of confinement in cramped quarters on the journey, and then the unimaginable isolation of being the only living things on a whole planet, millions of miles from home. The selection of the crew will be one of the most crucial mission elements of all. That's what I was researching."

"Sounds like casting a reality show."

Michael laughed. "On a reality show you *want* conflict. On a space mission, it's the last thing you want."

"So, what did NASA say about your research?"

"I sent it to them—with a special copy for Ryan Cassidy—but they only responded with a polite letter. Thanks for your interest ... I mean, NASA does have its own team of psychologists who do nothing but work on crew dynamics, but I was sure I had come up with some fresh and important ideas. They just didn't see it that way."

"Maybe it's not what you were meant to do. Maybe you were meant to be the one to contact aliens."

He turned sharply toward her and realized that she'd stepped closer while he was pointing out Mars. Much closer. There was enough light from the pool area to reveal the rich blue of her eyes, framed by naturally extravagant lashes. Delicate eyebrows. Prominent cheekbones. Perfect complexion.

He was shocked when their lips touched—had he kissed her, or the other way around? Hers were full and moist. He drew their warmth to him and breathed in a scent of coconut from her skin. The sarong fell away from her shoulders as she wrapped her arms around his neck. He let it drop and enjoyed the cool smoothness of her skin beneath his fingertips.

Then they were apart, and she backed off a step or two. Her eyes were large.

"I'm sorry…," he began.

"No. No, I just…" She looked at his body, then back to his face. "Was I kissing you, or was I kissing…*both* of you?"

He shook his head, confused. "There's no separating us—she's always here. But she doesn't get involved in everything I do, if that's what you mean."

She raised a hand to her lips and tried to smile, then quickly bent down to retrieve the sarong and replace it around her shoulders, shivering a little and trying to hide it.

"She's not contagious."

Dominique nodded. "Of course not. But is there any way to, you know…suppress it? Just for a little while? I'm not sure I'm ready for a threesome." She pulled the sarong tighter.

"Suppress it? No. At least, I don't think there is." Michael turned back to face the darkness. "Look. It's probably just as well. It's no one's fault." He reached for his glass on the railing, but it was empty. "I think I need another drink. Do you want anything?"

She shook her head. He gave a little nod and walked away, shielding his eyes from the glare of the lamp above the doorway.

# 35

Sakiko drew a brush through her hair, cursing under her breath. *Argo* had great showers, but too much sun, salt air, and shampoo had left her hair frizzy and easily tangled. Maybe she should tie it back in a ponytail—it would be incredibly hot in La Paz and it wasn't as if she'd see anyone she knew, apart from her team.

And Michael. If he came along. For the past couple of days, he'd been a hermit, keeping to his cabin or standing in one spot at the deck rail getting drunk. He'd probably stay aboard the ship. Probably.

She left her hair down. Damned if she was going to put on makeup, though. Just a little eyeliner. She brushed her fingers over her too-thick eyebrows. Why couldn't she have delicate eyebrows like her Japanese friends? All the plucking and shaving had never seemed worth it, but....

As she made her way toward the limo tender, she nearly ran into Michael in the hallway. He was just standing mid-corridor with his back to her. After a moment of indecision, she cleared her throat.

"Are you coming?"

"I didn't know if I was invited," he said, his face blank.

"Nobody got an engraved invitation. You seemed to want to be alone."

He opened his mouth but changed his mind. Instead, he swept his hand forward, inviting her to lead the way. When they got to the tender, she noticed some startled looks among the crew before they could hide their reactions. Michael seemed to ignore them, but he couldn't miss Sunita as she quickly shifted along the seats to be closer to Yuri. Sakiko rolled her eyes. Sunita had played hard to get with Yuri for so long; but since the accident, she kept fussing over him, making sure he wasn't over-exerting himself. Yuri was lapping it up.

Dominique looked a little uncomfortable, too, but didn't flinch when Michael and Sakiko sat close to her. Maybe it was something else.

No one but Yuri said much as they crossed the harbor. He'd been in La Paz before and wanted to show Sunita the cathedral and a museum, but she protested that shopping would be more entertaining.

"The *Plaza de la Constitucion* has some interesting little places," Dominique said. "Right near the cathedral. The locals shop along the *Calle 16 de Septiembre*, which is within walking distance; but if you're looking for keepsakes from the local artisans, the *Plaza* is probably better. Of course, we'll start out at the *Malecón*—a gorgeous beach, though the shops and restaurants are expensive."

Sunita gave Yuri a "told you so" look and patted his leg.

Sakiko had only been to eastern Mexico, diving south of Cancun and in Cozumel. La Paz offered slightly wider roads than she expected, but the same quaint flat buildings in pastel colors, though it disgusted her to see many whitewashed walls spoiled by graffiti tags.

Palm trees were everywhere near the beach, but inland along the *Calle 5 de Mayo* the streets were flanked with much bushier varieties. The beachside area of the *Malecón* was especially beautiful, with immaculately cobbled roadways and lush vegetation, and Dominique led them to a few shops there to get an idea of prices before moving on to other shopping locales.

Sakiko found herself walking with Michael a few meters behind the others, both spending more time admiring the view of the beach and the sparkling water than the fancy storefronts. At a jewelry store, they elected to stay outside, though she did spare a few glances at the selection of beautiful gold-coin pendants in the window, and especially a large disc pendant with an Incan motif in antique silver on a chunky chain. Then she thought about how it would look like cheap costume jewelry compared to pieces Dominique wore every day, and she turned away with a sigh.

While they waited, a group of seven- and eight-year-old children surrounded them. With hands outstretched, the kids chattered at them in local Spanish, far too quickly for Sakiko or Michael to recognize any words. The children were all fairly well-dressed, obviously not poor—but tourists were an easy mark. It was probably a game to them.

Sakiko hadn't brought a lot of Mexican currency, but she dug into her purse and placed a coin in each outstretched hand. The bright eyes and smiles they returned were worth more to her than trinkets she would never wear again.

"If you do that, you'll be swarmed everywhere you go." Sunita had just come out of the store, followed by Yuri and Dominique.

"I know."

"She's a sucker for kids." Yuri said.

Dominique spoke some words in Spanish and the children cheerfully resumed a game that involved kicking a ball. The adults moved on, with Sakiko and Michael again falling behind.

"Is that true? You like kids?"

"Of course. Who doesn't like kids?"

"My ex-girlfriend for one. She totally focused on her career. Would never have considered having a family."

"Something tells me you didn't agree with her."

"Let's just say I didn't bring it up again after the first time. But I would love to have kids, yeah. I always assumed I'd be a dad someday. And I'd do things a whole lot differently from the way my parents raised me."

His last words were so emphatic that Sakiko laughed. It felt good to laugh again.

"Everybody thinks that. And then everybody makes the same mistakes. That's part of the human condition."

"You've never had kids, though."

"No. I get such a big kick out of my nieces and nephews, I always figured I'd have kids myself, but that's obviously not going to happen. Doug—that's my guy friend—he's a magician. *Definitely* not interested in kids—probably did too many birthday parties when he was working his way up. Anyway, he's always traveling—we never see each other. Come to think of it, I don't even know where he is right now."

Her voice had grown softer and Michael didn't say anything right away. Then he stepped closer and nudged her shoulder with his own.

"It's not like you're too old to have kids. Lots of people wait. I just would have figured you were more of a career woman too."

"So, women shouldn't be able to have both?" she said with an edge to her voice, then she shook her head. "Sorry. That was a pissy thing to say. It's just not happening—let's leave it at that."

They quickened their pace to catch up with their friends and followed them into a boutique.

The rest of the excursion had passed far too slowly for Sakiko, shops and stores all blurring together in her mind. She hadn't bought anything at all, though she had given most of her cash away to other children who ambushed them while Michael had taken pictures of her with her phone.

That night she sat on her bed and looked at the pictures. Her favorite was a pose with a young mother proudly showing off her new baby girl. The woman wasn't pretty, but her smile of pride and love lit the screen. Sakiko felt a twinge in her chest as she zoomed in on the baby's face.

It wasn't fair that she could still feel so much pain from something that had happened fifteen years ago.

It had felt like a thoroughly adult decision at the time, but in retrospect she was so young then, and so frightened. She wasn't ready to be a mother—she was just about to start a career. Brent would have been a lousy father. They weren't even in love, just careless. The worst part was that her mother had found out, thanks to an unguarded moment on Facebook, and had barely spoken to her since. Her mother so badly wanted to be a grandmother.

Strangely, it had probably been the aftermath of the abortion that had set Sakiko on her career path. In her post-grad work, she'd already been narrowing in on the effects of ocean chemistry on sea life, but it took on a broader scope: she wanted to do something to protect the planet and preserve it for children, even if none of them were her own.

She swiped through more pictures and came upon one of Doug.

He was in Europe, somewhere, on a tour—a big career step for him—but neither of them spent much time on social media, and they hadn't even exchanged email for a week. No, more like two. He was probably in Germany by now.

A sudden thought struck her, and she called up his last email. He was in France then. It mentioned partying, a sexy tour guide he'd met, the wine and the food. He hadn't asked about her at all.

He hadn't even said he loved her.

She went back through his other messages. They'd always ended with "I love you" or some variation. Six weeks earlier there were a couple that said, "Love, Doug." After that, just his name.

She slowly put the phone down on the bed and stared at the wall.

*What do you know?* she thought. *The magician performs a vanishing act of his own.*

They hadn't even been together for very long. Less than a year.

But when she lay down to sleep, the pillow was wet against her cheek.

# 36

At first Michael was glad that something had awakened him from the dream because he was able to remember it, and it was a good one. As he rolled over, his leg felt a cold touch. He checked the front of his shorts.

Damn. His second *wet dream* in a week?

He flung back the sheet and turned on the light. Fortunately, he'd only been covered by the single sheet, and it wasn't noticeably damp. The housekeeping staff probably saw that kind of thing all the time, but he would have been mortified to have them find it. He rinsed out his shorts in the bathroom sink, dropped them in the laundry hamper and put on a dry pair.

Maybe he'd just gone without sex for too long.

After spending most of the day together, it wasn't a surprise that he'd dreamt about Sakiko. They were scuba diving along a pristine reef, but he'd spent as much time admiring her in the short wetsuit as looking at the flamboyant coral. Then she wasn't wearing a wet suit, but a bikini. They were snorkeling, occasionally surfacing to flirt with each other, inventing reasons to touch. Time slowed for the delicious moments of slippery skin on skin. Sometimes they were so close he could nearly feel the coolness of her lips.

He ducked under the water and gazed at her body, more defined than covered by the triangles of fabric.

Then his head was in the open air again and she was slowly rising from the waves like a nymph, water sheeting from her shining skin, naked and perfect.

The image was still intense in his mind, and he tried to distinguish every detail so he could remember it for a long, long time.

Sakiko, Yuri, and Sunita were just finishing breakfast when he arrived. He gave Sakiko a quick smile, afraid that a memory of the dream was showing on his face. Sunita excused herself to go on deck.

Yuri gave an appreciative nod at Michael's heaping plate.

"I have to admit, I had wondered how you could scarf down so much food and never show it. I guess now we know."

"Yeah, it's a blessing and a curse. Sometimes I don't want to eat so much, but my metabolism is crazy fast. Even if I don't feel like dessert, my arm reaches for it anyway."

"Are you serious?" Sakiko's eyes opened wide.

He realized his mistake and quickly turned back to point at Yuri's tablet lying on the table. "Is internet service back on?"

"Not for everyone, but the captain trusts some of us not to spill the beans, so we've got special passwords. I almost wish I didn't."

"What do you mean?"

Yuri slid the tablet toward Michael. "Your friend Ryan Cassidy has been busy. We hoped he'd be satisfied with hearsay, and the story would just go away? Well, he wasn't, and it hasn't."

Michael read with growing alarm. Cassidy had changed his tune after hiring divers in special suits to investigate Evergreen Lake. They'd found some residue of an 'unknown substance.' It was hard to believe they'd been so persistent. Evergreen was a small lake, but a whole lot of territory for divers to cover, even if they'd somehow managed to track down Phil Rodriguez to narrow the search zone for them.

"Nobody's going to pay much attention to that," Michael said. "Chemical waste had just been poured into the lake—of course they'd find some weird stuff."

"It gets worse."

He read on. A woman had witnessed a car crash and the driver's amazing rescue from a river by a stranger. She'd identified a picture of Michael Hart.

"Holy shit."

"So that was you?" Sakiko asked.

Michael shrugged. "It seemed like the right thing to do at the time."

"Aquaman." Yuri laughed. "Fantastic."

"It's not fantastic. I told Cassidy about the outpost myself—I wanted to help prepare the world for the knowledge that there's more advanced life out there. But I didn't tell him anything about Naïda. Now he knows that something happened to me. He'll try to track me down. Is there any way he can? I didn't tell anyone at the university where I was going."

"You weren't included on the crew list I gave to my funders," Sakiko said. "Sounds like Cassidy tried to talk to your girlfriend, but she didn't cooperate."

"No, the mayor wouldn't acknowledge anything like this. She loves having staff who can say she's not available for comment." He looked at Yuri. "This stuff is just on Cassidy's personal blog, right?"

"It's been getting plenty of shares on social media—the guy has a lot of followers. The only mainstream media that have picked it up were two small newspapers in Sudbury, I think. Big news that a former astronaut was in town, especially if they can make him look like a flake."

"I wish he were just a flake." Michael pushed his plate aside, with some scrambled eggs still on it. "The guy used to be my hero."

Sakiko stood and gave a tug on her blouse.

"I'll try to convince the captain to keep the internet restricted for a while longer. That would probably be best for all of us. We're lucky no one recognized Dominique when we were in La Paz." She put her sunglasses on and left.

Michael sighed, lifted his coffee cup, noticed it was empty, and put it back down.

"Don't worry, she likes you," Yuri said with a smile.

"It feels like all I do is bring her trouble."

"Ryan Cassidy isn't the only trouble on her mind. There are questions being asked about our funding."

"Questions?"

Yuri hesitated, then reached for the tablet and shut it off. "That's not my story to tell. Sorry."

After a moment of awkward silence, Michael placed his hands on the table and stood up.

"There must be someplace on this boat that a guy can get a drink at nine o'clock in the morning"

The rift with her bondmate has been the worst experience of Naïda's life. It still isn't clear to her how she came to do wrong, but there must be some way to make things right again. So much depends on her next actions.

She has a plan, but is she truly ready for such a step?

She knows the technical process of reproduction, though she isn't sure if the knowledge is innate in her species or was planted by the Controller.

However, human reproduction is vastly different. Could there be a way to reconcile the two extremes?

This is the second time that Michael has expressed a desire to have offspring. He engaged in reproductive activity with the female human called Nicole but explained to Naïda that it was for a recreational purpose and would not generate spawn. There is no equivalent to that in her memories, so she concluded that he had not reached the life stage appropriate for reproduction and was only practicing.

It seems that was incorrect.

She has now seen immature humans firsthand. *Children.* They were at many dissimilar stages of growth, yet their female parents were *still involved in their care and development.* That was very difficult to accept, a concept so utterly alien. But what was immediately clear was that these parent humans were physically less mature than Michael. She is sure that some had barely reached the human adult stage themselves. So, she reasoned that Michael must be capable of reproducing, but his society did not yet require it of him.

Another incorrect assumption.

Her understanding of human aural communication is far from perfect, but the female named Sakiko expressed a readiness for parenthood very overtly through her behavior. And not simply the production of progeny, but the continued *nurturing* of the offspring, as if both are *elective behaviors* and not species imperatives.

Naïda does not know why Sakiko has not produced children when she is so strongly motivated to do so. Further thought has failed to produce an answer. But the thorough analysis of recent events, mental images, and human speech has resulted in a compelling conclusion.

Michael wants children.

Naïda has already felt powerful curiosity about the immature forms of the human species. Could it be that her own interests and those of her bondmate are meant to coincide in this way? Could that be the intent of the Creators? If so, why has the Controller not made it evident to her? Again, she is frustrated that she has not been given a much greater knowledge of human ways, and especially of her role in the joining.

Some things are clear. She is bonded—it is her duty to act in the best interests of her bondmate, and even fulfill his desires when possible. Michael wants offspring. Naïda can produce offspring. Humans expect the DNA of the male to come from an individual that is almost as close as a bondmate, and not simply drawn from a common genetic pool. Naïda has plenty of formative substance from Michael, thanks to her ministrations during the night. It was convenient that his sexual organs had readied themselves on their own. With additional stimulation they provided all the genetic material she requires.

Will this act please Michael *and* the Creators? She wishes she could be certain, but she is learning that existence on this planet rarely offers complete certainty.

There is a decision to be made. Delay will not help.

She begins the process.

In the mixing of her DNA with that of her bondmate she finds a satisfaction greater than she has ever experienced. *Pleasure*. Extravagant pleasure. So much so that she produces far more material than necessary for a single issue.

Some hours later, the budding starts. She is able to direct its location and chooses sites around Michael's body that will offer the greatest protection, yet also the least visibility. She is not entirely sure what motivates her to make that choice, but there is ample space in the areas of his groin and upper thighs, and behind his ears. The buds are very small and match the color of his skin. Some she plants between his shoulder blades, where he does not see and cannot reach, though she does not think the budding process will trigger an itch.

Finally, she feels an even more powerful swell of emotion. She cannot define it, cannot understand it: a form of pleasure that is almost painful. Yet, through it she knows that she is done.

The buds will stay dormant until encouraged to mature at an appropriate time. She does not know when that time might come and is not sure how or when she should inform Michael about their progeny.

*Their children.*

For now, it will remain her *secret.*

# 37

Michael didn't hear the voices until he rounded the corner. Sakiko had her back to him and Sunita was glaring out to sea, but he quickly stepped back so they wouldn't see him. It was probably the first time he'd heard Sakiko angry at anyone but him.

Sakiko kept her voice down, and the wind snatched most of the words away, but he heard "lazy" "careless" "disappointed," along with Yuri's name a few times. He turned around quietly and found another way topside.

As he came out on deck, he nearly ran into Yuri.

"Hey, Aquaman. Out of your cabin for business or recreation?"

"I was thinking a beer or two at our favorite hangout. You?"

"The aft deck? Absolutely, my friend. It's always important to contemplate where we've been."

Drinks in hand, they sauntered into the sunshine. The pool beside them was bright and clear, but Michael found the ocean waters more inviting. They sat on the steps aft of the pool and looked out over the ship's wake.

"Were you looking for Sakiko?" Yuri asked.

"No, I just saw her. It sounded like she was giving Sunita a chewing out. Does that happen often?"

"This might be the first time. It's not so easy to reprimand the boss's niece. Yeah, Sunita's uncle, a guy named Edward Ryder, is in charge of our department. She's fully qualified for the job—Sakiko didn't even know the connection when she hired her—but Sunita does take advantage. Maybe she's been slacking off with the water sampling or checking over the equipment." A strange look came to his face. "Either that or Sakiko suspects she's discovered something and passed it on to her uncle."

"About me, you mean?"

"That's possible, too, but I was thinking of something else." He looked at Michael, hesitated, then downed the rest of his beer. "OK, look. The thing is, the funding for this trip didn't exactly get approved in the official manner."

"I don't understand."

"Sakiko's application was brilliant, but somebody on the judging panel didn't agree. So, a little...creative paperwork was required."

Michael's face tightened.

"Are you saying she fudged the funding approval?"

"You didn't hear me say anything of the kind because you're my friend and her friend. I'm just hoping Sunita didn't hear anything like that either."

"Holy shit."

Yuri nodded.

"Time for another beer?"

"You bet."

As Michael stood, he saw Captain Fox coming up to them. Even in the heat of Baja, California, the man was dressed in full whites and looked as crisp as an Arctic nautical chart.

"Gentlemen. I'm a little surprised to find you without feminine company."

"Not by choice, Captain. The ladies appear to be otherwise occupied."

"Not for long, Mr. Hutchings. Ms. Swan has asked that I stop the ship for a few hours. I believe she has an ocean swim in mind, so I expect her on deck soon. Mr. Hart, my crew tells me you seem to have captured the attention of *two* women. An enviable circumstance, to be sure."

"I guess there really are eyes everywhere," Michael said.

"Don't complain. Once you reach my age, young women think of you as a *father figure*, perhaps a substitute for the father they've each disappointed. A humbling state of affairs, but better than not being thought of at all, I suppose. Enjoy the attention while you can."

"Dominique can't be a disappointment to her father if he's willing to pay for an operation like this, even provide one of his yachts." Yuri gave a wave of his hand.

Fox's wry smile brought his beard up into the breeze, where it looked positively playful for a second or two.

"What a pleasant thought. But not in keeping with the man I know. He does love his daughter, but that doesn't extend to the indulgence of her every whim."

"Then how is it that you're aboard?" Yuri asked. "I'd heard you'd retired after being the favorite captain of Cartwright's navy. He didn't ask you to grant him this favor?"

"I'm sure he still thinks I'm in the Turks and Caicos, where he last saw me."

Michael and Yuri exchanged looks, but further questions remained unasked as Dominique came on deck. As they watched her approach, Yuri thoughtfully whispered, "Close your mouth, Michael."

She was stunning in a cream-colored swimsuit with scarlet accents. It was one-piece, but with cut-outs in the middle—daring, yet entirely elegant, and it clung to her tenaciously. The sway of her hips bore no trace of conscious artifice.

"Captain, this is as good a place as any," she said.

There was only a bare hint of land to the north. Cabo San Lucas, Michael thought, on the southernmost tip of Baja, California. Obviously, Dominique wasn't interested in exploring its beaches with their thousands of tourists. As the wake of the ship died away, crewmen prepared boarding ladders to hang over the stern.

"Coming swimming?" she asked him, her gaze holding his for just a little longer than necessary.

"Sure." He already wore a pair of blue shorts that doubled as a swimsuit and moved to strip off his light gray T-shirt. Somehow, while sliding over his head, it managed to catch on his dive watch. Dominique laughed and stepped close to help him.

As Michael freed himself of the shirt, he saw Sakiko at the top of the steps. Her eyes shifted from him to Dominique then down at her own bikini top. The turquoise bikini was simple, with a touch of webbing at the cleavage and the high-cut hips and fit her perfectly. After her hand had lingered over the webbing for a moment, her shoulders straightened, and she came down the steps to the ladder.

Michael watched her until she was below deck level, then found Dominique scrutinizing him with a smile on her face.

"Thanks," he said.

"You're welcome." She turned and dived into the water with the form of an Olympian.

"What a perfect ass," Yuri muttered.

"I didn't mean to do it."

"No, I mean *hers*."

Michael gave an embarrassed laugh and tied his t-shirt to the nearest railing. As he did so, he saw Sunita coming toward them in a black bikini and dark sunglasses, looking like a beachwear model. He took a deep breath, bemused to find himself in the company of three such striking and formidable women. To clear his mind, he turned and plunged into the sea.

The water was magnificent, cool enough to be refreshing on such a hot day, and calm as a pond. Michael felt Naïda in his skin, but she didn't cover his head. He didn't need protection. She simply wanted to revel in the touch of the ocean. Even that much of her presence enabled him to glide through the sea in a way he could never do on his own. It was a shame she couldn't provide him with such agility out of the water.

Dominique was both agile and graceful as she took a second dive from the deck.

Sakiko was treading water nearby, but he didn't look to see if she was watching him. He dived down and stayed under, feeling Naïda rise to the surface of his face. He was grudgingly pleased that she understood his different intentions and responded to them. Although he didn't choose to breathe water, she used the rest of his body to draw oxygen, enabling him to hold his breath much longer than normal. His eyes recalibrated, too, and he thoroughly appreciated a crystal-clear view of Dominique and Sakiko as they swam overhead.

Was there really a choice to be made, as Fox had said?

He sensed a sweet, intelligent personality beneath Dominique's rich girl exterior. But he couldn't believe she was seriously interested in him. A little shipboard romance was probably the extent of her plans, if she had any.

Sakiko was another story. He'd begun to fall for her the first time they met, admiring her unassuming expertise and her obvious passion for the undersea world. He was seriously infatuated, at the very least.

Yet, in truth, there wasn't any choice to be made at all, because neither woman could stand the thought of Naïda being a part of him. End of story.

He burst through the surface and gulped a lungful of sea air. Yuri and Sunita were flirting on the aft deck, Dominique climbing the ladder. He sculled his hands, pivoting to look for Sakiko, when he heard her voice.

"Look! Dolphins!"

Within moments the sleek creatures were everywhere, frolicking and chattering. Most of them swam in a wide circle around Michael and Sakiko, some diving under the ship to appear on the other side. He kicked harder to raise himself in the water and see them better. Sakiko laughed with delight as one came close enough for her to touch.

Michael felt the pressure wave as a dolphin streaked past him a meter away, then dived into a somersault and came back, passing even closer. It gave a long stream of clicking sounds, and suddenly another dolphin slid by within arm's reach. And another. Their splashing made it hard for him to catch a dry breath, so he submerged and let Naïda adjust. He took in a breath of water and dropped three or four meters, astonished by the supple gray forms that flashed by him, their speed and their size. Each time one passed it seemed to come closer, until each dolphin was rubbing against his skin on its way by.

*Too close!*

They seemed to back off a little.

Maybe they thought he was drowning—he'd heard tales of dolphins helping struggling swimmers. Except their attentions had begun even before he'd gone under.

Could it be Naïda? Could they somehow sense her presence?

His vision tinted briefly to yellow, and the word *YES* formed in his mind.

On the spur of the moment, he reached out for a nearby dolphin. It slowed, giving him time to wrap his arms around it, then surged ahead with him trailing along its side. The pressure of the water flow threatened to take his shorts with it, but as Naïda made another adjustment to his eyes, he was able to keep them fully open. He cautiously shifted his hold to make sure he wasn't impeding the dolphin's pectoral flippers, his arm sliding until stopped by the dorsal fin.

Expecting the dolphin to push him to the surface for a breath, he was surprised when it dived deeper, arrowing toward the bottom. After a short sprint, it gave a snap of its flukes and flipped over, aiming for the surface again. Another burst of speed, like a submarine missile launched at the rippling sun, then the two of them—dolphin and man—breached the surface with a plume of spray. Flinching from the brightness, Michael squeezed hard on the rubbery body in abject fear as they arced backward and crashed into the sea. Yet the impact was no worse than when he did a backward roll entry from a boat in scuba gear. He couldn't laugh with his lungs full of water, but the next time the dolphin breached, he forced his eyes to stay open and the exhilaration of the moment was like a fire in his chest. Even bearing the weight of a man, the dolphin must have reached a couple of meters above the surface.

After the second breach, it was content to race in circles while its companions joined in the fun. Michael saw dancing columns of bubbles appear all around them as leaping dolphins re-entered the water and charged downward to do it again.

He didn't know how they'd so quickly sensed that he and Naïda were different. A normal human being might be injured by a ride like that with such rapid pressure changes.

Michael's dolphin slowed until it was barely moving through the water and began a series of muted clicks.

There was no pattern he could discern—that was far too much to expect—but he was content to feel a powerful companionability, a shared recognition of intelligence.

After five minutes or more, it rose to the surface. Michael took his cue and let go, coughing up a heavy spray of water and becoming an air-breather once more. The dolphin chattered and dived away. Its companions followed it, although they periodically arched to the surface. It was obvious that they weren't in any hurry to leave *Argo*.

Michael was watching them, nearly breathless with the wonder of it, when other images began to come to his mind. Ocean depths. Rocks rising into blue sky. *Gelid structures on the sea floor*.

He was barely conscious of his actions as he climbed the ladder onto the ship. His friends crowded around, and at first he couldn't distinguish their individual sentences.

"That was incredible. How did you...?"

"Lucky bastard."

"What was that all about?"

He held up his hands.

"It was Naïda," he said. "The dolphins recognized her...alienness."

He gave his head a shake and smiled.

"They've encountered it before."

# 38

"That's the one."

Michael leaned toward the laptop screen as Sakiko enlarged the image.

"Rocas Alijos" Dominique said from behind Sakiko's shoulder. "Is that really likely? I mean, the Alijos Rocks are remote, but a lot of scuba charters stop there. What are the odds that there could be an alien installation without anyone finding it?"

Michael shrugged. "The images Naïda got from the dolphin are pretty vague, especially above the surface, but none of those other pictures are similar at all. This one is a match. It's either there or someplace that looks the same. How far away is this place?"

"A few days cruising," Captain Fox answered.

Sakiko stepped back and crossed her arms. "But even if this image did come from the dolphin and not just your own memory, how do we know it isn't because they think it's a great fishing ground? The Pacific Current begins turning westward in that area—it's probably rich with sea life."

"Wouldn't a place like that be a good choice to spread chemical or biological agents into the broader ocean?" Yuri asked her.

She replied with a frown. A little more support from Yuri would've been nice.

"So would a hundred other places," she said. "Not to mention that we don't know how the ocean currents ran ten thousand years ago. And these rocks are volcanic peaks."

"The image of the alien artifact is similar to the one I discovered, and the one I expected in the Gulf, but not exactly the same," Michael offered. "It's spread out over a larger area and has some prominent spikes or pillars that the others didn't have. I can't explain where a picture like that would come from if the dolphins hadn't actually seen it."

"Your imagination?" Woodward leaned against the wall of the room. No one answered him, but the looks on the faces of Sunita and Parzifal Fox were reply enough.

Dominique reached out a hand to Michael's shoulder and, a moment later, did the same to Sakiko.

"Well, the dolphins haven't left us, and Rocas Alijos is on our way back north. Why don't we sail in that direction and see what the dolphins do? They might lead us, or leave us, or tell us we're heading the wrong way." She smiled. When no one said anything more, she looked at the captain, who merely nodded and left the room. The others soon followed leaving Michael and Sakiko behind.

Michael stood staring at the laptop for another minute before lifting his head toward her. "I guess we'll find out when we get there." He stopped in the doorway. "I think I'll take a shower."

It was in her mind to offer to share his shower, but she knew she couldn't say it. She pulled her robe tighter and raised a hand in a half-hearted wave. He turned away and left with lips pressed together.

When he was gone, she let the robe fall loose again and shook her head. He might have been flirting and she'd shut him down as if she were a spinster schoolmarm. Couldn't she just think of him as any other man?

Except he wasn't. He had an *alien* inside him. And worse, this was an alien with a mind of its own. Who really knew which mind had control?

For some reason, she thought of her parents. She loved her father and had spent years trying to earn his respect but hadn't made a similar effort to fulfill her mother's desires for her. She hadn't even known what those desires were. Her mother had been a 'free spirit' in those days. Yet, ten years into her second marriage, she'd seemed to have little spirit of her own left at all. She'd become totally absorbed in her second husband's world.

The idea that marriage partners could be like two halves of one soul appealed to a younger Sakiko's notions of romance, but the reality she'd seen was no fairy tale. If the joining of souls had to mean the smothering of one by the other, it was not for her.

And human relationships were a joining by ritual and choice only. How much more must it be true of an actual joining like that of Michael and the alien?

Surely one of the personalities in that duo would eventually dominate. The alien came from an advanced civilization. Maybe it was bio-engineered to be of service to its host, as Michael believed; but it was dangerous to assume that. There were far too many unknowns. And the greatest unknown was the true intentions of the aliens Michael thought of as the explorers. How often in human history had the term 'explorer' really meant 'conqueror'?

No, she needed to maintain her self-control and push any romantic feelings for Michael aside.

She nearly laughed as she thought about the number of times she'd complained that relationships were too complicated.

The whoop of a siren outside her window nearly made her wet the bed.

She rolled to her feet and stumbled through the dark to the window just as a beam of light passed over it, painting the far wall with sweeping shadows from the curtain's pattern. She pulled the cloth aside but all that could be seen was a pivoting spotlight floating in the air perhaps a hundred meters away. The siren had only lasted a second or two, but now she could hear a voice, magnified electronically. A bullhorn?

She threw on her beach pants and robe as quickly as she could and padded into the hallway. There was a commotion near the elevator: Woodward talking to Michael and Yuri under a light dimmed for the night hours. Woodward turned to her.

"We're being boarded by a coastal patrol of the Mexican Navy. No idea why."

They felt the subtle vibration of the engines stop and the ship lose way.

"I think we can make some good guesses." Yuri turned to Michael. "You might need to hide."

"You think they're after me?"

"Would the authorities stop one of Blake Cartwright's yachts for a random drug search? My bet is that Ryan Cassidy has something to do with it."

"Cassidy wouldn't have any influence with the Mexican Navy," Sakiko said.

They didn't have a chance to argue it further. The elevator stopped at their deck. Dominique stuck her head out.

"It *is* the Navy," she said, "but there's an American aboard. Military type, by his bearing."

"Where am I supposed to hide?"

"There are very few places they won't look, and we have no time to get you to one. I'd suggest going overboard." Even now she could smile as if a clever joke was being played on them.

"Right."

Before he could move, Yuri said, "Wait," and dashed into his cabin, returning with a couple of bed sheets.

"I don't..."

"Do you want to *jump* from the foredeck? There's no time for you to get aft without being seen."

Michael nodded and they ran toward the far side of the ship from the Mexican vessel. Sakiko and Woodward followed Dominique's lead as she slowly walked to the outer deck to greet their visitors. Sakiko was glad of her robe, but she saw Dominique deliberately loosen hers.

By then, lights flooded the aft deck: *Argo*'s own and a couple of spotlights from the cutter floating alongside. If they'd been welcoming invited guests, the captain would likely have extended the "sea terrace" off the main lobby on the starboard side. Instead, the Mexican boarding party arrived in two small boats that pulled up to the stern. The boats disembarked more than a dozen men, all in uniform except one, the American. A darker man climbed aboard with easy confidence and doffed his cap as Parzifal Fox stepped forward.

"This is most irregular and inconvenient, *Capitán*," Fox said. "I hope you have a very good reason."

"My apologies, Captain," the man said in perfect English. "We have reliable reports that a fugitive has hidden himself aboard your vessel."

"A criminal—is that what you mean? You can't be serious, sir. *Argo* is not so large that someone could stow away without being discovered. And the crew and passengers all know each other." That wasn't true but sounded believable.

"The fugitive may have come aboard very recently. I am certain you have no reason not to cooperate with the Mexican government, and I assure you that we will finish our task and be gone within a very short time." The Mexican officer knew the yacht's captain had no choice but to comply.

Dominique stepped forward and a flash of white showed through the part in her green robe.

"I hope you're a man of your word, Captain," she said. "Some of us need our beauty sleep." The Mexican laughed and his men joined in. "Follow me and I'll show you around our humble home."

Fox gave a sharp nod, stepped aside, and gave a hand sign to the first mate, who hurried off, presumably to inform the crew and housekeeping staff. The Navy contingent jostled to be close behind Dominique and their captain.

Sakiko was impressed with the Mexican captain's pleasant composure. He looked very young compared to Fox. Handsome, even, with hair as black as the night and a clean-shaven face.

She shifted her gaze to the American and found that he was giving her his full attention. *Not* looking at Dominique. That had to mean something. She returned his frank stare, but it took all her effort.

*Cassidy*—she was instantly certain of it, though he didn't look at all the way she'd expected. It was in the crystals of ice that crawled up her spine, nerve ends signaling that she faced an adversary of unknown menace. He was completely unremarkable, yet it was as if at any moment his hands might slip from his pockets clutching deadly snakes. Or hand grenades. Or a warrant for her arrest.

She's been wrong picturing Cassidy as a hulking Marine with a jaw of stone. Cockpits of fighter jets and spacecraft weren't welcoming to tall builds. But something about his smaller-than-average size made her fear that if she glanced away for an instant, he would vanish to reappear behind her. His hair and thin brows were of such light color that they failed to give his face any expression. His eyes seemed to slide away from her gaze yet penetrate her at will.

Someone had to keep a watch on this man. Though she fought the urge to flee, her face turned away of its own will, her ears intensely attuned for any hint of movement.

But he said nothing and remained utterly still.

It was likely that he'd been warned to stay out of the way. He had no authority here. Did he also expect an easy search? What cover story had been prepared should the Navy ship return with Michael in tow? She hoped Yuri had managed to return his bed sheet rope before they searched his room.

After nearly thirty minutes, the Mexican captain stepped onto the rear of the upper deck and spoke into his hand. A few minutes later raised voices and the clang of metal on metal came from the cutter, followed by large splashes. She walked quickly to the rail and looked out.

Divers were going into the water. One diver was still on deck and was lit well enough that she could see thick bulges on his lower back and outer thighs. Soon after he made a giant stride entry into the ocean, he sped away much faster than a man could swim using leg power alone. *Diver jet-boots*—she'd seen a demonstration of them once before and had been childishly envious.

Now she felt fear. She could only hope that Michael had been able to get a good head start. To keep from pacing, she looked for a deck chair, but they'd been put away for the night. Instead, she sat on a step beside the pool and surreptitiously watched Cassidy as he stood staring out over the ocean.

"They'll find him, you know."

His voice startled her after such a long silence. It wasn't what she expected, either. Higher, softer. More penetrating.

"I hope they do," she said. "I'd hate to think we've had some criminal stowaway on the ship."

He slowly turned to her and smiled.

"Play it that way if you want. It won't make any difference. You might be in the market for a new boyfriend, though."

She stifled a flinch. Did Cassidy have a source of information on the ship? But she and Michael had never shown any affection that the crew would have seen. Quite the opposite. No, Cassidy was making a wild guess.

"You have a strange imagination, Mr. Cassidy." He reacted to the name. "It wasn't hard to figure out who you are. What's harder to understand is why you're bothering us, and how you persuaded Mexican authorities to let you waylay a rich American's yacht in the middle of the night."

"Let's say I have friends in high places. Many of my former colleagues have done very well for themselves in the corridors of power."

"It must really sting to know that you haven't."

His smile died. "I wouldn't be too cute, Ms. Matthews..." A flurry of splashes just astern interrupted him. Sakiko stood to see and gave a surprised laugh.

"I think you could say that we have friends, too."

The pod of dolphins was stirring the ocean surface into a froth, individuals darting erratically in seemingly random directions, but never colliding. Then, almost as one, they dived beneath the ship and didn't reappear for several minutes. The pattern repeated soon after, and by the time they reappeared, the Mexican captain had returned to the deck, walking briskly toward the stern. He barked snatches of Spanish at his crew members as they followed him and shot a glare at Cassidy. Within another five minutes, they had all boarded the Mexican cutter's small boats and launched. Sakiko saw Cassidy at the stern of the second boat, sitting straight and still as if this turn of events had nothing to do with him.

The Navy ship came back to life. Presumably it would take a few minutes to get its divers back on board, but Sakiko sighed in relief at the rumble of its engines.

"Yeah, that could have gone badly!" Yuri stood behind her and gave an ironic wave to the departing craft. "Who knew dolphins had such a good sense of timing?"

"Did Michael get away? Are you sure none of the divers caught him?"

"Not judging from the look on the face of the cutter captain. Unless I miss my guess, Michael will be showing up any minute now. Considerate of the Mexicans to leave the boarding ladders in place."

It actually took ten full minutes before they heard a spray of water and Michael's cough. His head rose into view a moment later, and he gave them a nervous smile.

"Beautiful night for a swim!"

# 39

The research team gathered a half-hour later in Dominique's suite to be out of earshot of the crew. Sunita and Fox were the last to arrive. Sunita looked at Michael and gave a surprised laugh.

"What?"

"You're darker than my brother," she said and laughed again.

He looked at his arms in the light of the stateroom and his eyebrows lifted.

"Naïda, did you do this?"

*Yes.*

"It's melanin," Yuri said. "Normally the body uses it to pigment the skin for protection against the sun. Your symbiote must have control over it."

"Right. I guess that made me a little less conspicuous in the dark water."

Michael explained that he'd stayed under the keel only a few meters deep for the first part of the search. The movements of the Mexican crew were easy to hear as they stomped the length of the ship, calling to each other and slamming doors. Then the first divers hit the water and he knew he'd have to go deep. He hadn't counted on their using jet boots and they nearly caught him.

The perfect clarity of the water, so enjoyable at any other time, was a serious handicap as he tried to elude his pursuers. He dived to a depth he estimated to be nearly seventy meters, but the Mexican scuba divers with their underwater searchlights were still far too close. Down another thirty meters. The beams didn't seem to reach that distance. Luckily, he'd been wearing dark blue shorts, and Naïda had found a solution to his white skin. He'd kept still and resisted the urge to look up, but his breathing became more and more labored. He was afraid of passing out. If the search went on much longer, he'd have to rise, and they would catch him.

It was like cavalry riding over the hill when he heard the dolphins arrive. From their clacking exchanges, it sounded like it was all a game to them. He was startled by a single dolphin that swam down, nodded its body, and shot away. Almost immediately, a small group of dolphins began to make crisscrossing patterns between Michael and the searchlights. The rest were clearly getting in the way of the divers, first circling then charging at them head-on and turning aside only at the last moment.

It wasn't long before the divers gave up.

"Did the symbiote call to them for help?" Yuri asked.

"No. I guess the dolphins heard the Navy ship approach and figured it wasn't a good thing. Don't ask me how they'd know."

"They must be able to sense the two of you from a good distance," Yuri persisted. "They didn't come until you were in the water."

Michael shrugged. "There was nothing they could do about it until then."

"It's still amazing. And you were down near a *hundred meters*? That's far deeper than last time. Your body must still be adapting, getting more efficient at producing oxygen." He grinned. "Are you sure I can't try on this symbiote sometime? Just borrow it for a little while?"

Michael's vision turned red. He laughed. "Even if that were possible, Naïda isn't keen on the idea at all."

"You two act as if this was all fun and games." Sakiko thrust her face forward. "We were stopped by the Navy of a foreign country! Who the hell is Cassidy to have clout like that? It obviously isn't a game to him. He wants Michael and he wants him badly."

"He's obsessed with the idea of contacting extraterrestrials," Michael said, "and either he sees me as a hated competitor or a map to the motherlode."

"I did some checking on the internet a few minutes ago," Yuri said. "Cassidy does have a powerful friend, a former astronaut crewmate who's very near the top in the US State Department. There was scuttlebutt that this guy made a major blunder on a mission, but it was covered up. If I had to guess, I'd say Cassidy has some dirt on him."

"Could that give him enough pull to call out a foreign Navy?" Michael asked, instantly afraid that Cassidy had presented his suspicions about him to the CIA or NSA or some even less savory intelligence branch with powerful influence and minimal oversight. And now Michael had not only thwarted him but embarrassed him. He'd turned Cassidy into an enemy.

"That man. *God*. He's like an eel lying in ambush under a rock." Sakiko shuddered.

"He *will* return, I'm certain of that," Fox said. His face showed discomfort that was more than just anger. Maybe it had felt like a personal attack to have someone forcibly board his ship.

"If he does, he won't let dolphins stop him," Dominique said. "He knew you were here, Michael, and he'll have guessed where you must have been during the search." Her mouth curled in a sad smile. "Maybe the only answer is for all of you to leave."

"*What?* We had a deal."

"I know that Sakiko. I don't mean leave for real. I was thinking Yuri could plant some sort of false trail on the internet suggesting that you'd been spooked by the Mexicans and caught a flight back to the States. We're still close enough to Cabo San Lucas. We could turn back and send a boat ashore. Maybe even make sure you're seen at the airport."

"No disrespect ma'am, but you sound like a spy novel," Woodward said. "Cassidy would get wind that *Argo* was in port, for sure. If we send Hart ashore, we might be delivering him right into their hands."

"I agree, Ms. Swan." Fox nodded sharply. "But the internet idea is a good one. At least it will sow some doubt. Then if Cassidy manages to board us again, perhaps Ms. Matthews, Ms. James, and Mr. Hutchings could hide in the steering gear room at the stern while we insist that they've left the ship. Mr. Hart would still be safest in the water." He looked into the faces around the room and received nods of agreement.

Sunita gave a prodigious yawn, reminding them that there were still a few hours before sunrise.

As they walked together back to their rooms, Sakiko said to Michael, "Cassidy told me they would find you. And...he said I'd be in the market for a new boyfriend."

Her words produced a strange mix of feelings in him.

After a long pause, he said, "Wild guess."

"That's what I thought too."

# 40

The next few days were drizzly and cooler. Bad timing, because people's nerves were on edge and everyone needed distraction. Sakiko spent a few hours in the gym and got a massage, but mostly passed the time by running ocean tests herself instead of sloughing them off on Sunita. Since Sunita was devoting more and more of her attention to Yuri, it was probably just as well.

Michael often kept Sakiko company. He had nothing else to do and seemed genuinely interested in the equipment and testing procedures. Most of the time he watched what she was doing. Sometimes he just watched her. And that was OK. She'd foregone her usual grubby clothes when handling the equipment, and instead wore a halter and shorts. Then the drizzle turned cold and the slickers he found for them ruined the effect.

"Why are you taking so many temperature readings?" he asked as she hit a switch. A small winch began to rewind the cable of the bathythermograph and retrieve the instrument from a few hundred meters below them. He'd helped her a few times with a bucket thermometer for surface measurements.

"Well, there could be some kind of chemical or other physical agent that's suppressing the algae, but we can't be sure it isn't just environmental conditions like water temperature or dissolved gases until we check for such anomalies. That's why I've got the salinometer and the probe, too."

The size of a small flashlight, the probe connected to a box that looked like a short-wave radio. It measured dissolved oxygen. It had already detected differences between this area fed by the Pacific Current and the waters of the Gulf of California they'd recently sailed. But so far, no pattern stood out from the data.

"You still don't think it's alien intervention?"

Sakiko still found it bizarre that a serious conversation could include the subject of aliens.

"I can't say for sure; you know that. If it is something they've done, enough testing should enable us to see the mechanism they used. Maybe even figure out a way to counteract it. Whatever the cause, the more we know, the more likely it will be that we can do something about it."

"I almost don't know what to hope for," Michael admitted. "What would be harder to fix: an unknown technology that should at least be traceable to specific sites? Or a manmade process that's so widespread it can affect something the size of an ocean?

He helped her enter the data from a pH meter into her laptop. The acidity of the water had been higher over the past few days, but a lot of factors could produce localized effects.

Once the bathythermograph was aboard, Sakiko waved to a crewman on the bridge deck and *Argo* got underway again.

The weather had cleared by evening, but it remained cool. Sakiko suggested they try out the hot tub on the foredeck. It was one of the few passenger areas of the ship that neither had frequented very often. As they were about to climb in, she touched his shoulder.

"The symbiote isn't going to be hurt by this, is it?"

"No, I checked it out soon after we came aboard. She's learned how to regulate my body temperature zone by zone, so she can shift most of her substance to someplace cooler if she needs to. But thanks for asking." He was completely sincere.

Sakiko realized that he probably considered her unfairly antagonistic toward the symbiote. There were very good reasons to be concerned, but in the weeks they'd spent together she'd never seen any indication that it meant Michael harm. Maybe she could be a little more open-minded.

"It doesn't object to alcohol, either?" She reached for a tall mojito perched on the decking.

He laughed. "She keeps most of it from being absorbed because she doesn't like to have my mental functions impaired. I should have called her Buzzkill." He took a long sip of his own mojito and slid deeper into the fizzing water.

The bubbling jets relaxed muscles that Sakiko hadn't even realized were tense. The stars were sharp dots on black velvet, and she imagined what the great ocean might look like from far above the Earth.

"I watched Cassidy while the Mexicans were searching the ship," she said. "Have you ever met him?"

"Only once when I'd just graduated from high school. He was still a big deal at NASA—that was before his fall from grace after he claimed to have seen the UFO."

"I guess that would change a person; but after seeing him, I just couldn't figure out why you'd ever liked the guy."

"Maybe because he was a bit of an underdog. He had a tough childhood, wasn't very big, but managed to rise through some of the toughest training in the world to become the commander of space missions. And he made time for a seventeen-year-old with dreams."

"You dreamed of being an astronaut?"

"Not exactly. I was fascinated by the idea of colonizing other planets, but I didn't expect to do it myself." He took another long drink.

"You didn't play astronaut when you were a kid?"

"No, I wanted to be a superhero—doesn't everyone?" His laugh was a little forced. "Except I was a chickenshit."

"That sounds like an exaggeration."

He shifted in the tub and looked up at the stars. When she didn't say anything more, he shrugged.

"I went to a small rural school for a couple of years—grade seven and eight. Let's just say there weren't a lot of brainiacs there, so it was easy to be top of the class—but not such a good idea. Turns out it's more important to be *fast* than to be smart." He paused, swirling his glass. "Thankfully, by the time I went to high school, we'd moved, and I'd learned my lesson. I didn't stand out anymore."

"But you went on to get a doctorate. Become a professor."

"It was either that or work for my dad's accounting firm. My grandfather's influence with the university alumni counted for more than my grades, I'm sure. What about you? I'll bet you aced every class. Voted most likely to win a Nobel Prize for biology."

"Most likely to be a spinster librarian is more like it. I think it actually says that in my yearbook."

"You sure don't look like a librarian right now."

She gave a light snort.

"Are you sure the symbiote blocks alcohol?"

The first sight of Rocas Alijos made Sakiko shake her head in amazement. The rocks were eroded tips of volcanic cones, a handful of stone pinnacles rising from the ocean in the middle of nowhere, but so slender that it was hard to believe they wouldn't break off in a strong wind. Up close, they appeared more robust; but the total horizontal surface area of the three main rocks and a scattering of others only amounted to about a thousand square feet. Occasionally visited by scuba divers and a favored spot for fishing charters, the area was deserted when *Argo* arrived. The waters were a little rough for tourists, but Sakiko had half-expected to find Ryan Cassidy waiting for them.

He wasn't, but the dolphins were. They swam around the ship, then became even more active when *Argo* launched a dive boat, leaping into the air and chattering until Michael jumped into the water. One of the dolphins pressed close to him for several minutes before swimming apart. He couldn't be sure it was the same one that had given him a ride days earlier, but its message was received.

The dolphins couldn't lead them any farther. Either there was no longer an alien presence in the area, or they just couldn't tell where it was. Twenty minutes later, as the team prepared dive gear, the dolphins swam away to the west into open ocean.

Underwater, a rock bottom sloped outward for some distance, then plunged precipitously. The shallows were still a vast area to search. They began with the largest islet, Roca Sur, and the string of rocks north of it. Sakiko and Michael made one dive pair, swimming clockwise,

Yuri and Dylan Woodward the other, travelling counterclockwise. Both teams swam grid search patterns.

Like every other diver, Sakiko tended to swim in curves rather than straight lines, thanks to a kick stronger in one leg than the other. Without a firm knowledge of the local sea-bottom topography, it took regular monitoring of the compass to maintain anything like a straight course. She and Michael agreed that she would navigate while Michael did most of the searching with his enhanced vision. He would have led the way if the symbiote had detected any alien presence, but it had not—or wasn't admitting to it. Michael had had trouble getting any answer at all regarding nearness of another outpost

Sakiko wasn't surprised. If the aliens had an agenda, the symbiote would be a part of it, whether knowingly or not. Sooner or later, it would have to realize that Michael and his friends were pursuing goals that probably conflicted with the aims of the aliens. Withholding information was the least it could do, but it might be able to do much more.

She watched Michael as closely as she could, but if the symbiote did choose to interfere it wouldn't be in any overt way.

Seeing him swim without scuba gear except for dive boots and fins made her envious. Although his fingers and toes developed translucent fringes when he was in the water, the long manmade dive fins still gave a bigger push. A second advantage was more significant: a skin surface that became like a sea mammal's, creating far less friction through the water. Pores sealed and the hairs on his head fitted together into a tight shell. Sakiko wondered if there might also be some kind of electrostatic effect that helped to part water molecules.

Michael balked at swimming naked, but Dominique had found a Speedo swimsuit in his size among spare clothing kept onboard for guests. The way he avoided swimming above Sakiko showed that wearing a Speedo was still outside his comfort zone.

The water was clear and a sublime blue. Though the seascape was nothing like the vibrant coral reefs she loved to explore, its hugely varied terrain had a rugged beauty, with steep walls, sculpted rocks of every size, and abundant fish. Parrotfish always drew her attention with their rainbow hues or bright blue chins. Schools of mackerel darted between the divers and the surface, their twisting moves through the rays of sunlight making scales flash like dozens of strobe lights. A curious Mexican hogfish followed them for ten minutes or more, its protruding forehead making it look surprised.

Michael easily slid into the midst of a passing school of yellow-tailed surgeonfish, causing them no concern. Sakiko had done the same thing often enough in full dive gear. The fish simply didn't see a human diver as a predator. The school did react to the appearance of a yellowfin tuna about twenty meters away, making a sharp diving turn that left Michael behind. Wahoo and dorado came into view from time to time, too—it was easy to see why the place was popular with sport fishermen.

Then there were the sharks. At one point on the second dive of the day the light suddenly dimmed and Sakiko looked up to see thirty hammerheads or more swimming past. They paid no attention to the divers, but she and Michael kept their distance. A few shark species like black-tips were so common she barely noticed them anymore, until one had the nerve to pass Michael within a couple of meters, giving him a thorough once-over with a coal black eye. She knew that one would be back.

It carved a lazy slalom path away from them, skimming over the bottom twenty meters away. Then it turned in their direction. Sakiko tugged at Michael's arm and pointed. He knew better than to make any erratic moves. They shifted close together to look more intimidating while she reached for her dive knife with her right hand and her 'safe second' air hose with her left. Sometimes a loud burst of bubbles could deter aggressive sharks.

The shark's approach seemed to take forever until the last ten meters, when it put on a burst of speed. But at three meters away it veered aside and simply lost interest, swimming hurriedly off into the depths.

Michael looked as mystified as Sakiko. It was only later, after they'd climbed aboard the boat and he was helping her strip off her gear, that he gave a schoolboy's grin.

"Shark repellant," he said. "Naïda made my sweat glands give off some kind of smell that the shark didn't like. I had no idea she could do that. Impressive, huh?"

"Definitely. Now if it would only tell us where its friends are hiding, we could save ourselves a few more encounters like that." She checked her dive computer and sat heavily, letting her body hang over her legs. "I've logged enough bottom time for the day, unless something urgent comes up."

He nodded. They ran the boat a few hundred meters to where Yuri and Woodward's inflatable orange dive marker tube bobbed in the waves.

An hour later, Michael went on his own to cover much of the same territory, but at a greater depth. He towed a dive flag behind him, and a boat stayed near it with a diver suited up and ready to go if he ran into trouble. Sakiko regretted that they hadn't brought any high-tech communication gear, but she'd just seen evidence that Michael was pretty capable of handling things by himself.

Because, of course, he never *was* by himself.

The first day of the search was a bust. Not having seen an example of what they were looking for, Yuri and Woodward had wasted a lot of time getting close to outcrops of vegetation and shadows cast by rock formations. There were a few cave-like hollows formed by fallen boulders, but none bore any trace of anything unnatural.

That night they drank little and went to bed early.

The second day they managed to fit in three dives each, but with no greater success. They covered the immediate area around Middle Rock and the smaller islets and pushed themselves in the late afternoon to finish searching the shallow parts of North Rock—but nothing stood out from a jumbled debris field. that had all begun to look the same. Even Michael's attentiveness flagged badly by the end. He climbed wearily from the water and had to admit that they could easily have missed something.

That night, the cooking staff prepared an especially sumptuous meal of sushi and sashimi featuring fresh-caught tuna and shark, artfully arranged around the remains of the small shark's head and jaws. Sakiko and Michael shared an awkward laugh, but the display didn't impair their appetite. The meal, and some perfectly brewed cappuccino, did a lot to renew their spirits.

"Let's be smarter about this," Michael said as they sat sipping their drinks in the overstuffed couches of the salon. "If there is an alien installation here, and its purpose is to disperse some kind of chemical or physical agent, where would be the best place to catch the current out into the broader ocean?"

"From what we've seen, I'd say the slopes to the south of Roca Sur," Sakiko replied. "The first place you and I looked. And we were fresh then."

"Yeah, but we were just getting into our rhythm. I don't know about you, but I was easily distracted by the fish and the number of sharks."

"We were also new to the terrain," Yuri said. "It takes a while for our brains to get a sense of the topography: what shapes are normal and what aren't. We could have missed something subtly different."

"The outpost I discovered back in Canada *wanted* to be found—it lit up like a glowworm when we came near. But maybe other installations weren't meant to be discovered. They might even be camouflaged."

"Crikey!" Woodward had passed up a cappuccino in favor of a beer. "You're not saying we have to search the whole place all over again are you, Mike? Can't you persuade your girlfriend we mean business, and get her to lend a little abracadabra?"

Sakiko gave him a sharp look. Michael didn't notice.

"She doesn't sense anything alien here, I'm sure of it. And anyway, there's nothing I could do to *persuade* her if she's reluctant to help. I just think I should go over that area again in the morning. Especially the deeper sections, where the drop-off is steep."

Dominique gave a wave through the window to one of the serving staff and ordered some liqueurs. When the man had gone, she said, "You're putting a lot of faith in a hunch that's only based on some playful dolphins."

"Crazy, I know. But I have a feeling I left *sane* behind weeks ago."

He didn't say "I told you so" the next morning as he surfaced holding a piece of something that looked like transparent plastic. It was about the size of a sheet of paper and disintegrated into slippery sludge by the time the small boat had returned to the *Argo*.

"There were just a few patches of this on the underside of a canted slab of rock," he said. "Right at the edge of a drop. It was caught in a small crevice."

"You think there was an installation on that slope but it's gone now?" asked Yuri. Michael nodded.

"I think it left recently, too, headed for somewhere beyond our reach."

"Beyond *our* reach?" Sakiko sat forward.

"I'd say these installations are in communication with each other. They know about us and they don't intend for us to stop whatever they're doing.

"Our job just got a whole lot more complicated."

# 41

It was clear to Michael that the Rocas Alijos installation had moved to deeper water because it had been forewarned. How, and by whom? Naïda was the obvious suspect, but when asked directly, she denied it. She claimed that she hadn't sensed any alien presence near the Alijos Rocks.

Could it be that the aliens had eyes in the sky—a satellite left behind or a newly-arrived scout craft? Earth's radar installations were able to track tens of thousands of pieces of tiny debris in orbit, so alien craft would have to use a stealth technology to remain hidden, but that certainly wasn't impossible. Even so, he thought it was much more likely that an artificial intelligence in the installation near Puerto Peñasco had sent a signal before its destruction. Either it had correctly predicted where *Argo* would go next, or it had broadcast an alert to any other alien installations on the planet to hide. If that were the case, finding and disabling those devices had just become impossible for a small team acting on its own. Full marine resources of all the nations of the Earth would probably not be enough.

Any scenario he could imagine seemed to confirm his fears about an invasion. Although he and his friends weren't to blame, two alien devices had been destroyed, and if the rest had gone into hiding for protection, it must be that they expected further attacks.

That was a conflict humanity could not win.

Though Michael was nearly sure that artificial intelligence, not living beings, had monitored the Evergreen Lake outpost for ten thousand years, Naïda had managed to stay alive that long. What if explorer aliens had survived somewhere else on the planet? Or was it that advance scouts *had* arrived and were beginning to coordinate a counter-offensive?

He asked the question out loud.

*No,* Naïda responded. *If there were Creators on this planet I would know.*

Creators. It made sense that she would call them that. He wasn't convinced that she would be aware of their presence, though. They'd be cautious, knowing that she might be compromised by being bonded with a human.

Or could they be completely confident that she would obey their will?

"Where to now?" Sakiko asked him from a lounge chair as he came on deck. She and Yuri had been taking measurements and were running the data through software on their laptops.

"I have no idea. I suppose we could try to guess what invaders would need their advance posts to do. That would affect where they'd be located. I'm sorry. I wasn't expecting them to go into hiding. I don't have a contingency plan. For now, I'm just going to go for a swim."

"To see if the symbiote can pick up anything?"

"Because I need to get wet."

With no new destination, *Argo* was staying put for the time being, running the engines or thrusters only when needed to keep the bow into the waves. At the moment the sea was flat, and Michael dived off the stern after putting a ladder in place.

Each time he returned to the underwater world he enjoyed it more, no longer afraid to draw water into his lungs, relishing the feeling of becoming a denizen of a liquid world. Even salt content wasn't an irritation anymore—his body had adapted to it, inside and out.

He dived deeper, arrowing toward the indigo realm far below. Not searching this time—the sea floor was thousands of meters beneath him—he was testing his abilities against the forces of the ocean: pressure, cold, darkness.

He sensed that he was as far as he'd ever gone, and still he dropped. Naïda made no protest. If anything, she seemed as eager as he to push their limits. There was nothing to see nearby, but his eyes adjusted frequently, so the clarity of his vision remained good. He put a hand in front of his face and could still distinguish flesh tones, though only the tiniest trace of red or yellow light could penetrate these depths.

He stopped his descent, closed his eyes and executed a tumble and a roll. Could he still tell which way was up? Yes. Could he still breathe? Yes, with effort. Wouldn't want to exert himself too much, though. The cold? Noticeable, but not a problem. However, there was a sensation much like he experienced after prolonged dives in scuba gear: a feeling that his metabolism had been revved-up and he was probably burning through energy stores very quickly.

Hopefully the kitchen staff would put on a big spread for lunch.

He should have brought a depth gauge with him. There was light, but not much. He smiled at the thought of Ryan Cassidy sending divers after him now, but reminded himself not to get cocky. There was no way he could outdive a submersible. Or an automated weapon.

He slowly rose to the surface, enjoying the changing shades of blue. In his imagination, *Argo's* hull was a castle in the clouds, and he was flying to meet it.

Sakiko and Yuri met him as he came aboard. While he toweled off, he told them about his dive.

"We lost sight of you in the first few minutes," Yuri said. "Even with that white suit. You two are getting better at this each time down."

"Definitely. There must be a limit, but...." He rubbed his hair with the towel and noticed a twinge behind his right ear. Running a finger along it, he felt a small lump. Strange. He gently plucked at it. There was a little resistance, but it came free and he held it out between thumb and forefinger: a whitish ball the size of candy sprinkles on birthday cakes.

"Have you ever seen anything like this?" he asked the others. "It's not some kind of sea lice, is it?"

Yuri bent close. "No, those have small tails. That looks more like an egg of some kind, but I couldn't tell you what it's from. Why would it be behind your ear?"

"Don't ask me. I just hope I didn't pick up some kind of parasite."

Sakiko knitted her eyebrows as if he'd said something ironic. Then she smiled.

"Want me to check you over?"

Yuri laughed. Michael blushed. And Yuri laughed even harder.

*It is offspring.*

A magnified image of the tiny sphere appeared in his mind.

"Naïda says it's an egg," Michael told them.

*It is my offspring.*

He nearly dropped the little white ball, then quickly let go of the towel and cupped his left hand under his right.

"Oh my God! Naïda says it's *hers*. *Her* offspring!" He licked his lips and placed the dot in his palm to give the others a better look as they leaned in. "Holy shit. I had no idea."

"Jellyfish reproduce by budding," Sakiko said. "That makes sense from the way you described the symbiote before it...joined with you." Her eyes opened wider and she stopped talking.

"It's fantastic. I thought she was the only one left of her species. It never occurred to me that she could reproduce."

"Quite a few species reproduce asexually," Yuri said. "Takes all the fun out of it, but useful if you're stranded on a desert island. That's kind of like your symbiote's situation, right?"

"This is great! Now we can learn more about them without my having to be a guinea pig."

"Are you so sure Naïda will be happy about using its babies in lab experiments?"

*These are our offspring. The offspring of bondmates.*

Michael's hand began to shake. He tried to steady it with his other arm.

*The offspring of Michael and Naïda.*

His knees gave way. Yuri jumped to his side and helped him to a lounge chair.

"What's wrong? *Michael*! Are you OK?"

He couldn't speak. He looked into their eyes, his head slowly shaking. Sakiko grabbed her glass of orange juice and gave it to him. He spilled some on his chest, then drained what was left. With a cough, his head drooped, and he stared at the deck, breathing hard.

"She says it's *our* offspring—*hers and mine.*"

"Oh my God." Sakiko sat on the edge of another chair, facing him.

"Wow," Yuri said in a whisper. He cleared his throat. "What does she mean? A combination of DNA from both of you?"

Michael waited for the answer, then nodded. He had an image of his wet dream from a few nights earlier but didn't feel inclined to explain.

"Well, she's always had ready access to your DNA," Yuri continued. "That's...incredible. I don't know what to say."

"Neither do I," Michael growled. "What would make her think she had the right to do something like that? Without telling me. Creating some kind...some kind of..." He stood abruptly and swung his arm back as if about to throw the offending speck into the ocean. A painful tingle surged through the arm, then quickly subsided, and he slowly lowered it. He'd never known Naïda to exhibit such alarm.

"You can't just kill it," Sakiko said softly. "It's...*life.* And part of it is you."

After a long moment he nodded, hanging his head, but the muscles in his arms and neck were rigid. He hesitated, then put the white bud on the tip of his finger and placed it back behind his ear, holding it until he felt it would stay.

"Just like a woman," Yuri smirked. "Get pregnant then spring it on you."

Michael's face was stony. He turned his head to the side. "How many of these things did you make?"

Naïda didn't answer.

"How many? Where are the others?"

No response. When he felt behind his ear again, the bud was gone.

"We need a group meeting," he said. "I need to find some way to control her."

It was Sunita who presented the solution.

"What about Botox? It paralyzes selective muscles temporarily. If most of the alien thing is in or near your skin...."

Michael nodded reluctantly. "I suppose there'd be clinics in tourist towns like Cabo San Lucas, if we could find a practitioner who could keep her mouth shut."

Dominique gave a light laugh. "You, sir, are forgetting that you're aboard a yacht owned by Blake Cartwright, ever the gracious host to the rich and famous of the world. She hasn't had much to do on this trip, but we have a cosmetician aboard who's also fully trained in Botox treatments. Daddy's friends aren't all young, but they must be beautiful, mustn't they?"

Michael was relieved to learn that the cosmetician was actually a licensed doctor who'd tired of treating trauma and been lured aboard by a yacht lifestyle. Dr. Carly Cardinal had a head of tight black curls and a set of startlingly white teeth that disarmed him when she smiled, which was often.

"Ms. Swan tells me you're interested in Botox treatment. I certainly can't imagine why."

"I'm sure you can't," Michael tried to smile. He did his best to describe his situation. Dr. Cardinal's eyes grew, and her smile vanished.

"I'd heard rumors, but I didn't believe them." She kept looking from Michael to Dominique, who nodded in confirmation. "Jesus, you poor man. But I'm not sure Botox will help you. It blocks certain neurotransmitters from getting a signal through, so it can quiet unwanted spasms as well as preventing facial wrinkles. I've used it on cerebral palsy patients and Parkinson's patients back when I was practicing. But no one's ever needed it to subdue selective muscle activity throughout the body. Not that I've ever heard. I don't really *know* how you'd do it. And the dosages..."

"It's a lot to ask, I know," Michael said. "We just don't have any other ideas. I want to interfere with the *symbiote's* control of my muscles but not my own control. Could we test a little for a few minutes, to see if it does anything?"

Dr. Cardinal's smile returned, though briefly, as she looked at Dominique. "This guy's never been to Hollywood, has he? Mr. Hart, Botox treatments are typically effective for three to four *months*. You want me to dose you for a few *minutes*?"

"Months? No, I can't do that. Not without knowing what the effects will be."

The doctor sat down hard on the countertop of her mini-clinic space and rubbed her chin.

"Sheesh, are you sure I'm not dreaming this? Oh, wait a minute. There might be something worth trying." She turned and rummaged through a cupboard. "There's no way I could give you injections that would have a widespread effect and only last a short time, but this cream version...." She pulled out a tube, carefully read the labelling, then did some checking in her computer.

"This is a topical form of Botox for certain types of issues like crow's feet. Its effects last just as long, normally; but maybe if we try a very small amount on your skin for only a minute or two instead of the usual half-hour...it could tell you if we're on the right track."

After a long pause Michael nodded. "Sure. Let's do it."

"Were you checking with the symbiote?" Dominique asked.

"Wondering what she'd have to say, but I'm not getting anything." Which wasn't completely true. He felt a nervous chill that might not be entirely his own.

Dr. Cardinal spent the next three-quarters of an hour applying the cream to more than a dozen places on Michael's skin in amounts so small he could barely see it, carefully removing each patch after only two minutes.

"Short applications *should* reduce its absorption and limit its effects to a smaller area—I don't know for certain."

"Why did you pick those particular places?"

"Well, I can't cover all of you. A friend taught me the most basic *chi* points of the body—the ones they use for acupuncture and related treatments—so, I figured why not start with some of those? We're shooting in the dark, here, right? Don't worry if you're not noticing anything yet. Results don't usually show up for hours, or even 'til the next day."

Michael thanked her and got dressed. He didn't feel any different, and there was still no reaction from Naïda. He shrugged off a touch of remorse. How dare she use his DNA to make offspring without telling him? Maybe a hybrid wouldn't be viable and would die on its own. But it could also be a monster, an abomination. He shuddered.

Right then it seemed that trying to get drunk would be an effective way to tell if Naïda was being suppressed, even though it was still before noon.

Yuri and Sakiko looked on with obvious discomfort as he downed a string of tequila shots. They tried to talk him out of jumping into the pool, but he wouldn't be dissuaded. Naïda didn't interfere or react in any way. Even when he deliberately pictured a mermaid to call her, and loudly spoke her name, there was no response.

"I think it worked," he said with a lazy smile as he wrung water out of his t-shirt. "I just might be in charge of my own body for a change."

"Either that or the thing is hiding because it's pissed off," Sakiko said in a low voice, but Michael just shrugged.

He spent the afternoon sleeping off the alcohol. At dinner he didn't feel like talking. No one spoke about Naïda, but Sakiko looked the question at him. He only shook his head and ate a little more. There was still food on his plate when he left.

Shortly after sunset Sakiko came up to him as he stood at the starboard aft railing, looking out over the sea. The ship still wasn't far from Rocas Alijos, but the rocks had been swallowed by the night. Something about them held his imagination: tiny tips of a vast mountain peak that stretched into unreachable depths.

"Sorry to ask, but have you noticed anything more? Do you still think the Botox worked?"

"I think it did," Michael said, but didn't sound happy about it. "I've tried adjusting my eyesight to the darkness. Nothing happens. Other sensations like extra body awareness and balance, fine muscle coordination...I hadn't even noticed that she'd affected them until now."

"That's sooner than Dr. Cardinal expected, isn't it?"

He nodded. "Which makes me wonder how long it will last. There was no way to know. Maybe it's done something...something permanent." His voice was husky, and he cleared it, a little ashamed.

Sakiko stepped close and took his arm.

"I'm sure it's not permanent. But you sound...disappointed. Have you changed your mind?"

"I was furious with her for producing offspring with my DNA. *Really* furious. And I've thought about that. It was fear, I guess. I was so thrilled when I thought she'd just kind of cloned herself, but revolted when she said half of it was mine. She took it from my sperm, you know. She figured out how to get some. Which makes them even more like...like babies. Like *my* babies. And I was just *disgusted*." He bent over the railing, not sure if he might cry or be sick. Sakiko wrapped her arm over his shoulders.

"Don't be so hard on yourself. We're talking about a being that isn't even from this planet. We know almost nothing about it. It could be the most dangerous thing to ever happen to humanity, and you've got it living inside you, without any choice in the matter. Now it is reproducing without asking you." She reached for his face and turned it toward her. Her voice grew quiet. "It's perfectly normal to be afraid. God knows, *I've* been afraid of it all this time. Afraid of what it might be doing to you."

"I know."

"And most of that fear is just xenophobia, I'll admit. I'm not proud of that because I've always thought I was as accepting and open-minded as they come. I'm a scientist, for God's sake. I shouldn't be acting on gut reactions like that. But I have. That feeling has kept me away from you, Michael."

"I know that, too."

"To be honest, I'm kind of glad to...well, to have you to myself for a change."

The deep feeling he read in her eyes made his throat tighten. He turned from the railing, bent his head, and gently kissed her.

As he pulled away, she softly bit at her lip and turned to face the sea.

"I thought maybe you and Dominique...there have been a few rumors."

Michael took a deep breath and slowly released it.

"Dominique...well, she's very attractive. But I didn't sleep with her. I couldn't." He gently turned her face back to him. "You're the one I want."

They made love in her room. It was even better than he'd imagined.

Then they held each other close, cocooned in the warm dark.

# 42

Paralysis.

Catatonia.

Naïda searches for words within Michael's specialized vocabulary. Her own species has no terms to describe this state: like a waking stasis, but hypersensitive, not restful. Definitely not that.

There is a sensation like sensory feedback, yet with no original stimulation; a silence so profound it is like a pressure, or maybe endless vibration with no causal movement.

Those are only the physical sensations. Terrible as they are, the intangible ones are much worse, the *feelings* she would never have known without human contact. Far better if she had not.

She has failed. She is a failure.

Failed her bondmate. Failed the Creators. Failed her own species.

She still cannot comprehend how she so completely misunderstood Michael's desires. She wanted only to *please* him. Instead, she has awakened in him an anger so powerful he will poison his own body to keep her immobile.

*Poison!* There can be no greater betrayal of a bondmate. Yet she knows that it is a sense of betrayal that motivates him. How inconceivable that he should feel such a thing when she had intended only the greatest gift she knew.

He does not need her companionship. He now has the woman Sakiko for that.

She has lost his affection. She has lost his trust. The emotion this causes feels like her very substance is being torn inside out.

Clearly, the Controller no longer trusts her, either. In trying to please both, she has satisfied neither. Following the Controller's directives, she nearly caused the death of her bondmate and herself. In acting on Michael's behalf, she is now shunned by the Controller. Is she at fault? She does not know. The result is the same. She is no longer of use to either. To anyone.

Although she knows it is only another unwelcome trait learned from humans, she does now have a desire to shelter and nurture her offspring. To see them develop and grow. To discover how much of them will reflect her own DNA and how much Michael's.

She does not believe that Michael would harm them—not anymore. His kind of human is more likely to sacrifice himself than take another's life. The same cannot be said for the evil man, the one pursuing Michael. He might find the offspring and bring them harm or even death. The pain of *that* thought is almost more than she can stand.

As a last act before her paralysis became complete, she was able to hide the offspring from easy discovery, but she can no longer protect them. In truth, if they do remain hidden and survive, there is nothing more she can do for them, and they do not require it. The Creators have always provided protection and ready access to nourishment: but, if necessary, the young of her species can develop with complete independence until near the time of maturity.

She is not even needed by...her *children*.

There is no longer any reason for her to exist.

She can do something about that. There is a way.

If the paralysis eases at all, she can extrude the bulk of her being to the surface of Michael's skin in thin layers, where it will slough off and peel away by abrasion in the same way the dead cells of his own skin are removed. Once the amount of lost material reaches a certain level, she will be unable to function and will die.

Yes, that may be for the best.

# 43

At first, Sakiko thought she'd awakened from a nightmare. As she listened to the noises in the night, she realized she'd awakened *into* a nightmare.

"*Michael.* Wake up! It's Cassidy!"

He wasn't a light sleeper but came awake quickly.

"You've got to get into the water," she said.

In the dim glow from a deck light, she could just see the large whites of Michael's eyes.

"I can't. The Botox."

"Jesus!"

They scrambled into shorts and t-shirts and opened the door to find Dominique about to bang on it. Her eyebrows arched, then she motioned them forward and began to jog down the hallway. Yuri and Sunita waited ahead and joined them.

"The steering-gear room," Dominique said. "We might just have time."

Their destination was at the very stern, past the crew lounge, the engine room, and the garage for the smaller boats. Their route was convoluted since they couldn't risk going on deck and had to travel most of the length of the ship. At times they could hear voices shouting above but didn't dare stop to listen. The entrance to the room was unobtrusive, and since it was just below where Cassidy and his companions were climbing aboard, it might be the last place they'd look. The drumming of booted feet overhead made Sakiko's mouth go dry, and for a horrifying moment she was sure she would sneeze.

Sunita sneezed instead.

Dominique said, "No one will have heard that on deck. There are two ships this time and they're making a lot of noise themselves. I'll put on a show and do my best to convince them you've left *Argo*." She closed the door and left them sweating in the dark.

"Do you think they'll believe we left?" Sunita asked, her near-whisper full of fear.

"It won't stop them searching every square inch," Yuri replied. "I don't know how Cassidy convinced them to try again, but he won't quit this time. He's got too much on the line."

"There's no way one former astronaut has that much clout," Sakiko said. "Especially not with a foreign nation. He must have persuaded one of the nastier shadow services that he's got a line on the intelligence coup of their dreams."

"Why isn't Captain Fox kicking up more of a stink about *Argo* being boarded?" Sunita asked. "This is the second time!"

Yuri gave her arm a squeeze. "We're on a private yacht surrounded by gun-carrying Mexican authorities in their own territorial waters. What's he supposed to do?"

"I should give myself up," Michael said. "I have no right to put anyone else in danger."

"Don't you dare!" Sakiko snapped. "And anyway, they'd still interrogate all of us, to find out what we've seen."

No one spoke for several minutes. As the commotion overhead subsided, the silence that followed felt even more threatening.

Michael cleared his throat softly. "If they do capture me, there's something you need to know." He hesitated, then began again. "There's another reason I've been so sure an alien invasion is coming.

"*I sent them a signal.*"

"What? What the hell is that supposed to mean?"

"I'm sorry, Sakiko. I told you I communicated through Naïda with the intelligence in the outpost. Mostly images. It showed me...amazing things...important science. Advanced knowledge. And it promised to show me more."

"If...."

"If I sent a signal to the aliens. I just had to physically trigger it by touching the outpost—I don't know why. I refused at first, several times. But... I thought it was the right thing to do. A way to solve the world's problems."

"Jesus Christ!" Yuri hissed. "It didn't occur to you that the rest of the world should have a *say*? You're an egomaniac!"

"Shit, Michael. *What were you thinking?*"

"I was thinking that a super-advanced race would have no interest in conquest. The outpost computer could have sent a signal itself, anytime. The only reason for me to be involved would be to show cooperation. That we're intelligent enough to welcome peaceful visitors."

"That sounds like rationalizing after the fact," Yuri said. "At least tell me it gave you the secret of the meaning of life."

"No," Michael answered after a deep breath. "It didn't give me anything. It shut down and was totally unresponsive from then on. Soon after that it was destroyed by toxic waste dumped into the lake."

There was another long silence as they tried to process what they'd heard.

"So, you figured you'd been tricked?"

Michael reached out in the dark for her hand, but she pulled it away.

"Yes. And if the artificial intelligence chose to trick me, that meant...well, they probably weren't as friendly as I'd hoped."

"Why couldn't you tell me...us?"

A long sigh turned into a moan. "We'll be like ants to them. It might mean the end of our species. And I'll be responsible. The greatest traitor humanity has ever known."

It was quiet enough to hear the breaths of the others and the rustling of limbs as they fidgeted. Sakiko didn't know what to say. Until then she'd thought Michael was being paranoid expecting an invasion. Now that possibility seemed all too chillingly real.

"I'd hand you over to Cassidy right now if it didn't mean landing the rest of us in shit," Yuri said.

"Amen to that," Sunita added.

"Shut up, both of you," Sakiko said. "Michael had no right to do what he did, but if the aliens wanted a race to conquer, the damage was already done as soon as he entered that lake and was detected. Anything after that could make no difference."

Sunita scoffed. "You should have turned yourself in to the authorities right away..."

The door swung open and blinded them with light. As Sakiko's eyes adjusted, she could see the Mexican Navy captain with Ryan Cassidy beside him and Parzifal Fox a few steps behind.

"You couldn't bring yourself to leave such hospitable surroundings after all," the Navy captain said with a smile. "I don't blame you. But I'm afraid you'll all have to come with us. I have warrants for your arrest...as spies."

They protested loudly but there was no resisting the guards. A few steps brought them onto the aft deck, beside the swimming pool.

"All four of you. Good." Cassidy said, his face expressionless. "Or is that *five*?

His arm snapped out and shoved Michael into the pool. With a quick gesture from their captain three Mexican crewmen jumped in too, grabbing Michael and holding him under. He thrashed fiercely but could not raise his head above the water.

"God, no! He'll drown!" Sakiko screamed.

"Come now, Ms. Matthews. Why do you think I'm here? Do you think I don't know about Mr. Hart's extra abilities, and how he managed to hide from us last time?"

Shocked, she looked at Parzifal Fox, but he wouldn't meet her eyes.

With a curse, she launched herself into the pool and onto the back of one of the Mexicans, knocking him away from Michael, but another man replaced him. The one she'd attacked yanked her arm viciously behind her and forced her face under the water until she had to release her breath in a furious scream. He pulled her head up and shoved her to the wall of the pool.

Gasping, she looked at Michael. He hung limp, still held a half-meter below the surface.

*"He's drowning, Goddamn you!"* she shrieked.

The Mexican captain snapped his fingers and his men lifted Michael up. Water slopped from his mouth. His eyes were open and staring. His chest didn't move.

With a string of obscenities, the captain gave orders to his men. They hoisted the body onto the deck, rolling it onto its side. A Navy crewman in a uniform with different insignia pushed Michael hard from behind, forcing out another gush of water, then rolled him onto his back and began to give mouth-to-mouth resuscitation. For an endless minute there was no sound but the forceful breaths.

At last, Michael coughed, and more water spilled from his lips. He rolled sideways, spitting fluid and drawing rasping breaths. Sakiko tried to run to him, but two Mexicans pulled her back.

"I'm impressed," Cassidy said drily. "It takes a lot of guts to drown when you could save yourself. But maybe a first taste of death is enough to cure that foolishness." He nodded, and the three men pulled Michael back into the pool and under the surface.

"*No!*" Sakiko wailed, struggling so hard it took two more men to hold her back.

"Cassidy!" Fox snapped. "I did not let you on my ship to commit murder. Let him up, or I'll see you charged the instant you set foot on American soil."

"Really, Captain. You yourself told me the man has an alien inside him that lets him swim like a fish. Are you saying you were lying?"

Fox squirmed under the glare of his friends.

"You don't understand," Sakiko sobbed. "It's *gone*. The symbiote's gone. Into the ocean. Without it, he'll drown." It was a gamble, but only six people had known about the Botox, and Fox wasn't one of them.

"Is that true?" Cassidy snapped at the yacht captain.

"It might be. I am not with him all the time."

Cassidy gestured at the crewmen holding Michael and they raised him up again. The man who'd revived him before rushed to help again, but this time it looked like he was too late. Two minutes passed, nearly three, before Michael suddenly writhed and sprayed water over Cassidy's shoes. Even then, he couldn't catch a good breath, his eyes wide in terror. In time, his gasping began to ease, and he collapsed on his side.

Sakiko fell to her knees and vomited on the deck.

The voice of the Mexican captain was a snarl. "Mr. Cassidy, I will not be a party to murder. You assured me that this man could survive underwater. I should have known it was a fantasy."

"If it was a fantasy, it wasn't mine." Cassidy glared coldly at Parzifal Fox. "But I don't think so. I have a laboratory in Cabo San Lucas standing by. My people there will be able to tell who's lying."

Two Navy crewmen hauled Michael to his feet.

"The rest stay," Fox said, without raising his voice. "We all know that they are not spies. However, they *are* guests of Mr. Blake Cartwright, and he is not a man you should provoke."

Cassidy's jaw clenched. His right hand slowly curled into a fist.

"No problem," he said. "You've all had plenty of time to coordinate your stories anyway."

As the Mexicans and their hostage began to return to their boats, Sakiko cried, "Take me with you. I've been with him longer than anyone."

Cassidy actually showed surprise. He gave a questioning look to Fox, who shook his head in disgust, then simply shrugged. Cassidy swept his arm toward the boat and Sakiko stepped forward.

As she passed Yuri, he quietly said, "I hope you know what you're doing."

# 44

The laboratory was an old one, but it was clean, and some of the equipment looked new. Cassidy left Michael alone in a small room while he questioned Sakiko. She stuck to her story that the symbiote had left Michael and vanished into the ocean when he'd gone swimming the previous morning.

Cassidy seemed especially eager to know if the symbiote was aware, or even intelligent, but she only smiled as if he were pulling her leg. The ploy wouldn't work for long if they were to get answers from Michael, though. She'd had no chance to talk to him alone.

A doctor came into the room and appeared surprised to see her. He looked Hispanic but spoke English with a slight British accent. He introduced himself as Dr. Mendez.

"Our clinic will have nothing to do with torture or coercion, Mr. Cassidy, no matter who you're working for," Mendez said. Sakiko had the feeling he was speaking to her, and she was grateful. She couldn't be sure that Cassidy wouldn't threaten her with violence to force Michael to talk. Cassidy's mouth twitched in displeasure.

"There won't be any need for that, Doctor," he said. "We're all friends here. We're just trying to get at the truth, for the sake of our race, our whole species." He gave Sakiko a look. "Now, can we get started with the tests on Mr. Hart, please?"

"I'm afraid not," the doctor answered. "I could do some very basic tests, but I need the help of some others for magnetic scanning or DNA tests, and that help is not available until tomorrow."

"You might have told me that."

Mendez shrugged an apology. "I'm sure you'd rather get the cameras and recording equipment in place before we get too far into it anyway."

Now Cassidy looked pissed.

"Doctor, maybe it would be best if you don't say anything more. We can discuss these things alone. I suppose we'll just have to pass the time by having a little preliminary conversation with Mr. Hart."

He opened the door to the adjoining room. Michael sat in a single chair in the middle, without restraints, but looking as if he were handcuffed. Imprisoned and defeated.

Before anyone else could move, Sakiko ran in and threw her arms around him.

"Michael, I'm so sorry. I had to tell him about the symbiote, about it getting away yesterday morning. He already knew everything from Fox." It was a risk, letting Cassidy know they were a couple, but he'd probably assumed it anyway.

He grabbed her arm and yanked her back.

"That will be enough, Ms. Matthews."

"Fox told you?" Michael asked Cassidy in a weak voice.

"Everything. So, there's no point lying. I have to say it's an honor to meet a man who actually has an alien living inside him."

"We've met before. But I think you've forgotten the meaning of the word 'honor' since then, Mr. Cassidy." Michael sat straighter. "I thought you were a hero. But you're obviously nothing more than a thug."

"Yes, you mentioned our meeting in your email. Do you know how many nerdy teenagers I met in those days? And not one in a thousand of you had what it takes to be an astronaut. I don't know how in hell someone like you was picked to be the ambassador to an alien race. Pure dumb luck, obviously. But I'm sure we can correct that situation."

It was the first hint of Cassidy's motivation for pursuing Michael. If anyone was going to bring advanced extraterrestrials to the people of Earth, it should have been Astronaut Hero Ryan Cassidy. He claimed to have encountered UFOs more than once. Maybe that had made him believe he was *chosen*. Until now.

Cassidy would see Michael as a usurper. And all of his bitterness about his transformation from hero to laughingstock might be transferred to the man the ETs had chosen in his place.

*How far would that jealousy go?* Sakiko wondered. *What was this man capable of?*

Cassidy began to ask pointed questions about the outpost in Canada and the symbiote. He wasn't a trained interrogator, but his attack was intelligent. Sakiko was impressed as Michael avoided verbal traps and deflected the most dangerous lines of questioning. He told the truth about the outpost—presumably Cassidy knew most of those details from other sources anyway—but he left out everything about the signal and the fact that the symbiote was the go-between.

He refused to be baited about special 'abilities.'

"What difference does it make anyway?" he said. "You'll never find it in the ocean. You scared it off, Cassidy. Brilliant move. Congratulations."

Cassidy took a slow breath then pulled a chair from the corner of the room, turned it around and sat with his arms resting on the chair back, the picture of an average Joe just looking for a friendly chat.

"Look, Hart...Michael. We don't have to be enemies. We're not so different. We've both been interested in space travel since we were kids. For you it was Mars, right? You even wrote a university thesis about a Mars expedition." The man had done his homework. "I'm betting you've always dreamed that extraterrestrials would visit Earth in your lifetime—that they'd usher in a wonderful new era for the human race. So have I. You probably know that I've seen UFOs. Twice! And now that bright future for humanity hinges on us—you and me, right here in this room."

Cassidy eyes were alight with conviction as he shifted forward on the chair.

"Contact with another species—probably a more advanced species—has to be handled the right way. Friendly, but not submissive. Cooperative, but with something held in reserve. We're talking about diplomacy at the highest level. Surely you can see that something so important can't just be left to one or two individuals playing it by ear! I'm sure you've done the best you can, but now you've got to hand it over to the professionals. For the sake of all humankind."

"You mean professionals who kidnap people at gunpoint? Nearly drown them to soften them up a little? Those professionals?" Michael's face was coolly blank.

Cassidy clenched his jaw and tried again. "It can't have been easy . . . having some kind of alien inside you. Now you say it's loose—it could spread anywhere, infect anyone—and maybe the next person will die from its infiltration. Or...or maybe the next person it encounters won't be so open-minded and will kill *it* the first chance they get. Is that what you want?

"I'm betting you have some idea where it will have gone, maybe even some way of contacting it. We could bring it in and protect it, while also keeping people safe from any risks it poses. Why can't you see that? Why won't you help me?"

"Help you make it a prisoner, a lab rat, like you've made me?" Michael shook his head in disbelief. "Yet you somehow still think you're the right person to represent humanity? The great Ryan Cassidy, anointed emissary to the new gods!"

They stared at each other: a standoff. Michael showed strength that Sakiko hadn't suspected. Cassidy held all the cards, but that wasn't obvious from the scene she was watching.

"All right, Hart. Tomorrow we'll run some tests. Many of them won't be very pleasant. You could still avoid that by telling me what I want to know." He stood up. "Don't delude yourself that you have any rights here. The local officials will take as long as they want—as long as *I* want—to contact the Canadian embassy. Maybe the message will even go astray, who knows? Mexicans don't waste a lot of worry on petty legalities, and they take the idea of an extraterrestrial incursion into human space very seriously."

"Don't believe him," Sakiko said.

"Ms. Matthews, I've allowed you to be here as a courtesy. Don't abuse it. So far, I've been able to keep the local soldiers from *interrogating* you, but I'm not sure I can stall them forever." His eyes were cold slits.

She drew a sharp breath and looked at Michael who seemed more afraid for her than for himself. That gave her strength.

"You're wasting your time and ours, Mr. Cassidy, and when this all comes out, the world will see you for the pathetic has-been you really are. Be sure of that."

Cassidy's eyes blazed for just a moment, but then he shook his head and laughed. His confidence frightened her more than any threat.

"Words, Ms. Matthews. Just words. No more than used-up air."

He knocked on the wall and a uniformed guard entered.

The guard took Sakiko to a small room with a chair, a desk, and a cot. As he left, she heard the lock click on the door. She was locked in for the night, and she had a feeling Michael's accommodations would be even worse.

Michael's rumpled appearance the next morning confirmed it.

"Sleep on the floor?" she asked. He only replied with a nod. The interrogation room smelled heavily of sweat, but not urine, so maybe their captors had some compassion. They were surprised when the guard left them alone to fetch Cassidy. Michael beckoned her close.

"I've done everything I could to warn Naïda about the testing, and not to reveal herself under any circumstances, but I don't know if it worked. I still can't sense anything from her. I mean she's *there*—I know that much—but she's not communicating. I think she's helpless."

His eyes showed that he felt the same way. She reached out to caress his face.

"How touching," Cassidy said from behind her. "If you really cared, you'd save him the pain of what he's about to go through by telling me what I want to know.

"Neither of you?" he pressed. "In a way, I'm disappointed. But part of me is very much looking forward to what comes next, Hart. You've caused me a lot of trouble."

Two guards returned Sakiko to her room, a cell in all but name. The intent seemed to be to subject Michael to a battery of invasive procedures and let Sakiko imagine the worst. That way Cassidy could attack the psyches of both.

Their situation wasn't hopeless, she thought. If the symbiote could only manage to withdraw itself from the blood and tissues where samples were taken, there might still be a chance to convince Cassidy that it was gone. Naïda was probably too diffuse to show up on magnetic imaging. It's offspring, though. Who knew how many there were and where Naïda had hidden them?

Nothing could be done about that.

For the first time, Sakiko tried to imagine how Naïda, was feeling. Did it experience fear? Jealousy? Anger? Did it feel imprisoned like she was?

They shouldn't have used the Botox treatment, no matter what the provocation. They simply didn't know enough about its effects on a living, thinking organism. It was the worst kind of selfishness, callousness. Bigotry. And Sakiko's own intolerance had probably pushed Michael into it.

She had lots of time to contemplate her shame.

At mealtimes, her guards allowed her to go to a small snack room. Soon after midday she was surprised to encounter Mendez, who looked uncomfortable but didn't avoid her.

"What are you doing to him?"

"Nothing vicious, I promise. Much of it is very routine health testing: blood sampling for contaminants, blood gases, stress tests, EEG, EKG, X-rays. We don't have an MRI scanner available here, but he'll be flown to one tomorrow. DNA testing, of course. That man Cassidy actually expects results within a day! Too much television, that one."

"Doctor, don't pretend to yourself that you're doing something noble here. Helping anyone. There's nothing wrong with Michael Hart except that he's being held prisoner, subjected to lab experiments against his will. If you don't report this to the American embassy, you're just as guilty as Cassidy is."

There was pain in his eyes as he brought his face inches away from hers.

"You think the American government doesn't know? Who do you think is paying for this? I'm just a preliminary examiner. If these tests do turn up something disturbing, specialists will be brought in. Then there'll be nothing more I can do for him."

Sakiko's stomach turned over, her suspicions confirmed, and she simply stared as he walked away.

They allowed her to see Michael for a few minutes in the early evening. He looked horrible, but still tried to smile for Cassidy's sake.

"I've had every orifice probed more times than I can count, and they should've just put faucets in the veins of my arms and thighs. They haven't found anything. There's nothing to find. But dickhead here is a little slow. I now have a lower opinion of the astronaut program's intelligence screening."

"I don't know what satisfaction you'll get from making me angry, Hart. Do you think I'll take a swing at you and then you'll use *kung fu* to make a getaway? You don't look like you could wrestle my grandmother right now."

Cassidy leaned his back against the wall. "Why won't you believe that I want the same things you want? A peaceful meeting of humans and extraterrestrials. The elevation of humanity to a place among other spacefaring races in the galaxy. I'm not evil. I don't want to use alien technology or biology to make weapons. Although I can't say the same about the men you'll meet in a few days if you don't help me out."

He moved to Michael's chair and leaned on the arms.

"Talk to me. Tell me everything you know, and I might be able to protect you from those others. Once they get here…."

Sakiko took a deep breath. Was Cassidy telling the truth? The doctor had told her much the same thing. She looked at Michael. He gave a small shake of his head.

"Screw yourself. The only one you want to help is Ryan Cassidy."

The man backed away, again allowing anger to show.

"It's too bad you feel that way. We might all have reason to regret that before long."

He walked stiffly away, followed by the guard and Sakiko; but when she was taken to a restroom just before lights out, she heard a rustling sound coming through a vent shared with the bathroom next door.

"Michael?" she ventured.

"Yeah, it's me."

"Are you sure you don't want to cooperate? You don't know what they'll do to you. Remember that you *wanted* to alert the authorities about the possibility of an alien invasion, but you didn't know how. This actually would be a way to do that."

"Cassidy can't be trusted, and any covert government agency will just keep the information secret for their own purposes. If they ever got their hands on Naïda they'd tear us both apart to find more exotic ways for the military to kill things. No, we either have to go public or tell no one."

After a long pause she said, "Please don't get yourself killed."

"I'll do my best."

Cassidy brought them together again for only a few moments the next morning.

"I'm not even going to bother asking anything," he said. "I just wanted you to know that your friend Yuri has tried to use the internet to tell the world about some kind of alien invasion. He seems very earnest, and also very skilled. Sadly for him, a ship at sea is easy to isolate. We've blanketed *Argo* with interference. Even the old Soviets couldn't have done better."

As he stepped toward the door, he turned to face Sakiko. "I'm afraid you won't be seeing Mr. Hart for a day or two. He'll be going on a little trip for some more testing. But then, you might be busy anyway. Shall we have a little chat?"

She followed him to a tiny office with a desk and two chairs. Her heart sank as she recognized the letterhead on a large envelope lying on the desk. The Foundation. Cassidy paid no attention to it as he sat in the chair behind the desk and slowly swiveled. Sakiko settled into the other chair of uncushioned hardwood.

"You know, my first wife was a marine biologist. Roz Quinlan. She even remembers you. Says you were one of the brightest students she ever had. I'm not sure she'd agree now." His eyes flicked to the envelope. "We sometimes saw Edward Ryder at parties. Kind of a prick—I can see why you wouldn't like him. But I couldn't understand why he didn't like you, why he'd be calling up old contacts like Roz trying to track you down. Until I read this, of course. Imagine my surprise to find out that the Sakiko Matthews I was looking for had *faked* her funding."

"Your *delight*, is what you mean."

"At least you don't try to deny it. I just hope there was nobody else involved who'd be dragged down with you. There was? Yuri Hutchings, if I had to guess. The thing is...it's such a small amount of money. I could get my hands on that much with a phone call."

"I suppose you'll buy Ryder off if I tell you everything I know about Michael and the alien symbiote." The answer was a shrug.

"What is Michael Hart to you, really? You only met him a few weeks ago, and he's been nothing but a pain in the ass since. Your research expedition—years of work establishing your reputation, busting your butt to get the stats, spending as much time on funding pitches as on publishable papers. A cause you believed in so deeply that you were willing to risk your entire career, even *go to jail*, and suddenly along comes this guy who hijacks the whole thing, chasing after aliens. The sooner you can put Hart behind you, the sooner you can get back to your real work, your real life. Reputation and career intact."

"What if Ryder won't be bought?"

"I remember Roz telling me a story about a grad student Ryder tried to pressure into sex. Yeah, I thought it was you. The story never came out. But it could."

He leaned over the desk and spread his hands over the folder. "I could make all of this go away."

She stared at the damning letterhead. Nothing he'd said was untrue. It was hard to believe how her whole life had been derailed in the past few weeks. It would feel so good just to have things back the way they were, to do the things she knew how to do. And a whole lot better than jail.

"You're very smart, Mr. Cassidy. But you don't know everything. There are things more important than *status quo*. Sometimes it just takes the right situation to open our eyes."

"Am I to take that as a No?

"The funny thing is, I'm beginning to believe that if you were me, you'd make the same choice. I never thought I'd give you that much credit."

Cassidy stood and called to the guard outside.

"Don't get too used to your accommodations, Ms. Matthews. You won't be in them for much longer."

# 45

The rest of that day and most of the next were a mix of excruciating boredom and the anticipation that the next time a guard appeared they'd be accompanied by some US law-enforcement agency come to arrest her. It didn't happen. Likely Cassidy still believed she'd be of use to him and didn't want to give away any of his cards.

As she was finishing her lunch on the second day, she encountered Doctor Mendez again. He didn't smile.

"What's wrong? Is there something wrong with Michael?"

"Wrong? I'm not sure how you define that."

"Has something happened to him? Is he still all right?"

"He's healthy. Oh, yes. In fact, I've never studied anyone healthier." He gave her a strange look.

"It wasn't supposed to be a trick question."

"Michael Hart has better blood chemistry, cholesterol, blood pressure, respiratory performance, endocrinal regulation—you name it—than anyone I've ever met. Every single measure is absolutely optimum for a human being."

"What's wrong with that?"

"Well, perfection is hardly normal! I didn't want to believe Mr. Cassidy's outlandish suggestions, but something is regulating Michael's body systems to a degree that can't be explained by chance." He rubbed his eyes. "I've never believed in aliens. I still don't but..."

"But what?"

He avoided her eyes. "But I had to report that there is something...*superhuman* about those results. I shouldn't have used that word."

"Why?"

"Because it has set things in motion that I can't control. The DNA samples we took have been sent for top-priority analysis to one of the most sophisticated DNA labs in the world. I've only ever seen measures like that...well, at the outbreak of a new fatal disease, for example."

Sakiko pressed him to explain further, but he would say no more.

Late that afternoon, she heard Michael and Cassidy return, and caught a glimpse of a man with them that she hadn't seen before. A bulbous head that appeared to be completely bald sprouted large ears and thick blond eyebrows above a pair of wire-rimmed glasses with round lenses. The nose was unusually flat and the mouth thin but curved in a perpetual smile. He reminded Sakiko of a Muppet, and she felt a surge of hope. Maybe someone from the Canadian embassy?

A guard near her said something in Spanish that she didn't understand.

"What?"

"*Interrogator*," he said.

Cassidy came to her room. He'd lost a lot of his cockiness and looked very unhappy.

"The man's name is White...supposedly," he said. "I told you that if you didn't cooperate with me, you'd have to deal with someone worse. I don't even know who he works for, but I have a feeling there's no official record of his visit here."

"I don't understand. If the American government is behind this, why haven't they moved Michael to the States?"

"Are you that naïve? There's a big advantage to not being on American soil, subject to all those annoying human rights laws and government oversight committees."

"If I didn't know better, I'd think you actually disapproved."

Cassidy's eyes turned to her with a rare touch of sadness.

"I'm really not a villain, Ms. Matthews. I simply think that contact between humans and extraterrestrials must be handled the right way. You and Hart have been given an incredible opportunity, and you're blowing it. Wasting it. Playing with fire. Protecting you from yourselves is a kindness, and an obligation to our race."

"I think you spent too long looking down from orbit, Cassidy. You think you're still somehow above the rest of us."

He shook his head and walked out, locking her door.

Soon after, a guard came to take her to Michael. He was in the same chair in the middle of the room, but now he wore handcuffs. The man who called himself White stood beside him, hands behind his back. Again, Sakiko was struck by the interrogator's air of bonhomie and harmlessness. How long must it have taken for him to perfect that? she wondered.

"Ah, Ms. Matthews, thank you for joining us. Would you like to take a seat?"

"I can do without the handcuffs, thanks anyway."

White smiled. "Just a precaution. I've been told many things about Mr. Hart. Until I can be sure which of them are true...." He shrugged his shoulders. "I'd like this to be friendly, but so far, Mr. Hart isn't very receptive. I hope you can help me convince him of what an important contribution he can make to our country."

Michael scoffed. "I'm Canadian. You've imprisoned a Canadian citizen on Mexican soil without charges, haven't let me speak to my embassy, and you want me to believe we're all friends?"

"Then let's say, a contribution to humanity. From what I understand, you've made contact with an envoy from an extraterrestrial race. You've even had an alien species inside you. You represent a pivotal moment in human history, Mr. Hart. You could be a hero—the most famous person in the world."

"Then why aren't we standing in front of cameras on the lawn of the White House?" Michael leaned back. "Don't pretend that you're going to let the world know about me, Mr. White. I'm no genius, but I'm not that naïve."

The bald man gave another smile—more tight-lipped this time—and slowly paced behind Michael and back again.

"You're right, that might not happen right away. Consider the kind of panic news like that would cause. The world needs to be prepared for such a thing, and we need to be prepared first, for what might come if these visitors aren't quite so benevolent as you seem to think.

"So, help us, Mr. Hart. Tell us everything you know about these...alien outposts. Give our scientists all the information you can about what this symbiote did to your body. Tell us where it has gone and how we can contact it."

"Even if I could, do you expect me to believe you'd treat it as an honored guest? You'd bury it so deep in your secret labs it would never see the light of day. Take it apart, piece by piece, hoping to make a weapon you could use against its host species, or at least against your human enemies."

Tightly under control, White turned to Sakiko.

"You're a scientist, Ms. Matthews. Tell him how important it is for us to know everything we can about these creatures. A whole new biology! Their genetic makeup might reveal a cure for cancer, a means to prevent aging!"

"Or secrets to ensure that the US stays at the top of the global power-pyramid, anyway," Sakiko said coldly.

"You're American. Would that be so wrong?"

"I'm also a citizen of the world. Forgive me if I don't accept that when we make contact with a species from another planet, our military-industrial complex is our best hope to make a good impression."

Michael snorted. "What she said!"

White no longer looked like a favorite uncle. His jaw was clenched and his skin even more pallid. He turned his back to them.

"You could both be extremely wealthy for the rest of your lives," he said.

Michael's honest laugh startled the guards.

"You're as pathetic as Cassidy over there," he said. "If you want me to be cooperative, set me free."

"I can't do that."

"Didn't think so."

Michael looked at Sakiko as if to make sure she was still okay with his resistance. She gave a reluctant nod.

White turned back and signaled to a guard.

"How disappointing," he said. "I've given you both the opportunity to do the right thing. What happens next is all on you."

The guard led Sakiko back to her room. Her last view of Michael, sitting up straight and determined, made her proud.

And terrified.

She was awakened by alarm bells and the sound of running feet. An endless twenty minutes later the doctor and two guards came for her. They took her to a room that looked as if it were equipped to handle surgery, its walls lined with myriad machines that flashed lights and emitted strange noises. Racks of floodlights overhead aimed at a mechanical bed in the middle holding Michael Hart, thrashing weakly against restraints. As she got closer, she saw that his eyes were staring at nothing and there was foam at his mouth.

"*Oh my God.* What did you do to him?"

The man named White raised a hand and the guards held her back. Mendez took her by the shoulders.

"Look at me. Does Mr. Hart have any serious allergies?"

"Not...not that I know of."

"Any history of epilepsy? Other seizures? Has he traveled to Africa? *Ms. Matthews!*"

"No. I don't *know*! We never talked about anything like that. We didn't require a medical history. What have you done to him? What's wrong?"

"We think...we think it might be a bad reaction to drugs that he was given."

She gasped. "Like *truth serum*? My God, you people are unbelievable!" She shot toward White with her hands spread like claws, but the guards were on her instantly.

"Do I have to have you removed, Ms. Matthews?" White said in a voice like scratched glass. "It would be much more helpful if you would tell us something that could save Mr. Hart's life."

"This is a trick to get me to talk?"

"It's no trick," Dr. Mendez said forcefully. He swept a hand toward the machines. "His vital signs are crashing. This shouldn't have happened. We have no idea what to do. Anything we try might make things worse. Unless you can help us."

A sob wrenched from her throat and her legs went limp. The guards dragged her to a chair near Michael's head, but she threw her arms over his middle, giving in to tears. A male nurse moved to stop her but White waved him away.

"Tell us something, Ms. Matthews. Before it's too late."

"I don't know anything, you bastards!" she screamed. "He's not like us anymore, don't you get it? You can't go pumping poisons into him. The symbiote changed everything. It could regulate his breathing, his metabolism—probably all of his body systems, but..."

"But it's no longer inside him—yes, so you've said." Incredibly, White still wore his penciled-on smile. "That's a great shame. It appears there's nothing more we can do. If you and your friend had only chosen to be more cooperative...." He turned his back to her and drew the doctor and Cassidy into the hallway where they began talking in low voices.

Sakiko put her head to Michael's ear. The burning skin turned moist from her tears.

"Naïda. *Naïda!*" she whispered as loudly as she dared. "You've got to do something! Michael never meant to harm you. We just didn't understand. Please, Naïda. Don't abandon him. Don't give up on him. You can't..." Sobs overwhelmed her, and she could only hold Michael's hand and cry into his shirt.

The rare moments that sleep claimed her that night were filled with evil dreams. When she couldn't lie still on her cot any longer, she would go to her door and knock. At first the guard didn't want to tell her anything, but a look into her face made him take pity. After that, he would simply say, "Still alive" when he heard her knock. It was better than nothing.

Soon after first light, they allowed her to go to the operating room. Cassidy was there, but not White. Michael still looked to be at death's door, but his eyes were open, and he tried to smile when he saw her.

"How are you feeling?" she asked.

"*Twice* as good as yesterday." He gave her a pointed look. She fought to keep surprise from showing on her face.

"The assholes gave you sodium pentothal or some shit like that. It must have caused a fever. I thought I was going to lose you."

He nodded. "Not a hundred percent yet, but the paralysis is starting to pass."

She smiled, and it felt so good.

"I'm truly glad. It was a bad mistake."

He nodded again. Even this short exchange had taken Michael a lot of effort, and he laid his head down and closed his eyes. His lips began to move as if he were mumbling words to himself.

They let her stay with him for the rest of the day, but never alone, and the room was equipped with cameras. Michael slept most of the time. Even though Sakiko's only knowledge of the medical monitoring machines came from TV shows, she felt sure their readings were improving. Michael's color slowly returned, and his raspy breathing fell into a gentle, quiet rhythm.

Cassidy shattered the relative peacefulness in the early evening as he stormed into the room. Dozens of men and women were visible in the hallway behind him, wearing something like hazmat suits and carrying rolls of plastic and coiled hoses.

"What's going on?" she asked Cassidy.

"We're in quarantine. Every last one of us. And soon, anyone else who's come into contact with Michael Hart."

It was an hour later that the doctor appeared, followed by White. Cassidy had spent a lot of the hour pacing the floor.

"What's this all about?" Cassidy snapped.

Mendez looked at White, who shrugged and smiled.

"It's all right, Doctor. You can tell them. It may be instructive for Ms. Matthews to hear this, too."

With Sakiko's help, Michael was able to sit up in the bed. She took his hand and was reminded of all the scenes in movies where a hospital surgeon tells bad news to a husband and wife.

"It's your DNA, Michael," Mendez began, sweat evident at his hairline. "That's not my specialty, but I was briefed. They...didn't want any more people coming here and being exposed."

"The symbiote was never contagious," Michael said.

"*You* might be." Mendez looked for a place to sit and finally perched on a piece of counter beside a scrub sink. "How much do any of you know about *non-coding* DNA?"

"Junk DNA?" Sakiko asked.

"Some of it might be junk, or at least inactive leftover scraps not needed anymore. But much of it, if not most, does serve a purpose. DNA is just bits of data that give instructions. Less than two percent of human DNA actually provides the codes to make the proteins that build living cells. In many cases, the coding DNA is controlled—activated and regulated—by non-coding DNA nearby. Those sequences might be switches, data backups, specialized instructions—we're far from knowing all the possible uses made of it, but we know what's there. It has been mapped."

"Tell them what this has to do with Mr. Hart, Doctor."

Mendez coughed nervously, covering his mouth with his hand.

"The lab discovered that Mr. Hart's DNA has many, *many* differences from a typical human being, differences almost entirely within the non-coding DNA, including a great many sequences that are unmistakably viruses."

"*Viruses!*" Cassidy's arms uncrossed and he rubbed his palms on his thighs. The doctor raised a hand.

"A lot of human DNA sequences originated in viruses and have either been neutralized or put to some effective use. We've lived with them for thousands of years. They're very easy to identify. It's *not* so easy to identify the ones in Michael's cells, however. I'm told there are dozens, perhaps hundreds, that follow the viral patterns but are—no pun intended—totally alien."

"Contagious?"

"We have no way to know. Until we do, we have to assume the worst: that Michael has been transformed into a biological weapon that could cause devastation to life on Earth."

"Come on, doctor," Sakiko said. "That's total paranoia." But no one else in the room seemed to think so.

Not even Michael.

"How will we know if Hart is carrying a deadly virus?" Cassidy asked.

The doctor gave up trying to be nonchalant and wiped sweat from his brow with his hand.

"Well, it will almost certainly kill him first."

# 46

Naïda is weak. Weaker than she has ever been since her near-death just before bonding with Michael. At that time the replication and deliberate mutation of her genes was interrupted in transition and her body had begun to fail. The new weakness is only fatigue from a profligate expenditure of her resources for far longer than was safe. A simple cause, but no less dangerous. It has been necessary. It has saved the life of her bondmate, and her own.

Despite the lethargy, she revels in the feeling of restored freedom.

For days she used every method she could just to shift her substance away from areas where strange humans were withdrawing quantities of Michael's cells. He felt it was crucial for her to do so, though she still cannot truly understand his desire to keep her hidden. Surely the benefit of interacting with the Creators would be evident to anyone.

Even such small actions were nearly impossible, caught as she still was in the web of the poison the humans called Botox.

Then new toxins attacked his body, and for a time she welcomed defeat, since his death would also result in hers. She would have let it claim her if it had not been for the woman Sakiko.

Through a few spoken words, the touch of skin on skin, and the shedding of fluids, she came to understand that this woman was experiencing the kind of intolerable pain that Naïda herself had come to know. Much worse than physical pain.

Nothing less than *the loss of a bondmate.*

That Sakiko can feel such a thing is a revelation to Naïda. It does not seem possible. Humans remain forever in separate bodies—she knows this. Yet she is sure that she was not mistaken, and the woman's words made Naïda ashamed that she ever considered abandoning Michael to his fate.

The Botox had disabled certain nerve receptors, and she could not revive them. The toxin itself was gone, but its effects remained, and would last until the body replaced affected cells in the normal course of its maintenance. It was a deeply held racial memory that finally revealed the answer: a powerful capacity of hers and Michael's combined DNA to create non-specialized cells able to become any kind of cell the body required.

She made new nerve cells to replace the damaged ones.

The effort required has been immense. When new chemicals were poured into Michael's system, she should have diverted them as she did with alcohol, but she simply had no resources to spare. His body had to fend for itself for a time, and its temperature climbed dangerously high. At last, as she began to make real progress with cell regeneration, she could turn some of her attention to other battles.

Full recovery would still be a long way off, but Michael's improvement is dramatic. Her own condition is a concern. She does not dare draw any more energy from Michael—he has none to spare. If she could only get some rest.

Still, even with her reserves of strength so badly depleted, she no longer contemplates defeat.

Her bondmate needs her *and wants her.* In spite of his new human bond with the woman Sakiko. Naïda had held out no hope for that.

He has told her over and over that his treatment of her was a terrible mistake. He asks for something humans call *forgiveness.* She would gladly give it if she knew what it was.

The only stain on this reunion is Michael's new fear that the Creators have distributed deadly diseases throughout his DNA as a potential attack against the humans.

*That cannot be.*

The Creators would not design her to bond with a human only to use the bonding to kill him and others of his race. That would be pure evil.

She tries to reassure Michael, but she has no proof to offer, and he remains deeply fearful.

She must allow herself to be *happy*, and trust that the happiness will find its way to him, like oxygen, water, and energy.

Hours pass in this state, as she tries to carefully distribute the nutrients Michael consumes for optimal healing. It does not leave much for regular processes, including those with which Naïda is most inextricably linked, but she can endure that a little longer. The fulfillment of purpose is bliss.

The peace does not last. The dangerous humans have come back, speaking information that she can tell is profoundly disturbing to Michael and Sakiko.

As the others exchange angry words, Michael communicates with Naïda. He asks her if she understands the concept of sacrificing one's own life for the sake of others.

She says that she does.

# 47

"Well, Hart, it looks like your aliens have already gone on the attack!"

White's ever-present smile had vanished, and his face was approaching crimson. His ears had already reached it.

"What are you talking about? Attacking Earth?" Michael struggled to sit up, but he was still weak. He fumbled around and found the controls for the bed, raising the upper half. Sakiko hurried to his side.

"They've attacked a goddamn submarine. And you could have helped us stop this. I'll see that you pay for it."

"Cassidy, explain what this lunatic is raving about. I don't know anything about a submarine."

Cassidy took a few steps into the room and glanced at White, who gave an angry nod. Doctor Mendez entered too, looking as if he was having the worst day of his life. He perched on a small filing cabinet in the corner but couldn't stop fidgeting.

"It's a Brit sub," Cassidy began. "It happened to be on patrol a few hours from Rocas Alijos. We...the U.S.

Government asked the captain to take a look around: with sonar, and whatever else they've got."

"Looking for the outpost we couldn't find. God, Fox did tell you everything. But it would be organic and I doubt if it would show up on sonar."

"We don't know whether it did or not. The sub has gone down. Its only communications were emergency messages."

Michael felt their eyes probing him, but he was completely mystified, and it must have showed. Cassidy gave a heavy sigh and sat on a stool.

"As far as we've heard, *HMS Torrance* was cruising along with no indication of trouble when ship's power suddenly failed. They lost everything for a few seconds, including sonar and navigation. Long enough to cause a collision with the seamount. Emergency power cut in soon after, but they've only got enough for life support and some instrumentation. No way to move the sub."

"*Fucking aliens!*" White snarled.

"We don't know that," Cassidy said.

"How bad is it?" Sakiko asked.

"The sub is lying at an angle on the seamount slope. A hundred and seventy meters deep. About a hundred and fifty crew on board, although some are probably dead and the rest...well they soon will be." Cassidy ran his hand over his face. "The collision made a hole amidships on the starboard side. Flooded a few compartments—some of the most critical, including the reactor itself and the reactor control room. There are diesel generators right below the reactor, but they're flooded too. Luckily, most bulkheads closed as designed, and the crewmen everywhere else are still getting air."

"You said they'll soon be dead. Why? Is the rest of the ship flooding? Why can't they use the escape hatches?"

"There's no further flooding as far as we know. A U.S. Navy vessel is on the way with a remote-controlled submersible that can mate with the escape hatches, and transport survivors to the surface. But it will take more than half a day to get there. The *Torrance's* crew doesn't have that long." He sucked a harsh breath. "The collision must have caused a leak in the reactor's cooling system. The captain says core temperature is climbing slowly but steadily. The reactor should have scrammed automatically, but didn't. Attempts to scram remotely from the command center haven't been successful. Scram controls in the maneuvering room are watertight and should be getting emergency power, but that compartment is flooded."

"A meltdown." Sakiko's words were an awed whisper.

Cassidy nodded. "Probably within the next four hours. There'll be steam explosions that will tear the ship apart. Even before then, radiation levels will be devastating."

"There's no way the crew could survive a free ascent from that depth," she added.

"No," Mendez spoke up. "The deepest I've ever heard about was just over sixty meters, and the survivor suffered lifelong health problems."

White stepped forward. "Enough chatter. Hart, if you know anything that can help those British crewmen and you don't tell us, then God damn you to hell."

Michael stared straight ahead, unable to speak. What could he possibly know that would help?

"He can't contact the aliens," Sakiko said. "Fox must have told you that we tried to find an installation near Rocas Alijos and failed. It was gone. We believe..." she looked at Michael, but continued, "that artificial intelligences run the outposts—not live aliens. I won't accept that one of them would do something like this, then do nothing to help, either."

White thrust his face up to Sakiko's. "What you accept or don't accept..."

"*Send me*," said Michael.

The others were shocked into silence.

"*No!* You've never gone that deep!"

"What do you mean, Hart?"

"No!" Sakiko grabbed his shoulders, her voice cracking. "You're barely hanging on as it is."

"I don't understand. What could he do?" Mendez slipped off the cabinet. "You said the symbiote had left you."

"I did say that."

"You said we would never find it in the ocean. Are you saying it will find you?" White growled.

"Just send me."

"Michael, *please!*"

"A brave gesture, Hart," Cassidy said, "but you're forgetting that steam has already escaped. The reactor will be bubbling out more before you can get there. That reactor compartment will be flooded with radiation. Even if you could get the reactor to scram, you'd be committing suicide."

Michael swallowed and shook his head. "We can handle it."

Cassidy turned to Sakiko. "Is he lying?"

"Yes."

Michael felt his chest tighten as he reached out a hand to cup Sakiko's chin.

"I'm full of alien viruses, remember? If I'm going to cash out anyway...I'd rather it *counted* for something."

The crew of the MH-60G Pave Hawk helicopter were protected by hazmat suits—the huge aircraft had been used to ferry the quarantine team to Mexico but now was on a different mission. Michael, Sakiko, and Cassidy wore headsets to enable them to hear instructions from a Royal Navy specialist as they closed in on the site. The rich blue of the ocean below calmed Michael, and his breath caught as they overflew the starkly beautiful Alijos Rocks.

He was shocked to see *Argo* not far away flanked by two smaller vessels at some distance, probably the same Mexican Navy ships that had come for them...how many days before? He found he didn't know. Time had blurred together like a bad dream.

"Probably the piping," the RN specialist was saying. "It's a Trafalgar-class sub that's decades old, and leaks have happened before in that class. Temperature sensors are included in the emergency-power priorities, and at last word from *Torrance*, the reactor pile is still below critical but won't last much more than an hour. We still feel there won't be any irreversible damage yet—not from heating, anyway. Pray the collision didn't jam anything. So, nothing should prevent a scram if you can get the mechanism to trip. As I've said, the reactor controls in the maneuvering room should be intact, but to get to it from the aft hatch would require flooding another big section of the ship. That may not be necessary.

"An ROV was dropped from a helicopter, and it shows a large hole amidships starboard. Right about where the switchboard room is, just below the maneuvering room. The hole in the outer hull *looks* like it's big enough for a man—we can't tell for sure about the pressure hull inside, but if it *is* big enough for you to fit through, be bloody careful of the edges. They'll be like knives."

Michael thanked him and stared again at the sub's layout on the screen in front of him. Normally he had a great visual memory, but with the stress of the situation he was afraid he'd forget everything the moment he hit the water. He did his best to reassure the navy officer and the others that his instructions were simple and clear and that he understood them. Even he couldn't screw them up.

The plunge of the helicopter startled him. They were directly above the submarine. The Pave Hawk settled slowly to a hover only meters from the water. Michael didn't want to waste time using the hoist.

"It's going to be dark down there, and it's a big ocean," Cassidy yelled over the rotor and wind noise as the side door opened.

"Don't worry." Michael gave a weak smile, then turned to squeeze Sakiko's hand.

"How long do you think it will take for the symbiote to find you?"

Michael just smiled wider.

"She never left him," Sakiko answered.

And he leaped into the sea.

# 48

As the cloud of bubbles surrounding him began to disperse, Michael had an exhilarating feeling of wholeness. Naïda quickly prepared him for the underwater environment as he dived toward the deep blue. His first breath of water made him cough—his lungs were still weak—but now he belonged to the sea as much as the land. Naïda gave a warm yellow glow to his vision in agreement.

He asked if she sensed any alien presence.

*I am in contact with The Controller now,* she said.

The Controller? The artificial intelligence of the Rocas Alijos outpost, presumably.

It hadn't even revealed itself to her when they were there. Had that been a snub? Apparently, the new situation changed things.

*How do they communicate?* He'd never asked before.

She didn't answer right away. The increase in water pressure and diminishing light were becoming noticeable. He could tell she'd boosted his metabolism to fight off the cold.

*There is a device under the bone near your ear, implanted just after we bonded. It is transparent to the energy used by human detection systems.*

An implanted transceiver. A *bug*! And she'd never told him. That was an unwelcome reminder of his recent mistrust. Were there still crucial things she wasn't telling him? Their lives might depend on it.

*The Controller insisted. The Controller acts for the Creators. And my species.*

Of course. What a painful position she'd been forced into, owing her very existence to 'the Creators' and yet irrevocably tied to a creature of another species. Like an arranged marriage between potential enemies. He had no right to judge her. He owed her his life.

*Secrets are not good. They hurt.*

Amen to that.

They were leaving the world of light behind. His eyes adjusted, but they were still too far from the bottom for any shapes to resolve out of the murk. A small but powerful flashlight was mounted on a band around his head like a miner's light, since the spaces inside the flooded hull would be pitch black. Even Naïda couldn't boost light where there was none. He could detach the unit and hold it in his hand if needed.

Why was the Controller contacting her now?

*It does not want me to continue. It wants me to stop.*

Oh shit. *Why?*

*There is a high probability that we will die, Michael and Naïda.*

Of course. If the artificial intelligence was tasked with carrying out the directives of the Creators, then Naïda might be its only agent on Earth with freedom of movement to take action. More than that, she was the last of her species. Even her offspring would be hybrids, and they had apparently disappeared. Michael had no right to ask her to sacrifice herself for people of his race.

If she wanted to stop him, she had only to stiffen his limbs, leave him vulnerable to the cold, or reduce the oxygen reaching his blood. His lungs were already laboring. He didn't know how they could go any deeper and still function, especially as weakened as they both were.

They had no business being here at all except that the plight of the submarine's crew had vividly resonated with Michael—as part of his research for a Mars colony, he had studied the psychological implications of the life submariners lived. Although his focus had been on spacecraft and space colonies, living conditions weren't so very different: personal bonding from living in close quarters surrounded by a hostile environment, commitment to a shared duty, constant awareness of sudden danger to self and companions.

The sunken submarine would be a pressure cooker, forcing relationships, professional and personal, to the breaking point. Extremes of human behavior would be manifesting themselves, from the most cowardly to the most heroic, from heartless self-interest to courageous self-sacrifice. Now, only he and Naïda could do anything about it. They were the only ones who could prevent the ultimate social collapse—and a most cruel communal death.

He had a sudden flashback to the woman trapped in the sunken car in the Wanapitei River: the panic in her eyes and the fear in his own heart that he didn't have the right stuff to save her. Yet he had saved her.

Maybe it had been a practice run for this vastly greater challenge.

His eyes had been seeing the submarine for nearly a minute before he realized it—his brain had taken it for some vast feature of the seamount. Seeing all of it meant that he must still be a good distance away. He swam harder, but as his eyes began to resolve more detail, he slowed.

The starboard side was facing a steep slope, the keel lodged against giant boulders; but the sub looked as if it might slide farther at any moment. It wasn't vertical but tipped perhaps thirty degrees to port. As he swam across the top of the superstructure, he watched for signs of damage. He had to follow the hull's curve downward before he finally saw the hole, like an obscene cancer.

There were more than one hundred and thirty souls still trapped within the cold steel cylinder. He tried to imagine what they were doing. There wouldn't be much they could do but wait and keep their oxygen needs to a minimum. Their emergency batteries wouldn't last forever.

He had no idea what the crew had been told—almost certainly not the whole truth. Maybe a more optimistic prediction for the arrival of the SRDRS submersible and its capabilities. Waiting helplessly for a terribly slim chance at life would be a refined torture.

He turned his attention back to the hole. Some radioactive water would already have leaked into the surrounding sea, but that black, ragged mouth was truly a point of no return.

What was Naïda prepared to do? Would she help him? Or would she remain loyal to the race that had been linked with her own for millennia?

*I have blocked communication with the Controller. You are my bondmate. We are one.*

A surge of emotion gripped his throat, and he couldn't afford that. He forced his mind back to the job at hand. It was only a few more meters to the jagged rent in the thick steel. There was a gash about twelve meters long, parallel to the keel, but only a third of that length was a complete puncture. Short as it was, it had exposed several compartments to the open sea, including the reactor compartment itself. Width was going to be a problem. The rent in the outer hull was a meter across at its widest, but the pressure hull breach was much narrower. He might not fit through.

The sea water oozing back out of the hole was noticeably warmer—it must mean the runaway reactor core was getting a small measure of cooling from the surrounding liquid. Where there was heat, there was radiation.

Suppressing his dread, he pushed his head close to the inner hole and raised the flashlight. Any obstruction would mean he'd be out of luck. The beam reflected off a flat surface a meter away, or less. He'd need to be a contortionist.

Fighting discouragement, he paused to rest and think. The simple act of drawing water into his lungs was a constant gasping for breath, like a marathon runner at the finish line. How could they possibly accomplish anything in that condition?

*There is no one else.*

Unquestionably true.

He rolled over, face tilted up, and carefully gripped the upper edge of the hole in the pressure hull. The naval officer hadn't exaggerated: it felt like grabbing the blade of a giant's bread knife. Dive gloves would have helped. Very slowly, he thrust his head through the hole. The tough part would be his shoulders. He slipped inward and felt a pair of daggers dig into his shoulder blades. His arms were in the way. Backing out a little, he slid them up the inside surface, feeling for a seam or anything his fingers could grip. There was nothing. He had to give a light kick with his feet and ignore the razor claws down his back. Bend at the waist, slide a little more. He could barely raise his head and saw nothing but blank wall. Now his torso was in. His back bumped the flat surface, and he rested for another few seconds.

There was just enough room to turn his hips to the right, bringing his left leg under and then drawing his knees toward his chest. It worked, with the addition of a few more cuts, but he had to push with his feet on the jagged edge to straighten his body. After that, he was able to rotate and rise to the top of the obstacle that had blocked him: a cabinet or piece of machinery maybe.

As he swept the flashlight, he braced himself for a sudden appearance of a bloated drowned face—it always happened in horror movies. But he was spared that—the cabinet extended right to the ceiling. He was in the switchboard room, as predicted, filled with boxy racks of equipment and little else. He eased to his right around a corner. Something dragged across the skin of his back, weedlike. It made him shiver, and he pointed the light beam upward.

Into the face of a corpse.

He started and banged the back of his head.

She was floating face down, her staring eyes less than an arm's length from his own, her face partially obscured by strands of blond hair. Long for a navy crewman. Probably she'd had it restrained, but it had come loose in the water.

His initial revulsion gave way to a devastating sadness, as if this one dead woman represented the deaths of the whole crew. But that wasn't true. Not yet. If he didn't damn well pull himself together and get moving, it *would* be true. He swam along the outer wall and found an exit.

*This water will kill us.*

She meant the radiation. *How soon?*

*Within days.*

No, he wanted to know how much time they had before they received a fatal dose.

*Unknown.*

He could have borrowed a dosimeter, but its readings wouldn't have changed anything. The very water he breathed was poisoning him. He had to forget that. Just get in, get out, and hopefully save the lives of others—lives that weren't already forfeit.

The compartments to his right were also flooded, he knew. The maneuvering room he needed to get to was directly above him, but the nearest stairwell was on the other side of a bulkhead.

The swinging flashlight beam lit up another corpse, floating with legs and arms splayed. Michael swallowed his fear and gently pushed it out of the way.

The bulkhead door swung open smoothly, but it admitted a gush of water that nearly scalded him. He frantically backed all the way down the corridor, bumping into the dead man. The heating of the water had created pressure that forced it into the cooler compartment, but he didn't know if the mixing of the liquid would be enough to produce a safe temperature.

He waited a couple of minutes, aware that each one that passed brought the reactor closer to a meltdown. Then he moved ahead, but the water there was still blistering hot, and he had to retreat.

That corridor was right outside the reactor room—the temperature of the water would only continue to rise.

There was no other choice.

He sensed that Naïda understood. She would do everything she could to distribute the heat away from his skin without spreading it to his vital organs or brain. And she would have to do it for as long as it took for him to swim through that next corridor, up a stairwell to the compartment above, and through at least one bulkhead.

His head already pounded from lack of oxygen—he didn't know how he'd be able to expend that much effort. But he couldn't put it off any longer.

Fitting the flashlight into its headband mount, he eased back against the bulkhead behind him, and gave a powerful push with his legs. His water-adapted limbs rocketed him through the black water as if he were traveling through the tunnel carved by the beam of light. Breathing was unthinkable—he didn't dare let the scorching water into his lungs. It seared his skin, and he stifled a groan.

A bulkhead. He rapped it, heard no difference in sound, cranked the wheel and pulled. Dragged himself through, but the water was still far too hot. Up the stairwell. Another bulkhead on the left, and another only a couple of meters beyond that. It felt like his skin was roasting away and a scream forced his lips apart, but his teeth clenched in pain. He passed through the second bulkhead and closed it behind him with barely enough strength left to turn the wheel, then leapt away from the heated water that had followed him in and gasped a breath.

For five precious minutes he could do nothing but breathe, sucking in lungfuls of water and expelling them, sucking in more. His head felt like it would explode. Sparks of light flashed in the darkness, but he knew he was imagining them. At least, he prayed he was.

He'd made it to the maneuvering room. If its shielded electronics were intact, he could complete his mission.

He couldn't sense anything from Naïda. She might be in shock. Utterly, utterly spent.

Please, God, don't let her be dead.

He slowly turned his head to sweep the room with the narrow flashlight beam. There were several bodies this time. Four. No, five. All but one floated very near to him. The other, a woman, was farther in, illuminated by a single glowing monitor screen. She'd probably been sitting in the chair in front of it when the water began to gush in.

The hole into this room was smaller. Its inhabitants would have seen their deaths coming, and most had tried to escape through the bulkhead. Perhaps she'd known that it was no use. Or maybe she'd understood the need to stay at the reactor's controls as long as she possibly could. She might have received the captain's order to scram the reactor—if only she'd lived that long.

Michael swam over next to her. The wide screen showed several readings that he couldn't understand, but its temperature gauge was obvious. It was flashing bright red. The core was far into the danger zone. Freed neutrons were ricocheting through the reactor splitting uranium atoms at a rate that would be increasing exponentially. A lot of radiation would now be hitting the crew.

He refused to think about his own exposure.

The lower half of the monitor was a touch screen, and the emergency manual scram command was right where the Brit navy guy had said it would be, but it required a code. Michael pressed the icon on the screen.

Nothing happened.

He pressed again, and again. A fourth time. A fifth.

Wait. The computer station had been sealed to be waterproof, but he didn't know if it used a resistive screen technology, or capacitive. What if it couldn't sense the conductivity of his skin because it was wet, and the water was very warm?

He tried again, pressing the screen firmly and dragging his fingertip a little.

A virtual keypad appeared. He pressed in the code he'd been given, but the screen flashed red and gave an error message. He was sure the code was right, but the screen still wasn't reading his touch properly.

He tried a second time, pressing much more carefully.

The error message again.

Jesus! Systems like that often shut down after three failed attempts. Another failure would cost more than a hundred lives.

Desperately, he tried to reach Naïda.

*I am here.*

Was there any way she could increase the electrical conductivity of his fingertips? It was all he could think of.

She didn't respond.

He called her with the full force of his mind.

No answer. But he couldn't wait any longer. The temperature gauge now strobed in mute panic.

He keyed in the code.

It was accepted.

The entire screen flashed with a message indicating an emergency scram. Control rods would be sliding into the reactor to absorb the cascading neutrons. If only the tremendous heat hadn't warped the core or the rods. If it had, they were dead.

The screen flashed green. The color that signaled life. Life!

Michael closed his eyes and shook with relief.

The successful scram meant the core hadn't melted out of shape, and risk of it's doing so should be over. Seawater would gradually draw the worst of the excess heat from the reactor.

That would take time, though. Too much time.

Michael couldn't afford to wait in this irradiated hell. Yet to escape meant running the gauntlet of superheated water again. His skin already felt on fire.

He had to *think*, when it was all he could do to stay conscious.

The water in the maneuvering room was significantly cooler. When he opened the bulkhead the hot water beyond it would surge through, but there would be a layering: for a short time, it would rise over the denser, cooler water which would run down the stairwell like a waterfall. It would absorb the heat quickly, but....

He took the deepest breaths he could to oxygenate his tissues. It made no difference he could feel, but stalling any longer was a sure death sentence. He yanked open the bulkhead door and launched himself through, hugging the floor. A soundless scream burst from him as the near-boiling water touched his ravaged back. He slid down the stairs and kicked through the frame of the open bulkhead below, into the worst of the furnace. On into the switchboard compartment, shoving aside a corpse that suddenly seemed to wear a face far too much like his own.

By then everything had become a blur. He was conscious only of impacts and scratches, squeezing and stabbing. A pulsing throb buffeted his eardrums. His lungs no longer did anything—he worked them, but nothing happened.

Suddenly he was in open ocean and rising. Light called to him and he reached for its embrace. Dimly, he sensed that he was bleeding all over, and hoped there weren't sharks.

Naïda was back with him, though. She'd channeled far too much heat into her own structure, but the cold water was reviving her.

An eon later, they broke surface and he cried at the brightness of the light, sobbing water from his lungs to mix with the waves. Air invaded his chest like the return of the fire. Nausea wrenched at his stomach, and he vomited.

*The radiation?* he thought. *Did we...did we receive a fatal dose?*

*Yes. Long ago.*

He sagged in the water and looked into the clear blue sky, as if to find welcome there.

*It will be all right,* Naïda told him. *I can remove the pain.*

Couldn't she replace mutant cells, or repair DNA before the tissue damage went too far, or...something? Anything?

*I don't know how.*

He thought deeply, struggling in the mounting waves as a new roar grew steadily in his ears.

"That's it, then," he said aloud. "It's time for you to make your peace with the Controller."

The roar got very loud and he passed out.

# 49

The piercing light slowly, slowly resolved itself; and in the middle of it was the face of an angel.

Sakiko smiled at him so hard it squeezed tears from her eyes.

"Where...?" His voice was little more than a whisper.

"You're in the Naval Medical Centre in San Diego and they've been looking after you like royalty. You're their hero. You've basically been in a coma for eleven days. Part natural, part deliberate, because they didn't want you moving while your skin healed. You were like a cooked lobster."

The room was lined with plastic, like a bubble, and Sakiko wore scrubs and a mask, though she'd pulled it down to speak.

"Still in quarantine?"

"No. The positive-pressure environment is because you were at high risk of infection. They'll probably be able to end that in another couple of days. The doctor will be in this afternoon to do another assessment. Do you have any pain?"

"Not too bad." His face felt too stiff to smile, but Sakiko smiled enough for both of them.

"Good. They didn't want to give you much pain medication in case it caused a problem for Naïda. There was no way for us to tell."

"The radiation. How did we survive?"

"I can't tell you that. We have some guesses, but I think I'll leave that to the experts when you're strong enough. It's safe to say you owe your life to Naïda. *Again.*"

"No more Botox?"

"Over my dead body! We were *so* off base. It finally hit me: Naïda's a *teenager*. God, can I remember what that was like—willing to do anything to please a guy but always messing things up. Worst time of my life." She gently pressed his hand and spoke in a softer voice. "She certainly shouldn't be punished for loving you."

Michael couldn't say anything right away. He pictured Naïda's name and water nymph image.

*I am here.*

Her terrible weakness shocked him, and he tried to will some strength into her along with the most profound gratitude he could convey. Sakiko dabbed wetness from his cheek.

It was then that he noticed dark smudges under her eyes.

"Have you been here the whole time?"

"Where else would I be?" She gave his hand another quick squeeze.

"Well, now you should go somewhere and get some rest."

And he fell asleep.

Three days later, a nurse pushed him in a wheelchair to a small conference room on another floor. He'd insisted he could walk but hadn't made it to his door. Sakiko went with them. The room was tastefully appointed with light gray acoustic panels on the walls and thick, navy-colored carpet supporting a long, polished mahogany table. As they entered, Michael was happy to see Yuri and Sunita rise from their chairs to hug him. From the way they stood together, it was obvious that they were now officially a couple.

"After we saw what you and Sakiko went through," Yuri said, "we realized that life's too short to play courting games." He put his arm around Sunita's waist.

"Yuri..." Sakiko began, "have the police come to see you? Or Edward Ryder?"

"No, and they won't be coming after you either, thank God. And thank Sunita."

The younger woman dipped her head.

"I should be apologizing for my family. Uncle Ed told me on the phone that he hadn't wanted me going on your expedition, and *thought he'd made sure it wouldn't happen*. Yuri and I got suspicious, so I contacted the Foundation and sent them Yuri's original copy of the funding application." She shook her head. "Uncle Ed falsified your data to make sure the application failed. He couldn't believe it when the money went through, but even though he was sure you'd forged the approval, he couldn't know if you'd planted copies of the original data somewhere with it. So, accusing you might have backfired on him, and he kept his mouth shut until he could figure out what to do. Once they saw the original application, the funding panel retroactively approved your grant."

"All charges have been dropped," Yuri said. "Except against Ed Ryder himself."

Sakiko put a hand to her chest and fanned her face with the other. "Oh, Sunita, thank you so very much. I can't tell you what that means to me."

"Yuri told me Ed tried to force himself on you years ago. I'm so sorry."

Sakiko gave her a warm embrace and Sunita's carefree smile returned.

Yuri rubbed his hands in excitement, eager to continue telling his news.

"After the submarine rescue, they stopped blocking us from the internet. Dominique has some great media contacts too. Only official circles have been told about Naïda, but we've spread the word about an alien presence on Earth and it's getting a lot of traction. There were some wild stories that the aliens caused the sub to crash, but we've been able to spin it that they actually helped with the rescue. Which is true, right? Speaking of Dominique...."

Michael turned to see her walk through the door. She gave him a warm kiss on the cheek and a bone-crushing hug, but Sakiko didn't seem to mind. Behind her came three men in richly tailored suits. Although the first man had short white hair instead of Dominique's vivid black locks, there was no mistaking the family resemblance.

"Mr. Cartwright," Michael said. The man's handshake was firm and sincere.

"This is Dr. Sandeep Cameron." The shorter man had very dark skin and a winning smile. "He's a genetics specialist who works for me. You can thank him for the fact we're not wearing hazmat suits, though it was an understandable mistake on the part of your captors. When testing showed unknown virus sequences in your DNA, it would have been reckless not to take full precautions. And the true interpretation is...well, hard to believe."

"That's an explanation I can't wait to hear," Michael said.

"And this is Tim Doherty, COO of my Galaxa Corporation. I think you'll be equally interested in what he has to say. First, I'd like to know the latest from the doctors."

Sakiko gently took Michael's arm. "It's all pretty good news. Michael's skin will be tender for a good while, but it doesn't look like there'll be any scarring. I expect we can thank Naïda for that. His body systems are all approaching normal function again; he just needs some more rest to get his strength back. But he should be able to leave the hospital the day after tomorrow."

"I think there's a yacht in the harbor that might be available for some R & R." Dominique winked.

"Of course, he's the talk of the medical community," Sakiko continued, "because no one can explain how he survived such a massive dose of radiation."

"Did they do a marrow transplant?" asked Dr. Cameron.

"*No.*" She looked sheepish. "In fact, I told them I was his wife and, uh, wouldn't let them do anything like that. Ryan Cassidy surprised the hell out of me when he backed me up. The thing is, there were *two* lives at stake—a radical treatment for one might kill the other, and they'd both still die." She gave a little smile. "I told them to just get as much energy and nutrients as possible into him any way they could: intravenous glucose, Gatorade, whatever. Then Michael mumbled '*chocolate*' and I knew who was really doing the talking!"

Michael laughed, and the others followed, a little slower in understanding.

"The hospital staff treated his scalded skin, but Naïda had to look after the radiation damage pretty much on her own." She squeezed Michael's arm and looked up at the ceiling, blinking back tears.

"Naïda is the name you've given the symbiote?" Dr. Cameron smiled. "Interesting. And I think I can shed some light on how it was able to perform its miraculous healing."

"This could take a while," Cartwright said. "Maybe we should all sit."

"I'll try to keep it short," Cameron said, laughing. "As Mr. Hart and Ms. Matthews were told in Mexico, Mr. Hart's DNA has some significant additions the rest of us don't enjoy, primarily in what's called the non-coding DNA. Many of the sequences appear to be virus DNA, but not any types we've catalogued. Given that aliens from another star were involved, we shouldn't blame the first analysts for jumping to the conclusion that he might be a walking bio-weapon. But happily, there's another explanation. Mr. Hart's..."

"*Michael*, please."

"Very well. Michael's special viral DNA sequences are able to turn on and off like switches, producing what we call *totipotent* cells: all-purpose cells capable of becoming any specialized kind of cell the body needs. Stem cells in embryos are the best-known examples. Cells damaged by radiation—or any other injury—can be replaced much more effectively with these cells, so the potential for self-healing is...stunning. Michael also has never-before-seen, long, repetitive strings of DNA that we've come to believe provide much greater certainty of gene replication without error, thereby preventing unwanted mutation."

"Like checking fixtures for manufactured parts," Tim Doherty said.

"Yes. Quality control at the molecular level." Cameron laughed again. Michael couldn't help but smile at the man's enthusiasm, as long as he didn't become Doctor Cameron's pet project.

"Are these differences in DNA what give Michael his, uh, special abilities?" Cartwright asked.

"Most of those seem to involve physical manifestations by the special substance of the symbiote itself."

"*Her*self."

"Oh, very good, Ms. Matthews. Yes, *her* structure is not cellular, but more like lattices of proteins and other molecules which interact in fascinating ways with human cells, sometimes bonding together as one, other times acting as a separate agent. But I have no difficulty in believing that the two bodies are now inextricably linked. In the DNA there are a lot of what have been called 'orphan genes.' I prefer the term *de novo* genes, meaning 'new' genes, which haven't been found in any other species. These genes have *start sequences*: the early coding on a DNA strand that tells the cell to duplicate the gene. Some of them *may* be involved in the special things Michael can do, or they may indicate whole new abilities we can't yet imagine." His eyes sparkled. "Fortunately, my colleagues and I have convinced the appropriate government agencies that these genes are *not* about to trigger worldwide biological Armageddon."

"Do we really know that?" Yuri asked. "No offence, Michael, but can we be sure that alien-engineered DNA isn't a danger when we still don't know what the aliens' intentions are? An invasion force could arrive any day and a Trojan horse would be a big help to them."

"We have no evidence that Michael Hart is a Trojan horse," Tim Doherty interrupted. "But if the aliens meant for Michael to create an advantage for their side, I'd say they've done the exact opposite by creating a new space-capable human being." He turned to face Michael.

"I don't know what you mean," Michael said.

Doherty was too keyed up to sit and had to walk around the room.

"One of the most daunting obstacles to operating anywhere outside Earth's magnetic field," he said, "is that long term exposure to cosmic radiation is deadly to us, and every form of shielding we've thought of presents serious difficulties, especially the enormous mass involved in shields of heavy metals or water. Your symbiote could make travel to other planets survivable."

"Radiation is just one..." Michael began.

"Let's add everything up." Doherty ticked off each point on his fingers. "You're totally at home underwater—a weightless environment. I suspect that involves the ability to alter your center of gravity and make adjustments to your inner ear that would probably make you immune to space sickness. Self-healing is also a great trick when you're millions of kilometers from any medical facility. Your eyesight not only adjusts to intensity, but wavelengths of light the ordinary human eye can't see. The symbiote can alter the melanin in your skin—a bit of extra protection against solar radiation on a planet not protected by an ozone layer. It can speed up your metabolism as needed to generate body heat, or provide muscle endurance, to a far greater degree than the ordinary human body. And it can control such things *deliberately*, rationally, not just through autonomic responses. Your ability to 'breathe' dissolved oxygen in seawater tells me you'd tolerate other low-oxygen environments, too."

"I can't breathe a vacuum."

"No, but how about the atmosphere of Mars—not on the surface, but perhaps in deep places where it might be thicker? Worth investigating, anyway. Your tolerance to atmospheric pressure—or lack of it—must be way beyond ours. I'm betting your symbiote could toughen your skin against low pressure much the same way it smooths your hair and skin surfaces to lower friction. Very handy in the event of an air leak."

"You don't understand. These adaptations—the purpose of bonding with the symbiotes in the first place—was to enable the explorer aliens to live in the *oceans* of their home world. I've seen it."

"Yet where did they go after that? Into space. Because those same adaptations gave them an advantage there, too."

"You make a good case, Mr. Doherty." Yuri fidgeted with a pen on the tabletop. "But I think some super-secret advanced weaponry would be a bit more reassuring."

The ring of a phone interrupted. Blake Cartwright reached into his inner jacket pocket to answer it. The others continued the conversation in lower voices until they saw the shock on his face. It sounded as if he were talking to several people at once. Cameron and Doherty gave him questioning looks, but he ignored them. Finally, he ended the call and stood deep in thought, his expression unreadable.

"What's going on, Blake?" Doherty stepped closer to his boss, but Cartwright looked at Michael.

"I'm afraid we're going to have to break up this little gathering. One of my helicopters is coming to pick you up, Michael. A former search and rescue aircraft. For a critically important ocean assignment."

"You can't," Sakiko protested. "He can barely get out of bed."

"There isn't any choice. Only Michael and Naïda can do this." He turned to Yuri with a strange smile. "You wanted to know what the aliens' intentions are, Mr. Hutchings. We might just have a way to find out.

"The Navy believes it's located another alien outpost just off the coast and plans to give it a warm welcome. They've given us a short window to get Michael there first."

# 50

This time, Michael was willing to let the helicopter lower him into the sea. He wasn't sure his fragile body could stand much of an impact.

Sakiko had been allowed to come along. Together they'd looked down in dismay upon an ocean covered with Navy ships that a helicopter crewwoman identified for them. Because they were only a few dozen miles from shore, there was no need for an aircraft carrier, but a hard-charging cruiser took its place. Michael counted three destroyers and four other ships of unusual shapes that the crewwoman called littoral combat vessels, since they were used for warfare close to shore. She also revealed that a submarine lurked somewhere beneath the waves.

The navy had told the media that it was an exercise, but to Michael the deadly intent was palpable as floating weaponry made a continuous circle through choppy seas. Such a formation would require unflagging alertness and close coordination, but only ships on the move could take evasive maneuvers on short notice.

As the helicopter lost altitude, they'd been able to see the circle within the circle—a parade of dolphins swimming around and around an unmarked center. Apparently, they'd been doing so for more than a day. There were dozens of them.

"It was the dolphins who found the thing," the crewwoman said. "Then one of the Navy's littoral craft confirmed it with an underwater camera."

Michael nodded. This was not a friendly gathering. He'd been told that all the ships and a half-dozen aircraft were on high alert and ready to deploy weapons if the alien presence made any move to escape the cordon. He hoped that wouldn't happen while he was in the water, but it had been made clear to him that his presence wouldn't prevent an attack. As far as the Navy was concerned, the alien had most likely caused the sinking of an allied submarine. If it took any action that was perceived as a threat, missiles would launch, and Earth's first interstellar war would have begun.

At least they were allowing Michael to try diplomacy first.

The feel of sea water was invigorating, especially to Naïda. A good thing, because she was the key component of this plan.

As soon as they'd submerged, a delegation of dolphins came to greet them, darting past excitedly on every side. He felt Naïda protest even before he could ask her to, and the creatures backed away, but two accompanied them down toward the sea floor. As one, they dropped through the deepening blue—and then a familiar, gelatinous structure gradually became visible on the featureless bottom. Michael was acutely aware of the capriciously powerful presence before him and the bristling display of navy weaponry above. Directly between two such forces was not a comfortable place to be.

Was the artificial intelligence of the alien formation aware of the deadly armament arrayed against it? It must be, but there was no movement. Then, suddenly, it began to glow with the greenish white radiance that he could not forget.

He approached within ten meters and motioned for the dolphins to leave. They didn't, but increased their distance from the outpost.

Was Naïda making contact?

*It says it's about time we showed up.*

Huh? If her translation was accurate, the Controller didn't sound like it felt threatened. That might be unfortunate.

*It wants to speak to both of us.*

And Michael's head began to fill with images: the original outpost, the hand-shaped depression he had triggered to send the signal, the aliens' home world. Human physiology. Chemical structures. The double helix of DNA. Worlds, stars, galaxies. Brighter and brighter the images became, their presence in his brain gaining strength.

There was a brief moment when he struggled to prevent his mind from losing all control, but it was too late.

He had a fleeting vision of tons of high explosive unleashed.

The universe turned white.

His next memory was of breaking the surface into bright sunshine and bobbing in the waves until an inflatable boat from the cruiser raced to pick him up. It was disconcerting to be hauled aboard the great ship and reach the deck only to find a dozen automatic rifles aimed at him and the ship's guns still pointing toward a specific patch of ocean. At least they hadn't fired. That must have been his imagination.

He bent to catch his breath, then waved his hand wearily toward his greeters.

"It's all right," he gasped.

*"We have a peace treaty."*

There was a wheelchair waiting, which was a good thing because gravity wasn't his friend right then. They took him to the officers' wardroom where he was introduced to an admiral named Schellhorn and no one else, though there were several other high-ranking officers present. So, strangely, were Blake Cartwright and Tim Doherty. Sakiko walked to Michael's side and took his arm.

"The admiral and I are golfing buddies," Cartwright said, and Schellhorn laughed.

"It's all right, Mr. Hart. Despite all the stripes, you're in friendly company. Now tell us what you mean by a 'peace treaty.'"

"I mean the aliens are no threat to us, Admiral. Not now, not ever."

"Just how can you be so sure of that?"

"Let's say that I was given information that was extremely convincing, and there's a part of me that would be able to tell if that weren't the case."

The admiral gave a knowing nod and after a moment of deliberation he dismissed the rest of the officers, but made himself comfortable in a chair as if expecting a tale he wouldn't want to miss. As the last of the other Navy people left, Dominique, Yuri, and Sunita came in, followed shyly by the geneticist Dr. Sandeep Cameron.

Michael must have looked surprised. The admiral said, "I allowed Cartwright to bring your people aboard my ship in return for a personal briefing, so let's hear it."

"Have you been told about my...companion, Naïda?"

"I've been told. I'm not sure I believe it."

"Oh, she's real, Admiral. She just happens to inhabit the same body that I do. That has its disadvantages; but in this case, it means I have an utterly reliable translator. And lie detector, among aliens."

"I'll have to take your word for that. I'm told she's an alien herself."

"She wasn't born here, but she's more than proved her loyalty to me, and to us."

Admiral Schellhorn nodded acquiescence.

"So, tell us what happened," said Blake Cartwright who wasn't used to being kept waiting. Michael eased back in the wheelchair and took a deep breath.

"We believed that the three alien installations we knew about—in Canada, the Gulf of California, and near Rocas Alijos—were controlled by artificial intelligences. In fact, there is only one. One AI put in charge by what I call the *explorer* aliens to look after several emplacements they left behind. Naïda knows it as the Controller. When she and I were recovering in hospital, she believes the Controller unobtrusively guided her in repairing the radiation damage. That seemed to suggest one of the emplacements wasn't far away, but she didn't know where.

"The AI decided to allow itself to be found to bring us to a face-to-face meeting. A dramatic performance, too, though the AI was never really in danger itself. Your weapons could destroy the alien structure, Admiral, but the AI is just as present in others elsewhere around the world. In fact, it was more concerned about the safety of Naïda and me, but believed this short standoff was the best way to convince government authorities to listen to us."

"I *am* listening, Mr. Hart. And I have a direct line to the president."

"Good. Because we've finally learned what the aliens want.

*"They want us to join them among the stars."*

The instant babble of voices made Michael want to cover his ears. He laughed and waited for them to stop talking over each other.

"What about the signal? The alien invasion?" Yuri asked.

"The Controller persuaded me to send a signal from the outpost in Canada," he explained, "ostensibly to invite the aliens back to Earth. It promised a treasure trove of knowledge in return; but when I sent the signal, it gave me nothing.

"I was certain I'd been tricked—that the aliens would invade the Earth and were already preparing the oceans to be more like their home world."

"That's why you wanted aboard *Argo*, with Sakiko's team." Cartwright's arms folded over his chest.

"Yes, and the AI—the Controller—let me believe that." He hesitated, suddenly embarrassed. "It was a test."

"A *test*? For what?"

"One test of several. The alien explorers placed the first outpost at the bottom of a lake ten thousand years ago so humans couldn't reach it until we'd developed the technology to do so. Then, bonding with Naïda was another test—the ultimate, most invasive way to learn not only about our physical structure and behavior, but our beliefs and principles. Human character. During everything that's happened, the Controller has been monitoring and evaluating our actions." He shrugged an apology to his friends.

"Tell me it didn't cause the submarine to crash," Dominique said.

"If it did, it wasn't on purpose. When it detected the sub approaching, it sent out a pulse of energy to investigate, like we would send a sonar ping. It's possible that pulse caused the power outage—at the worst possible time. If so, the AI is truly regretful and will share information about shielding methods to prevent anything like that from happening again.

"But it did command Naïda *not* to sacrifice herself, to see what she would do. We know what she *chose*, and she chose the right answer. She learned that from *us*."

"So, the signal *you* triggered didn't actually go anywhere?"

"It did, Yuri, but God only knows how far the aliens have travelled in ten thousand years, and they're not about to come back soon. They've moved on.

"Instead, they want us to follow them. The signal went to the *Moon*, to activate a data vault that will reveal information to us—if we can get to it! Information that will help us get to the *next* outpost, on Mars. That outpost has archives of information that will lead us to the outer planets, and so on...steppingstones, one at a time, to the stars. It seems they've used this method to help a number of other species reach outward. Each cache will offer knowledge appropriate to our level of development by then. But before you ask, it won't give me any more samples of that knowledge. We must work for it."

Sakiko took his hand. "So, the AI judged the human race *worthy*?"

"To be honest, I think the biggest factor was Naïda. The kind of person she's become."

"You've *both* become," Sakiko said.

Michael spun his wheelchair. "I'm still wondering about your presence, director Doherty, the head of a private space exploration company. You couldn't possibly have known what I was going to say."

Doherty laughed, his eyes bright with excitement.

"A brilliant coincidence, perhaps, Mr. Hart. Or Fate. Here we decided that you're the key to the human exploration of space, and now it turns out that's why the explorer aliens left the symbiotes for us to find. Not so that the human race could return to living in the oceans—as beneficial as that might be—but to follow them to the stars."

"OK," Michael said finally. "Give me a few more days of rest and you're welcome to take more samples of our DNA for copying. Try it out on other humans."

Tim Doherty shook his head with a look of puzzled amusement.

"Thank you, Mr. Hart. But you misunderstand. *We want you to be the first astronaut of our Mars program.*"

Michael sat on the edge of his hospital bed and slid his wheelchair out of the way. He could hardly wait to get out into the San Diego sunshine that teased him through the window. Two more days!

Sakiko had gone to lunch with Yuri and Sunita.

"We're serious about the offer of the *Argo*," Dominique said. "If these aliens aren't behind the acidification of the oceans, Sakiko's work is still needed."

"The Controller insists they're not to blame," Michael said. "But it *has* identified a few man-made chemicals that it strongly suspects are the culprits. Sakiko thinks she knows some solutions that are worth testing. Together, they might not be able to cure the whole ocean, but they hope to be able to protect the reefs, at least."

"Perfect. Use *Argo*. That will give you a place to think over our *other* offer." Blake Cartwright stood just behind her, smiling. "We won't be ready to start intensive training for another six months anyway."

"Is Captain Fox still aboard?" Michael asked softly.

Dominique sat on the bed beside him.

"When you were held captive and Cassidy's people had *Argo* smothered in radio interference, Captain Fox had the crew tender loaded with as much fuel as it could carry and personally sailed it through a major storm to Cabo San Lucas to try to get local authorities to find you. He alerted Father and then called in every favor he could from former comrades in the navy to keep you out of the hands of the special ops people after the submarine rescue. Otherwise, they'd still have you."

"Parzifal Fox had a wife who was convinced she'd been abducted by a UFO and it drove her into a mental institution, where she eventually committed suicide. Don't judge him too harshly." Cartwright's voice was surprisingly gentle. "He didn't understand. In fact, I'm not sure the rest of us really do, yet."

Michael nodded. Fox, Nicole, Phil Rodriguez...he had no right to judge any of them. Or anyone else. But . . .

"What happened to Cassidy, do you know?"

Cartwright laughed. "Would it surprise you if I said he's in Washington, lobbying to have you recruited for the space program? The man isn't stupid. I think he realizes that he let his ego call the shots. But he regrets that now and seems to be genuine about his hopes for humankind and alien races. Of course, I hope you'll decide to run with our team." He stepped forward to shake Michael's hand, then turned to his daughter. "I'll be downstairs."

When he was gone, Dominique looked into Michael's eyes.

"I won't be on *Argo*, if you decide to use it. But we just might end up working together. Somebody must have told Father he should make use of all the education he paid for, so he's putting me on the team at Galaxa. It's a junior position, but I don't intend to let that hold me back."

"That's fantastic! I couldn't be happier for you. And you deserve it. I'm sure you'll blow them all away." He took her hands. "Good luck, and thanks for...more than I can say."

She gave him a warm kiss and held him tightly for a long time.

"You've got a wonderful woman in Sakiko—the right one for you, I'm sure. But we could have had some good times."

"I hope you know that the right guy for you won't be some shallow rich-boy type. You deserve the best."

She blew him a friendly kiss from the doorway, and then she was gone.

# 51

Naïda has recovered her energy but has nothing on which to use it. That is becoming intolerable!

The human concept of *hospital* will never make sense to her. Even human bodies are equipped to heal most injuries and illnesses they're prone to, if properly triggered.

It is true that the damage she and Michael suffered was nearly catastrophic. For the first days, she was far from certain that death would not prevail. Decisions of priority were agonizing, especially having to allow radiation-damaged cells to wreak havoc in Michael's body while she repaired her own substance, because she could not do what had to be done without first regaining some of her own strength. It is very fortunate that her kind does not respond to injury with loss of consciousness. The process of repairing the damage she and Michael had suffered required every spark of her mental faculties at full-focused attention for hour upon hour.

After the Controller had subtly given her the crucial knowledge she needed, it had withdrawn to let her do her work.

Then, as she finally believed the tide had turned in their favor, she was shocked when the humans decided to keep Michael in a sleep state, leaving her with no one to talk to for endless days!

Relief was indescribable when he finally awoke.

Naïda's whole world has changed since then, emotions swirling until she feels as if there may be a problem with Michael's system of balance. If so, she doesn't want to fix it—the sensation is too pleasurable.

For so long it has seemed that she could do nothing right. Now, the humans behave as if she can do nothing wrong.

Wondrous, though oh, so confusing!

The revelations from the Controller came as the greatest shock. Far from being a failure, Naïda had fulfilled the will of the Creators in ways even they had not envisioned. She still is scarcely able to process such a success. Michael seems to understand it much better than she.

Perhaps most gratifying of all is the way Sakiko now values her presence and even her feelings. That is very unexpected. And, strangely, that new relationship has brought her into a greater closeness with her bondmate.

She has a hard time comprehending all the concepts Michael has tried to explain to her, especially the thought of being on other planets without the Creators. Yet she thinks she has begun to understand what Michael calls *hope*.

She has great *hopes* for their life together.

She just wishes they would leave the hospital and get to it!

It is puzzling, though, that Michael still has not told Sakiko about the offspring.

# 52

The San Diego beach was beautiful, but too crowded for Sakiko's taste, even so late in the evening. Michael badly needed to work off the stiffness of his muscles and feel earth beneath his feet before they took a cab to the harbor. In some ways it would be great to be back aboard *Argo*—far nicer than anything she had to look forward to back home. She was excited about testing the theories she and the Controller had developed to re-energize oceanic algae. For the first time, she felt truly hopeful that she might be able to save her beloved coral reefs. It would be so easy to throw herself into the venture to the exclusion of everything else.

Except there was the unavoidable question of how soon she might lose the man who'd come to mean more to her than she could ever have imagined.

"How long do you think it will take to make your decision?" she asked Michael.

"I don't know. I couldn't bear the thought of leaving Earth forever. God, it's beautiful. Land, sea, and air."

"You wouldn't have to. Doherty's plans include return flights every couple of years when Earth and Mars line up right."

"Sure, unless your body gets too used to one-third gravity. Then you could never return to Earth."

"Maybe Naïda can help with that, too."

"Would you want to go to Mars, by way of the Moon?"

"I think it would be amazing to stand on another planet, to have a whole untouched world to explore."

"Interesting."

His smile made her suspicious but when she asked about it, he only shrugged.

"You've truly become one-of-a-kind, Michael Hart. You really could be the key to our future. You should be proud."

"I just happened to be the one who stumbled onto the outpost. Everything I can do was given to me by the aliens. I can't take credit for any of it."

She stopped him and took hold of his shoulders, shaking her head in frustration.

"You still don't get it. Cameron and Doherty did. Yes, the aliens altered your DNA through Naïda, but *that would have meant nothing* without the things *you* did. All along it was you who was pushing, exploring what you and Naïda could do together. Learning to communicate, learning to cooperate. Every crisis forced you to stretch your abilities to the limit, tap into those hidden resources, *remake yourselves*. Even going to the brink of death. All of those steps were what activated the altered DNA—I'm convinced *that's the way it works*. It couldn't have happened otherwise. Those abilities aren't a gift—you've earned every one. You nearly killed yourselves for them. And if there are more lying hidden inside you, you'll earn them, too."

He gave a little shrug, but his face was thoughtful.

They walked on in silence. Soon they'd reached a rocky area with no one else nearby.

"Could I…could I talk to Naïda?"

"She's listening. But if you girls want to share secrets, I'm afraid it's kind of hard not to eavesdrop."

She gave him a playful shove, then held him close.

"Naïda…I just want to say I'm sorry. I was wrong about you all along. Stupid and blind. Scared. *And jealous.*" She gave Michael a sheepish smile. "But you're…amazing, and wonderful. We all owe you so much. And please don't take this the wrong way, but I'm proud of you for the *adult* you've become. You've had so much to overcome, but you did, and…*you're an inspiration.*"

Michael gave her a squeeze of agreement.

Sakiko bent closer, her throat tight. "And I'm so very, very sorry about your offspring. I can't imagine what it must feel like to lose them."

A laugh burst from Michael before he could stop it. She was stunned.

"How can you think that's *funny*?"

He held her shoulders and looked into her eyes.

"I didn't know how to tell you. I've tried a few times…."

"What?"

"Naïda's children—*our* children—they're not gone. They're perfectly safe." He put his hand on her stomach.

"I don't get what you're saying."

"She had to hide them quickly, before the Botox took full effect, and it had to be just the right place because she knew she wouldn't be able to help them afterward."

"So…?"

"So she put them in my *testicles*. Then you and I had sex, just as she'd hoped."

Her mouth fell open, her heart suddenly hammering.

He nodded.

"They're in *you*, my love. In your womb. They have been all the time."

She had to sit down on a rock.

"Don't worry, they're not going to make you pregnant. They're not going to develop at all. They would need to be removed and incubated by one of the alien outposts. The Controller will lead us to it."

Sakiko took a ragged breath and tears fell from her eyes.

Michael squatted in front of her and took her face in his hands.

"Don't cry. They haven't hurt you in any way, and they won't. They won't affect you at all."

"That's not it. It just reminded me again that you and Naïda have a closeness that you and I can never have. You even have *children* together. When you told me they wouldn't affect me, I...I realized that I wished they *would* have made me pregnant, as if I could be part of both of you that way."

She let the sorrow pour out. Michael held her tightly and kissed the tears that fell.

"It's OK, it's OK," he whispered. "If that's really what you want, there is a way."

She pulled back and wiped her face with her hand.

"What do you mean?"

"The offspring grow pretty quickly once they're in the right environment. In six months, they'll be juveniles, like Naïda was when I found her.

*"You could join with one of them."*

She suppressed a sob and looked at him, unable to believe what she was hearing.

"Why not?" he asked. "We could share thoughts, feelings. All three of us...*four* of us. We'd be closer than human beings have ever been. And it wouldn't stop us from having children of our own, if you want. Human children."

"But what about the genetics? Wouldn't that be incest? Wouldn't it be like having a child with one of your daughters?" she asked.

"I asked the Controller about that. Incest is about inbreeding: having too much of one set of genes. The eggs in your ovaries have been there since you were born. They don't change and the symbiote won't alter them—they're all yours. My sperm don't carry the hybrid DNA either. And the fetuses of a host develop on their own for that very reason, to protect the variety of the gene pool of both hosts and symbiotes."

He took her hands.

"You could go into space. We could go there together. I know the oceans are your first love, but you'll have six months to test your theories before training begins. A couple of years before we launch. We might even learn something out there that could help all of the Earth's ecosystems. Only...whatever you choose, you can't do it for my sake. It's too big a decision. You have to be certain that it's what *you* want."

"You're a good man, Michael Hart."

"I'm a much better man than I was, believe me."

She bent her head and touched her abdomen. "I think I'd like to meet these little people and get to know them. And you. And Naïda."

His face broke into a huge smile and he lifted her to her feet. "She says, *Me too!*"

She looked out over the ocean and thought about the wonders beneath its waves. Then she turned to the east, to the hills.

A bright, full moon was just beginning to rise. Beckoning.

# Acknowledgments

Writers spend countless solitary hours weaving scenarios in our heads and tapping away at keyboards. Then we set our creations free. But that journey into the world at large never happens without help.

I want to thank my beta readers who read the unedited manuscript of *Naïda* and offered their honest comments: Louis Leduc, Melanie Marttila, Liisa Kovala, and Todd Gale. Your feedback helped me make the book so much better.

More and more, I appreciate the skills of my editor Robin Carson who not only catches my mistakes of spelling, grammar, and fact, but also diagnoses the weak spots in a manuscript and encourages me to remedy them my own way. That's a very special gift for which I'm forever grateful.

Mentors like Robert J. Sawyer and David Mitchell, and fellow authors like Mark Leslie Lefebvre not only share their knowledge so generously but also lead the rest of us by example. My hat is off to you.

Juan Padrón consistently surprises me with cover art that's nothing like I expect and always knocks my socks off. Thanks Juan!

Just like in centuries past, it seems that artists need the financial support of patrons to be able to pursue their passion. I truly appreciate the Ontario Arts Council for filling that role in the creation of this book.

And I owe the most, always, to the unshakable faith of my wife Terry-Lynne whose belief in what I do is a hundred times greater than my own and keeps me from turning aside when the path ahead looks like more than I can handle.

## THE PRIMUS LABYRINTH

A woman's bloodstream has been seeded with destruction.

Curran Hunter almost died at the bottom of the ocean. Now an innocent victim will die unless Hunter can purge her body of deadly devices by piloting the *Primus*, a prototype submersible the size of a virus. Its control system uses *Virtual Reality*—its creators assure Hunter there can be no danger.

They are utterly wrong.

"Loved it! I give this book an enthusiastic four stars for its political intrigue, discussion of moral dilemmas, exciting action scenes, and fully fleshed characters..." Charlotte Graham—Reedsy Discovery reviewer

## BEYOND: Stories Beyond Time, Technology, and the Stars

Ride a bright flame of imagination across time and space with fifteen mind-stretching stories beyond time, beyond technology, and even beyond the stars.

A man who can walk through walls.

Agents who repair the mistakes of the past.

An invasion from beneath our feet.

A man who learns his replacement body was previously owned and died mysteriously.

A disastrous experiment to harness the awesome power of a hurricane.

Don't be afraid to go BEYOND.

"Scott Overton is a storyteller of boundless skill...a writer to watch." —Mark Leslie, author of *Haunted Hamilton* and *I, Death*

Buy your copy: https://books2read.com/u/mV6Xr2

## DEAD AIR

*It's a hard thing to accept that someone wants you dead. It forces you to decide if you have anything worth living for.*

When radio morning man Lee Garrett finds a death threat on his control console, he shrugs it off as a sick prank—until minor harassment turn into undeniable attempts on his life. When the deadliest assault yet claims an innocent victim, Garrett knows he has to force a confrontation.

"A gripping, insightful debut from a veteran radio personality and gifted wordsmith." —Sean Costello, author of *Here After*

Find out how to add these compelling reads to your own collection at www.scottoverton.ca .

Or https://books2read.com/u/mV6Xr2

## ABOUT THE AUTHOR

A radio broadcaster for more than thirty years, Scott Overton described that world in his first novel, the mystery/thriller *Dead Air*, published by Scrivener Press. *Dead Air* was shortlisted for a Northern Lit Award in Ontario, Canada. But the rest of his writing is science fiction and fantasy, including his 2020 science fiction/thriller *The Primus Labyrinth*. His short fiction has been published in numerous magazines and anthologies, many of those stories brought together in his *BEYOND* collections.

Now a freelance author and voice talent, Scott works from his home on a lake in Northern Ontario. His distractions from writing include scuba diving and a vintage sports car.

You can learn more and read free stories at Scott's website www.scottoverton.ca .

## *A Word to the Reader.*

Authors cherish their readers and readers can become devoted to their favourite authors. We always hope so!

If you enjoyed this book please consider leaving an honest review wherever you bought it, or with any reading communities you participate in. After buying our books, that's the absolute best way you can help us continue doing what we do and bringing you the stories you want to read. Just a few lines will do, and I'd truly appreciate it.

Thanks, and I hope you'll look for my other books too.

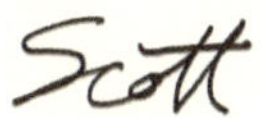

www.ingramcontent.com/pod-product-compliance
Lightning Source LLC
Chambersburg PA
CBHW020232110726
47898CB00004B/1239

* 9 7 8 1 7 7 7 4 3 0 8 2 5 *